"Wondrous, not just in the feats of imagination, which are so numerous that it makes me dizzy to recall them, but also in the humanity and tenderness with which Sequoia Nagamatsu helps us navigate this landscape, to find a way to survive while holding on to the things that make us human. This is a truly amazing book, one to keep close as we imagine the uncertain future."

—Kevin Wilson, *New York Times* bestselling author of *Nothing to See Here*

"Sequoia Nagamatsu is a writer whose imagination is matched only by his compassion, the kind we need to light our way through the dark."

—Chloe Benjamin, *New York Times* bestselling author of *The Immortalists*

"A celebration of the resilience of the human spirit."

—*San Francisco Chronicle*

"Sometimes a novel comes along that feels so prescient—so startlingly aligned with the happenings of the real world—it seems plausible that the author was attuned not just to scientific foreshadowing but to some divinatory reading of the stars. . . . Humming beneath the fantastical, scientific and mystical imaginings of this book are quiet and tender stories of love, family, and belonging. . . . This polyphonic novel reflects our human desire to find meaning within tragedy. To feel our innate interconnection with all things, to care for one another—strangers, even—during times of immense loss, to learn how to say goodbye, to make things of beauty, and, most essentially, to inhabit and tend a livable planet for all."

—*Scientific Ameri*

"Weirdly wonderful and weirdly powerful, a book of speculative fiction so close to real life that its heart-stopping events feel almost inevitable."

—*Minneapolis Star Tribune*

"Nagamatsu's imagination is boundless, taking readers from hotels for the dead to interstellar starships. Fans of sci-fi and post-apocalyptic stories, look no further."

—Hey Alma

"Fans of *Cloud Atlas* and *Station Eleven* will love this spellbinding and profoundly prescient debut."

—The Millions

"*How High We Go in the Dark* is not a plague novel; it is an *after*-plague novel. Sequoia Nagamatsu nimbly bounds through time, space, and species while tackling the question 'Where do we go from here?' My favorite kind of speculative fiction: philosophical and hopeful, endlessly inventive, with a beating heart."

—Gabrielle Zevin, *New York Times* bestselling author of *The Storied Life of A. J. Fikry*

"A novel that is both grimly timely and moves past our usual notions of time to reveal a wider view. Sequoia Nagamatsu allows his story to unspool with such a great sense of scope, freedom, and clarity, creating a stunning mosaic of experience and humanness."

—Aimee Bender, *New York Times* bestselling author of *The Particular Sadness of Lemon Cake*

Spectacular Praise for
HOW HIGH WE GO IN THE DARK

"Moving and thought-provoking. . . . You'll be impressed with Nagamatsu's meticulous craft. . . . Well-honed prose, poignant meditations, and unique concepts. . . . Offering psychological insights in lyrical prose while seriously exploring speculative conceits. . . . *How High We Go in the Dark* is a book of sorrow for the destruction we're bringing on ourselves. Yet the novel reminds us there's still hope in human connections."

—*New York Times Book Review* (Editors' Choice)

"Thoughtful explorations of how the survivors process death and loss. . . . Even the bleakest stories conjure up a memorable image, and often that visual involves reaching upward: to the stars, to a memory, or even just stretching your arms skyward at the roller coaster's peak, whether or not you know how the ride ends. . . . Ambitious . . . achingly poignant . . . an emotional roller coaster."

—*NPR*

"Exactly the white-hot missive of hope, humanity, and compassion you need. . . . Each story is a marvel of imagination. . . . Rich in scope and vision, with each nested story masterfully rippling across others, this is a visionary novel about grief, resilience, and how the human spirit endures."

—*Esquire*

"Done artfully. . . . A heartbreaking tribute to humanity."

—*Entertainment Weekly*

"Lovely and haunting."

—*Wall Street Journal*

"A truly genre-transcending work in which sense of wonder and literary acumen are given boundless opportunity to shine."

—*The Guardian* (UK)

"Haunting and hopeful. . . . Deeply moving."

—NBC News

"Hauntingly beautiful. . . . A lyrical adventure that feels fantastical yet familiar."

—*Good Housekeeping*

"[A] searing literary dystopia. . . . Each character is intimately drawn as they grapple with a future that gives very little freedom to hope or dream. . . . It feels like an archive of personal stories about what the future may bring."

—BuzzFeed

"Ambitious and intricately plotted. A beautiful meditation on the way everything in this world—no, in the universe—is connected. . . . The writing is beautiful and immersive and, at times, hypnotic. It asks both the big questions and the small questions of what will become of us, and even when the answers are complex, there remains the bright beacon of hope."

—Roxane Gay (Audacious Book Club Pick)

"Haunting and luminous, *How High We Go in the Dark* orchestrates its multitude of memorable voices into beautiful and lucid science fiction that resembles a fitful future memory of our present. An astonishing debut."

—Alan Moore, creator of *Watchmen* and *V for Vendetta*

HOW HIGH WE GO IN THE DARK

HOW HIGH WE GO IN THE DARK

A Novel

SEQUOIA NAGAMATSU

WILLIAM MORROW

An Imprint of HarperCollins*Publishers*

Earlier versions of the following chapters originally appeared in the following publications: "City of Laughter," *Redivider* (2013); "Through the Garden of Memory" originally published as "How High We Go in the Dark," *Pleiades* (2019); "Speak, Fetch, Say *I Love You*," *Willow Springs* (2017); "Before You Melt into the Sea," *West Branch Wired* (2011); "Songs of Your Decay," *Day One* (2016); "Melancholy Nights in a Tokyo Virtual Cafe" originally published as "Melancholy Nights in a Tokyo Cyber Café," *One World: A Global Anthology of Short Stories,* ed. Jhumpa Lahiri (2009); "Life around the Event Horizon" in *ELEVEN11* (2016); "Pig Son" in *Craft* (2019); "The Scope of Possibility" in *Black Warrior Review* (2016); "Grave Friends" in *Iowa Review* (2020); "Elegy Hotel" in *The Southern Review* (2020)

A hardcover edition of this book was published in 2022 by William Morrow, an imprint of HarperCollins Publishers.

FIRST WILLIAM MORROW PAPERBACK EDITION PUBLISHED 2023.

Library of Congress Cataloging-in-Publication Data

Names: Nagamatsu, Sequoia, author.

Title: How high we go in the dark : a novel / Sequoia Nagamatsu.

Description: First U.S. edition. | New York, NY : William Morrow, [2022]

Identifiers: LCCN 2021018637 (print) | LCCN 2021018638 (ebook) | ISBN 9780063072640 (hardcover) | ISBN 9780063072657 (trade paperback) | ISBN 9780063072664 (ebook)

Classification: LCC PS3614.A423 H69 2022 (print) | LCC PS3614.A423 (ebook) | DDC 813/.6—dc23

LC record available at https://lccn.loc.gov/2021018637

LC ebook record available at https://lccn.loc.gov/2021018638

ISBN 978-0-06-307265-7

23 24 25 26 27 LBC 12 11 10 9 8

IN MEMORY OF CRAIG NAGAMATSU

1958–2021

HOW HIGH WE GO IN THE DARK

30,000 YEARS BENEATH A EULOGY

In Siberia, the thawing ground was a ceiling on the verge of collapse, sodden with ice melt and the mammoth detritus of prehistory. The kilometer-long Batagaika Crater had been widening with temperature rise like some god had unzipped the snow-topped marshlands, exposing woolly rhinos and other extinct beasts. Maksim, one of the biologists on staff and a helicopter pilot, pointed to the copper gash in the earth where my daughter had fallen shortly before discovering the thirty-thousand-year-old remains of a girl. We circled the research outpost, a network of red geodesic domes peeking right below the tree line, before landing in a clearing. Maksim helped me out of the chopper, grabbed my bags and a sack of mail from the back.

"Everybody loved Clara," he said. "Don't get weirded out if people don't talk about her, though. Most of us keep that kind of stuff to ourselves."

"I'm here to help," I said.

"Right, of course," Maksim said. "There is, of course, another matter . . ." I half listened as I studied the land, breathed air that, like the fossils beneath us, seemed trapped in time. He explained that a quarantine had been put into effect while we were in flight. No one had expected me to come finish Clara's work, let alone so soon.

Inside, the outpost's central dome looked and smelled like a dorm common room, with a big-screen television, worn recliners, and a stockpile of mac and cheese boxes. The walls were covered with a mixture of topographical maps and movie posters—everything from *Star Wars* to *Pretty Woman* to *Run Lola Run*. Down the accordion-like halls, I could see unkempt people emerging from their bunks or labs. A woman in a purple windbreaker and running leggings sprinted across the room.

"I'm Yulia. Welcome to the end of the world," she said, and disappeared into one of the eight tunnels radiating out from the central domes, punctuated with bunks like cells in a beehive. The team emerged from their workstations, slowly enveloping me with the musty scent of more than a dozen researchers.

"Everybody, this is our guest of honor, Dr. Cliff Miyashiro from UCLA—archaeology and evolutionary genetics," Maksim said. "He'll be helping us out with Clara's discovery. I know all of us lab rats will get even weirder now that we're not allowed to leave the site, but try to be nice."

Maksim assured me the quarantine was precautionary since the team had successfully reanimated viruses and bacteria in the melting permafrost. He said government officials watch too many movies. Standard protocol. No one at the outpost seemed sick or concerned.

Unwanted orientations into how Clara lived her life here soon followed—where she drank her coffee and gazed up at the aurora; the route she jogged with Yulia, the botanist; the tabletop lotus aromatherapy fountain she and Dave, the epidemiologist, used for their morning yoga sessions; the cubby where she kept her snow gear, which would become my snow gear since we're about the same size—and how for birthdays, some of the team would make the trip to the nearest big city, Yakutsk, for karaoke, to forget for a moment that the buildings around them were slowly sinking into ancient mud.

"Can somebody take me to the girl?" I asked. There was a notable pause. A researcher in the kitchen put away the plastic cups and bottle of whiskey he was no doubt bringing over to welcome me. The cluster of disheveled scientists, most of them in flannel or fleece, felt like a repeat of Clara's memorial a month ago, a church filled with her friends and coworkers, most of whom we'd never met before. I'd shaken their hands as they lined up to tell me and my wife, Miki, how sorry they were—a man with spiky blue hair said he'd once tattooed a star system onto Clara's back, a purple planet orbiting three red dwarfs, and called her *a fucking trip*; our old neighbors reminisced about how Clara used to babysit their twin girls, helped them gain confidence in math; a bald gentleman, her project supervisor at the International Fund for Planetary Survival, gave me his card and invited me to continue my daughter's work in Siberia. After the crowd left, I held Miki as we rewatched the slideshow I'd prepared, pausing on a photo of three-year-old Clara at her foster facility. She held the purple crystal pendant she'd had when we adopted her. We both swore we saw her eyes light up with tiny stars whenever she gazed into it.

Outside the funeral home, our granddaughter, Yumi, played with her cousin despite the heat waves rippling the street. I could smell the smoke from the burning Marin Headlands to the east beginning to creep over the neighborhood. "Our daughter never seemed to need us," Miki said, her voice barely above a whisper. "But Yumi does." I clutched the business card in my pocket.

At the research outpost, Maksim led me away from the awkward stares of the crew to the mummified remains Clara had found before she died.

"Annie's in the clean lab," Maksim said.

"Annie?" I asked.

"Yulia loves the Eurythmics—her parents are still living in the eighties. She named the body after Annie Lennox."

The clean lab consisted of a plastic sheet duct-taped from floor to ceiling, separating one side of the bone lab from the other. He handed me a box of nitrile gloves and a respirator face mask. "We don't have funding for anything else, but we try to be mindful of the pathogens we may bring back with us.

"Probably nothing to worry about ninety-nine percent of the time," he added.

"Right," I said, a little taken aback by his cowboy attitude.

"Some of our colleagues at Pleistocene Park, about a thousand kilometers east, have made progress reintroducing bison and native flora to the land. More vegetation, more large animals roaming the steppes packs the topsoil, preserves the ice below the surface—helps us keep the past in the past."

I doubled up my gloves, pulled on my mask, and stepped through a slit in the plastic.

Annie rested on her side, fetal, on a metal table.

PRELIMINARY EXTERNAL EXAMINATION NOTES: Preadolescent *H. s. sapiens* with possible Neanderthal characteristics— slight protruding brow ridge. Approximately seven or eight years old. 121 cm in length, 6 kg in weight (would have been approximately 22 kg in life). Remnants of reddish-brown hair remain at temples. Tattoo on left forearm—three black dots surrounded by a circle punctuated with another dot. Body is covered in stitched garment—likely a mixture of pelts. Seashells not endemic to the region woven into stitching—further study needed.

The tissue around her eyes had shriveled, as if she were staring into the sun. The skin around her mouth had begun to recede, revealing a pained cry. I couldn't help but picture Clara as a young girl, or Yumi, who was about this age, traversing barren plains in search of big game, stalked by giant steppe lions and wolves. I ran my hands over her clenched fists.

"Big fucking mystery," Maksim said, coming up behind me. "Most of our research here is funded, in partnership, with the International Fund for Planetary Survival. We keep busy with soil and ice core samples and the occasional ancient animal carcass, but I'd be lying if I said all of us haven't been distracted by Annie and the other bodies we recovered from the cavern. And of course, there's the unidentified virus that Dave found within them in our preliminary samples."

"Have you run any other scans, tested samples? The shells, for one thing . . ."

"From a small sea snail native to the Mediterranean. *Trivia monacha*. I mean, there's evidence of Neanderthals and early humans in Siberia near the Altai Mountains as early as sixty thousand years ago, but nothing this far north. The complexity of how the shells are woven into the fabric is highly unusual. Honestly, this needlework would put my grandmother to shame."

"It's strange that Annie's the only one with such clothing. The other bodies in the cavern showed evidence of simple fur cloaks. The station debrief file you guys sent over left me with more questions than answers," I said.

"We've been waiting for someone to take up the task, fill in Annie's story. Clara said she was here for the animals. She wanted to understand the Ice Age biome so we might re-create it. But it always seemed like she was searching for something else. She'd linger at the dig sites longer than any of us. And for someone whose job it was to study what was hidden in the earth, she spent a lot of time staring at the sky. I bet she would have seen Annie as part of her charge, too. She was always talking about how the unknown past would save us. For a scientist, she dreamed more like a poet or a philosopher."

"Got that from her artist mother," I said. As a child, Clara would spend entire afternoons in her tree house creating—her teachers called her a genius and we encouraged her as much as we could. She wrote reports on nebulae with crayons. We'd find lists of the constellations she'd spotted, alongside mythologies of those she'd made up, the cousins of the Pleiades, the dipper that was neither big nor little but just right.

"I think I can see that," Maksim said. "It's normally easy to get to know people around here, but Clara kept to herself. It took some sleuthing through her belongings to even find your contact information."

"She was always about the work," I said. Our eyes both fell to Annie, whose cry seemed to fill the silence of the lab.

Maksim nodded and said I should get some rest after the long trip. He told me Clara's belongings were in a box in her sleeping pod, waiting for me.

When I departed for Siberia, my granddaughter, Yumi, sobbed at the airport even though, at almost ten, she insisted she was fine. Miki asked me again if I was absolutely sure about doing this. At least wait a few months, she said, so you're not heading into winter. But I knew that if I stayed, I'd delay indefinitely, and the specter of my daughter would have faded from this faraway land.

I never could picture the place where Clara had chosen to disappear in her final years. When Yumi asked Miki and I where her mother was, we would point to a map, search Google Images for the

Batagaika Crater and northern Siberia. My wife helped Yumi make papier-mâché dioramas of the region that they populated with tiny toy bison, dinosaurs, and 3D-printed facsimiles of our family, on an expedition where time didn't matter.

"Your mother loves you," I'd reassure Yumi. "Her work is important." And part of me believed this, but I'd also given Clara an ultimatum the last time we were all together, telling her she needed to come home, that it wasn't fair to Yumi or to us. Apart from the postcards and the occasional video calls with Yumi, I hadn't spoken directly to my daughter in over a year.

Before I realized her research outpost was an international effort, I'd imagined Clara roughing it in a yurt, falling asleep beneath animal fur, cradled by the light of the Milky Way. I saw now that her sleeping pod was a three-by-ten-meter cocoon, nested into the wall of one of the domes. Lined with thermal fleece, it had LED lighting, bookshelves, a fold-away worktable, and cargo netting for storage. I searched a duffel of her belongings that I found tucked into the netting—clothes, toiletries, one of her disaster journals, a personal diary, an old iPod, a few artifacts she'd procured on her travels—but the item I'd most hoped to retrieve, Clara's crystal necklace, was nowhere to be found. I hoisted myself onto her bunk and removed my hiking boots, peeking under the mattress and inside a ventilation grate, anywhere she might have hidden her pendant for safekeeping. My feet had baked during the long journey, and the cheese-like odor filled the bunk, mixing with the stale scent of cigarettes and sweat that permeated the rest of the station. I lay back for the first time since leaving America and searched through Clara's iPod, stopping at the *Planets* suite by Gustav Holst. The triumphant horns of the Jupiter movement transported me to happier times when Clara's wonder was still caught up in the stars, like when she insisted her third-grade solar system project had to be at the correct scale or got into trouble at science camp for inventing a story about the lost star sister of the Pleiades that was once visible in the ancient African sky. What did Clara think of when she looked at the cosmos dancing above the gray of the tundra here? I grabbed her diary and began flipping through it, trying to hear her voice again.

Day 3: *It's amazing how the interior of the crater has already given birth to patches of green. Mammoth tusks protrude from the mud, while new plant life takes root. With the frequent landslides and ice melt creating temporary streams, the whole area has become a washing machine, mixing up the new and the ancient. Everybody here understands what's at stake. It's hard to ignore the Earth when it slowly destabilizes beneath you as you sleep, when it unlocks secrets you never asked for or wanted. On my first night, I stood outside and listened. And maybe it was my imagination, but I could have sworn I heard the soil churning, the dance of a million dead insects, early humans, and wolves.*

Day 27: *In the wild, most parents will fight to the death to protect their young. On some level, I know my parents understand this. I do not answer their messages because I've said all that's left to be said. I believe Yumi hears the song of the Earth when she sleeps. I have to believe she knows why I can't be there for her plays and soccer games and all the other things. She'll be okay. My colleagues here have children, too. They say their kids don't understand or that they aren't as close as they would like to be. But we're here to ensure that they and their children and their grandchildren can breathe and imagine—and so they don't have to deliver the eulogies of so many species. Happy birthday, Yumi. If you ever read this, know that I never stopped thinking of you.*

I set the notebook aside and returned the iPod to the duffel bag, noticed another item wedged in the corner, wrapped in a pair of fleece socks: a worn photo and a carved figurine. The picture was taken three years ago, when we'd met up with Clara in southern Alaska. Yumi had just turned seven, and I was excavating a four-hundred-year-old Yupik village that was slowly washing out to sea.

I recognized the squat brown dig site trailer in the background. I used to sit inside and watch over my grad students while I finished my morning paperwork and coffee. The day this photo was taken, Miki and I looked on as Clara fit Yumi into a pair of oversized waders. Whenever Yumi saw her mother, on average every three or four months, for a week or two at most, it was as if Clara could do no wrong. "We only have the week," Miki told me that morning, when it seemed like I was about to go lecture our daughter. "Don't cause trouble."

I walked from the excavation office to the edge of what my assistants called the mosh pit and watched as my daughter and granddaughter sifted through the sludge. Clara was telling Yumi a story about seal hunts.

"I think I'm going to start a painting of Clara and Yumi together like this, knee-deep in the mud," my wife said from behind me. "For my next gallery show. Maybe it'll remind Clara that the two of them need each other."

"It's almost too perfect," I said.

"Look, Grandpa. I'm a big poop!" Yumi yelled.

Afterward, Miki took Yumi back to the motel to get cleaned up and I urged Clara to stay behind so we could talk.

"Your mother says you're coming home for a while once we finish here," I said.

"A week at most. I told you about the opportunity in Siberia," she said.

"You see how much Yumi misses you, though."

Clara stood next to one of the folding tables that overlooked the lip of the mosh pit. It was strewn with artifacts. She was focused on a wooden doll we'd found at the site, no larger than a soda can.

"I'm doing this for her," she said.

"Sure, I get that," I said. I've always been proud of how much my daughter cared about the world. After school she'd study the news, comb the internet for disasters, wars and hate and injustice, write it all down in these color-coded journals. Once, I asked her what she was doing, and she said she was just trying to keep track of it all because it didn't seem like anybody else noticed or cared that we kept making the same mistakes, that hate in a neighborhood or injustice in a state ran like poison through veins, until another ice shelf collapsed or another animal went extinct. *Everything is connected*, she'd say. And I'd tell her, *You're only one person and you only have one life.*

"You'd rather I come home, wouldn't you, and maybe teach in your department? Pick up Yumi every day after school and pretend like everything is going to be fine." She waved the wooden doll in the air, studied its simplistic carved smile. "Whoever played with this had a hard life, you know. Probably a really short one."

"I just want Yumi to have a childhood with her mother," I said.

"You and Mom are in no position to talk about being there for your child."

"That's not entirely fair," I said. Every time Clara made this accusation, I felt like a pill bug curling in on itself. Once she had her own money, she'd wasted no time escaping to the farthest corners of the planet with only postcards and photos to let us know she was alive. Clara turned and left me standing there, grabbed her messenger bag, walked toward the ocean, still holding the wooden doll. By the time I caught up to her, she'd pulled out another one of her journals.

"Have you seen the new sea rise projections?" she said, reading off a list of cities that might be submerged within Yumi's lifetime—most of southern Florida, nearly all the major cities in Japan, New York City turned into Venice. "Are you watching the news of Appalachia burning? Brain-eating amoeba population explosions at summer camp lakes?"

"Things are bad in every generation." I looked at the opened pages of her notebook, each one covered in disaster. "But we still have to live our life."

"Your research here wouldn't be possible if it weren't for climate change," she said.

"I know," I said.

"Tell Yumi I'll take her out for breakfast tomorrow. We can talk later if you want." She turned and walked toward the research tent, flagged down one of my assistants, asked for a ride into town. While she was waiting for her lift, she came back to the dig site and found me in the mosh pit, half sucked into the earth.

"By the way, don't think I don't want to be with my daughter," she said. "You're dead wrong if you think that."

But the next day, when Miki and I went to meet Clara and Yumi for breakfast, we found Yumi in tears. Clara had changed her plans, said something about travel being too difficult to the site in Siberia, things were out of her control. She hugged Yumi, who was sniffling over her banana split, and then her mother, who told her to be safe. But I didn't say anything. I drank my coffee and ordered chocolate chip pancakes.

"Cliff," Miki said.

I peered through the blinds of the roadside diner, watched Clara climb into her rental. She didn't start the engine, though. She sat there for a long while until I finally got up from the table, went outside, and knocked on her car window.

"I love you," I said, cracking open the door. "Stay safe."

"I'm sorry this is the way things need to be," she said.

Back in Clara's sleeping pod, I tucked the photo in my wallet and picked up the two-inch dogū figurine I'd found wrapped in the sock. It was a squat stone humanoid with a bulbous torso and globular eyes occupying most of its head. I had bought her this replica as a junior high graduation gift at a museum of ancient Japanese history, explained that it was likely a form of magic for the Jōmon people, capable of absorbing negative energy, evil, and illness. I told her to keep it close, that it would keep her safe in the world. I ran my fingers across the crevices and contours, feeling for some last shred of my daughter—a bad day at work, the distance between her and Yumi, a final breath.

From across the dome, I heard someone sprinting closer, their footsteps echoing through the aluminum halls. I slipped the dogū into my pants pocket as Yulia entered the room, glancing at her wrist health tracker.

"Phew. Moscow Marathon, here I come. So, I'm not sure if you're hungry or just want to rest," she said, still catching her breath. Yulia had changed from workout clothes to the unofficial uniform of the station: faded jeans and a hoodie. "But we made fish tacos and we're about to watch *The Princess Bride*."

"So, you're the one who named Annie," I said. "The Eurythmics fan."

"Maksim wanted to name her after a Beatles song," Yulia said. "Like how Lucy was named after 'Lucy in the Sky with Diamonds' when they found her in Ethiopia. Our girl would have been Jude or Penny. I beat him at chess for the naming rights."

I followed Yulia to the main area and made myself at home on a recliner that was patched in several places with duct tape. The aroma of grilled trout filled the facility, and I realized I hadn't eaten a real meal since my first layover in Vladivostok nearly ten hours ago. Four of the researchers huddled on the sofa. Another used a supply chest as a stool. They all formally introduced themselves and the one on the chest, Dave, offered me a glass of vodka, which he said was mandatory for initiation. He lingered on the edges of his words and wore an Occidental College shirt, so I assumed he, too, was from California.

"Santa Cruz," he said. The bottle he tipped over my glass looked like a mammoth tusk. One of the other researchers noted this particular vodka was a true Siberian drink from the oldest distillery, made with local water, wheat, and cedar nuts. "You'll learn to hold your own soon enough," Dave continued. "Keeps us warm, keeps things interesting. Helps us forget that we're flying by the seat of our pants here." My face began to flush after the first few sips.

I sat on my pleather perch like a gargoyle, cradling my shot glass, observing the room like an awkward schoolboy, figuring out how I might fit in here. A few researchers clustered in the halls, dancing; most crammed onto torn furniture, either heckling the movie or asking me questions, including my thoughts on live-action role-playing games. Eventually I let Maksim create a *Dungeons & Dragons* character for me, an elf rogue named Kalask, a name that sounded like IKEA furniture. Dave snatched the character sheet away from him.

"This nerd has been trying to get a game started for over a year," Dave said.

"I'm building the perfect campaign," Maksim said.

"Forget that shit. I know a good initiation game," one of the mechanics said. His name was Alexei. He was a frequent staffer at Bellingshausen Station in Antarctica. "It's important that new guys like this don't keep to themselves."

"His father was at Bellingshausen in 2018, during the first attempted murder in Antarctica," Yulia explained. "So he's a bit sensitive to cabin fever. Alexei is our unofficial counselor. If he sees one of us acting weird, isolating, getting too caught up in work, he'll give us our medicine."

"Medicine?"

"Bear Claw!" Alexei yelled.

"You don't have to," Yulia said, sitting next to me. She explained the rules of Bear Claw: a full glass of beer is passed around the room and with each drink, vodka is poured in to refill the glass.

The entire room was chanting my name now—*Cliff, Cliff, Cliff, Cliff.* These kids understood I needed to forget, even for a moment, that Clara's presence still resided here. The station started to spin beneath me as the glass made the rounds. The laughter and conversation around the television seemed miles away when Yulia finally tapped my shoulder to check on me; the end credits of the film were scrolling and a glass half-full of vodka had landed in front of passed-out Alexei. In the newfound silence, we could hear the wind and hail pelting the outpost. Maksim rushed outside to protect the solar panels. Some of the others dispersed to their pods or labs. Yulia lingered. She was probably close to Clara's age, early thirties, maybe a little younger. She had studied at Moscow State University and completed a fellowship at Cambridge, where she continued her work on native flora, particularly low-lying shrubs as crucial carbon sinks.

"Clara always had that on her," Yulia said. "It was in her coat pocket when we recovered her."

I looked down and realized I had been fumbling with the dogū figurine the entire film.

"It was like a lucky charm," she said.

"I told her it would protect her," I said. "Didn't think she still carried it around. Of course, some say you're supposed to break the figurine after it absorbs any kind of misfortune or evil. There was a crystal pendant she always wore—like an uncut diamond the size of a thumbnail. Slightly purple. She wore it on a braided silver chain. It wasn't in the box."

"It wasn't on her when we recovered her body," Yulia said. "It must have gotten lost, or maybe it was stolen when she was transported to the hospital. I know it meant a lot to her."

I clutched the dogū tighter as she spoke, my eyes drifting past her to the map of the crater on the far wall. Yulia stood and helped me to my feet. I swayed from the vodka and pointed to an orange pushpin, an exposed cavern once sheltering ancient air.

"Clara fell into the collapsed part of the cavern ceiling not far from there," she said, shaking her head. "I didn't understand her at first—all she talked about was seeing Annie and the other bodies. Maybe she was delirious from blood loss, you know? Maybe she hit her head. But all she cared about was the discovery. *There are so many of them*, she said. *I can see her face.* I remember because she kept repeating it. *I can see her face.* She was saying so much—something about writing reminders to herself, about how it'll be all her fault. Do you know what she might have been talking about?"

"No," I said, and wondered if Clara blamed herself in the end for not being able to save the world. "I'd like to see where she was found."

"Weather permitting, a few of us will head out tomorrow afternoon. We're trying to get as much fieldwork done as we can before the topsoil freezes again. Everyone wants to get their samples and crunch the data this winter. Though Maksim seems to think it'll be another Siberian heat wave—which is nice for us but bad news for the planet."

———

The next day, after considerable time draped over a toilet due to the previous night's welcome, I pulled on Clara's waders and bundled up for what was forecast to be a beautiful Siberian October day, a balmy five degrees Celsius. The journey from the station to the crater's edge, a half-hour hike, curved through pine forests dominated by larches, modest trees whose upswept branches looked like they were in a constant state of shivering. I hung back with Yulia and Dave, followed the long line of researchers slowly trudging along behind the equipment.

"You know, the larch's root system helps maintain the ice in the ground," Dave said. He patted the trunk of one of the trees as he passed. "These trees are the descendants of the last ice age."

"Oh?" I said.

"He would have been a great trivia show contestant," Yulia said.

"Hey, don't pretend like your runs are all about fitness. You worship this place as much as any of us," Dave said.

"I do," Yulia said. "I just prefer to keep my mouth shut."

"Anyway, speaking of trivia: You know they call Batagaika the gateway to hell? Probably started when the locals cut too many of these trees. And vegetation, my friend, is what keeps this land frozen. This piece of the underworld is getting bigger every year."

As we approached the crater's rim, I imagined the land falling away from beneath my feet. In reality, it had slowly peeled away and sunk with the floods and permafrost melt. I stepped close to the edge and saw a somber Grand Canyon spread out beneath the perpetually gray Siberian sky. The researchers had carved out an entry point, a zigzagging soil ramp exposing a colorful palette of time—the burnt sienna and raw umber of a crayon box. Dave and his team broke away and started their trek to a section of the interior they'd nick-named "the gully," where they collected samples from a stream. But deeper in the crater was another cavern, an ancient cave uncovered by last year's melts. Yulia guided me beyond the others and pointed to a hole the size of a Mini Cooper.

"We didn't realize this was here until Clara fell through it. Prob-ably covered by a thin layer of ice and soil. We've since widened the opening for access, set up scaffolding and supports in the interior to prevent the ceiling from collapsing. But of course, everything is melting out here."

Yulia slowly descended using a metal ladder propped against the muddy lip of the cavern, her headlamp bobbing in the dark. Ice melt trickled on my head as I followed her lead, lowering my feet one step at a time into a void. I breathed into my coat sleeve, overpowered by the smell of rotten eggs, soil laden with newly released gas, microbes, and ancient dung.

"Here," Yulia said, handing me a bandanna to tie around my nose as I touched down on rock. "The smell was ten times worse before we widened the opening. But smells mean science. A lot of these gases are produced by bacteria that have adapted to the permafrost. Some even have their own kind of antifreeze."

Yulia turned on a string of lanterns suspended along the perime-ter of the cavern—a shelter, a home, a tomb. Save for stalagmites and stalactites lining the floor and ceiling like a sound wave, the interior was largely smooth. Once, these walls had been open to the sky. I imagined Annie sitting at the entrance, savoring the meat of a fresh kill with her family over a fire. Perhaps they ate in silence, or maybe they told tales. Did Annie and the others sing? Did a funerary dirge echo off these walls?

"That's where we found Clara," Yulia said, pointing to a portion of bedrock that looked like it was stained with blood. "She was gone by the time we reached her."

I knelt and ran my fingers along the darkened stone capillaries.

I wanted to ask if Clara had said anything about her family, though I knew it was more likely she was studying her resting place as she bled out, breathing in the Pleistocene epoch as consciousness faded. The remnants of a stone circle occupied much of the space, with a door-sized megalith at its center, carved repeatedly with the same design tattooed on Annie's body. The ground around the pillar, the resting place for most of the recovered bodies, crawled with a series of dots and swirls, patterns resembling a code or a language that shouldn't exist.

"These carvings," I said, running my fingers over the exact edges. "It's almost like they were made with a laser. I don't see any chisel marks. Some of these lines are incredibly precise."

"Related to cuneiform, but not quite. We sent photos of the walls to an archaeolinguistics professor at Oxford. He said the markings were impossible for the time period. What he could make out seemed to indicate that much of what's surrounding us is something akin to high-level math."

"You know, Clara always loved those documentaries about ancient aliens—how we had help building the pyramids, the legend of Atlantis having extraterrestrial origins. I told her there was always another explanation." I'd chastised her for entertaining conspiracy theories from people with mail-order doctorates. But whenever I questioned her beliefs, she just rubbed her pendant, as if it held secrets only she knew. Sometimes I wondered if her fantasy and science fiction magazines, her UFO phase, or how she dragged me to a Bigfoot convention in Sacramento had made her a better scientist than me—maybe it was the reason she saw things in the dirt that no one else could.

———

Once we were back aboveground on the main interior of the crater, I trudged my way to Dave and his research team, my boots sinking into the mud. Dave was crouched over a stream, collecting water and sediment into plastic bags. His entire team looked like they had gone swimming in a swamp, their faces mottled with dirt.

"Like a snapshot," Dave said, looking up. "All of it. It's amazing what survives down here."

"What are you looking for, exactly?" I asked.

"Best defense is a good offense," Dave said. "Eventually, whatever is in this land will make its way to cities, to the ocean, to our food. We've been finding largely intact bacterial life. Annie and the other bodies contained incredibly well-preserved giant viruses we've never seen before. No luck reanimating anything ancient as of yet. The oldest sample we've made viable was a century-old smallpox strain— that's why we're on quarantine."

"You're trying to bring those ancient viruses back?"

"We need to understand what's coming out of the ice as it melts," Dave said. "Most of what we're finding poses no threat to anything but amoebas, but that one percent of uncertainty is why I'm out here. The more we know about these pathogens, the better we'll be able to defend against them in the unlikely event they become a problem. Kind of like ignoring history. You can try, but it'll probably bite you in the ass later. The more we know about where our illnesses come from, the better we can prepare."

"And if you bring something back that's in the one percent?" I imagined prehistoric microbes crawling over Dave and his team, through their hair, inside every orifice, and suddenly became aware of a leak in my boots. I would have thought even a 1 percent risk would have warranted more funding for protective suits.

"We try to stop it from getting out or we prepare people," he said. "We get the world to wake up and pay attention to the fact that all this ice melting and the millions of years of shit it contains has to go somewhere." Dave reached for his belt buckle, twisted the metal square, pulled out a tiny flask and took a sip. "But the odds of us finding some completely foreign runaway pathogen that we don't already know about are incredibly small."

Later that day, I returned to the compound to continue my examination of Annie, carefully turning her over, cutting into the husk of her skin to prepare samples of tissue and bone marrow. Dave and his colleagues offsite were planning to run DNA and viral analyses.

"It's okay," I caught myself saying, as if Annie could hear me or feel my fingers as I cracked open her rib cage to inspect her hardened organs, black as the stone walls that kept her hidden. I was about to remove her stomach when Miki texted:

Don't repeat the same mistakes as she did. Yumi only has one childhood. She's already lost her mother.

I won't. I'm not. I'm here trying to understand Clara, I responded. Yumi will want that, too, someday.

Miki sent a photo of Yumi at the zoo, another of her napping, one of Yumi and her cousins biking through Golden Gate Park with giant sun hats and air pollution masks during a recent Smog-Free San Francisco Challenge week. I was happy for the update, but I didn't have anything else to say. I set the phone down and returned to my work. I was living at the edge of the world and everything else seemed like a distant dream.

I pried open Annie's mouth and found traces of crushed flowers and pebbles that evaded our understanding of Neanderthal and early human migration routes—too far a journey and distance for a young girl. The mysteries of Annie continued to compound as I explored the stories hidden in her body.

INTERNAL EXAMINATION NOTES: Stomach mostly empty but contains traces of marmot and several plants, notably *Silene stenophylla* (narrow-leafed campion)—low amounts make it unclear whether ingested for sustenance or as treatment for illness. Teeth and gums in near pristine condition with traces of wood found between molars, indicating possible dental care. Samples of plaque indicate a diet rich in plants, animals, and insects. Unidentified bacteria beneath gum line in addition to variants of *Streptococcus*. Signs of cerebral edema preceding cranial trauma. Cranial trauma exacerbated by deterioration and thinning of parietal bones and skull base. Genome results and analysis forthcoming from Far Eastern Federal University.

Rigor mortis had curled her fingers. I imagined her asking for help—if her family had possessed medicinal knowledge of plants that could potentially redefine our knowledge of early humans. How do you sing a lullaby in Neanderthal?

Miki and I first started caring for Yumi during her fifth Christmas, when she and her father came to stay with us. Her mother was on a research trip. I'd stay up with my granddaughter to give Ty a break, watching cartoons as she completed her breathing treatment; the wildfire smoke aggravated her asthma. Sometimes I'd fall asleep with her in my arms, and wake to Ty holding a breakfast tray. I'd watch Yumi and her father making weekend plans—a bike ride, a dinosaur exhibit, a ballet class—and remind them to take lots of photos because Clara was missing it all.

It seems like another lifetime that a coroner pulled my son-in-law out from a metal drawer. I had to identify his body after it was spotted floating in Baltimore Harbor by some diners at a dockside restaurant. At first they thought it was a seal. By then, Ty and Yumi had been living in our converted garage apartment for over a year. She had just started kindergarten and he was struggling to find steady work, freelancing as a graphic designer for local restaurants and cash-strapped dot-coms whenever friends passed him a lead.

"Hey, Pops," he'd say. "What do you think about this logo I made for that new Thai restaurant down the street?" Always enlisting my feedback, as if I had an artistic bone in my body.

"I'd eat there," I'd say. Or "Maybe this place should give you a full-time gig." And sometimes Ty would ask, but always the answer was no. He'd moved to the West Coast with Clara after attending college in Boston to give Yumi a better support structure and was never able to find his footing.

"Don't worry. Next time," Miki and I would tell him. "The next interview, the next freelance gig will lead to something steady." He never complained, always asked too little. So, when he wanted to leave for the weekend to attend a friend's wedding, we paid for his ticket, told him to go have fun. Two stab wounds. No witnesses outside his hotel. I had just tucked Yumi into bed when we received the call from Ty's friend. Clara was silent for a long time on the phone when I told her. She didn't cry; she asked me how Yumi was doing, if she knew. I told Clara that I didn't know how to tell her.

"When can we expect you back?" I asked. In my mind I saw her packing her bags and booking a ticket.

"I'll be there as soon as I can," she said.

But she missed the funeral despite Ty's family delaying it for nearly two weeks. They simply couldn't wait any longer. When she finally arrived, I picked her up at the airport and dropped her at the cemetery to visit her husband's urn niche, waited in the car for nearly an hour. After that, she moved through our house like a

ghost, continued to work on her laptop. She cooked and ate alongside us, saying little, leaving the house for hours to clear her head. I'd
later find dozens of movie ticket stubs in the trash, crumpled letters
to us and Yumi that never progressed beyond a few words—*Maybe
it's time . . . I know I've been . . . I want you to know . . .*

I watched her over the following weeks, slowly packing and donating all of Ty's belongings. One of the few things she kept: a photo
of the two of them and Yumi celebrating Yumi's third birthday at
Disneyland. I wanted Clara to feel the loss. Miki and I worried we'd
somehow failed in raising our daughter. But here in Siberia, I read
her journals and realized she dealt with loss in her own way. She had
a plan, and maybe when Yumi was older, she would have been able
to come home and say she played some small part in making the
world better.

Day 68: *Dear Yumi, the team went into a nearby village today and
we saw a girl that reminded me of you. Her mother and father were
holding her hands, all three of them bundled up to their eyeballs,
waddling over the ice. Your father and I took you ice-skating once.
You probably don't remember, but you pushed a metal walker across
the rink, grasping it for dear life. But then your father took off your
skates, held you in his arms, and the two of you flew around the rink.
I miss him. Maybe I should have stayed longer, explained better. But
all I can do right now is remain here, so very far from where I want
to be. Maybe it'll all be worth it one day. Maybe it won't, and we'll
have lost all this time (and your grandfather will have been right).
But know that what I'm doing here is trying to give you a future
filled with light.*

After I finished Annie's examination, I went outside to join Maksim and Dave for a cigarette. The temperature dropped quickly at

dusk. I tried to inhale without inviting in the cold like when I was younger and smoked outside of bars and restaurants, meeting people through our shared nicotine exile. I hung back for a moment as Dave practiced his Russian with Maksim, watched the sky as it transformed into an orange haze over a never-ending sheet of fresh snow. Somewhere, at that moment, footprints in powder recorded the day of small animals and the slow migration of bison. Somewhere, thirty thousand years ago, perhaps the snow recorded someone who loved Annie, walking far away from here.

"Beautiful, isn't it?" Maksim said.

"It is," I said.

"And depressing as hell," Dave said.

"It's Siberia," Maksim said.

"We didn't realize Clara had a daughter," Dave said.

"Maybe he doesn't want to talk about this," Maksim said.

I breathed the smoke in deeply and fell into a coughing fit. Maksim handed me a flask, which I gladly sipped to cool my throat.

"It's okay," I said. "She's almost ten." I pulled out my phone, showed them photos of Yumi and Clara and Ty, all of us together.

"It's tough having those kinds of connections out here," Dave said. "Pretty sure my marriage has been in the shitter for a while now."

"Any updates on how long the quarantine will be in effect?" I asked.

"We've seen some reaction from amoeba test subjects to the virus that we found inside Annie. It's like their cytoplasm began to either seep through their outer membrane or crystallize. We're not telling our governments just yet. We need to know what we have first, what it might mean, if anything, for humans," Dave explained. "Don't want them overreacting."

Maksim handed me the flask again, told me they'd make a Siberian out of me yet. If I closed my eyes, I could imagine Clara standing at the edge of the crater, looking back through the darkening forest, searching for a speck of light from the outpost.

A week later, mainstream news outlets called Annie "Another Missing Link" and "The Wonder Girl of Ancient Siberia" after the analysis of her genome was completed. Part Neanderthal and part something only superficially human, she possessed genetic traits similar to those of a starfish or octopus. What exactly this would have looked like in Annie was unclear, but the frail girl I'd previously imagined would have been highly adaptable to whatever the Ice Age had thrown at her. She was a fighter. She was filled with possibility. Most of the lab buzzed with video interviews and celebrations, the promises of research grants and new equipment. No news of the virus within Annie had been publicized, and we'd been instructed not to reveal anything. Dave and Maksim grew increasingly busy, trapped in their labs despite their assurances to us that everything was under control. I wondered if Clara would have told us about any of this had she lived.

I video-called my wife and Yumi. They were both wearing construction-paper crowns when they answered. I said I would be home soon, maybe a month or two, and I wanted to believe this was true. Yumi had been chosen to play the sun in a school play and had started taking violin lessons. My wife's sister and brother-in-law had moved in to help, since Miki held regular art shows in New York, and other relatives stopped by on weekends, resulting in regular potlucks.

"I sold two paintings of Clara and Yumi," my wife added. "A couple in Brooklyn said they could sense the love between them, and also a kind of longing. I didn't intend that, but I couldn't help noticing the sadness in Clara's eyes."

"I think she was happy out here," I said.

When Yumi chimed in after, I told her about an extraordinary girl who had the lungs and heart of an Olympic athlete, and who may have possessed the ability to heal from minor wounds in a matter of hours like a starfish or an octopus.

"Like a superhero?" Yumi asked.

"Kind of," I said.

"But you said she got sick."

"Everyone gets sick sometimes," I said. "And that's why I need to stay here for a little while longer. I want to make sure people don't get sick if they don't have to."

"But you're okay?"

"I'm okay."

After Yumi left the call, I reassured my wife that what I had said was true. I told Miki to make teriyaki beef for the next family dinner, to soak it in sauce overnight in the fridge, and to cut the meat extra thin because that's how Yumi likes it. I promised I would call if anything changed.

At night I wrote to Clara in her journal, instead of watching *The Goonies* or *The Shining* for the umpteenth time. Most of the researchers had dispersed to their own pods as the quarantine dragged on, as winter storms limited our research to the domes. The outpost alcohol and cigarette stash ran low between supply drops. Some took on new hobbies—learning how to play chess, crocheting, drawing, magic card tricks. Yulia was sketching a group portrait of the entire team. I opened Clara's notebook one night and wrote *YOU WERE RIGHT* on the interior cover in big bold letters, circled and underlined.

Dear Clara,
It's strange to think I've started to build a life in the same place I saw as your escape from home. But you saw something else, and I

think I understand now why you never could rest. It wasn't about us or a job or all the little things we call a life. You saw a future of dead soil and dead oceans, all of us fighting for our lives. You had a vision of what life would be like for future generations and acted like the planet had a gun to our head. And maybe it does. I was always so proud of you, but it took Siberia, a quarantine, and the mystery of a 30,000-year-old girl to help me realize that. Maybe tonight I'll look at the stars and make up a new constellation for the both of us, a woman standing at the precipice of a great chasm. I'll be here with you.

Love,
Your father

Sometimes, late at night, Yulia and I overheard Dave and Maksim talking in Russian as we were finishing our evening game of chess in the common room. They tried to be covert, but voices ricocheted off the walls around here. She'd translate what little she understood around the scientific jargon—video conferences with medical and government officials, reports that a strain similar to the Batagaika virus had been found hundreds of kilometers away in soil and ice cores. But no one had gotten sick and so maybe we were all okay. Perhaps we possessed an immunity to the illness deep inside of us because some of our ancestors had fought the virus. Dave reiterated this to us all: unless we're taking shots out of lab test tubes or snorting infected amoebas, we shouldn't be overly paranoid.

"But they're still going to keep us here," Alexei, the mechanic, said. "They can't keep us here if nothing is wrong with us."

"Actually, they can," Dave said. "Right now, we're their best bet for learning more about the virus."

We looked at the amoeba samples under the microscope every

day. Maksim and Dave explained any changes, how the cytoplasmic structures inside them had begun to disintegrate. We watched a rat injected with the virus inexplicably slip into a coma.

"It's like the virus is instructing the host cells to serve other functions, like a chameleon—brain cells in the liver, lung cells in the heart. Eventually, normal organ function shuts down," Dave explained. "There's still no reason to think any of us are infected, though, or could be infected."

"There's also no reason to think that we're not," Yulia said. "You said you haven't seen anything like this before."

"We should have left it alone," one of Maksim's assistants said, pointing to Dave. "Everything will be your fault. I have a family. We all have families."

Later that evening, Maksim assigned everyone to dining and common area groups.

"If you can't be civil with each other, this is the way it has to be," he said. "I will not tolerate arguments. We have enough to deal with right now."

Lately, I can't help but think about all the times the team was covered in mud and water from the crater, of the jury-rigged clean lab, the respirators that probably need their air filter cartridges replaced. I question Dave's decision to inject the virus into a rat, one of history's most notorious vectors for disease. We're told to report anything out of the ordinary. We're told the quarantine is to be extended and to expect supply drops every two weeks. We're told biohazard medical teams will be sent if necessary. I fall asleep every night video-chatting with my family, telling fairy tales to Yumi: *And they all lived happily ever after.* I wake up half expecting to find something wrong—a fever, a stiff neck, a rash. I examine every inch of my body in the mirror. We are all waiting for nothing or everything. I dream of going home and holding my family, telling Yumi that her mother has saved her. I dream of the last trip Clara took with us, flying over the Arctic National Wildlife Refuge, watching the last remaining wild caribou migrate. When Dave tells me he has a splitting headache, I tell him to take his own advice and not jump to any conclusions. But I tell him this while standing across the room. When Yulia says she has a stomachache, I tell her to drink tea. We'll be okay, I say, but I see the fear in her eyes. Dave tests positive for the new virus with both saliva and blood samples. I don't know if there's anything I can do to help Yulia. In the real world, people comfort themselves with ignorance, politics, and faith, but here in the domes only hard numbers matter. She has stopped running, her portrait of the research team left unfinished. We keep telling ourselves we're going to complete our work and go home—some days I even believe this. I put on my daughter's snow gear, take the dogū figurine with me, and walk out onto the tundra, picture Clara there beside me beneath the aurora. I don't take the ATV. I walk the mile to the crater's edge. I imagine the virus and anything else the ice has kept hidden from us being sucked into the figurine, its stone belly filled with all that can harm us. I tell my daughter I love her and throw the dogū into the crater, waiting for all that has been unburied to be retaken into the earth. I walk back to the outpost. I can barely breathe.

CITY OF LAUGHTER

I had been trying to land a paying stand-up gig in Los Angeles when the Arctic plague arrived in America, infecting the children and the weak. For almost two years I paid the bills as a sanitation worker, cleaning abandoned offices and shuttered schools, while at night I tried to fill dive bars with laughter in exchange for drinks. *But seriously, folks*, I'd say. *Tough crowd*. Patrons would applaud out of politeness, to maintain the illusion keeping them whole. I had all but given up hope for real comedy work when my manager called me for the first time in months.

"Have you heard of a euthanasia park?" he asked. It was early in the morning. I was pulling on my janitorial coveralls.

I paused. Of course I had. Everyone scoffed when the governor first announced plans for an amusement park that could gently end children's pain—roller coasters capable of lulling their passengers into unconsciousness before stopping their hearts. Critics called the proposal perverse, accused the state of giving up on the next generation.

"Yes," I said. "I mean, I've seen the debates on the news."

"You've also probably seen the plague projections. Parents are desperate," he said. "My niece, my nephew. Hospitals can barely keep up with the treatments. There's a waiting list at the funeral home. I don't know if you know anyone who has been affected."

"I think my second cousin is in the hospital," I said. "But not really."

"Anyway, some billionaire dot-com type who lost his son bankrolled a prototype euthanasia park on the site of an old prison between here and the Bay Area. They've been in operation for six months."

"Okay, what's this have to do with me?"

"Business is picking up for them and if these recent reports about the virus mutating and infecting adults are true, then this place is going to be booming. They need staff."

"But I'm a comedian."

"It's a paying job and it comes with housing," he said. "It's entertainment."

"Manny," I said, "you know my material. I talk about being a bad stereotypical East Asian—smoking pot outside of SAT prep classes, letting jocks copy my shitty math homework . . . Would I need to wear a costume?"

"I didn't need to call," he said. "Just check your email."

I hung up and stared at myself in the mirror in my hazmat coveralls. But instead of leaving for work, I BitPalPrimed my parents with news of my move, something real for a change, rather than the usual lies about my next big break being right on the horizon.

"Maybe something I can be proud of," I told my dad. "Not exactly what I imagined, but I'll be making people laugh."

In the background of the video chat window, I saw my mother walk in and out of my dead baby brother's room with a vacuum. He died in a car accident about a year before the outbreak and my mother still saw his face in mine whenever she looked at me.

"Your cousin Shelby died," my father said. "She may have infected her brothers. We don't know. Some people say this plague is airborne and others don't. Hard to know what to believe."

"How are you and Mom holding up?"

"Surviving, I guess. Might stay with your auntie Kiyo. Help plan your cousin's memorial. But I know you have work. What's the job again?"

"It's a firm," I began, "that provides comfort services to sick children. I'll be helping run their programs." I was already bending the truth to garner some modicum of parental approval. I had always had to fight for their attention when my brother was around.

"Sounds like a good opportunity," he said, nodding. But I could tell from his tone, the way he squinted his eyes as if he were in pain, that he either didn't believe me or didn't have the emotional headspace to really hear what I was saying.

A couple days later, I handed in the keys to my apartment and drove through the lifeless streets, punctuated by a handful of shops and the orange haze of wildfires over the Los Angeles foothills. The newly homeless slept in their cars. Soup kitchens attracted lines snaking through parking lots. Outside of city limits, billboards advertised funeral packages and antique barns that had been cleared for body storage or triage. No rest stops. No open diners. Jacked-up gas prices at the few remaining twenty-four-hour stations dotting the highway. I followed the uncivilized darkness of the road for hours, unable to avoid radio evangelists going on about the second coming, until I saw the park's angelic lights in the distance.

When I climbed out of the car, I felt like I was arriving at a prison that was pretending to be something else. The barbed-wire fences remained and while the old signage had been removed from the concrete walls, the discolored outline of the words STATE PENITENTIARY was still clearly visible. Inside the park, colorful murals of children in bumper cars, riding merry-go-rounds, and plummeting down log flumes covered the walls of the administrative building beneath the words WELCOME TO THE CITY OF LAUGHTER! A rainbow painted on the linoleum led me through the halls, passing old security checkpoints turned into gift shops and concierge desks. The minimally furnished HR office had been converted from a recreation room, judging from the sofas and old board games piled to one side. Only a table and a few filing cabinets took up the remaining space, along with a floor lamp and a stack of deconstructed cubicle walls. As I approached, leaving the rainbow path, the park manager, a balding man in a silver astronaut suit, leaned back in his chair and propped his feet on his desk.

"Your agent said you'd be here hours ago." He noticed me staring at the nameplate on the desk: WARDEN STEVEN O'MALLEY. He picked it up and tapped it against his hand. "It's actually Jamie Williamson, by the way. I kept a lot of the old shit we found around here."

"Skip," I said, offering my hand. "I'm sorry. I took a detour to fill up on gas."

"Skip," Jamie said, adding extra emphasis on the *p*. He studied me for a moment and then began searching his desk drawers with a shit-eating grin on his face, pulled out a form. "That short for Skippy?"

"Just Skip," I said.

Jamie pushed the forms across the desk and explained that I'd have to wear a generic mouse costume while prancing through the park, taking pictures with families, handing out balloons, helping children onto rides.

"It is imperative you exude merriment," he stressed. "No half-assing, Skip. The parents will know. The kids will know."

"No half-assing," I said. But I was still processing the fact that I would have to wear a costume. I thought about leaving the office, saying thanks but no thanks, but it's not like I had a job or an apartment or any other prospects.

"And there might come a time when the parents have second thoughts. Some might want to leave with their children, buy some more time with them."

"What do you mean?" I asked.

"We've come to an arrangement with the government and the

CDC," Jamie continued. "If we are to continue operations, no one with the virus is allowed to leave."

"And I stop them how? I weigh a hundred and thirty pounds. I write jokes," I said.

"Firmly, and with a big City of Laughter smile," Jamie said. "And of course, radio our security staff if a cheerful *no* ever fails."

A teenage girl named Molly wearing pink striped overalls escorted me to the employee dormitories. Beyond the old prison buildings, the park resembled a Six Flags knockoff—cracked pavement, kiosks filled with off-brand candy, papier-mâché dragons and enchanted fairy forests that looked like they were about to melt in the sun or dissolve with the next downpour. The central prison complex had been renovated into a pirate-themed shopping area and food court inappropriately named Dead Man's Cove with vendors and vending machines and food carts and animatronic displays occupying the cells. Above us, rainbow spotlights scanned the ground from the guard towers. I could see the silhouettes of their rifles amid the prismatic glow.

"Are they really necessary?" I asked Molly.

"People aren't likely to run with their kids if they think they'll be gunned down," she said. "It's mostly for show, but you never know. Some of the guards are real wannabe commandos."

Molly walked at a brisk pace, hanging a left at the Buggin' Bumper Cars, a right at the Wet and Wild Raft Adventure, and continuing past the Laughateria, where the manager said the cast members were encouraged to perform family-friendly improv.

"How long have you been here?" I asked.

She turned around without stopping, as if she were giving me a campus tour, waved to someone in a pink shrimp costume. "Couple months," she said. "My parents cook in one of the restaurants."

"You like it?" I realized this was a stupid question, but I wanted to understand what kind of life I'd signed up for, if I'd really be helping people.

Molly shrugged, muttered something like *Jesus Christ* beneath her breath before leading me past a roped-off roadway with a sign that read DO NOT ENTER. RIDES AND EQUIPMENT UNDER REPAIR.

We walked behind an antique merry-go-round dotted with seahorses and mermaids suspended on rusted poles. Asphalt became dirt and dust until we were surrounded by a circle of mobile homes and RVs. Lawn chairs and beer cans were nestled beside a burned-out fire pit. Farther away a cluster of small cottages sat atop artificial turf. From where we stood, the park lights looked like an oasis in the desert. Molly pointed to a rusted-out Winnebago and handed me a welcome packet.

"Read this," she said. "Someone will get you oriented tomorrow. There's no real training. Just don't make the kids cry."

I pointed to the cottages. "What's up with those?"

"For families, people with special needs," she said. "We'll also be administering experimental drugs here, running studies for a pharmaceutical company."

I shook my head. I could tell Molly was tired of me, or maybe she was just being a teenager.

"Well, good night," I said.

"There are probably bedbugs in there," she said, already turning away. "Nobody really cleans these donated vehicles."

I turned on the lights of the camper and discovered a faded mint-green bachelor pad with old *Playboys* stuffed inside the glove compartment, food stains on the chipped countertops, the result of what I imagined were hundreds of road trips. I sifted through the cabinets and found some canned food only a few months past its expiration date. I ate cold ravioli while staring at the park lights through the window before drifting off to sleep.

*   *   *

My first charge was a little boy named Danny (Group 5A: Non-contagious / Stage IV Illness). He had fiery orange hair and wore dinosaur pajamas. His parents trailed close behind as I pushed their son from ride to ride in a race car stroller. Over the next few hours, this family lived a lie where all that mattered was having fun, though I couldn't help noticing quieter moments—parents holding each other as their child waved to them from a bobbing ostrich on a carousel. Some of these kids were completely oblivious—too young or needing so badly to believe the happy-go-lucky marketing. But little Danny knew the score. Every now and then I'd ask him how he was doing, if I saw him take a puff on his rescue inhaler or he seemed too weak to stand from the stroller.

"Great," he would say, trying to be chipper through his coughing fit. "What's next?"

Danny's mom and dad stopped in the middle of the path, their arms wrapped tightly around each other as they looked up at the final ride, the Chariot of Osiris, with its nearly two-thousand-foot pinnacle that would launch the train to a speed of 200 mph through several inversions. Jamie had told me this was one of the hardest parts of my job, waiting for the parents to say goodbye, maintaining the illusion of cheer and merriment all employees were supposed to project. Tears streamed down the mother's cheeks as she exited the Maze of Tickles.

"Thank you for giving us a way to say goodbye. We didn't want him to die in some hospital overflow center," the father said, pulling me close, whispering in one of my giant mouse ears. "I know you're just doing your job, but you gave us one more day with our boy." He squeezed my furry mouse shoulders and crouched beside his son.

"We love you, Danny," he said. "My little Dan the man."

"We'll be right here, watching," she said. "You're such a good boy."

I couldn't imagine being in their place. I thought about the tiny body bags lining the streets in the early days of the Arctic plague, how crying parents could be heard at all hours of the night, the white buses that took away the deceased to be stored or burned or studied. At first, nobody knew what was happening. There were rumblings of illness in Russia and Asia. We expected that any viral outbreak would warrant a simple trip to the pharmacy or a walk-in clinic, until the first American cases revealed something much more serious. Breaking News: Children Collapse on the Beach in Hawaii. Aerial footage played on a loop, parents and lifeguards and bystanders circling the bodies lying in the sand.

"Are you seeing this?" my father asked. Having grown up playing on Oahu beaches, my parents felt especially connected to the events. We watched the news together as more and more incidents were reported.

"I feel weird," a little girl in pigtails and a neon pink swimsuit said to a reporter, before she was carried away on a stretcher. Leilani Tupinio would die a month later from organ failure; her lungs' cells and tissues had transformed to resemble a liver. Her heart had begun to form the structures of a tiny brain.

"This shouldn't be possible," a doctor said in an interview. At Hawaiian hospitals, doctors and nurses labeled infected patients as having the "shape-shifter syndrome," before the CDC publicized the link to a case in Siberia. By the Fourth of July in 2031, only a couple of months later, children had begun falling ill on the mainland—a case in San Francisco tied to infected oysters, an elementary school outbreak in Portland following a family's trip to Maui.

Before I pushed Danny down the path to Osiris, his mother gave him one final hug and a sip from his juice bottle before pulling out a syringe.

"Just a little poke of courage juice," she said, injecting her son with the sedatives that the park sells. Parents aren't forced to do this, but we encourage them to consider making their children's last moments as calm and peaceful as possible.

"Are you scared?" I asked, realizing I probably should have stuck to another joke, or made some bullshit balloon animal.

"Yes," he said, voice barely above a whisper, as I began to push his stroller. He started to sniffle, sucking the snot into his nose, leaving a snail trail above his lips.

"It looks like fun, though," I said. "For brave boys and girls."

"Yes," he said, a bit more chipper this time. As the drugs coursed through his veins, I noticed a final sliver of energy. He smiled as tears ran down his cheeks. He craned his neck upward, seemed to marvel at the height of the coaster as we approached its gates.

I knelt and wiped Danny's face before joining the other costumed staff with their charges as they readied the ride. When every child was secured, the staff stepped back, creating a wall between the tracks and the crowd of parents, who were cordoned off several feet away, security staff at the ready. The chain and hydraulics of the coaster began to hiss as the train rose to the sky. The staff clapped along rhythmically. At the halfway mark, I gazed at the cars, now at their tipping point, and closed my eyes right as the roar of the tracks and the joyous screams of the children grew to deafening levels and the train plummeted back to earth, through the first inversion, pulling ten Gs—and then the screams stopped. Brain function ceased in the second inversion; their little hearts quit pumping in the third.

When I opened my eyes again, the heads of the children were bobbing, as if they were in a deep, impenetrable sleep.

* * *

Two months had passed since my arrival at the park. In park time, this meant I had eaten every item on the menu at the Laughateria, except for the shrimp scampi (translation: the park needed more toilet paper when they served it), and attended team morale training twice, which consisted of trust falls and sitting in a circle talking about our feelings—*Hi, I'm Skip, and I guess I'm mostly okay now. I'm getting better about dealing with the guilt. But sometimes it's just hard, you know?* The group would nod at comments like these and twinkle their fingers in the air in solidarity. These sessions were followed by an hour of meditation set to a loop of Grieg's "Morning Mood"—images of wildlife and laughing children projected onto the walls, accompanied by a soft female voice over the PA system telling us that we were waking up to our calling.

"And remember," the voice said, "what is laughter but a moment of release where pain and memory are washed away? When we laugh, we are stronger. When we laugh, we heal the world."

But outside of these management-organized events, no one really hung out much. Once, Victoria, the churro kiosk girl who dressed like an elf, came into my trailer in the middle of the night, threw a condom in my face, and told me not to get any ideas. We spent the night together and when I draped my arms over her body the next morning, she immediately got up and got dressed, reminded me this wasn't the real world.

Sometimes, when I just had to shake up my routine, I'd drive to the Olive Garden in the next town over. The park keeps it open for the guests. A bartender there told me that serving people from the park feels like being surrounded by ghosts—they come in alone, drink quietly, and leave.

"I totally get it," he said. "Doing what you people do. Nobody wants to linger. People get hurt that way."

"I don't know," I said, sipping on my mango margarita medicine. But I wondered how long it would be before I became like the other staff, one foot in a parallel universe where nothing mattered except laughter and forgetting and sad fucks with whoever lived in the trailer next to yours. Two months at the park meant I had placed nearly one hundred fifty children on Osiris.

It was a regular Saturday when the drug trial patients moved into the cottages next to our trailers. Most of the staff sat on lawn chairs outside as the families arrived, some of the kids in wheelchairs, others walking at a snail's pace, holding the hands of their parents. We waved if the children waved. Otherwise, we just watched. One of the kids, maybe six or seven years old, arrived on a stretcher topped with a plastic bubble, as if he were some sort of buffet dish. He pressed his hands against the plastic, watching as one of the local coyotes made a snack out of someone's half-eaten basket of fries. The guards carried him. Behind the boy, a woman I assumed to be his mother struggled to drag two large suitcases. She was dressed in an oversized silk poncho that kept getting caught in the wheels. I looked around at my coworkers—watching, drinking, refilling their pipes with mediocre pot—and finally decided to offer my help.

"I'm Dorrie," she said, as I approached and took the luggage. "And the troublemaker in the bubble is my son, Fitch."

I followed them to their cottage, beyond the central playground area, and into a squat two-bedroom affair with a sloped roof punctuated by several skylights. The pharmaceutical company had furnished the place with modernist Swedish furniture prone to straight edges, except for a blue plastic coffee table that was shaped like California. A wicker gift basket sat on top of it. I waited in the living room with their suitcases, watched the guards bring Fitch into his room. Everything the boy could need—his bed, toilet, sink, shelves filled with children's books, a television with a gaming console, an IV stand, an array of medical machinery—was all separated from the rest of the house by a glass wall with a sliding door. The guards turned on what appeared to be an air filtration system from a panel built into the wall and the room hummed to life. Fitch quickly crawled out of the stretcher and closed the glass door behind him.

After the guards left, Dorrie invited me to stay for dinner. She inspected the fridge, which had been stocked with essentials and precooked frozen meals.

"I'll give him this," she said, still inspecting the freezer. "My ex-husband made sure we wouldn't starve."

"I didn't want to ask," I said. "I'm not sure what's normal for the study participants."

"My ex and I have different views on how we should care for Fitch," she said. "He's a research doctor. Convinced that any day now he'll find a way to save our son. I was tired of waiting and these studies are happening now. Some kids seem to be getting better."

I could hear Fitch settling in, playing a video game. I leaned back and saw that he was on the bed with a controller. He'd already peeled the paper adhesive off the ends of the monitoring electrodes and pressed them onto his chest, hung an IV bag at his bedside, waiting for his mother to finish the rest. As she went to help her son, I arranged a folding table on the other side of the glass partition.

"There's wine in the gift basket," Dorrie yelled from his room. "And can you blend one of the shake cups in the freezer? It's all he can keep down lately."

By the time we sat down to eat, Fitch had already sucked down his Very Berry protein shake and was playing a game of Pictionary with us, holding up a frenzy of squiggles.

"Um, windmill," I guessed.

"Nope," Fitch said.

"Helicopter," Dorrie guessed.

"Nope again," Fitch said. "But close!"

"Wait, I know. Hovercraft!" Dorrie said.

"Ding, ding, ding!" Fitch said.

We played three more rounds before he threw up his shake. Dorrie explained that the pills the doctors had given him when they arrived might do this for the first few days. She sanitized her hands and entered the clean room. It was supposed to help prevent anything else from compromising Fitch's already weak immune system. She removed his shirt and put on an audio version of *A Wrinkle in Time*, and rocked him in her arms. I watched the constellation of scars and welts on his chest rise and fall as he slowly drifted off to sleep.

"You don't need to stay," she whispered, still lying next to her son.

I took the dishes to the kitchen. Dorrie stepped out of the room and thanked me for the welcome.

"Fitch really doesn't have friends anymore," she said. "I think it meant a lot to him to have someone else here."

I poured us each another glass of wine, finishing off the bottle. I took a long sip, not really knowing what else to say.

"Can I ask you why you came to the park?" Dorrie asked.

"I was the class clown in high school," I explained. "But, you know, I came from a stereotypical Silicon Valley Asian family, which meant being a doctor or a lawyer or a banker or tech entrepreneur. I just wanted to make people laugh. I wanted to help people cut through the bullshit and see the world."

"So, you had a gift and you didn't want to waste it," she said. "Nothing wrong with that."

"Not sure me making fun of my cheap parents or telling stories about going to comic book conventions to pick up women is much of a gift, even if they are one of the few public spaces in America where it feels totally fine to be Asian, especially when the girls think you look like some anime character."

"Are you kidding me?"

"So many Sailor Moon dates."

Dorrie took a sip of wine and tried to contain her laughter, almost dribbled some onto her shirt.

"At least here I feel like I'm helping people, even if it's not the way I ever would have planned it," I said.

I showed up at Dorrie's cottage the next day and the one after that, devising a different excuse each time. I brought Fitch some of the comics I'd amassed as a kid, along with paints from the gift shop for Dorrie, since she'd mentioned attending art school before she became a mother. She immediately set about painting a solar system in Fitch's room, complete with spaceships. In the living room, she painted glowing orbs filled with light, flowers, and scenes from ancient history that Fitch told her he sometimes sees when he dreams. After about a week, I stopped making excuses and Dorrie knew to expect me at her door or outside her work most evenings. She was a part-time office assistant in the checkout facility, where parents went to collect the ashes of their children. We never really discussed a name for our arrangement, and I told myself that I wasn't responsible for Fitch, that the whole situation was more than I wanted in my life. Part of me worried that I was using her to feel like a decent human being.

Every time I talked to my parents, I wanted to tell them about Dorrie, but I didn't want to jinx whatever it was I had with her. Months later, I finally told them I'd met someone.

"She's beautiful and paints these fantastical dreamscapes. And she has a terrific son."

"A son?" they both said in unison.

"Is he—?" my mother began.

"Yes, he's sick," I said.

My mother's gaze seemed to reach across the state, through the screen. My father only shook his head.

"Hope you know what you're getting into, son," he said.

"Oh, Skip," my mother said. She held a hand in front of her mouth as if to contain her disappointment.

"It's a good thing, really," I said. "For me. For them." I looked out the window toward the cottages, imagined Fitch reading one of my comic books.

"We hope so," my mother said.

After ending the call with my parents, I walked to Dorrie's cottage and found her outside gazing up at the sky with a small telescope, swirling paint on canvas, creating an imaginary wormhole just beyond the moon, a maelstrom of violet and yellow. At the wormhole's center, perhaps millions of light-years away, she'd painted a tiny blue planet, not unlike Earth, orbiting a red star.

"What are you thinking about?" I asked, and saw that tears had stretched her mascara into tiny flames. I assumed she was upset about Fitch, since she never met the other kids at work like I do. Her job is to deliver a small wooden box of ash, with nothing but a name, photo, height, and age in her file to guide her through the process.

"I'm wondering if he'll ever be well enough to play on that jungle gym set in the courtyard. If any of them will be."

I stared at the swing set, the rainbow carousel, tried to imagine children playing. I had never wanted kids, but the fact that I could barely remember ever seeing one playing in the street, or on a crowded basketball court, or heading to school on a bus unnerved me.

"The park manager once told me the jungle gym was for morale," I said. "To give the trial patients hope. I think part of him really wants to see the kids out there one day."

We walked toward the playground. I followed Dorrie's lead, took off my shoes to feel the cool sand under my feet before sitting on the swing. The seat was damp from the misty air. I could feel it soaking through my jeans, no doubt leaving a dark spot. The lights from the windows of the other cottages and trailers played like a dozen tiny television sets—glimpses of people washing dishes, eating dinner, having a fight. One of the guards was punching a heavy bag. Molly was playing some sort of board game with her parents. Victoria was doing yoga.

"I wish people would come out once in a while," I said. "Apart from staring at the fire pit like zombies and getting shitfaced, I mean."

"We've gotten so used to keeping to ourselves, surviving. You can't blame them," she said. "You know Fitch talks about this park like it's some kind of promised land. He barely caught a glimpse of the rides when we got here, but he dreams about it. He asks me if I'll ever take him, why we can't go on one of his good days."

"And what do you say?"

Dorrie pulled the chains of our swings together so we drifted right next to each other, our feet tracing parallel waves in the sand.

"I don't know how to answer that question. I usually change the subject."

"It's amazing how all of this is invisible in the city," I said after a long moment, pointing at the sky. I didn't know how to respond to her comment. I just grabbed her hand and gazed up at the vast graveyard of long-dead stars.

We returned to the cottage and Dorrie watched Fitch toss and turn for a while. She told me the first sign of her son's illness had been abnormal sleep patterns. His eyes would flutter no matter how much he slept. He always felt like there was a fog wrapped around his head. He only had a few happy memories from before his illness. A swimming lesson, she explained. Holding her young son in the shallows of Hanauma Bay during a family vacation as he kicked, surrounded by schools of reef fish. One shot of infected water up his nose was all it took. Most of the first-wave victims in Hawaii died within six months or they slipped into a coma. That was before doctors introduced gene therapy and drug cocktails as a means to slow the morphing of cells. Fitch had beaten the odds with three organ transplants, clinging to a sliver of his old life for nearly two years.

"Hey, let's lighten up for a bit, if that's okay. Wanna watch a movie?" I began searching for something fun to watch, waited for Dorrie to give me the green light.

"Nothing depressing," she said.

"We are in the City of Laughter," I said.

I scrolled and scrolled; she remained silent.

"Anything?"

"So far he's been lucky," Dorrie said. "Because of my ex, Fitch had so many chances the other kids didn't have—a liver, a kidney, a lung. But there's no plan B for a brain. The treatments are slowing the spread, but it's only a matter of time."

"We don't have to watch anything if you're not in the mood," I said, turning off the TV.

Dorrie picked up the remote and turned it back on.

"No, let's watch something ridiculous," she said.

She curled into me, and I thought about all the nights these past nine months that ended just like this one—never acknowledging the future, desperately wanting to forget the past—taking small comfort in the equilibrium that we both knew couldn't last forever.

*   *   *

I awoke the next day to the distant bellow of Osiris making a test run. Dorrie was still asleep beside me, her legs tucked tight against her body. I was normally at the park by now, changing into my costume before she stirred in the morning. I peeked out the window and saw others doing the same, waiting for their turn to make their way to work with minimal chance of running into someone else. No neighborly chitchat or gossip, each of us holding a perpetual funeral in our heart and mind, eyes fixed on the peak of Osiris, where loudspeakers blared Grieg's "Morning Mood" right on time, every day at 8:00 A.M., and the soft female voice, sometimes adopting a faux-British accent, telling us to smile and laugh, to focus on the good we were doing for the children, for our country. "And always remember," the voice continued, "to turn that frown upside down!"

In the next room, I could hear Fitch watching an old episode of *Barney & Friends*. I climbed out of bed, walked up to the glass wall that separated him from the rest of the world. He looked over and waved, quickly returned to drawing a labyrinth with crayons. It was a good day for him, which meant a day of video games and comic books punctuated by visits from the park nurse who checked his vitals. Such spells of energy never lasted long, though, and it was too early to be certain of the treatment's effectiveness. The color had returned to his skin, but his eyes remained those of a person who's never known rest, sunken into bruised craters.

"I bet you can't solve this one," he said, crossing his arms. He held the labyrinth he'd drawn against the glass. "You have to get the prince and princess out. The prince came to save her but then he got trapped, too."

"What are those pointy things?" I asked. "And those rectangles in the middle of the path?"

"Spikes and trapdoors," he said. "And there's a half Pegasus, half shark that will eat the prince and princess if they don't escape soon. One Mississippi, two Mississippi, three Mississippi . . ."

After I saved the prince and princess, I gave Fitch his daily comic book. This had become something of a routine between us. It was the one hobby I'd shared with my little brother, eventually amassing nearly three thousand issues. Comics let us see a brighter world, forget our troubles, allowed us to dream. And I wanted this for Fitch. He deserved another world.

He was flipping through one of my brother's favorite issues of *Fantastic Four*. "Who is this?" He'd begun asking me for background on the characters. "And this?"

I pointed to each team member and explained they had traveled in a spaceship through a cosmic storm that gave them superpowers.

"I wish we could have a cosmic storm," he said.

"Oh? And would you want to be invisible, be a human torch, have your body stretch, or be a pile of rocks?"

"I'd want to shape-shift so I could be all of those things or anything I wanted," he said. I could tell that our brief interaction had drained him more than usual. He sank into bed, the comic book resting in his lap, eyes fluttering. I placed my hand on the glass wall to say goodbye and told him I'd check on him after work.

When I went to the living room, Dorrie was already there, combing over an email from one of the drug trial's doctors. She spent hours each day researching treatments that were in development both in the United States and abroad, emailing the various programs about Fitch's case. I sat beside her on the couch as she cradled her morning coffee.

"The trial doctors told me the first round of drugs are barely slowing the spread of the virus," Dorrie explained. "And the pills could create more problems if Fitch keeps taking them long term. He's on a lower dose now, but I'm searching for other trials."

"So, you'd move again?" I said. I was thinking about myself, the price of moving forward, of all the good days Fitch would have versus the ones that were almost unbearable to witness. Dorrie still seemed to believe, or maybe she needed to believe, that everything would be okay somehow. I tried to play my role for her, the supportive friend, part-time mediocre lover, coworker, sort of father figure to Fitch.

"We go wherever he might have a chance," she said.

*   *   *

My manager glanced at the clock when I punched in for work an hour late.

"I know," I said. "I'm sorry. Just some personal stuff."

But instead of a lecture, he warned me about a family who'd been red-flagged this morning as a flight risk. The six-year-old girl, Kayla McNamara, was a level 5 biohazard with open pustules on her body, wearing a CDC-approved pink hazmat suit in a teddy bear print. While symptomatic transmission to adults was rare, the park didn't want to take any chances, especially when an employee might pass the virus to kids in their family. The mother was incredibly devout and believed solely in prayer, so the girl hadn't been treated with any of the drug cocktails administered to most infected children. The mother had also refused to be apart from her daughter when instructed to join the other parents in the Learning

Land Room. He told me to keep an eye on her but not to interfere in any way.

"Call me directly if it escalates," he continued. "We want to avoid a spectacle. We need to maintain the illusion for the children. The father will join them this afternoon."

I was juggling bean bags as I tailed the high-risk family from a distance. Normally a small fan inside the costume keeps me from overheating, but on this day the battery had died. Beads of sweat dripped down my face, stinging my eyes; my shirt and boxers clung to my body. I lifted my costume headpiece slightly, letting in a rush of air. I focused on Kayla as she pointed to a kiosk with balloons, an ice cream stand, the bumper cars. Her mother ignored her. If this girl was lucky, she'd last the day without collapsing. The heat weighed on my limbs, creating a halo of light-headedness. I wanted to stop Kayla's mother from ruining her daughter's final day. The little girl dutifully followed along and I was reminded of Fitch, how he was always brave for Dorrie, even though his lungs burned and his stomach ached so much he could only ingest liquids. "Dance of the Little Swans" played from the loudspeakers as Mrs. McNamara held on to Kayla in line for the Dipsy Doodle boat ride, furtively scanning the crowd from behind her oversized sunglasses. When she turned in my direction, I began dancing wildly, diving deep into character.

"Just let the poor girl go on the damn ride," I whispered inside my costume. I wondered what Kayla dreamed about—maybe she wanted to go to space like Fitch. "Just let her have this one thing."

But right as they were about to step onto a boat, her mother slipped out of line, pulling Kayla behind her, quickly weaving through the crowd.

"We have a runner," I said into the radio, alerting my manager and security. "Repeat, we have a runner. Headed west toward the Laughateria. Requesting immediate assistance." I tried to keep up with Kayla and her mother, uncertain when security would arrive, afraid one of the tower guards might take a shot if they noticed them. I looked toward the fence, saw figures in black scanning the park through the scopes of their rifles.

"Tell the watchtower security to stand down," I radioed to my manager. "I still have the family in sight."

"A Roller Daze Security Squad is on the way," my manager said.

The mother and daughter slowed to a walk. I crept up behind them, ducking behind signage and bushes to remain out of sight. They were headed to a perimeter fence, and despite the signs indicating injury or death from high voltage, the fences were not electrified.

"Excuse me, ma'am," I said, slowly approaching, "but you're entering an off-limits area. Are you okay, Kayla? Do you want to go on a ride?"

The girl looked up at her mother and then at me. Her tiny chest rose and fell as she tried to catch her breath.

"You don't understand," Mrs. McNamara said, crying. "They're trying to take her away. I thought I could do this. But I can't let her go." The little girl leaned on her mother, barely able to stand.

"It's okay," I said, reaching out my arms like some kind of savior. I felt sorry for this mother. Sure, the park was better than an overrun hospital or a converted warehouse turned plague ward, but what parent wanted to say goodbye? "I'm here to help. Take my hand, Kayla."

I took a few steps closer. I was nearly an arm's length away when something knocked the air out of me and I found myself on the ground, head throbbing. A man kicked me in the stomach. He tore off my mouse head and told me to keep my hands off his family. I probably could have grabbed him by the legs like a calf and taken him down, but the entertainment staff can be fired for touching guests. I closed my eyes when he spat in my face and told him I was sorry. I winced as he pulled back his fist for a right hook and then, in a blur of blue sequins, the security team on Rollerblades whisked the entire family away.

*   *   *

"I don't understand why you didn't at least try to block him," Dorrie said as she examined my scrapes and bruises. She told me the girl's mother had collapsed in her arms when Dorrie gave her the urn filled with her daughter's ashes, and the father apologized for hitting the mouse before they left.

"I've never been in a fight," I said. I could hear the low hum of the nebulizer machine in Fitch's room, the wet breaths he took as he inhaled medicated mist into his lungs.

"Fitch was calling for you today, by the way. He's been bad since this morning. He has a headache and he's struggling to breathe. The doctors said we'll start to see other problems, since we're weaning him off the drugs. There's another trial next month at Johns Hopkins. I thought his father could pull some strings. He tried, but he hasn't made any progress."

I picked up a sketch that was sitting on the table—Dorrie, Fitch, and someone I assumed to be Fitch's father in front of a lake. I could feel her studying me, as if I had stepped into a part of her world she'd never intended to share with me.

"We barely had any time at all. My husband, I guess I should be calling him my ex, has been saying he's close to getting Fitch another lung, a heart, but he's been saying that for months. I don't know. I'm just so tired of this, Skip."

Dorrie walked over to the glass partition that separated us from Fitch's room, stood in the doorway. I went to the kitchen, poured her a glass of wine, marveled at the organization of her fridge and freezer: a week of meals in Tupperware, all of Fitch's medicine labeled and separated. I came up behind her and handed her the glass. She drank half of it in one gulp. I stood there debating who she needed me to be at that moment. We stared at the lights of the machines surrounding her son, a toy planetarium projector shooting stars across the ceiling as he struggled to breathe. We both knew that without medical intervention, Fitch would last another month, maybe two.

Fitch's crying woke us up at four the next morning. He complained of his head pounding, his insides burning. By the time Dorrie washed her hands, pulled on a mask and gloves, there was vomit in his bed. He said the pounding had gotten worse.

"Is there anything you want me to do?" I asked.

"No," she said. "I'll take care of him. I've already alerted the medical office. Just wait outside for the on-call doctor."

I sat on the porch, stared at the lights that ran the length of Osiris like a lightning bolt, a judgment from the sky. The doctor came and went. I remained outside until late morning, when Dorrie said Fitch had finally settled down.

"So, he's okay for now?" I asked.

Dorrie looked back toward the house, considered the question. The front porch was slowly filling with sunlight, heralding a new day at the City of Laughter. For this moment, we were caught in the silence, the sort of gravity the park did its best to hide.

"I don't think he was ever really going to be okay," she said.

*   *   *

The following day I was in charge of a small group of children—a little girl named Janey, who clutched her naked Barbie doll for dear life; Genevieve, with the loose front tooth; Phong, in the beat-up Bruins hat; and Madison, who just wanted to go home. It was a day like any other at the City of Laughter—which is to say that I laughed and told jokes during business hours and walked home feeling like a shell of myself after helping the crematory crew clear out the coaster cars. I stopped off at the Olive Garden after work to grab dinner for Dorrie and some ice cream for Fitch, in case he was feeling well enough to eat it. I had a beer while I waited for my order. The bartender told me I looked like shit.

"Well, shittier than the typical shit," she said.

"Haven't really been sleeping well," I muttered, and left the conversation there. I played with my phone, slid past the screen saver of my brother, thought about texting or calling my family for the first time in weeks. What would I say? You were right? I'm in over my head? The television over the bar showed families and wildlife fleeing their homes in and around the San Francisco area—Muir Woods, an ancient forest on fire sparked by a summer of unprecedented heat. A commercial advertised a new funeral hotel for prolonged goodbyes. In the dining area, across the restaurant, a couple ate silently, an urn on the table between them. A group of waiters sang "Happy Birthday" to an old man dining alone in the corner.

When I arrived at Dorrie's cottage, she was reading out loud from one of the comic books I'd given Fitch, nestled in bed beside him. I could tell from her bloodshot eyes that something else in his little body had failed him. Dorrie had painted a Martian landscape onto one of the walls—a barren red plain punctuated by a volcano in the distance and a solar-powered NASA rover.

"Can we talk for a minute?" she said. "Leave the ice cream."

She kissed her son on the forehead and followed me outside. We sat on the swings of the playground, gently gliding above the sand.

"I gave him a double dose of the old trial medication. We only had a few doses left. He should feel a little better soon."

"What happened?" I asked.

She looked down at the tracks from her feet, reached out for my hand. "I've been thinking. Maybe we should take him to the park while he's well enough to enjoy it."

I stared at the lights of Osiris and thought of the hundreds of children I had placed on the ride over the course of a year—the population of an entire school. Some had even requested to sit in the front, so they could have the best view of the drops. After a while, I lost track of their names, but I could still see their faces when I closed my eyes. In some parallel world, maybe I'd join Fitch on some other coaster where we'd look down at the drop, hold each other's hands as we screamed through the loops and inversions, enjoying the wind on our faces, coursing through the sleeves of our shirts as the world became one rainbow blur. I'd put him on my shoulders afterward, treat him to anything he wanted at the gift shop. It wouldn't be this place. No, it would be Disneyland or Universal or Six Flags (anywhere but here). We'd come home to Dorrie painting—maybe a portrait of the three of us—and Fitch would tell her about all the rides we'd gone on, how brave he was even during the inversions.

"Are you sure?" I asked.

"I received the dates for the next drug trial that might be an option for him. He's not even guaranteed to participate. They put him on a damn waiting list."

I got up and kissed her brow, pressed our heads together, trying to hold all that needed to be left unsaid inside of us, everything she was asking me to do.

"Okay," I said.

Before I fell asleep, I left a message on my mom's phone: *I love you. I miss him, too. Every day. But I'm still here. You're still here. And you were always there for both of us.*

The next morning the machines around Fitch's bed told us he had stabilized during the night, but we knew he might *feel* different once he woke up, and that the number of remaining good days were few. We snuck into his side of the room while he slept, hung streamers and balloons over his bed. On his lap, I placed a City of Laughter T-shirt with a logo of the Chariot of Osiris and its several loops.

"Wait, what?" Fitch said, confused, still half-asleep, when he woke and looked around the room. He studied the T-shirt and then, "Oh my god! Are you guys serious? Are you really taking me?"

Dorrie nodded and Fitch immediately began disconnecting himself from all the machines before hopping out of bed and packing a bag with his favorite toys, the last comic book I gave him, a juice box, a jacket. He asked me what else he might need.

"Just your awesome self," I said. "We'll leave first thing after dinner."

I gave Fitch a map of the park, pointed to the color-coded legend in the corner as he unfurled it on the floor. I traced my fingers along the brick path that was filled with the carved names of visitors, past the candy-striped entrance gates to the courtyard containing the Laughateria and other exploration zones.

"And sometimes the trainers let kids feed the seals a bucket of fish," I said, pointing to the Aqua Zone.

"Oh, I know," Fitch said.

"He knows," Dorrie said.

Fitch pulled out his handmade map of the City of Laughter from his toy chest, complete with annotations in crayon. In his version, he'd drawn himself on every ride, seated beside me and his mother. He drew us walking hand-in-hand along the brick path between the attractions. In one corner, he'd created a schedule, highlighting the rides he wanted to go on first, circling the shows he wanted to see. He pointed to the Laughateria, looked up, and asked:

"Will you be performing? Will you be the mouse?"

"Do you want me to be the mouse?" I said.

Fitch considered this for a long while and seemed to decide that he'd rather have me to himself. "Nah," he said. "Who's going to ride with me if you're a mouse?"

Throughout my workday, Dorrie texted me that Fitch hadn't stopped unpacking and repacking his bag and studying the maps of the park. I stopped by the gift shop during my lunch break and bought him an astronaut onesie, a hat that said *Junior Space Commander*, and a pair of glow-in-the-dark sneakers. I returned to Dorrie's cottage after work and slipped the gift box through the slot in Fitch's glass door. He picked it up and shook it, studied the wrapping paper printed with tiny roller coasters.

"What's it for?" he asked.

"Your birthday," Dorrie said. "A very early present since you've been so good."

I thought Fitch would tear through the wrapping. Instead, he methodically peeled the tape off each box, careful not to damage the paper. When he opened the first one, he held the astronaut uniform against his body. He put on the hat, examined himself in the mirror with a grin.

"This is awesome," he said. "Thanks."

"Our mission today, Commander," I said, "is to have fun. Can you do that?"

Fitch straightened his posture and saluted back: "Yes, sir."

"Then gather your gear. We will be embarking at seventeen hundred hours."

Hand in hand, Fitch led Dorrie down the path toward the park. I avoided looking up at Osiris as I followed along behind, studying the tuft of hair peeking out of Fitch's hat, the planet pins and dinosaur stickers he'd affixed to the brim, Dorrie in that purple summer dress she'd said she never had the chance to wear. She couldn't take her eyes off her son. I noticed the wildflowers growing through the cracks in the concrete, the way the air pollution had turned the sun nearly red.

"Hey, Fitch, you speed demon. I pulled some strings so you can have personal encounters with the animals. We'll have the miniature golf course all to ourselves."

"Prepare to get destroyed," Fitch said.

*   *   *

"I want to see the tigers," Fitch shouted as soon as we entered the park. "No, let's go on a ride."

He pointed to the Dipsy Doodle teacups. Around and around three times in a row, the world continued to spin after we finally stepped off. He climbed atop the dragon that was showing its chicken-wire interior, crawled through the fairy tree in desperate need of repair. But all Fitch saw was magic—and for a split second, watching him zigzag across the park, seeing him smile, really smile, for the first time since I'd known him, I almost forgot where we were.

For the most part, Dorrie remained quiet unless Fitch called her over for a photo or asked her to accompany him on a ride. She lingered in the background as we walked among the attractions, barely ate when we stopped for a snack at the Laughateria.

"Skip?" Dorrie said as we left the cafeteria, watching Fitch run toward the arcade. "Can you tell me how it'll happen?"

"Are you sure you want to know?" I asked.

"You're going to put him on the ride, right? I need to understand what I'm asking you to do," she said.

"He won't feel any pain," I began. "There's supposedly a period of euphoria. Most are unconscious after that. He'll be gone by the third inversion."

"No," she said. "I guess I want to know how you do it. If you didn't know Fitch, would he just be another kid you send on that ride? Do you remember them?"

Dorrie watched her son inspect the games as I told her about my charges, how I wrote their names and details in a notebook—Emma singing Disney songs, Colton covering himself with vending machine rub-on tattoos, Stacey wearing an oversized shirt that said CLIMATE CHANGE THREATENS BEER and who wanted to be a marine biologist.

After I was done, we purchased twenty dollars' worth of tokens, enough for Fitch to buy a stuffed tiger, and joined him at the Skee-Ball machine. But apart from today and all the nights I'd spent with Fitch, I wanted Dorrie to hear the words: "I care about him, too."

"I know you do," she said.

Our time was running out. Fitch was scheduled with Group 4B: Hospice-Sponsored Children, which meant we only had another hour. The park's animal trainers, neighbors of mine, gave us a special Big Cats show and let Fitch feed the sea lions. Afterward, without saying anything, I led us in the direction of the Chariot of Osiris. I saw Fitch looking up at it, his eyes returning to the map. I'll always wonder how much he knew in that moment.

"Are we going on this now?" he asked.

"Well, your mom doesn't like roller coasters, and I'm in charge of the control booth today," I said. And all this was true. I had told my manager that I wanted to be the one who pushed the button. "But this is a big-boy ride. You're a big boy, right? You're a space commander, right?"

"Yes," he answered. "I mean yes, sir. I'm a big boy. But—"

"Hmm?"

"Can the tiger come?"

Dorrie kneeled beside him and handed him the stuffed tiger. "I love you so much," she said. "Mommy had a really good day with you." She asked him for another hug before he sprinted off toward Osiris. Dorrie clutched onto me, sobbing as Fitch joined the line of children, her fingers digging into my clothes. I could feel the weight of her slipping, her legs buckling.

"I'll be right there," I yelled to Fitch as I helped his mother stand.

"I'm going to sit here on this bench," Dorrie said, barely audible. "Come get me after."

I moved as if the stone path had turned to quicksand. Each step had the potential to stop me in my tracks, my selfish thoughts racing, wanting to keep Fitch here with us somehow, the three of us together. I closed my eyes and breathed deeply, told myself to think happy thoughts about intergalactic victory with the help of Space Commander Fitch. I tried to imagine him at his worst, when his paper-thin skin turned impossible colors, as if every cell in his body had been set aflame. I reminded myself that the virus eating at his brain had wrapped around his synapses, stealing a little part of him with each minute—and then I opened my eyes and saw him more alive than he had ever been.

As far as Fitch was concerned, he was already in the sky with Orion high above, aiming his arrow at Jupiter or Venus. He was shaking with anticipation in his seat, rubbing his arms. I draped his never-worn denim jacket around his shoulders, pulled down the padded restraints, buckled him in tightly. He asked me if we could get ice cream after, and I wanted to tell him he could have all the ice cream he wanted. I studied his face and wondered if this was just the wish of an astronaut who knew he might not be coming home. I gave him a high five, told him to hold on tight. I told him he was on a mission to save the world and that I wanted to hear him shout at the stars and raise his arms as high as he could to rake the bottom of the sky.

From the control booth, I gave him one final salute. The orange shimmer of the electric torches dotting the tracks washed over him just enough so I could see his silhouette amid the excited horseplay of the other children. I pushed the red button and the chains of the ride clicked and clacked, pulling the train upward. Each sound vibrated through my body, striking at the temptation to stop it all. Dorrie was standing with the other parents near the guarded perimeter gates. I sat back in the darkness of the booth, waiting. And for a moment, I thought I heard Fitch's triumphant shouts, perhaps the happiest sound I will ever hear, until there was only the roar of Osiris and then nothing at all.

THROUGH THE GARDEN OF MEMORY

My parents and I were driving home to Palo Alto from a belated memorial in Minneapolis three months after my cousin Kayla had been euthanized. I fell asleep in the back seat on our final day of travel, the smell of smoke seeping through a cracked window reminding me of home. I felt hot and light-headed, and when I looked up, the stars seemed to streak across the sky as if the universe had been grazed with a paintbrush. My father refused to stop. He said we were making good time. I woke up in a hospital plague ward a week later, my parents watching over me from a quarantine observation room.

"The kids you babysat during the memorial tested positive," my mother said through an intercom next to my bed. "Their parents swore they'd been tested. We thought they were safe. I'm so sorry, Jun."

"Fucking germ factories," I said, allowing the room to come into focus. My throat crackled when I spoke, every word like coughing up pebbles. I thought about the gauntlet of toddler hands that smelled of actual shit, rubbing against my face during Twister, my aunt's stale basement air circulating with tantrums. Beside me, I saw several other beds filled with adults—some awake and staring at the ceiling, others unconscious and hooked into machines pumping air down their throats. "How are the kids?"

"Kenta is in the ICU; the others are stable, receiving gene therapy," my mother said.

I nodded, which sent a sharp pain down my back. I felt like I could sleep forever.

"The treatments for children don't seem to be working for adults," my father said. "It might be a new strain. They don't think it's air-borne anymore—of course, nobody really knows for sure. Some college students were infected at a beach, maybe from sewage contamination."

I felt like I was looking at someone else's body. I couldn't feel the sheet over my legs. The skin on my arms seemed abnormally pale, almost translucent, as if I were transforming into a deep-sea creature.

"What's happening to me?" I asked.

My parents shook their heads, held each other, a public display of affection I had rarely seen before.

"We don't know," my mother said.

Across the hall, I heard doctors and nurses rushing into a room, the steady tone of a flatlining patient, the tiny explosions of a defibrillator. I wanted to tell my parents that I loved them, but my lips felt cemented together. My muffled screams filled the room. I saw my mother putting her hands to her mouth, crying. The skin on my body quickly cycled from normal to see-through; stars seemed to float through my veins. My mother began speaking in Japanese, something she did only when she was upset. I heard my father screaming for help. I closed my eyes for a moment.

I awake in darkness. I can barely tell if my eyelids are open. I cry for help, for a nurse to turn on the lights, for any other patients beside me to make a sound so I know I'm not alone. I'm no longer in a hospital gown but in what feels like a T-shirt and jeans. There is no breathing tube in my nose, no drip in my vein muddling the pain. The charged air on my bare feet feels like how a child might imagine clouds—substantial enough to rest on yet capable of being traversed, an infinite expanse and cocoon at once. Above, the air feels light on my fingertips, as if gravity has dissipated, but such physics would suggest a grounding force. I wave my hands beneath my feet and cannot detect where my body finds purchase in the dark.

I start to wander, and soon other voices reach me: *Where are you? I can't see you. My phone won't turn on. Mine too. Everyone, keep talking.* Arms outstretched, bodies walking toward sound until we converge—chest against chest, heads bouncing off each other like billiard balls. At first, we count and there are ten of us. Most had been in hospital plague wards, like me; a few had still been living their lives. A lawyer from DC was getting ready for work, eating cereal with his daughter. An admitted felon had recently been released from jail for robbing his brother. A high school student and VR game vlogger said he was diagnosed only days ago. He'd been playing a game in his bed, hoping to finish while he could. An old woman had been talking on the phone to her daughter, who had just buried her children.

"My daughter had been coughing a lot lately," the old woman explains. She is almost shouting, even though I think she's standing a few feet away from me. "I needed to believe it was the flu."

"My parents were visiting me at the hospital," I say in perfect English, with no hint of my Japanese accent. I study the sounds emanating from my mouth—a perfect California boy, lingering on the ends of my words as if every final syllable is made of syrup.

The silences in our conversation fill my ears with a ringing tone, the sound of my own eardrums. I pinch myself to wake up. I want to see my parents watching over me. I close my eyes and open them again. I stamp my feet on the non-ground, hoping to break through whatever force or blanket of air is holding me.

"Maybe there's a way out of here," I say.

"But what if we're supposed to stay?" someone says.

"I'm not just going to wait here," the lawyer says.

"What if we get separated?" the old woman says.

"We hold on to each other," I answer.

"Who the hell put you in charge?" the felon asks.

"He's the only one suggesting anything useful," says the lawyer.

I can sense the shape of the others around me as we push through the dark like a conga line. The lawyer asks people for their theories, and it's not long until we connect the plague to this place. None of us can tell how long we have been gone. We aren't tired or hungry. There has to be an edge, a door or stairwell to somewhere else. If we cry out loud enough, someone will hear us. When the old woman begins to sing to fill the silence, we immediately join in, taking turns with our own selections—the Carpenters followed by the Beatles and the Talking Heads.

I'm in the middle of "Kokomo" when the lawyer matter-of-factly interrupts and confesses that he's been having an affair.

"TMI," the gamer kid says. "Random much?"

"I'm afraid my wife will leave," the lawyer says. "I have a family."

"A possibility," the old woman says. "But if you're not honest with her, things will never be quite right."

"We just sharing shit now? Okay, my older brother was murdered in a hit-and-run," the gamer kid says. "He was traveling with a bad crowd, you know. Not that I was a saint."

"Mom died of an overdose when I was a baby," the felon says. "Not what you think. She was just taking these pills to stay up because I wouldn't stop crying. My dad pretty much blamed me for her being gone. Been an asshole to me my entire life."

I wait a long time to confess anything about myself. I never snuck out at night to smoke. I never had an affair (never had a real girlfriend, for that matter). My parents and I moved to America after my father's job ended with the shuttering of the Fukushima power plant. We helped my uncle in Berkeley with his bakery. I received scholarships for college. But I also remember long lines in drab government buildings, my mother crying at night. I rarely spoke in class because I was ashamed of how I sounded. I rarely spoke to anyone, and yet I wrote constantly. I was afraid I wouldn't make my parents proud, even though they told me they were whenever I showed them my stories and poetry. I'd spend hours locked in my room the summers I was home from college. My father would take out his reading glasses and flip through my pages with an electronic translator.

"Yes, good. Very good," he'd say, passing the pages to my mother. He kept a notebook in his shirt pocket where he'd write the words and idioms that were unfamiliar to him, and he'd try to work this new vocabulary into conversation—*Isn't dinner a ball? This picture you took has good chiaroscuro. Wicked tasty, teriyaki. I'm stoked for your graduation.*

"So talented," my mother would say. "But when will you get paid?"

"Soon," I would tell my parents. "Art takes time. It's all about finding the right people who get your work. It's very complicated."

I think about my parents and uncle waiting for me at the bakery where I work part-time in the summer. Maybe they'll assume I'm wrapped up in my writing. I think about my family waiting for me at home, calling the police. I can see my father taking out his notebook from his top pocket, talking to detectives, telling them to *break a leg.*

We hear new voices in the void as we push on. A cry for help, a drawn-out hello. We instruct the newcomers to follow our voices—*over here, over here now*—until our bodies collide.

"I was driving the twenty-eight bus. Just pulled out of Fillmore, and suddenly all went black. Felt like I was falling," one newcomer says.

"Falling?" several people murmur.

"Like I was wearing a parachute."

"Anybody remember falling?" I ask.

Silence.

"My god, my passengers," the bus driver says. "My bus."

I consider the stories of the newcomers—what if we did come from above? And what does *above* mean in a place where we can touch the air beneath our feet? For all we know, we've been walking in circles.

"So, what are you saying?" the felon says.

"Maybe up is the only way out," I say.

"Or there is no way out," the gamer kid says. "Like an animal trap."

"Let's say there is a way out up there. How do we reach it?" the lawyer asks. "It's not like we have a ladder."

More voices reverberate in the distance. Too many to discern any kind of direction. The silence evolves into a steady hum like a crowded cafeteria. Fragments of English, Spanish, German, Chinese, languages I can't make out. I tell everyone to count off: 1, 2, 3, 4, 5, 6, 7, 8, 9, 10 . . . 26, 27, 28, 29, 30 . . . 63, 64, 65 . . . what if, what if . . .

"Are you fucking nuts?" the felon says. "This ain't no circus."

"Oh, I don't think I'd be able to do that," the old woman says. And maybe I have my doubts, but we need to try something.

"C'mon everyone, think about it," I say. "Whatever we are here, these aren't our real bodies. We're not tired or hungry. We don't feel hot or cold. I think we can do this. I don't think we can get hurt."

We try to arrange ourselves by size to create a human pyramid; figuring this out feels like it takes hours or even days. People shout their height and weight. But I'm not a doctor or a police officer and so the numbers mean little to me. We move on to broad descriptions— *pretty big dude, you know? I work out.* I picture a tank top and gym shorts.

"Okay, bigger folks down below. Crouch on all fours," I say.

Based on our initial math, which seems increasingly pointless due to the endless stream of people joining, we likely have the numbers for at least a fifty-layer pyramid. Surprisingly, everyone is communicating with ease, helping each other to their positions. I wonder if our work would go so smoothly if we were able to see each other.

I feel out the first layers of the pyramid for tightness, stability, running my hands across more bodies than I have touched in a lifetime. This is no time for shame or modesty.

"We need more strong people here. Follow my voice. Over here now," I yell, noticing a gap in the chain.

"Somebody just squeezed my ass," a woman yells.

"Seriously? Please stop," I say. "You don't want me to find you."

"Can we hurry this up already?" the felon says, crouched somewhere in the center of the base.

The next layers proceed to climb, slowly, regularly apologizing for stepping on people's heads. Again I inspect the pile, feeling for gaps, asking if everyone has a firm grip and foot anchor.

"I don't think I can do this. Someone get me the fuck out," a voice says, and I hear the muted thumping of a body falling down the pyramid, the slap of skin, the occasional *motherfucker*.

"Whoever that was, I need you to climb back up. You can do this. Think about your family and friends. Forget about what your body could do. That doesn't matter now." Several other people fall as I'm saying this and, again, I encourage them to find their places.

When it seems like all but the very lightest of us are in position, I tell the little ones to head to the top. It takes several moments for them to signal that they've arrived, long enough for me to again inspect the perimeter. Aided by my featherweight frame, I follow the last group—heads, hands, and backs serving as my steps toward an invisible sky. As I ascend, I hear snippets of chatter from within: *Whose brilliant idea was this? It's a wonder we're not all suffocating in here. I don't think I can hold on for much longer. Let me out. Let me out!*

Near the pinnacle the weight of the air begins to dissipate, as if I'm climbing Everest, punching through the boundary of Earth and sky. I stretch my hands up high, try to find a grip on anything, and scream for help: *Can anybody hear me?* As I shout, a tingling sensation weaves through my body; my hair rises above my head as if I were floating in water. I fumble with a button on my shirt and rip it off. I raise my hand and feel the button vibrate until it slowly floats off into the dark. A tremor stirs below, and the pyramid begins to buckle, undoing the platform of bodies underneath me. I feel hands holding tight to my ankles, and then their fingers slip away, and I topple down along with the rest of them, volleying off one another, flailing like a pinball. I crash-land on a bald man with a mustache, feel the weight of him as a web of limbs forming over me, writhing around me for purchase.

"Is everybody okay?" I ask. My voice sounds muffled underneath the pile of groans and complaints. I work to climb through, searching for empty space. "Is everybody okay?"

"Yeah, we're fine. We're invincible here, remember? So, you find Jesus or E.T. up there?" the felon asks.

"Not exactly," I say. "There's some sort of pull, though. A button floated out of my hand."

"Okaaay," the felon says. "That's a cool trick, but how does that help us? I mean, your sorry ass is still down here."

"Maybe the force will be stronger if we climb higher."

"And how many people will we need for that?" someone asks.

What little authority I'd attained by simple virtue of being the first to speak out begins to disintegrate. But people are still talking about getting out. People still need to pick up their children, feed their dog, say *I love you* to their spouses. For now, no one has brought up the fact that in the real world, our bodies are inhabited by an impossible virus. Perhaps we all need to believe in second chances.

"Look!" the old woman yells. I see her silhouette pointing as if someone or something has raised a dimmer switch; the darkness subsides but only just. A planetarium projects stars onto a ceiling, a zoetrope night lamp casting light on walls of black—except no, it's nothing that familiar or terrestrial.

All around us, spheres of iridescent light the size of hot-air balloons descend like a school of jellyfish. We are too mesmerized by the beauty of it to look away or even think about being afraid, as if we've been gifted with the sight of a cosmic occurrence like the birth of a star or the death of a planet, the aurora in a thousand snow globes. For the first time, we're able to see each other. Me in a T-shirt with Godzilla on it that I saw in the window of a store once but could never afford, the felon with a shoddy tattoo of a tiger on his arm, the gamer kid in a faded Stanford sweatshirt, the lawyer in salmon-colored slacks and a navy polo, and the old woman in a faded Bruce Springsteen T-shirt. We realize our numbers have grown far greater than we believed. The orbs descend as far as we can see, illuminating the faces of thousands, and as they touch down, scenes play within like movies—children running in a field, a couple having sex in a bathroom stall, a man crying in a hospital, children huddled on a concrete floor in an immigration detention center. The images shimmer as if made of water. The lawyer walks toward the closest orb. He sees himself in a deli flirting with the girl at the counter, giving her his card.

Farther ahead, the old woman recognizes her late husband. She looks back toward the group, uncertain what to do.

"It's my Francis," the old woman says. Her hands graze the orb and the entire scene ripples. "It feels like oil."

I take her hand, lead her into the orb, and others follow. The orb's membrane washes over our bodies as we pass through, as if we're walking through a waterfall. When we emerge, surprisingly dry, we're standing in the corner of a hospital room—the antiseptic smell wafts through the air. A past version of the old woman is feeding her husband in bed as they watch *Jeopardy!* on the television. *Who is Thomas More*, her husband says. His voice is barely audible. *What are mitochondria*, answers the old woman of the past. I squeeze her shoulders as we watch, and she begins to cry. I lead her out of the memory, pushing through the hospital room wall where we emerged. I wonder if all the various parts of our lives have been untangled and laid out before us to explore.

I push forward, half searching for an orb of my own, weaving through the crowds congregating around tiny planets of memory. *Excuse me, excuse me. Have you seen my childhood?* Some people are wandering into the lives of others as if connecting the dots toward enlightenment.

"That was a really amazing one," someone says as I pass. "Real salt-of-the-earth people. My great-grandparents also suffered through the Depression."

Out here, largely alone, I feel like I'm walking through the vast empty spaces between the stars of our constellations. I approach a lone man sitting on the ground, staring at an orb of himself. The memory shows him at a theme park, putting a little boy wearing an astronaut outfit into a roller coaster car. He slowly walks toward the control booth, watches as the train climbs toward the sky. He is crying in the orb. He is crying outside of it. I crouch beside him for a moment and rub his back.

"I thought maybe he'd be here," the man says. The orb shows the arms of children waving in excitement as the roller coaster plummets. "His mother is still out there. In the world. Alone."

"Maybe you should go back to the crowd and be with the others," I say.

"They'll make their way out here soon enough," he says.

"Walk with me for a bit, then." I hold out my hand and help the man up.

Together, we move through the orbs. Other scenes seem to exist out of step from the rest—more looking glass than memory. These ones are impassable, locked—a warehouse filled with people laid out on cots, attended to by medical staff. Those not sleeping seem catatonic. Their eyes follow the doctors like mannequins or dolls observing the world. The skin of some resembles my arms before I found myself here—translucent, filled with light. It's unclear if this is the natural course of the plague or a side effect of our attempts to cure it. In some orbs, white CDC vans collect the afflicted who have been cast out of their homes or fallen in the street.

"Is this what happened to us?" the man says.

"Who knows," I answer. I wonder how much time has passed *out there* and if my parents are safe. I do not want them to join me in this place.

Of course, some orbs seem to lack any explanation at all—a silver pod the size of a coffin darting across our solar system, crashing into the ocean; a large iridescent planet like the interior of an abalone shell orbiting three stars; a woman in a cave wearing animal skins and crying over the body of a little girl. We watch this cave woman sing in unknown languages, place flower petals over the girl's eyes. We watch her walk across a vast plain as she sheds her clothing and turns into light.

The orbs begin to tremble, sending ripples across our memories. The crowd slowly catches up to us. I can see the old woman and the lawyer. I wait for them, wave them over. Not far from where I stand, a scene of a girl eavesdropping on her parents fighting begins.

to disintegrate, evaporates into mist. And just beyond that orb, I finally see my life—my parents strolling through Japantown in San Francisco, me lagging behind, a preteen with headphones, peering into shops that reminded me of my childhood, smelling the aroma of grilled eel, riffling through the manga selection at Kinokuniya bookstore.

In other orbs I see my uncle Manabu give me my first bicycle while at a picnic in Golden Gate Park. I see my mother talking to a school counselor about my college options and the long nights I never knew about—my parents poring over legal and financial documents they only half understand, trying to buy my way into the future.

"We have to make sure Jun's going to be okay," my father says. "In case we're not here."

"Exercise more," my mother says. "Drink tea. I don't plan on dying anytime soon."

I stand over this incarnation of my parents and desperately want to hug them. I want to shout beyond time and tell them they were perfect—every bike ride, every sleepover, every toy we couldn't afford. All the prayers and lessons and after-school programs that helped me belong in this country even if I never fully believed it to be true.

"It's there," my father would say whenever I asked him why I needed to believe so hard in everything, why my friends didn't seem to have to try as hard. The man, the lawyer, and the old woman enter the orb, crowding into my childhood bedroom. "Opportunities are like little seeds floating in the wind. Your life is there. Some people have a big net to collect them all. Other people need to pray that the right seeds, the best ones, make their way to them with just enough bad ones to appreciate the good."

"Your family really did right by you," the old woman says. She's

sitting on my single bed surrounded by Gundam robots. She's studying my father, staring straight into his eyes.

"I didn't tell them that enough," I say.

When we leave the orb, I call out to the darkness and pray, thinking about each and every memory I have of my parents. I want to see
the moments I never knew, relive the ones I took for granted. The
lawyer leaves us to find his family. The man from the theme park
heads off in search of the orb where I found him, if it even still exists.
But the old woman remains at my side as I'm drawn forward. She
begins telling me stories of her thirty years as a nurse, her love affair
with a major league ballplayer.

"Once in the dugout," she says, laughing. "I didn't care if I was
only the side action. It was an exciting time in my life. I was using
him, too. Season tickets for five years."

When a new orb fills our path, I see a doctor talking to my parents
in a packed hospital waiting room. On the televisions hanging from
the ceiling, a talk-show host blames the plague on the governments of
the world, calls it an orchestrated attempt to reduce the population—
*Less people, more water and food, lower carbon emissions. Think about it!
This was the only way they could think of to dig us out of this mess.*

"We've stabilized him," the doctor says to my parents. "But you
need to understand that most patients at this stage will eventually
lose all brain activity."

"What happened to his skin?" my father asks.

"We don't know," the doctor says.

My mother studies the other families waiting, crying, each cluster
separated by clear cubicle dividers. A little boy in an enclosed biohazard gurney rolls past, staring dead-eyed at the ceiling. The talk-
show host on the television tells his audience that our utilities have
been compromised—*Don't drink the water. Don't take public transit.
They say the plague isn't airborne anymore. Okay, maybe. But they're*

*sure as shit getting the virus to people somehow. And do I need to say it?
Cut out the goddamn sushi. Cut out all food coming from over there—
Russia, Asia, all the first epicenters. If you don't hunt it, don't trust it.* I
see my mother looking down when the talk-show host says this, the
waiting room filled with other Asian families.

"Surprisingly, our readings show that his brain is incredibly ac-
tive," the doctor explains. "We've been seeing wave spikes before
activity flatlines."

"Can he hear us?" my father asks.

"We can't know for sure, but he's in there somewhere, dreaming."

Suddenly the orb shakes, the scene shifts to a hospital room I'm
sharing with a dozen other patients. A plastic partition surrounding
my bed prevents my parents from holding me.

"Find a way back to us. Believe. Any moment now. Wake up, Jun.
Wake up now," my father says.

The remaining memories, snapshots of the world, cluster and
wither into the ether, the last fragments of light extinguishing like
the afterglow of fireworks. The crowd is silent, shuffling about in the
darkness once again.

"What the hell was that about?" someone finally says. "If we can't
fucking change anything."

"I had forgotten a lot of my childhood," the lawyer says. "I got to
see my grandparents. Friends I hadn't thought about in years."

"Maybe we understand each other more now that we've sampled
each other's lives," the old woman says, as if she's standing on a soap-
box at a protest. "Maybe we can be kinder to one another."

"Again, lady," someone says, "what good does that do in the world
if we're trapped here?"

"Maybe it's a sign we're supposed to go back?" I answer.

"Maybe this is where we need to be," someone else says. "I can
relive my life with my husband."

"I had shit to do, you know?" the felon says. "I got a fucking life."

I can feel his breath behind me. My eyes are still adjusting to the dark.

"He's right. I mean, how many of us have families?" the bus driver says.

"I have a son," someone else adds. "He's working for Doctors Without Borders to help the plague relief efforts. The French have a drug that might slow the transformation of internal organs. Not a cure, but the drugs are being piloted in hard-hit villages in the South Pacific."

"Give me a break. Nobody knows how this virus works," says a man with an Australian accent.

Silence fills the crowd for a moment.

"I was watching my little cousin. We were playing Twister. I put a Band-Aid on him when he fell. I don't know. Maybe it was the contact. Maybe I accidentally drank out of the wrong juice glass," I explain.

"I slept with someone who turned out to be infected," someone else says.

"What if this is some kind of punishment?" the felon says.

"I'm pregnant," someone says. "I'm due next month. What could my baby possibly have done to deserve this? You tell me that."

For the first time in who knows how long, I sit down on the ground (or space or whatever it is). Something like static electricity fills my body, and I wonder if this is it—perpetual bickering, wallowing, or if, perhaps one day (whatever time counts for here), we'll find another way to occupy the dark, figure out how to fill it with all we were and all we know, now that we've been separated from the slog of life. But right now, all I want to do is cry, for myself, for my parents who I never thanked enough, for the long days and nights they'll spend beside my body, waiting. I see my mother bringing flowers to my room, my father reading stacks of my stories, practicing his English. Maybe he'll read the one I wrote about a salaryman in Osaka who falls asleep on the train and wakes in a world that has forgotten who he is. The old woman, no doubt searching for my presence, brushes her hand over my head. I let her frail fingers rest on my shoulders.

"Are you okay down there?" she asks.

"So much of their life was devoted to me," I say. "My mother prayed for a child for so long. The doctors didn't think it was possible. I was their fifth and last try with IVF. What are they going to do now?" The old woman doesn't respond. She crouches beside me and holds me in her arms.

The felon is standing one or two people away and seems to be picking fights with the others, screaming so loudly I can barely hear myself think.

"Yeah, why don't you come here and say that, asshole!" he yells. I can hear the commotion, feel the bodies around me writhe like disturbed bees in a hive. Someone pushes past me from behind. I hear what I think is a fight—clothes tearing, the successive cracks of punches, asshole bystanders who can't actually see anything cheering in the darkness. But then I hear something else. Crying. Others hear it, too. The wailing seems to be growing more frantic. It's so loud now that the hairs on my arms are standing on end. The fighting and waves of voices suddenly cease. I stand and what feels like the entire horde shuffles toward the cries. As the sound gets closer, the old woman and I crawl on all fours, feeling out in front of us, weaving through the labyrinth of legs. Nothing. I swear the crying is right in front of me. Hours might have passed. Nothing. Tiny toes. A foot. A chubby little head. "I have them," I say. *The poor thing. The kid didn't even have a chance. Can you do something about that crying?*

"The kid didn't even stand a chance," I repeat under my breath. I think about the unfairness of it all, the shit hand we've been dealt. "The kid didn't even have a chance, but maybe we can give them one," I say.

"Are you that pyramid guy?" someone asks.

"I am. And there are a lot more of us now."

"Are you saying what I think you're saying?"

"Maybe the baby's better off here," someone else shouts.

"Do you honestly believe that?" I say.

"What if we're just sending the baby to get sucked into some cosmic ventilation system?" a woman asks.

"We don't know," I say, my frustration growing.

Chatter erupts again, and so do the baby's cries.

Hell of a thing to be a baby in here.

You think the baby could tell people about this place?

Are you an idiot?

Wonder when the orbs are coming back. At least we had something to do then.

I walk through the crowd slowly, letting my void mates hear the child in my arms. Some reach out their hands, and I guide them to the baby's tiny body, head, and doughy hands, grasping onto my shirt. Perhaps in the world, my parents are sitting beside me. The hospital room televisions are playing the local news—a school shooting, another extinct animal, new statistics about the plague, people migrating from the heat. But my parents are telling me stories about a simpler life that I never knew, the kind where you could go to the beach and not worry about the sand or the city beyond it being swallowed by the sea, one where an earthquake never took away my father's job and we still woke up on a tiny street in a quiet neighborhood in a bustling metropolis where everyone grew old together. At night, my mother would read me folktales from Japan like the legend of the weaver and the cow herder, two lovers who abandoned their duties and were cast to opposite ends of the heavens, allowed to reunite for only one day a year—the day of the star festival, where I remember writing wishes on brightly colored chains of paper, hanging them on bamboo trees with my family—*I wish to be a famous soccer player (or maybe a writer). I wish to change the world. I wish for a long, healthy life for my family.*

"Okay," the felon says, standing right in front of me. He's touching the baby's head with his gargantuan hands. He's cooing and telling the baby to be brave. "Tell us what to do."

We begin to assemble, and I quickly lose track of the many layers forming the new pyramid. From all the rustling and small talk buzzing around, there seems to be a sizable population awaiting placement.

"Aren't we high enough?" someone shouts from above. "I think I feel what you were talking about before. My hair's floating. The air is different up here."

"I don't know," I shout. But perhaps it's time for us to try.

"Does anybody have a shirt or a jacket? Something I can use to make a sling?" I say. Someone hands me what feels like a nylon windbreaker—light and sleek and at least an XXL judging from how the jacket overwhelms my torso.

"It's the Charlotte Hornets jacket I had as a kid—bright turquoise, purple, and white. I loved that thing. Woke up here wearing it—perfect fit, even though I'm six-foot-seven now. I want it back when you're done," the man says.

I hand the baby to the old woman while I secure the jacket to my chest, tying the sleeves around my back, tucking the bottom into my pants, leaving a pocket for the child.

"Are you sure?" the old woman says. The baby gurgles in her arms as I reach for it.

"I've never been sure of anything," I say. "I wish we could see how high we've gone. I bet it's a sight, like something out of a Dr. Seuss book."

"If my grandchildren were little like this one, I'd want them to have a real life," the old woman says. "But part of me doesn't want to let go. What if the baby gets sick after we send it back? What if this is our second chance? I'm afraid."

The old woman kisses the head of the infant and hands them to me. I maneuver the baby into the pocket surrounding my chest, cinching the jacket arms tighter. The baby's breath and drool are moistening my shirt. The baby's fingers hold on to the collar of my T-shirt—*Yes, that's right. Hold on tight.* Like before, I ascend the pyramid, treading lightly to avoid stepping on too many heads and hands. I stop periodically to readjust the jacket, cinching the knots tight whenever I feel the sleeves coming loose, the sleek fabric threatening to untuck from my pants. With every layer, I check that the pocket is secure, afraid the baby might fall. Deep inside the pyramid the group shares more details about their lives, sings songs to keep up morale, reveals things they've never told anybody, because somehow not being able to see each other makes it all okay, like confessing to a priest or praying to the night sky. There are games of Twenty Questions and Truth or Dare alongside conversations about the soul and the future of humanity. It feels like I have been climbing for years, and perhaps in the land of life, years have passed. Will the child enter the body of a teenager or an adult, see through the eyes of an infant? Will they remember or be able to articulate any of this? The questions multiply as I reach the summit, as does the force of the pull from whatever resides above. I think about making wishes at the star festival and my parents trying so hard to read and understand the stories I've written. I think about my father telling me about opportunities in life floating in the wind like seeds. *May all the blessed seeds find their way to this child*, I whisper.

At the top, I can feel my body wanting to shoot upward into the black sky, as if a puppet master is pulling on marionette strings. Two hands grasp my ankles as I nearly lose my balance. But even at this height, the force is not enough to fully lift me. I unwrap the infant from the jacket and hold them tight to my chest. Breathe in the smell of innocence and youth.

"I bet you didn't expect to wake up to this," I say. "And who knows what you'll wake up to tomorrow. I hope you'll be okay."

As if the baby knows what is going to happen, they begin to cry.

"Throw the damn kid up there already," someone shouts from below.

"I hope I'm doing the right thing," I say. "Remember us."

And before I hesitate any further, I raise the infant above my head, feel their tiny squirming body sliding away from my hands. Almost immediately I regret letting go. The infant screams and I begin to sob. They are at the mercy of space now, the ether—all the invisible borders and choices between us. I remain at the pinnacle of the pyramid, looking up at nothing at all, waiting for the infant's cries to fade before climbing back down.

PIG SON

After my ex-wife mailed half of my son's ashes to me in an urn, I committed myself to growing the hearts and other organs that might have saved him inside of pigs. It's Fitch's birthday today, which means Dorrie texts me more than usual, which is pretty much never. Do you remember how I told you that he liked to fall asleep hugging his new collection of comic books? I've forgotten what he smelled like. I never respond to these messages. Dorrie doesn't really want a conversation. She still blames me for not being there in the end. She's never understood how hard I fought trying to save him. A real conversation would be too painful. It's the same reason I've never addressed Fitch's failed transplant in my peer-reviewed articles. His file sits inside my desk, rather than among the lab's program records, like a lost statistic.

My graduate assistant, Patrice, is shouting through the intercom, telling me to come to the lab quickly. I hear another voice I don't recognize, muffled and nasal and a little bit frantic, repeating the word *doctor* as if it's trying to convey an entire thought with a single word. I pull on my face mask and lab coat, open the outer door of my office. My staff is gathered around one of the glass holding pens where we keep our donor pigs. The pigs are all destined to help infected people like my son whose organs have given way to the plague. The timing is crucial, though. We need to reach the infected before they slip into the comas that mark the advanced stages of the illness. This one, donor 28, was nicknamed Snortorious P.I.G. after an intern put a gold chain and shades on him during a Halloween party. The pig studies me as I approach, wiggling its behind, and barely opens its mouth: *Dahktar*. The sound seems disembodied, like a ventriloquist is throwing their voice.

"Okay, very funny," I say, turning to my staff. "Who said that?"

They look at each other and Patrice points back to the pen.

"We think it's Snortorious," she says. Okay, sure. Forget that these pigs lack the necessary vocal cords for human speech, even if we have genetically modified them for accelerated growth and organ donor optimization.

Dahktar. This time the pig's mouth doesn't move at all. I'm starting to get annoyed, but there's something about the voice.

"Again," I say. I hop into the pen, nearly sliding on a piece of shit, and kneel, looking into the animal's blue eyes. "Say it."

Dahktar, he says. Jesus. The pig's strange voice, like a mouth filled with cotton balls, reverberates in my mind. After several more tests, there is no mistaking it. The pig's brain, not quite human and not quite swine, lights up like a firecracker on the MRI whenever he speaks.

"This does not leave the building. Not yet," I say. "We need to know what we have here. And we don't want someone else taking him away."

The staff simply nods, but that isn't good enough for me.

"I need to hear you say it: Yes, I won't say a word."

Yes, I won't say a word, they repeat in unison like we're in grade school. Okay, good. But this isn't some top-secret facility. There are no security clearances or repercussions here. The grad students were suspect even before the outbreak, swiping medical supplies for god knows what. I worry it's only a matter of time.

We divide the days between working with Snortorious and fulfilling our hospital organ orders. I pay Patrice's sister, Ammie, a speech therapist, to assist us in our research. We clear out one of the lab rooms to create a study/play area for Snortorious. We set up a television and a computer equipped with programmed paddle buttons specially modified for pig feet. I dig through my attic for my son's old books and toys. *Dahktar.* It's no surprise the word he heard the most around the lab would be his first. When Ammie and I work with him in his room, we break lab protocol and remove our masks and gloves. He seems to soak up everything we share with him—flash cards, cartoons, children's books, including *The Three Little Pigs* and *Charlotte's Web.* We treat him like a child, though it's hard to say where his mind is at any given moment. Ammie gives him treats, gold stars. Positive reinforcement is important, she says. He's learning so fast. At first, he has a new favorite word each day—*sheep, horse, farmer, bus, yellow, mud, Ammie.* Mornings and evenings, he screams the word *hungry* or makes a specific request from his rapidly growing vocabulary.

Apple, he says one morning. *Please.*

The other day he told Patrice *Thank you* after he finished eating. Good pig. He favors reruns of the old *Crocodile Hunter* show on Animal Planet, snorting excitedly whenever he sees a hippo. He also has a fascination with rocket launches, the test flights for a manned mission to Mars that somehow always seems a decade away. He counts down with mission control before running excitedly around the room at liftoff. We try to change the station whenever anything disturbing comes on—neglected and starving farm animals whose owners have died, rotting crops, the displaced clambering onto relief cruise ships after wildfires drove them from their homes. But he's seen the reports of hospital plague wards overflowing into trailers in parking lots and airport hangars. *Sick, people. Sick, people. Dahktar help.* He's seen the funerary industry take over our banking system, the footage of people paying for food at the grocery store with mortuary cryptocurrencies tied to ad-ridden phone apps. *Come laugh with us at the see-tee of Laugher*, Snortorious repeats like a mantra until he can form the words. *Come laugh with us at the City of Laughter. For only one thousand bereavement crypto-tokens, you can scatter your loved one's ashes on a one-hour cruise around SanFancisco Bay.*

And then tonight, right as I'm about to leave the lab, I hear Snortorious say a new word: *Lonely.* I approach his playroom and sit with him, scratching behind his ears. *Lonely pig*, he says. My phone buzzes; it's my ex again, a photo of Fitch holding a giant stuffed tiger on his final day. Snortorious repeats himself, and I feel guilty for having given him this life, one that would have ended weeks ago had he remained silent—a heart to Indiana, a liver to Michigan, lungs to Washington, DC. Of course, we've made other arrangements, sent other pigs. But something tugs at me as he speaks. I think about how when I go home, I'll heat up a microwave dinner, curl up in bed, watch one of the few videos I have of Fitch, a two-minute clip of him building a sand castle, over and over until I fall asleep. Instead, I grab the sleeping bag I keep in my office for when I'm burning the midnight oil and decide to keep Snortorious company.

He rests his chin on my shoulder as I read to him. His snorts create a tiny slimy pool in a wrinkle of my lab coat. We read *Where the Wild Things Are.* He points a foot when he wants me to linger on a picture, sometimes bringing his snout to the page as if he might inhale the words.

Max, he says. *Wild Rumpus.*

"That's right," I say. He can't quite read yet, but Patrice and Ammie are working with him. He's got his ABCs down and I linger over each word so he can put two and two together. We finish and switch to *The Velveteen Rabbit.* I try to flip past the title page and Snortorious sticks his foot on my hand, points to the orange stegosaurus nameplate pasted inside the front cover with my son's name scrawled in black crayon.

"Fitch," I say. I take out my phone and show him a few photos. I point to myself and then back to the pictures to drive home the relationship. "My son." I don't know if Snortorious can comprehend what I'm saying, though. He was raised in this building since he was a piglet.

Fitch, he says. *Fitch son.*

I recall how Fitch used to yell to me from across the hall after he brushed his teeth, telling me it was story time. He always asked for one more fairy tale, a few more pages, always falling asleep as soon as I gave him what he wanted. Snortorious is growing sleepy, too. His eyes are fluttering. At home, on my nightstand, story time has been waiting for years. There's a bookmark a few chapters shy of the end of *The Return of the King*, right as they're approaching Mount Doom. Fitch had been trying to read it on his own despite the book being much too advanced for him, but when he was admitted to the plague ward, he'd asked if we could finish it together, our words drowning out the sounds of the hospital. I put away the books and drape a blanket over Snortorious, lie down beside him, dwarfed by his body that's never seen an open field or another barnyard animal. I wonder if he dreams of that life (or if he dreams about the kind of life we once took for granted, until the plague threatened to take it away).

I wake to a still empty lab, mouth dry and head disoriented from breathing in the lab's recycled and sanitized air for so long. I find a sticky note on the plastic of my respirator mask that reads PRIZE SWINE. Typical juvenile pranks—even during a pandemic. Snortorious is snoozing in his holding pen near the workstations, alongside the other animal stalls. I slink back to my office and find my inbox filled with emails from friends in the department and beyond, asking about this pig they keep hearing about—Snortorious P.I.G. Someone leaked a video on social media. My colleagues outside of the lab no doubt believe it's some sort of joke, but the associate dean has scheduled an impromptu visit and seems less amused by the attention. Outside, Patrice is arranging our workstations for the day.

"Do you know anything about this video?" I hold up my phone.

Patrice is a good seed, albeit sometimes too buttoned up and serious. In contrast, her older sister Ammie spins flaming poi balls at raves, which I only know about from browsing her social media.

"I'm not accusing you, by the way. But if you have any idea who might have done this . . ."

"I don't know."

"Maybe one of the interns?"

"I really didn't see anything."

I grill the others as they arrive. I need to turn my attention to Snortorious and run damage control. Should I hide him? But how to explain his absence? Can I somehow get him to shut up when my colleagues arrive? He's outside yelling *hungry, hungry, hungry*. Ammie is already tending to him, rubbing her nose affectionately against his snout.

"Patrice, get in here. I need you to run interference. Let me know as soon as anyone shows up."

"What are you going to do?"

"Get the diazepam."

By the time Associate Dean Hayes arrives, Snortorious is knocked out in his pen. Hayes barely spends time with pig number 28, probably concerned that he might ruin his suit. He drags me to my office, lectures me about keeping a tighter rein on my staff.

"You're an asset to the university. The world needs labs like this now," he says.

I focus on the carnation on his lapel. Who the hell is this guy?

"My granddaughter has a fighting chance because of what you've done here. Don't turn the work into a circus."

"Of course not," I say.

I see Patrice waving her arms in the air as my colleague Dr. Brett Gaffney enters the observation gallery with her assistants in tow. They are snapping pictures of Snortorious, laughing along, taking group shots with one finger pushing up their noses in pig solidarity.

"One, two, three, oink!" Brett says.

I follow Dean Hayes as he rushes to the observation area to lecture Dr. Gaffney. I hastily grab reports from a grad assistant's work area, hoping he'll forget about the video if I play up our lab data.

"Sir, if you look at these figures, you'll note that our animal organ donor facility has helped stabilize more plague patients than any other research venture to date. We expect to quadruple our output if we can get federal approval to use a stem cell printer," I say, waving the files in front of the man's face. I'm pointing to the charts, mostly riffing, keeping one eye on Snortorious. "Some states have done very well in containing the adult strain. We're fairly positive transmission is no longer airborne. It's not a cure, but with more transplants, we can buy people time. And might I add, sir, that our organs are prime candidates for testing future vaccines, to observe if any cellular transformation has halted in a lab setting." I'm about to point him toward one of our other donor pigs, Sir Pigginsworth, when he pushes into the observation gallery and snatches Dr. Gaffney's phone.

"Your chair will hear about this!" he yells, attempting to delete any photos or videos taken of the lab. "All of you, leave. Now."

Dr. Gaffney ushers her students toward the door and waves back at me, as if to say *sucks to be you*.

"What exactly is going on here?" Dean Hayes asks. "This is exactly the kind of thing I was talking about." I can see Ammie and Patrice in the pen with Snortorious, rubbing his back. He's still mostly out of it but seems to be aware of the commotion.

"They weren't invited," I explain. "We really need to get back to work. Boston Children's Hospital is waiting."

Dean Hayes grunts and he's about to leave when Snortorious decides to speak.

Noisy, he says.

Ammie and Patrice are whispering into his ears, telling him to be quiet. Patrice is pushing down on his rear end, trying to get him to lie down, maybe the dean won't see him.

Noisy, noisy. Sleep, Sleep, Snortorious says, louder this time.

"What was that?" Dean Hayes asks. "That voice."

"What voice?" I say. Ammie is on top of Snortorious now, trying to hide him from view.

"I thought I heard someone," Dean Hayes says. "A very strange voice."

Many dahktars talking, Snortorious shouts.

"There," Dean Hayes says. He studies me for a moment before scanning the room, stopping at the pen where we can see Snortorious sitting up, staring right back at us. "Something is going on here."

Dean Hayes pushes past me, approaches Snortorious.

Ammie, Ammie. Scratch ear.

"Holy crap," Dr. Gaffney says as she walks back into the room. "Was that the pig?"

"I told you to leave," the dean says.

"You have my phone," Dr. Gaffney says, pointing to a table.

"Go. Now," the dean says. "And not one word of this to anyone."

"You." Dean Hayes points to me. "And you and you." He points to Ammie and Patrice. "Somebody better tell me what the hell is going on here."

Over the coming days and weeks, several meetings are held. Half the departments on campus want a piece of Snortorious. Initially, Dean Hayes wanted to relocate him (and this is still a possibility), but we've since convinced him that Snortorious only trusts us, especially after the many failed attempts to get him to speak without me or Ammie present. We've added security measures, of course—a guard at the door, limited access to the lab for preapproved personnel only. Today, neuroscience has their dedicated time with him. I'm sitting in the corner, overseeing the session. Snortorious looks to me frequently, letting out subdued, melancholy squeals as the doctors place sensors all over his body. *Dahktar. Dahktar.* I want to chase them off and hold him.

"Everything's going to be okay," I say. "It's okay, it's okay. I'm right here." But I honestly don't know if any of that is true. I don't know what the others have planned for him. And that's not to say we're not still studying him ourselves, and that I didn't see fame and fortune when I first heard him speak. But reading to him every night, getting to know him a little more each day has changed everything. He loves belly rubs and having the back of his ear scratched. He prefers *Star Trek* to *Star Wars*, and after we took him outside to the little Japanese tea garden behind our building, he asked me about the sky. I couldn't help but feel joy over the wonder in his eyes as he gazed upward. All the tiny little things we take for granted that he's been deprived of—fresh air, the feel of grass on bare feet. *Bird,* he said. *Bike. Girl on bike.* He looked down at his feet, his reflection in the pond, becoming aware of how different he was from the rest of us. *Tree. Many tree. Hot air.*

The researchers bring in all kinds of equipment. But they need my permission to break his skin. I always say no. Not yet. There must be another way. I keep waiting for the call where Dean Hayes or the department chair tells me I have no other choice but to let them conduct their research as they see fit. And where is the limit to that? Drilling a hole in his head? Turning him into pork chops to see if he'll taste the same? And as much as I hate all of this, we have learned more about why Snortorious decided to speak: First, the stem cells and genetic instructions that we used to grow human organs at accelerated rates went rogue, targeting his brain. Theoretically, this was always a possibility. The protesters outside of my lab never let me forget it. But after hundreds of procedures over the years, most of us had discounted the idea of a pig person, let alone one who could communicate telepathically. Second, Snortorious's brain is continuing to grow in size and complexity at an alarming rate. Most of the researchers are focused on his cognitive ability and telepathy. Patrice helped Dr. Gaffney with the projections. We know that if Snortorious's brain doesn't stop growing, complications will soon arise—headaches, seizures, and eventually death.

How do you tell a child that he's going to die? When Patrice told me the news, I couldn't help but think of my son—how I'd sit with him at night as he breathed his medication through a nebulizer. I lost count of the lies I told Fitch through the medicated mist of his exhales—about how we'd go camping, just the two of us, or how we'd see about space camp when he was a little older, feeling a little better. Sometimes, long after Fitch had fallen asleep, I'd stay in his room and watch the stars from his toy planetarium shoot across the ceiling, a grown man making wishes on a sixty-watt light. What lies would I tell to Snortorious now? I pace the lab and listen to the gentle oinks of the pigs and find myself calling my ex. She doesn't know anything about Snortorious, and I don't want to tell her. Maybe she'll think I'm full of shit anyway. I just need to talk to someone who loved Fitch, who remembers the moment when a doctor told us our son wasn't going to make it.

"Do you regret not telling Fitch about how bad his condition was?" I ask, as soon as she answers.

"He knew. But I think he appreciated not really knowing. We let him be a kid."

I don't say anything for a moment. I listen to Dorrie breathing on the other end. She asks if I'm okay, but sounds so incredibly far away, as if she's standing on the opposite end of a tunnel.

"David?"

"Yeah?

"What is all this about?"

"Nothing," I say. I open a video of Fitch on my phone. He's drawing one of his death-trap mazes in crayon—the last day I saw him before Dorrie took him away. "Are you okay there? At the park?"

"It's hard to explain," she says. "People don't look at me like someone who lost a son here. Our customers have all been through this. I hand them an urn—their son, their daughter. Lately, older people have been riding the coaster, too. Maybe a wife, an uncle, a grandfather. I hold the hands of people who check out of the park. We look at each other. And I tell them to smile just once before leaving. I tell them to laugh, to think about one memory. Saying goodbye is part of life here. I don't want to say that it's comforting. But it's something."

"I really thought I could save him," I say.

"I know."

"And I'm glad you took Fitch." I think about how I might have been there for his final months if I weren't so stubborn. I picture Snortorious at a park like that, asking me to help him into a seat, to end it all.

"I need to go," Dorrie says.

"Do you think if I had gone with you—" I begin.

"Look, I hope you feel better," she says.

"I'm sorry about your friend," I say. "I'm glad Fitch had him. He mailed me some of Fitch's drawings. I have them on the fridge."

I'm about to ask if I can visit her sometime, if she ever wants to come back. I want to hear her favorite stories about Fitch. I could linger in the silence of our conversation forever, imagining us able to talk to each other again.

"Goodbye, David," she says, before quickly hanging up.

You are a doctor. He is a doctor. Everybody doctor. Snortorious's speech abilities have improved dramatically over the past few weeks. We've reached a point where Patrice, Ammie, and I think it might be time to have a serious talk with him, our pig son, as Ammie refers to him. When we're near his pen, we clear our minds as much as possible. We still don't know for sure how his telepathy works, if he's able to hear our thoughts or not. *I am a pig. What job is pig?* He has begun placing people into categories, purposes, asking the big questions, like why are we all here? Why can't he talk to other pigs? He asks about love and friendship when he watches soap operas, war and the Arctic plague when watching the news. He asks about people in Washington fighting over a moratorium on gas automobile production and aid to California towns destroyed by wildfire. He asks *What is a moratorium? Kissing means love. Many sick people. Nobody agree on anything.*

"We can't keep telling him that we'll answer these questions later." Ammie corners me in the lab parking lot, climbs into my car. I've forgotten what it feels like to spend time with someone outside of the lab. She squeezes my hands. I linger on how that feels.

"I know," I say.

"I know you're only trying to protect him. But it's not like he's a boy. As much as we might wish it, he doesn't have the same rights in that lab as we do. He's going to have even less freedom once the government gets involved. You know they'll move him away from us. Soon."

"It's just that . . . what is he going to do with what we tell him?"

Ammie remains silent, looks out the window. Her dangling crystal earrings cast tiny rainbows on the dash.

"We help him," she finally says. "We give him options."

At night, after the lab has cleared, I let the guard know that I'll be working late. I disconnect the security camera in Snortorious's room.

Story time? he says.

"Yes, soon," I say. "But first I need to talk to you about something. You asked me yesterday about a pig's job."

Snortorious comes closer and sits in front of me. He's wearing a bright red cardigan that Ammie knitted for him. Now, fully grown, he towers over my head when I sit on the floor. I knew I would choke up if I tried to tell him the truth, so I've come prepared with a slideshow, videos on a tablet to help illustrate my points.

"You might have had a very different life," I begin. I show him a vegan activist video. I explain to him that the "Old MacDonald" song he learned with Ammie has another side and it isn't just about animals living together with their human. Snortorious takes a moment to process this.

Pig is food?

"Yes, sometimes," I say. "But some people keep pigs as pets and there are wild pigs like the ones you see on your nature shows."

People eat pig.

Snortorious's snorts become frantic, like he can't quite catch his breath. He is squealing, a shrill, somber wail that shoots through my body. I stand and scan the lab, make sure the guard didn't hear anything.

"Shh, shhh." I embrace Snortorious, rub his back, his ears, allow myself to feel my pig son for the first time without my gloves. "But that wasn't your job, okay?" I continue my slideshow. I come to a diagram showing the anatomy of humans and pigs, our organs. "Inside," I say, pointing to my heart, to his heart. I pull up the ultrasound cart and run the probe over my chest. "See?" *Thump, thump, thump thump, thump, thump.* I tap my hand to the beat. When I run the probe over Snortorious, his ears automatically perk up.

Heart make us live, he says, studying the next slide.

"Yes, that's right. The heart is very important." I pull out my phone and show him a photo of Fitch.

Son Fitch, he says. *Son Fitch. Fitch sick, too?*

"Fitch had a bad heart," I say. "He had the sickness you saw on TV." I tap Snortorious's normal heartbeat on his side—*babumbum, babumbum*—and then mimic arrhythmia—*bababumbumbum bumbum bababum bababum bababum*. "Your heart is a human heart." I advance the slide to a diagram and trace my finger along a big yellow arrow from a pig's heart to a human body. "Your job is to save people."

Again, Snortorious takes time to process this information. He rolls on his side, his ears twitch. *Pigs not save Fitch*, he says.

"No," I say. "But pigs have saved many other people."

Pig die without heart.

"Yes," I say. "Pig die without heart."

Snortorious lumbers across the room in deep thought and hits the paddle button for the TV. He flips through several stations before finally settling on the Travel Channel, a program depicting Machu Picchu. The snort-sniffles start again.

I never go this place, he says. He flips the channel again to two people kissing, an old episode of *Dawson's Creek*. *I never do that.* He's about to change the channel again. I place my hand on his foot.

"You're special," I say. I almost tell him the whole truth—*But the thing that makes you special is also killing you*, I say in my head, hoping he can hear me. "What do you want?" I ask.

I want home, he says. *Not here.*

I call Patrice and tell her to bring Ammie and the lab's van to the service entrance as soon as they can. Half the time, the rent-a-cop is busy playing games on his phone or looking for other jobs, so there is little to no chance of us getting caught, so long as we're back by morning.

"Pig Express is here," Ammie says, holding the van's sliding door. "Where we going?"

"My house." Before I hop in the back with Ammie and Snortorious, I swing over to the driver's side.

"Thank you for doing this," I tell Patrice. She's visibly shaken. Her hands are clenched tightly to the wheel. "If we get caught, I'll tell the university that I forced you to do it. Don't worry."

"It's not a problem," she says, but I can tell it totally is.

Back in the van, Ammie and I try to stay out of Snortorious's way. He's fixed to the back window, taking in his first glimpses of the world outside of campus, narrating everything to us as we pass. *Blue car. Truck. Statue. Tall building. Lady running.*

"So, what's the plan?" Ammie asks, pushing Snortorious's prodigious behind out of the way.

"This isn't a jailbreak," I say. "At least not yet. We need to think this through. Where would we take him? He doesn't exactly belong anywhere."

"Why take him out in the first place then?"

I rub Snortorious's sides. His mouth is half-open; his tongue hangs out in a goofy smile. "He asked for home. I wanted to give him that, if only for a night."

We herd Snortorious into my bachelor pad duplex. I'm trying not to alert what's left of my fraternity house neighbors. But, of course, a group of kids smoking a hookah in the back of a parked pickup truck spots us.

"Hey, hey doctor dude! Cool pig!" one of them shouts. "Can your pig take a hit?"

"That's legit," another student says. "I love *Babe*!"

I give them a thumbs-up. Three months ago, I saw an ambulance outside of their house, the small group of them diminished by one. They stood outside with their Greek hoodies and T-shirts, huddled in the rain, chanting their friend's name: *Luka, Luka, Luka*, howling at the moon like warriors on a battlefield. After their brother's death, I walked over with a typed-out list of dos and don'ts: *Don't swim in the ocean. Don't eat imported meat or seafood. Wash your hands frequently. Do practice safe sex. Do seek medical care immediately should you experience fever or any unusual pain.* I left them my card with my personal number written on the back.

"That'll do," I say.

"Oh, shit!" one of the students says. "A film aficionado."

"So, this is where the magic happens," Ammie says as I usher everyone inside and into my living room.

"I'm barely here," I say. I pick up the trash and dirty laundry from the sofa, lay a blanket near the fireplace for Snortorious. *Fire, fire, fire. Christmas fire.*

"Christmas isn't for another month. But maybe we do have a present for you," I say. I search the house for Fitch's old soccer ball that he never really got to use and kick it over to Snortorious. It's already past midnight. We only have six hours at best before we need to head back to the lab.

"What are we going to do?" Patrice asks. She's huddled in the corner of the sofa, clearly a ball of nerves.

"Apart from getting you a drink?" I slink to the kitchen and return with a bottle of bourbon and three glasses. We bounce around a few ideas and settle on watching classic holiday movies. Ammie and Patrice select *It's a Wonderful Life.* Snortorious chooses *A Charlie Brown Christmas.* This is us now. This is family.

"Maybe we should get something to eat," Ammie suggests. I look in the kitchen and heat up all the remaining frozen dinners that I have—three beef stroganoff, two veggie lasagnas—and run to the twenty-four-hour market for a cake and some candles. By the time I return, our weird little family is watching George Bailey promise the moon to Mary. I can tell Snortorious is preoccupied by the new environment, looking around at the photos on the wall, sniffing all manner of stains and spills on the carpet. I curl up beside him and pull out a family photo album, try to keep my mind wide open for him. Snortorious asks questions about every memory. *Who? Where? How old?* I have never had someone so genuinely interested in my life before. *Ocean*, he says.

"My ex-wife and I went to Hawaii for our honeymoon."

So big, he says. *So blue.* I try to visualize Dorrie and me scuba-diving off the coast of Maui, bearing witness to the long-dead coral reefs, and hope Snortorious can feel the water surrounding him.

Midway through the second film, we pause for cake. Patrice comes in with the candles already lit, and we sing "Happy Birthday," even though Snortorious was released from his gestation pod in March of last year.

"Make a wish," I say. And I wonder what goes through his mind, knowing that whatever he wished for will never come true. Maybe he knows this, too.

Charlie Brown is decorating his pathetic tree when I receive an email from Dean Hayes. Effective later this week, Snortorious will be relinquished from our care and permanently transferred to a facility off-campus under federal supervision. Ammie and Patrice, both sitting beside me, see the message, too. We share a look, remain silent on the couch behind Snortorious, allow him to enjoy the rest of the movie. I attempt to clear my mind of fear, muddle my thoughts with noise—an image of Fitch singing "Rudolph the Red-Nosed Reindeer" during a school play, the lyrics to "Frosty the Snowman," funerary television promos from Sal the Coffin King and Ernie's Urns. Ammie types out a message on her phone, holds it in front of me: What are we going to do now?

We give him choices, I type back.

When the film is over, I turn off the TV. Patrice has tears in her eyes. Ammie sits on the floor, rests her head on Snortorious's belly.

Sad friends. Sick pig. Sad friends. Pig go away.

"Yes," I say. "Pig knows?"

Snortorious snorts, shakes his head. If he knows about being sent away, about his growing brain, what else does he know?

"We want what's best for you," Ammie says.

"We don't want you to go away," Patrice says, the words barely intelligible through her sobs.

"We'll find a way to keep you safe," I say. "We'll find a way to make the rest of your life as happy as we can."

The awkward silence and Patrice's sniffles are killing me. I turn the stereo on low for background noise, realize we need some music from happier times. Snortorious sways his head to Hootie and the Blowfish's "Only Wanna Be with You."

Pig sick, he says. *Friends get trouble.*

"We can take care of ourselves," I say. "Don't worry about that."

We go through two more songs before Snortorious speaks again. At this point, I've decided that we need to either return him to the lab or make a break for it.

Pig go back. Pig sick. Pig help people.

"I don't understand," Ammie says. But Patrice begins bawling again. She knows Snortorious is asking us to free him in the only way we really can.

Pig heart help.

"No, no, no, no," Ammie says. Her voice breaks. "You can stay with us. See more of the world. Whatever time you have left."

Pig go back. Pig help people.

"Are you sure?" I ask. "Do you understand what you're asking us?"

Snortorious sits up, touches his snout to Ammie's forehead before walking over to Patrice and doing the same.

Pig sure.

On the campus quad, I sit with Snortorious and let him take in the first glimmers of sunrise. Orange. Purple. Yellow. Pink. Ammie watches us from afar. Patrice is already back in the lab making the necessary calls to hospitals in the tristate area in need of organs. I sit with our pig son on the frosted grass.

Beautiful, he says, shivering. I drape my jacket around him.

"It is," I say.

Story time?

"Sure, what kind of story?"

Finish Fitch story, he says. Snortorious turns his head and looks straight at me as if to say *I know about that, too. I know more than I could ever tell you.* And almost as a reflex, I pull him closer and kiss his forehead. He rests his head on my shoulder, and I do my best to remember how the story goes. I tell him about the King of Gondor. On our short walk to the lab, I tell him about the hobbits returning to the Shire. Home, I say—family, like you. And in the operating room, as he's slowly fading from anesthesia, I tell him about Frodo's final journey, leaving Middle Earth with the elves, before I place my hand on his heart, now beating steadily for a boy two hundred miles away, and tell him thank you.

ELEGY HOTEL

They gave bereavement coordinators like me studio apartments on the top floors of the elegy hotels. Some of my colleagues had naive ideas about saving the world, but really we were just glorified bellhops for the mountains of Arctic plague victims awaiting cremation, for the families who wanted to curl up in a suite beside the corpses of their loved ones and heal. On any given day, the deceased from local hospitals lined the basement halls in biohazard bags, waiting to go through the three-part preservation process: sterilization, embalming, and our antibacterial plasticizing treatment. This bought families time to say goodbye while our crematoriums struggled to keep up with the demand. The job wasn't rocket science and the pay didn't suck if you could stomach it. For the nearly three years since the elegy hotels opened and cornered the funerary market, I had kept my head down, barely speaking about my past, carting bodies from the California king beds to the oven. But three months ago, my golden-boy science-fair brother showed up in the hotel lobby to invite me to dinner and to discuss our mother. I assumed his plan was to guilt me into coming home.

My mom and brother were already waiting when I arrived at the Lucky Fin on Fisherman's Wharf, one of the last seafood places still open in San Francisco. Each table was contained inside its own little plastic bubble latticed with fairy lights, a throwback to earlier plague days, the fear that it was airborne. Many public spaces now kept these around for the ambiance.

"Here's my other boy," my mom said as I entered the bubble. She had a breathing tube running across her nose and wheezed after she spoke. Her frail skin hung from her frame like a shawl.

"It's good to see you, Mom," I said.

I remembered this same pinched look too well, the way she'd bite her lip when my father yelled at me over dinner as a teenager. *I'm just disappointed. We're trying to help you*, she'd say after lecturing me for my grades or for getting into fights. She'd tell my father to let it go, that I knew what I'd done, though sometimes, for weeks afterward, she'd float through the house, avoiding me, handing me my dinner without a word.

"And what will the great Dr. Bryan Yamato be having this evening?" I asked my brother as I sat down. He glared at me for a moment before handing me a menu.

"The abalone can't be beat here," he said. "This place is famous for it."

I ordered the halibut with summer squash, a Manhattan, and took the last remaining oyster on the table while my brother stalled, sharing the details about the renovations on his house in Vegas, where Mom had been living the past couple of years, and some science project of his having to do with black holes that seemed wholly superfluous considering the world was being sucked up into its own asshole. Oh, and did I know his daughter, Petal, had just started junior high and was learning to ride a horse? And that his son, Peter, was learning how to play the electric guitar? No, of course I didn't.

"And Dennis, you're working at one of those death hotels now," Bryan said. "Isn't that right?"

"Few years now. They don't have employee of the month or anything, no bonuses or stock options, but I'm doing okay. I'm the manager of two floors." Of course, the floors in my charge, the econo-rest rooms, had never been renovated and still retained the building's faux-Victorian aesthetic. Even in a hotel for the dead, life gave me scraps. Floral wallpaper peeled at the corners, a large water stain skirted the carpet of the broken ice machine, a growing colony of gum wrappers dotted the hall.

"Manager?" my mom said incredulously.

"Yep."

"And what do you do, exactly?" Bryan asked.

"A little of everything, really. Part host, part mortician, part concierge. I take care of our customers' needs," I said. "Including the dead ones." In the lobby of the hotel there's a rack of literature—brochures and books on the grieving process, the services we and our affiliates provide. The covers are always ill-chosen and decades-old stock photos: A few depict people strolling through Golden Gate Park, laughing at god knows what. One just has a man in a neon tracksuit holding a Walkman over his head as if in victory. Life will go on. Room service is available until midnight. Outside delivery and catering should be arranged with Golden Dragon or Buca di Beppo. Dial 9 for maid service. Dial 8 for the on-call mortician. I always hide a bottle of Jim Beam and an emergency joint in the dryer of a defunct laundry room, so I can sneak away when the questions of the bereaved become too much—*Excuse me, but my husband seems to be leaking. Does the hotel have erotic films for rent? But how can you be sure my sister isn't contagious anymore?* Of course, at the lower price point, I didn't have it half as bad as the other floor managers with their bougie customers. Before the state started offering economy packages at a discount, finding bodies in the bay or in Golden Gate Park wasn't uncommon. Most people were happy to be able to responsibly dispose of their loved ones at all.

"Oh," my mother said. "How interesting." I glanced at my phone for the first time since sitting down and felt Bryan's eyes watching me. I checked my crypto holdings—fifty funerary inc tokens and 0.000068 Bitcoin.

"I'm buying, by the way," Bryan said, clearly annoyed.

I ordered another Manhattan and concentrated on my food.

When our after-dinner coffee arrived, my mom gave Bryan a pointed look. *Here we go.*

"So, here's the situation," he said. "Mom's real sick. We thought we got all the cancer cells a few years ago, but there are spots all over her lungs. We need help, Dennis. At home."

"Okay, but what about a home aide or nurse?"

"Yeah, we've tried those. We're paying out the nose for those. We were hoping you'd help out here. You weren't around when Dad died."

"I don't like strangers in the house, poking around my things," my mom said.

"So, I'd live in your house?" I asked.

"That's the idea," Bryan said.

"You'd have your own area," my mom said. She leaned over the table, held out her hands, palms facing upward as if she wanted me to hold them. "I know this isn't ideal—for any of us."

I drank my coffee. I looked at a sea lion swimming outside, Alcatraz off in the distance. I once got into trouble there in middle school for leaving my field trip tour group. I snuck into a restricted part of the prison with a girl to smoke Parliament Lights and practice sticking our tongues down each other's throat. Before that, my family thought I was a pretty good kid, I think, anyway. I folded my napkin into a shitty swan and tried waving down the waitress, sticking my arm out of our bubble for another drink. I did everything except look straight in front of me at the desperate old woman shrinking into her chair.

"Can I think this over?" I said.

Bryan shook his head, leaned over the table like he was going to grab me. My mother looked as if she was about to crumple like a sheet of paper.

"What is there to think about?" Bryan said, loud enough for the people at the other tables to hear and turn to look. "You were god knows where when Dad died. Figured you might give a shit this time."

"You're causing a commotion," I said. "Don't do this in front of Mom."

"I'm causing a commotion?" Bryan stood and stepped outside of the dining bubble, holding open the flap for me to follow. I could see our waitress talking to the manager. "I thought there was a slim chance you might actually step up to help Mom, but if you can't do that, then you need to leave."

I turned to my mother, finally reached for her hands. They were unbelievably soft and delicate, like the skin of an infant, punctuated by a filigree of veins.

"I wish you would listen to your brother," she said. Her voice had shriveled to a wisp.

"I'll call you, okay?" I stood and kissed my mom on the cheek, half expecting her to pull away. She smelled like a medicine cabinet and wet wipes, rather than the menthol cigarettes she used to smoke when I got in trouble. She held tightly to my hands as I slipped away.

"I'll be in touch," I said. I pushed past my brother, who was still outside the bubble as if he were standing guard. "Thanks for dinner." I sprinted toward the door before Bryan could say anything else. When I looked back, I saw my brother consoling our mother, who was crying into a napkin.

Between my day shifts of changing towels and rolling bodies to the crematorium, I liked to chill on the fire escape with my only floor mate, Val, a young widow who dressed like a 1960s flight attendant: scarves, pencil skirts, an aura of cigarette smoke. My boss,

Mr. Fang, didn't like us going out there and would always say during meetings, "You have to at least pretend like you care about these people. I can't have you dangling off the side of the building with a bottle like some lowlife." His hoity-toity sensibilities kept him away from me, usually—he didn't like associating with people he considered low class if he could help it. I probably exuded no class in his eyes. Most of the time, Val and I were on the fire escape offering each other free therapy. This meant listening to Val wax poetic about why I continued to ignore Bryan's calls and, more generally, why I was such a fucking screwup. But sometimes, usually on hump day, we'd hit happy hour with what little money we'd saved and treat ourselves like royalty.

The week after my family dinner we went to the Lumberyard Club, a former pool hall turned adult entertainment emporium. These days, the only industries that half thrived in this city dealt in sex, death, or the means to distribute those things on the internet. I ordered chicken wings and an IPA from a waitress named Ambrosia dressed like Princess Leia in that purple-and-gold bikini from *Return of the Jedi*.

"Den," Val said, short for Dennis. Also: Den of iniquity. Den of despair. A den, she told me once, was a place where things just settled in their own filth. "Have you still not decided what to do about your mother?"

"Val, what about him?" I said, changing the subject, pointing to Hung Solo gyrating his hips across the room. I guess it was *Star Wars* night. She rolled her eyes. "Look, I'm still getting my ducks in a row. I don't even have a suitcase anymore. I can't just up and leave. I'm needed at the hotel."

"I think you're full of shit," she said. "Your brother's rich. Mr. Fang can replace you with some reject in a second. Unlike most of the other dipshits in this place, you actually have somewhere to go."

"Don't you have a sister in Philly?"

Val talked all high and mighty with her tiny-liberal-arts-college superiority, but she always got real silent when I turned the tables on her. Once, not long after she moved in a little over a year ago, she asked me to help hang a painting that her late husband had bought her—an impressionist portrait called *Clara Searching*, a mother and daughter digging in the mud by some Japanese artist named Miki. We'd been exchanging firsts—first album, first kiss, first toy we could remember getting during the holidays. I thought we were in a place where I could ask about her husband. She had a little shrine devoted to him in her television entertainment center—a bunch of photos, a watch, a pair of glasses, all surrounded by votive candles.

"Was this an anniversary gift or something?" I said.

"More like an 'I want to seriously date you and you said you liked art once' gift."

"Sounds like a good guy," I said, after we'd finally managed to hang the piece so it wasn't tilting to one side. "How long were the two of you together?"

She got real quiet after that, pulled out her client files, began flipping through their family requests, something I was often too lazy to do. But I knew from the way her eyes were moving that she wasn't really reading.

"I'm sorry if I . . ." I said a minute later, over the whir of the vacuum as she started straightening the room. I stood by the doorway, watching her tears drop onto the carpet before letting myself out. Val ignored me for weeks after that, and I never really knew what to say to her. When we passed each other in the halls, I'd complain about the water pressure. If I saw her at the employee continental breakfast that the hotel provided once a week, I'd hand her a plate of mini muffins. I knew she liked them, and they tended to run out.

"Thank you," she'd say, barely looking me in the eyes.

"Don't mention it," I'd say. "Want some company?"

"I think I'm just going to eat in my apartment," she'd say. And I'd watch her slink across the lobby into the elevator. It wasn't until the company held a training seminar about our loyalty card program that Val apparently decided we could be friends again.

"Welcome back to the land of the living . . . sort of," I said when she sat beside me during the lunch break. We ate our turkey sandwiches, shared our chips, and when I asked her if she wanted to marathon a few selections from the Criterion Collection, she didn't run away.

My tenuous friendship with Val was a constant reminder of how close I was to being entirely alone, which I think made me more thoughtful 50 percent of the time, the kind of person Val might want to hang around. The only other coworker I talked to was Mr. Leung, our head janitor. He had a long, wispy beard and bushy eyebrows reminiscent of an old master in a seventies kung fu film. It made watching him work an almost meditative experience. I confessed as much to him once and was immediately afraid that I'd come off as one of those Asians who knew jack shit about being Asian, which was mostly true. But he smiled and a few days later asked for my help in providing under-the-table services for some impoverished families around Chinatown.

"We have bio bag," he said in a thick accent. "We need to burn. No money."

I spent that night mulling over Mr. Leung's request, realized that I'd be helping someone while also sticking it to Mr. Fang, who hated the idea of assisting the needy or desperate. I almost didn't tell Val about it at all, since she seemed like a rule-following whistleblower, but when she saw me passing a note to Mr. Leung, I let her in on the plan. We would wait until Friday evening to begin, when Mr. Fang went to see *La traviata* for the umpteenth time with his wife. I'd wait by the service entrance for Mr. Leung and his friends to roll in the bodies they'd been storing in the freezers of local restaurants.

"Den has a heart after all," she said on the first night of our covert mission, climbing into the biohazard suit the sterilization techs wore when handling unprocessed bodies. And who wouldn't want to help?

"We can only give you this," a teenage boy with his grandfather told us after we presented them with a cardboard urn. He pulled out his phone and transferred fifty funerary tokens to my account, handed me a tote bag filled with food. After the initial group of families left, Mr. Leung, Val, and I ate the dumplings they gave us on the embalming table.

Everyone Mr. Leung brought to us over the next few nights was solemn and thankful.

"Is that enough?" they would always ask. "We're sorry we don't have much to offer."

"It's fine," I'd answer. Because money was never the reason and, honestly, I would have done it for free if they hadn't insisted. It made me feel good. They burned incense and held each other and cried while gazing at photos of their relatives. I bowed my head in respect. Once upon a time this was how we dealt with death. But something snapped in us when the dead could no longer be contained, when people didn't really get to say goodbye. Cryogenic suspension companies proliferated, death hotels, services that preserved and posed your loved ones in fun positions, travel companies that promised a "natural" getaway with your recently departed. I remember Mr. Fang reminding us upon hire to always exude customer service, to never upset the guests, to remember that we were a hotel first and foremost, a funeral home second.

One night after helping Mr. Leung on my own, I grabbed my bourbon from the dryer and headed to the fire escape. Val was already out there, blowing smoke rings around the silhouette of a ballet dancer projected at the top of the Salesforce Tower. It was advertising the mayor's Festival of Resilience, meant to boost city morale. Of course, most people just needed better support services— soup kitchens, counseling sessions, government-sponsored funerary packages.

Val wiped the tears from her face and handed me the joint. "I wonder if places like this will last now that they're rolling out new treatments. People are lingering in comas. There's hope. Maybe we're all working on borrowed time."

I shrugged and took a long drag.

"How'd it go today?"

"The usual," I said. I felt a little bad saying this, but helping Mr. Leung dispose of the bodies had become a routine. "I mean . . ."

"Yeah, I get it," Val said. "Don't think too much about the job."

"Do you like Starship?"

"The what now?"

"Like the band."

"No feelings either way, I guess."

"Do you mind?" I took out my phone and found the album *Knee Deep in the Hoopla*, and pressed play. My father had given me the cassette when I was little, and I couldn't shake these tunes that I'd once fallen asleep to as a kid, no matter how hard I tried.

"This is really bad," Val said. "But like in a good way."

We dangled our feet in the air, draped a blanket across our shoulders. I continued to ignore my brother's messages buzzing in my pocket, finally switching off my phone. I could tell Val wanted to say something, but she let it go for once. She rested her head on my shoulder, and we counted the tiny explosions from the welders attaching wind turbines that looked like gigantic tulips across the otherwise dark Financial District.

My brother tried to call me repeatedly when my father died of plague complications. Most would say I should have learned a lesson from this, grown from the experience, but I've been too busy running away from it. And then there was the voicemail my mother left after the funeral, a duration of eight minutes and thirty-two seconds, which I deleted without listening. Sometimes I fantasize about that message, waffling back and forth between "We love you, Dennis. Please come back," and "Your father died disappointed in you."

The last time I saw my father was ten years before his death. I had crawled back home after failing to launch a career in my twenties, my credit cards maxed out from years of trying to keep up with my more successful friends, buying drinks for strangers who I thought could open professional doors. I'd started stealing from my job at Patagonia—a few dollars here and there, a fleece, a hat. When my parents finally bailed me out with a ticket home to Nevada, my mother greeted me at the airport, waiting outside our twenty-year-old station wagon, arms crossed.

"You think you're Mr. Big Shot?" she said. "We dipped into our retirement funds to cover your debt. The invoice is in your room. You're paying us back, in case you didn't get the hint."

My dad played the good cop and hugged me. I was shaking and he probably saw that I'd turned into a thirty-year-old kid waiting for the business end of a belt. "You messed up," he said. "We'll look into AA for you, therapy. We'll get through this together." He told my mom to back off. But I was just so far deep, living in sad-sack city. I didn't fully appreciate how my parents were going out on a financial limb for me.

I was home for only a few days when everything exploded. My

dad told me to pick up our beagle's shit from the pads in the basement, and I sassed back.

"I'll do it when I feel like it" is what I probably said.

"You'll do it now!" he yelled. "Right now, your job is picking up d'Artagnan's shit. In return, you get to live here. Do you understand?"

Of course, I did not like that one bit. I stormed out of my room, leaving my futile online job search, and got in his face in the kitchen. When my dad was pissed, he puffed himself up like he must have done as the only Asian kid in a rural New Hampshire school district, defending his lunch money from the white bullies who'd taunted him, asking if he could see in widescreen.

"You want to come at me like that?" he said. "I will knock your goddamn teeth in if you're going to be a punk."

And maybe that was true when I was a teenager, but even if I was scrawnier than him, I had a few more inches and I didn't have arthritis. I wanted him to punch me, just so I could hit him back. Right then I fucking hated this guy. So, without really thinking, I took it up a notch, pulled a butcher knife from the Cutco set some salesman had duped my mother into buying. Sweat pooled around my grip. I imagined plunging in the blade and running out the door, a fugitive. Temporary insanity, my lawyers would call it. I'd sleep under a highway overpass, eventually hitchhike my way out of state and on and on.

My mom heard the commotion and came running from her craft room downstairs. I dropped the knife as soon as she turned the corner, but she'd already seen me—and in the split second it took for the knife to fall, my father landed a halfway decent right hook. I answered in turn, tackling him to the floor. One. Two. My father's nose cracked. Three hits before I felt my mother prying me off him. She cradled my father's bloodied face, shielding him from me. She stared at me for a moment, sobbing. I might as well have been an armed robber.

"Get out of my house!" she yelled. "Get out now and don't come back."

So, it doesn't take a rocket scientist like my brother to figure out why I'm not close with my family. I probably should have returned home at some point to patch things up before my dad died. Instead, I did what my mother told me to do: I left and never went back. It was easier pretending I was alone.

Business at the elegy hotels had been on the downswing lately due to new treatments and organ donor programs. Mr. Fang referred to it as *an opportunity to restructure the brand*. He started sending bereavement coordinators out into the city to talk to residents about our funerary and crematory services. Send off your loved ones in our luxury suites! Say goodbye to morgues and cold storage and hello to a 3½ Star Resort Treatment! Low Interest Payment Plans Available! One of our competitor hotel chains in Oakland—Elysium Suites— was now selling itself as a care facility, linking to early reports that the experimental plague treatments produced memory loss. I'd been excluded from the past few community outreach endeavors, thanks to what management liked to call *a dickhead attitude*, but other nearby chains and even our sister locations had been ramping up their marketing efforts, so one day Mr. Fang partnered Val and I together, probably hoping her hospitality skills would rub off on me or something.

Val really hoofed it in the field, as if we got a commission based on the number of brochures we handed out. I enjoyed watching her work and learned that a lot of people will let you into their homes once they know you've experienced a tragedy of your own. Val began with her broken widowed smile and ended with a foot in the door. She always asked for sparkling water. This was the balance between customer service, door-to-door sales, and funerary stoicism that I'd never quite mastered.

"Maybe try not smiling like a friggin' serial killer when you walk up to their door," Val said on our first neighborhood assignment.

"'If you act now, you can get two—two funerary urns for the price of one. We'll even throw in a box of chocolates and a gift certificate to Fisherman's Wharf's world-famous wax museum!' Do you ever think about how messed up this job is?" I asked.

We were approaching the next house on our canvassing list. Val turned back, looking more than annoyed—and here I thought I was just fighting the man, shooting the shit with a coworker, but something I'd said had offended her, like I'd uncovered a deep wound.

"Yeah, it's messed up," she said. "Maybe we are company lackeys, but our potential clients have a basic right to process their grief with our help. If you're not going to be serious about this, shut up and hang back."

"It's not that I don't think people should be able to choose how to say goodbye to their loved ones," I explained. "I was just trying to lighten the mood." I rushed to catch up to her, but she was already knocking on the door.

"Not everything is a party, Dennis," Val said.

I brushed my hand across her shoulder, tried to get her to turn back and listen to whatever excuse I could come up with, stepped back when someone answered. I waited outside on the stoop for her to finish, fumbling with my phone, wading through the swamp of my BitPalPrime social feed—ads for elegy hotels, vids of wealthy friends glamping on their quarantine retreats, notifications that profiles had been turned into memorial pages. My thumb hovered over a memorial for the father of a college friend who'd invited me over for Thanksgiving every year.

It seemed like Val was going to be a while, so I decided to head back to the hotel, taking the long way past the Ferry Building, down Market Street. When I reached Union Square, I sat and watched the city pretend to be what it used to be, realized it had been years since I'd seen a homeless person napping on a bench, panhandling outside a restaurant. No doubt, we failed them, too—did they die in shelters? In the street? Did we burn or bury them en masse? I searched my phone for a news article on the subject, found nothing except personal blogs and social media posts wondering the same—*Where did the homeless go? Who will answer for their deaths?* Outside the mall across the street, an LED billboard thanked everyone for doing their part: LIFE MUST PREVAIL. SPEND YOUR FUNERARY TOKENS ON THE LIVING. A new elegy-hotel-consortium-owned bank was being constructed next door to it, in the lobby of the old Wells Fargo building. I got up and walked for a while, let myself join the rhythm of shoppers and workers streaming in and out of buildings. I listened to a canvasser for a rival death hotel making his pitch—*Sleep with your loved ones on their way to eternal slumber!* I guess it didn't sound so horrible if you had someone to grieve, if you knew people would be grieving for you. Sometimes I wondered if anyone would come when I died, dreamed about what my father's funeral might have been like, how the crowd would have gasped if I'd entered the church, sat next to my mother, held her hand while my brother fought the urge to hit me. I would have waited to approach the casket until everyone else had paid their respects, and then stared down at some noble approximation of my father.

"I'm sorry," I'd say. And maybe I'd cry or break down completely, my mother and Bryan picking me up off the floor. Everything was always so goddamn dramatic and perfect in my head.

When I returned to the hotel, I slipped in through the side entrance, hightailing it to the elevators to avoid another lecture from Mr. Fang. When I reached the fire escape, I had a blunt hanging from my lips. Val was there staring at me like I was the biggest idiot in the world.

"Den, it's a two-way street," she said, almost immediately. It seemed like she'd been waiting to give me this lecture. At first, I thought she was talking about my piss-poor performance at work, but she was a better person than me, always thinking about the bigger picture. "You can't just wait for things to happen. You're lucky your family is reaching out at all."

"What if I bulldozed the street?" I said. "What if they're only calling because they're desperate?" I pictured holding a View-Master to my eyes, scrolling through all the times I'd let my family down—getting held back in third grade for not being able to multiply, cocaine in my backpack senior year, my dad picking me up from the county jail right after graduation, when my boss at Outdoor Outfitters called the cops after he caught me stealing from the register. The time I brought Nikki Ishio home and my family loved her. She was on the cheer squad, the honor roll. I took her to prom and my parents told me not to fuck it up—and then I fucked it up. And there was, of course, my father's bloodied face. The funeral I never attended. All the times I told my brother that I hated him and meant it.

"It's almost never as bad as it seems," Val said. It sounded like she was trying to convince herself as much as me. "You have a chance to make amends. That's something I can never do even if I wanted." But the thing was that I didn't want to reach out. Sure, I missed them, but who were they really? Who was I to them? The apologies and drama seemed like too much to bear. Here, I was in control. I was somebody without a past.

"I just don't see that happening," I said. But I'd be lying if I claimed I never thought about being a better person, a better son. She took out the photo of her husband she kept in a locket around her neck, handed it to me.

"I know you're curious," Val said.

"It's not my business."

"I was in Mexico when the first symptoms began," she said. "Some of my friends were going, the vacation was paid for, he said I should join them and have fun. I was touring the Aztec ruins, sitting around bonfires on the beach while he was throwing up in a toilet. He didn't say anything until I was ready to come home. Ridiculous, right? Never wanted to bother anybody about anything. If a neighbor hadn't seen him passed out in the hall with pustules on his arm, he probably wouldn't have gone to the doctor at all. His family flew out. My sister was helping him. When I got home, I thought I'd take care of him. That's what people expected me to do. But when I saw him, I didn't know how to handle it. His skin was sloughing off his face like wax. He had no hair. He could barely speak. I was afraid to be near him. They say he contracted a strain of the plague during a business trip, some aggressive flesh-eating bacteria in the water that had the virus. I let my sister do the heavy lifting. I went to school. I stayed at the library. I did everything I could to avoid his hospital room."

Tears streamed down her cheeks, outlining her eyes with a wavy blue corona from her eyeliner. I let her head rest on my shoulder and thought about how my life could have been different if someone like Val had bothered to be my friend when I was young. I left the fire escape and returned with a box of tissues from a nearby guest room.

"When he passed, I didn't get the call right away. I was at a movie, stuffing my face with popcorn. I never got to say goodbye. I didn't even try."

"What was the movie?" I asked. I knew it was a stupid question, but that's how I'd always been: attaching the little things to the stuff that hurt me, the jar of licorice with my high school principal's office, the smell of Old Spice aftershave and my father's belt.

"*Night of the Living Dead*. It was part of some classic horror festival."

"I probably would have been at the movies, too," I said. "In case you haven't already figured it out, I'm pretty shit with family." I wanted to hold her hand. I passed her the blunt instead.

"Well, you need to ask yourself what the hell you're waiting for," she said. "I like you, Den, but I'm tired of hanging out on this fire escape having the same damn conversation. You only get one good-bye."

When I went back to my room, I reviewed my missed calls, listened to my brother's numerous voicemails. He didn't sound angry, just tired. I'll call him tomorrow, I told myself, definitely sometime this week. If not for myself then maybe for Val. I sat on the fire escape outside my room and gazed at the city trying to resuscitate itself—a blimp floating over the bay, an ad projected onto its side for a new school of mortuary science, the bells of cable cars running up and down Powell Street for the few tourists brave enough to visit, someone playing a saxophone down below. Back inside my room, I did the dishes and packed all my belongings into garbage bags, caught up in the comforting idea of a reset, those transitional movements toward all that might be possible. I played music as I swept. I thought about patching things up with my family, making my mom proud. I'd learn Dad's recipes (even his famous curry chicken bowl), redecorate her room the way she wanted, and maybe, on her good days, I'd take her to one of the few remaining Vegas shows, the revival of

Cirque du Soleil with its surviving troupe members—*V: The Odyssey of a Virus*, an acrobatic journey of our will to survive. In my mind, I heard my mom telling me she loved me. But my phone remained on the kitchen counter, untouched for hours. When I finally bothered to pick it up there were several missed calls, voice messages from my brother, each angrier than the last. I considered calling him back this time, but I didn't need all the drama. I deleted his holier-than-thou lecture and again told Val that the next day would be the day I called home. Until Val finally said she was done with me.

"I can't, Dennis," she said. "I don't know what to do for you. You need to grow up and stop being so damn selfish."

"I know," I said. "I promise I'll call today. I'm sorry." But a few days passed and then a few more, and Val quickly became a ghost, moving through our shared hallways as if we were strangers. She'd nod, make small talk about work. She no longer asked about my family. Drinking out on the fire escape suddenly felt more pathetic. Outside of my tiny life I could feel the world reaching for the light— after an unexpected wave of thunderstorms, the air was marginally comfortable to breathe again, washed from the veil of wildfire smoke. People were starting to go out, filling restaurants and bars. I thought about finally calling Bryan, asking to talk to Mom. Maybe if I promised, heard her voice, I wouldn't be able to back out afterward. Maybe if I told her I really wanted to help this time. I imagined the conversation for so long it almost felt like it had happened.

I was removing a body from one of the rooms when he called. Several times in a row. Bryan was the brother I didn't deserve, the kind of person I'd never know how to be. How had he turned out so different? Was there something in his upbringing? Soccer? The fact that my parents had spent so much time trying to help me not fail out of school? All the attention they wasted on me, leaving him alone? I remember him crying on several occasions, saying how I always got everything, that it wasn't fair. My thumb hovered over the decline button, but this time I picked up. The entire summer had passed since I'd held my mother's hands.

"I don't know why you deserve this call," he said. Everything after that sounded like it came from the bottom of a well. When he stopped talking, I thought about hanging up, wallowing in the purgatorial red lights of some strip club or bar. I stared at the body on the gurney in front of me—a man named Bobby whose three grandchildren had visited him the other night. I'd heard them singing, laughing, celebrating a life, when I came to his room to deliver their chicken tenders. The children had been reading bedtime stories, nestled in beside their grandfather. I hovered the phone several inches from my ear, half listening as Bryan switched back and forth between explaining how our mom had died and yelling at me. Finally, there was a lull. He asked if I had anything to say for myself.

"I don't need you talking to me like you're in charge," I said. "I'm a fuckup, okay? But please let me take care of things for Mom. Just give me this." I saw my mother standing at the door of my teenage bedroom, me telling her I was sorry. I waited for my brother to hang up, still holding the phone away from my ear, sure he was about to really dig in. But he didn't hang up and he didn't yell because he had always been better than me.

By the following afternoon, my mother had been moved from the hospital morgue to our presidential suite. It would cost me my stipend for the next two years even after factoring in my employee discount. When I walked into the room, my brother was already there. He had been busy, decorating the walls with family photos, replacing the bedspread with a quilt our grandmother had made. On every conceivable surface, he had placed a vase of flowers. I sat next to him on a love seat near the edge of the bed. He was watching some travel show about Rome and crying into a glass of pinot noir.

"I never really did anything for her either, Den," he said. "She never went anywhere. It's not like I didn't have the money. This is probably the nicest place she's ever stayed."

"Remember those KOA campsites on our family road trips?" I said. "Helping Dad pitch the tents, waiting for Mom to come back from the grocery store because we always forgot something."

"Mom hated those trips," Bryan said. "She slept in the car because Dad never thought it was necessary to buy sleeping pads."

"It wasn't all bad," I said, thinking about my brother and me creeping through the forest with flashlights, waiting for our father to jump out at us in his ghillie suit.

Bryan shook his head and poured me a glass of wine.

My mother looked like she was taking a nap. The mortician had done a nice job. I could picture her getting up, asking us what was on the agenda for the day. *Shall we go to Alcatraz? I've never been. Can we get some hot chocolate and ride the Powell Street cable car?* Or more likely: *You're still on my shit list, Dennis, but I want to have fun for once in my damn life.* Whatever you want, I'd say. I'm so sorry, I'd say. In this fantasy, I hold my mother's hands as we stroll Ocean Beach collecting shells, roasting marshmallows over a bonfire. I ask her about her trip around the world that was cut short when she stumbled upon my father backpacking in Greece, her friends who've mostly passed, the old camcorder tapes I found as a kid that showed her kissing a man who looked a lot like David Hasselhoff. I never really tried to know her at all. In two days, I will cart my mother to the basement and watch her be reduced to ash. I will present our top-of-the-line urn to my brother. By the following evening, we will be joined by relatives and family friends. I'll retreat to the shadows after the awkward handshakes and niceties and feel unworthy of being there. For now, though, I walk over to the bed, surrounded by candles and flowers and photos of the small but remarkable life that

I never really knew. I thank her for everything she and my father gave me and that I never appreciated—the karate lessons and birthday cakes, the many second chances. I drape myself over her body, an ear where her heartbeat should be. I tell her I'm sorry. I tell her I love her. I wait for her embrace.

SPEAK, FETCH, SAY *I LOVE YOU*

I'm sifting through a nearly empty bin of spare parts, trying to repair my neighbor's robo-dog, yelling to my son to ask if he's seen any second-generation leg servos, when a customer walks through the door, a little girl carrying a PupPal 3.0 Pomeranian model in a bright pink tote bag.

"Aki," I yell. "Aki, I need help." I message him on his phone. I'm about to go search for him when he finally emerges from his room wearing headphones, giving me that same look he gave me when he said he wished the plague had taken me instead of his mother. He's become a master of emotional manipulation, saying anything to hurt me, to avoid being punished for bad behavior: staying out late, getting caught with alcohol and cigarettes in his bedroom. I'm not worried necessarily. It isn't like he's going to run out and join the yakuza. Mostly he just spends hours in his room trying to cover pop songs with his mother's shamisen, while her old robo-dog shimmies at his feet and plays recordings of her singing in the hospital, the only original record we have of what she sounded like.

"What is it?" he says.

"We have a customer," I say. "I thought we had a deal. You help me and you get pocket money." Of course, he used to help me for free, but these days I'm willing to bribe the kid for face time.

"No, *you* have a customer," he says. He goes into the kitchen, pours himself an orange juice, grabs a rice ball wrapped in plastic wrap.

"Very mature," I say.

His demeanor softens when he glances at the little girl. He sits at the service counter, and I see him studying the tiny pink supernovas on her face, a side effect of one of the most recent experimental preventative drugs used to manage the spread. It's been over a year since his mother died (followed by two aunts, an uncle, a cousin), and while Aki's a good kid, he's always holed up in his room or moving through the house like I don't exist. The pigtailed girl takes out her unit and activates it on the counter, sending the dog two unsteady steps forward before it collapses on its front legs. The head twitches uncontrollably, shifting its focus between me and its owner. The girl reaches deep into her overall pockets and stacks some coins one by one on the counter, followed by a couple of wrinkled yen notes.

"What's wrong with Mochi?" she asks. I could show her the spreadsheet of dissatisfied clients on my computer; my reputation as a miracle worker is spiraling out of control, people bringing in their robo-dogs with blind hope—dead on arrival, dead on arrival, dead on arrival. I could do that, but this girl is too young. I lie constantly to my customers, even to the adults, about the chances for their plastic best friends. It's hard to tell the truth when, for so many, these robo-pets are the most tangible memories they have of the loved ones they've lost.

Mochi begins playing "Happy Birthday" and then unexpectedly changes over to one of the preprogrammed techno club beats, LED eyes flashing flower patterns in rainbow colors. The dog sways from one side to the other, pointing its paw in the air like it's *Saturday Night Fever*. Left paw. Right paw. Right paw. Right paw—and then it collapses, nearly rolling off the counter as the music turns to static. The little girl looks like she is going to cry.

"Why don't you introduce our customer to Hollywood," I tell

Aki. "Get her a snack. I have some work to do here. It'll take some time."

"Can he fix her?" the little girl asks and pushes the money across the counter. I wave away her pocket change, slide it back toward her.

"She'll be here when you get back," I say. "Good as new." Aki shoots me a look as if to say *Are you just going to keep lying to people like you lied to me about Mom getting better?*

I've seen cases like this before—corrupted firmware, third-party programs that can barely run on their five-year-old operating systems. I can't do much, but I always try to find a short-term solution when there are kids involved. If the girl had come to me six years ago, before the pandemic, I could have helped her easily, but the 2RealRobotics Inc. canine plant where I'd worked has since laid me off, converted to exclusively producing robo-friend and robo-lover lines. Spare parts are hard to come by these days. There are scuff marks all over Mochi's body from where the dog has fallen. A piece of paper covered with tape instructs anyone who finds the pet to return it to an address in Meguro ward. I open the head panel—the serial number indicates a 2025 model. The little girl likely has no memory of a time before Mochi.

In the kitchen, Aki is introducing the girl to my late wife's robo-dog, a husky puppy she named Hollywood. "Sit," the girl says. "Shake hands, speak, let's dance!" She tells Aki how she carries her dog everywhere in a bag and how Mochi likes to press her paws to the train window on the way to school. She tells him that her father died last year but still tells her stories every night through the recordings in Mochi's memory bank. I'm inspecting Mochi's head cavity with a penlight when I hear Aki whisper something to the little girl—and then after a few clicks of Hollywood's paws, I hear my late wife's voice singing.

———

I'm certain I won't be able to return Mochi to her former self, but I bring her to my workshop anyway, sifting through the dozens of robo-dogs I've collected for spare parts—some donated by their owners in an effort to move on, others found online or in second-hand shops. Each has a name tag, and if I activated one, I might get a snapshot of their former life: a child's prayers, a math game where numbers flash on the head screen, brief recordings of their family during happier times. I've promised their former owners that when I'm done salvaging their dogs for parts, I'll hold a service so they can say goodbye. Somewhere among their ranks should be a replacement memory board. It won't be Mochi, per se, but for a little girl who needs her best friend, who needs to believe her robo-dog will always be there for her, it's something, at least.

I replace the motherboard and return to find the little girl sitting on the living room floor with my son, petting Hollywood. I set Mochi down in front of her. I've given the dog a pink collar and affixed a floral bow to her head.

"She's just like new!" the little girl say, opening up her tote bag on the ground. It's nearly as big as her, and she stuffs Mochi inside.

"Remember, Mochi is going to need some help getting back to her old self. Play with her, remind her of all the fun you've had together. Teach her the rules because she might have forgotten." The little girl nods. I feel both heartened and guilty for how excited she is to have her best friend back. Maybe she'll realize what I've done when she's older and forgive me. I do know that one day, hopefully far enough in the future for her to outgrow the comforts of a plastic dog, Mochi will falter—a misstep leading to a fall down the stairs, an unbreakable audio loop, a failure to charge. I realize these are realities for Hollywood, too, that I've been pretending the occasional glitch or failure to respond to a command is simply a quirk in the technology. "Speak," I say. Mochi lets out an excited series of barks and the girl's bag shakes. "I'm glad I could help," I tell her.

Before my wife, Ayano, was infected almost three years ago during a visit to her mother's fishing village, I never understood the fascination with robotic pets. My job at the robotics factory was merely a paycheck. Since then Hollywood has given me a bridge to my son. In our old life, I would come home, ask Aki about school, and if he was doing well, I'd tell him to keep it up. If he was doing poorly, I'd yell and take away his game consoles. And that was that. But when his mother was admitted to the hospital, I tried to step up as a father, checking his math, practicing his English with him. We'd watch the news together over dinner—endless reports about how the worst of the plague would be over any day now, the government committing to a decade-long seawall project to protect Osaka and Tokyo from rising sea levels. Mostly, we pretended to be absorbed in these reports to avoid speaking to each other.

It was Aki's idea to buy his mother a robo-dog, something to keep her company when we couldn't. He met me at a closeout sale where the last robo-dogs were being sold, and I let him take charge, questioning the vendors, playing with the robo-Pomeranians, -Akitas, and -poodles, adding bandannas and other accessories to our purchase without asking my permission.

"Dad, check it out," he said, pointing to a husky puppy. "I think this is the one."

I shook the dog's paw and it barked cheerfully. "I think you might be right," I said. Aki hoisted the gigantic box onto the cashier's counter and for one of the few times in his life, he looked me square in the eyes and thanked me without being prompted.

We wrapped a red bow around the dog's neck, sanitized it to protect Ayano's compromised immune system from any germs it might be carrying, and took it to the hospital, set it on the tray table over her bed. When she woke up, I told her to pet the dog's back and command it to shake hands. Ayano beamed and shook its latex paw as the dog wagged its tail, barked, and said hello in a digitized English accent.

"It's a slightly older model," I explained. "But we know how much you like snow dogs, dreamed of going dog-sledding one day."

"Tiny Balto," she said. She held the dog close to her chest. "Hollywood."

I pointed to the robo-dog welcome packet on the tray table that outlined its popular features: facial recognition, voice commands, audio recording and playback, an expandable library of songs, games like go fetch, eating a plastic milk bone. The Husky 3.0 model can pick up the beat of whatever music is playing and dance in time. Its LED eyes can display the weather forecast, personal calendars, and journal entries, and help with arithmetic. Its personality changes the more its owners interact with it and, if it's ever lost, a GPS beacon can be used to track it online. Ayano flipped through the packet and triggered Hollywood's myriad sensors. After that, anytime I slept over, I'd hear barking and electronic jingles throughout the night, my wife telling Hollywood how she really felt. *So tired*, she'd say, thinking I was asleep. Panting bark. Melodic chime. *I know I'm getting worse, pup. I don't know if you can understand me.*

A few days after receiving Hollywood, Ayano hosted a show in her room for some of the children on the ward. Aki was already there when I arrived, helping with the musical arrangements, playing his mother's shamisen while she sang and clapped. The kids danced and watched as Hollywood jumped around excitedly, eyes displaying fireworks. He sat up on his hind legs and waved his arms in the air. Ayano and Aki noticed me watching from the doorway. I felt like I'd intruded on something special that was just for them. Even Hollywood settled down and looked at me as if I'd taken a piss on the floor. "Okay, it's time to say goodbye, Hollywood," Ayano said.

Hollywood scanned the children. "Goodbye," he said.

"And I love you," she added.

"I love you," he repeated, and this time the voice was different, not the pre-programmed foppish Englishman's, but my wife's. The kids filed out of the room and Ayano commanded Hollywood to say it again. "I love you," he said.

"That's your voice," I said.

"I've been teaching him a lot of things," she said. "I wish we had gotten one sooner."

*　　*　　*

Next weekend we're holding a group goodbye ceremony for three robo-dogs. I'm meeting with Toru, a Buddhist monk who helps with the services I hold once a month in our small yard—incense, sermons, cakes from the grocery store, even tiny pine caskets I make myself. In the shed, there are nearly twenty dogs waiting to be used for parts, and for Toru's blessing, to ultimately be reunited with their families when they are nothing but shells. Each one sits on a cushion, and at night, thanks to the donation of a client, strings of miniature LED lights surround them like fireflies. Toru prays over the three we're preparing today. I notice how his eyes linger on the empty cushions that grow in number with each visit.

"It's almost impossible to fix them now," I say. "But people need to hope."

"This one, I remember"—Toru points at a shih tzu missing its front legs—"was with Mrs. Ito from down the street when she died.

The dog was already gone, of course. Had been for a while as far as I know. But she didn't know that. And this one—" He picks up a white pit bull with a painted brown spot over its back and studies its face. "This is Kogi. His owner lost his real dog who looked just like this. His ex bought him this one secondhand. He was drinking, missing work. Almost got fired from the post office. Kogi saved him, allowed him to connect to the world again. These dogs will be remembered—their spirits will be rewarded." I know Toru has to say these priestly things, but spiritual rewards don't mean a whole lot when your life has been cut in two—you want your wife back, not her voice trapped in plastic; you want your son to love you again.

Across the street, I give him the contact info for the owners and show him out.

My neighbor, Kigawa-san, is restocking his vending machine. He runs a small beer and sake shop. Most days, he sits on the sidewalk in a folding chair watching the time pass, punctuated by the chimes of bicycle bells, children petting Astro. His Akita robo-dog sits on the ground beside him. The neighborhood grandmothers, friends of his late wife, power walk up and down the street for exercise, stopping to chitchat, asking him how Astro is doing. "Is he being a good boy? Is he helping his master guard the shop?" Always the same questions. And always Kigawa-san pets Astro and answers: "He's a very good boy." Of course, Astro does not respond. His eyes are devoid of a single pixel. Months ago, I sat down with Kigawa-san over drinks at the corner bar and broke the news: I could not save his robo-dog, and it would only be a matter of time before he stopped functioning altogether.

"I see," he said. He poured a shot of sake and asked me to help him finish a small bottle.

"Okay," I said. "Look, I can try switching out the motherboard, but Astro would lose his memory, everything your wife programmed into him." He waved the idea away, said he'd rather the dog die with that part of his wife still inside than lose her entirely. We took turns pouring without saying a word. When the flask was empty, he thanked me and told me everyone missed Ayano. I didn't see him for two weeks after that and when I finally did, the flickering light from Astro's eyes had already disappeared.

"Have the Kirin autumn brews come in?" I ask. Kigawa-san sets down his newspaper. His baseball team, the Yakult Swallows, has lost again.

"You'll have to wait two weeks. Do you want me to save you a case?"

"I'll stop by," I say. I hate the stuff and only asked because I was scrounging for small talk that didn't have to do with his dog.

"Okay then." He scratches Astro's head, silent and dead still, and returns to his paper. I can tell he's waiting for me to leave.

*　　*　　*

After two years of transplants and gene therapy and experimental trials, Ayano's will to live was stretched about as thin as her skin, which looked as fragile and translucent as rice paper. In the hospital waiting room, Aki was working on his final assignments. It was the eve of his middle school graduation. He hoped to attend in person, not just virtually.

"Don't you dare have the doctors keep me alive," my wife told me, struggling to speak. "This is no way for him to grow up, waiting for me to die." And maybe part of Aki hated me for that, even though he knew it had been his mother's decision.

"Do something. Why aren't they doing anything?" Two days later, Aki ran from her room, screaming for help. Hollywood was beeping and barking from all the commotion. I dragged my son back to her side and told him it was time to say goodbye. A nurse handed us masks and gloves and opened the quarantine curtain that surrounded my wife's bed. The sting of antiseptics filled the room, mixing with the strong scent of her body odor. She hadn't had a proper shower in days.

"I want to see you," Ayano whispered, pointing at our masks.

"It's for your protection," Aki said.

"Little late for that," Ayano said. "I want to see you."

Aki looked at me for a moment before both of us slipped off our gloves and masks. We reached over to hold her hands as she struggled to take a breath. I placed Hollywood on her lap, noticed her gaze drifting to the night table. She reached for a paw and pressed three times. "I love you," she said through Hollywood. "Take care of each other." She sang a lullaby she used to sing to Aki, one of the only recordings we haven't heard again since that night, no matter how many times we've tried. She tugged on his ears, more songs followed, and we sat listening to her sing as her body succumbed to the morphine, and the beeping of a heart rate monitor rang flat.

At Ayano's wake, Hollywood sat front and center between a row of photos, flowers, and the vases she sculpted. He lit up and looked around whenever the altar bell rang. We charged him with entertaining the children outside when the service went long. Aki didn't cry once. He sat silently, excusing himself early to join Hollywood outside. He said these people didn't have the right to be there—these aunts and uncles and cousins he hadn't seen in years. No phone calls, no cards. Suddenly everyone is talking about how his mother was such a great person.

"Did you even bother to tell them she was sick?" he asked after the ceremony. "Did they know how bad it was?"

"Yes, they knew," I said. This was, of course, only partly true. I hadn't told anyone that Ayano was quite so close to death. I was worried her relatives would try to move in with us or always be at the hospital, that I wouldn't have the chance to care for my wife. Aki and I stood beneath the leaking wooden roof that covered the cement basin where people washed their hands before entering the temple. Outside, a light mist seemed to envelop our conversation, as if we had stepped out of Ayano's memorial and into our own bubble. "But you know how things are now. Everyone has their own problems. A lot of people are dealing with this sickness. Your cousin Reo died in the first wave. Uncle Yosuke isn't expected to make it through the week."

"So, you told them the truth," Aki said. "And you said she was getting better."

"I wanted to believe she would get better," I said. "Until the very end."

For months after the memorial, I allowed Aki to float through the house like a ghost, holding my tongue, trying to maintain the peace when he wanted to pick a fight.

"Don't touch my things," he yelled at me once when I was cleaning his room. "Don't touch those pictures. You have no right to be in here."

"I took that photo of you and your mother," I said. "I bought that frame. And last I checked I'm paying for this house and you're not taking care of your room. I let you get away with a lot around here."

He clutched the photo of his mother to his chest, the two of them on a boat ride circling Tokyo Bay. Beside his futon, Hollywood slept, powered down. Most of the time we didn't pay the dog any mind, often forgetting he could self-activate until he reacted to something—a television commercial jingle, a broken glass, one of our shouting matches. It wasn't until Aki picked up his mother's shamisen again that Hollywood left his charging station and truly reentered our lives. I watched my son open the case as I was preparing dinner, inspecting the instrument that once belonged to his grandfather, hands hovering over the strings, as if afraid to break anything. One note. And then another. And another. After several false starts, I could discern an unsteady "Moon River." Aki continued to play. I heard Hollywood activate behind the sliding door separating the living room from my son's bedroom, the mechanical whirring of joints as the dog waddled across the tatami. And then came *her* voice. Aki stopped. We both regarded each other as if a veil had been lifted. I slid open the door. Hollywood looked up at me with his pixelated eyes and wagged his tail. If I threw his Bluetooth ball, he would fetch it and bark. If I asked him to dance, he would sit upright and wave his front paws in the air. A robo-dog, a toy, a pet. And yet. Even though I had never subscribed to the traditional idea that all objects contain a spirit, I couldn't deny that a part of the woman we lost remained somewhere inside Hollywood.

"Keep playing," I told Aki.

Ayano slipped between English and Japanese as she sang, humming along with the instrumentals. Hollywood swayed from side to side. And for the first time in recent memory, I saw my son smile. For the first time since she left us, we sat in the same room and ate.

After that day, Aki moved Hollywood into the main room. We made a point of incorporating him into our lives. Aki still avoided speaking to me when he could avoid it. Instead, he used the dog as a conduit for connection.

"How about a car ride?" Aki would ask Hollywood in front of me. "Hollywood, maybe we can go to the movies and eat some popcorn. What do you say?" I once blew up at him for playing these games.

"I'm your father," I said. "You need to learn how to talk to me." But we weren't there yet.

Aki stormed out of the room with Hollywood in his arms and didn't acknowledge me again until he asked Hollywood if he wanted to go to the mall. Does Hollywood want a chocolate-covered pretzel? Does Hollywood want a Gundam model?

My son acted tough, but once, not long after his mother's funeral, I overheard him talking to the dog. His bedroom door was closed. I walked closer, leaned in to listen: "We're okay. I finally got a job at the corner store to help out Dad, but I haven't told him yet. His cooking is horrible. He can be a real dick sometimes, but I guess I can be, too. I miss you. I love you. I miss you so damn much."

Beep, blip, chime.

"Say it," Aki said, louder. "I love you. Say 'I love you.'"

Ayano's voice: "I love you."

"Repeat."

"I love you."

When Aki was at school, I'd play Ayano's music from her phone and sing along, horribly off key—"Yesterday" by the Beatles—and wait for my wife's voice to emerge from Hollywood's mouth. I wanted her to tell me she loved me, too. If I closed my eyes, I could imagine Ayano in the room with me, but the recording always stopped, followed by a digital chime, and when I opened my eyes, I was alone on my knees with a plastic dog running on a lithium battery.

*   *   *

In my workroom, I finish constructing the pine caskets for the upcoming memorial service, affixing a photo of each pet to the top with a coat of polyurethane. Some owners bury their dogs with their charging station and toys; others use the casket as a shrine, standing it upright to form a nook for candles and photos. The mail carrier delivers two packages. In the first box: spare parts I found on eBay. In the second: a first-generation poodle model named Samson all the way from Austin, Texas, accompanied by a letter from its owner explaining the problems he's been having. I told the owner not to send the dog. But people still seem to expect miracles.

I sent you an email months ago about my son's dog. Samson won't bark anymore. Just these strained mechanical wrrr wrrr sounds. His eyes light up, but we don't think his cameras are working on account of him walking into walls and heading in the opposite direction when we call. Last week, I thought he was gone for good. It took forever for him to charge again. All the forums say you're the best. I know you said things have changed, that you might not be able to help, but if there's even the smallest chance . . . we're prepared to pay whatever it costs. Please, help us. My son doesn't have much time left. He fights to breathe. The doctors say he's got maybe a few months. Samson is a part of him. When Samson was working, it was like my son could run and play. We just want our boy to be with his dog while he still can.

Attached to the letter is a photo of the man's son with Samson. The kid's hooked up to all manner of wires and tubes. He's so pale you can see the veins branching across his body. I take the dog out of the box, brush away the packing peanuts, and hear a rattle inside, telling me that this pup is likely dead on arrival. Poor kid. I open Samson up to confirm before emailing the owner. *I regret to inform you* . . . I think about the boy in his bed, waiting, hoping, maybe already deep in a coma in some crowded plague ward. I think about his father, skimming from monthly paychecks to buy his son something new that can never replace this dog. As a kindness, I include a cushion for Samson and refurbish the exterior as best I can. I'm preparing packing materials to send him back express when Aki emerges from his room, sees the poodle stuffed in the box.

"I told the guy not to send it," I say. "Nothing to be done."

"You should update the website and be honest with people," he says. "All you do anymore is open them up, shake your head, and send them back. It's pointless. Maybe it's time for you to get a real job."

My face grows hot and part of me wants to smack him on the back of his head, put him in his place, even if I know he's right. I still cling to the belief that I can do some good for these dogs and their owners. Aki goes into the other room and begins playing the shamisen. Soon, I hear my wife's voice, a song from her favorite enka singer, Keiko Fuji. I've begun to preserve all the artifacts of my wife's voice that she stored inside Hollywood on a digital recorder, in preparation for his eventual failure. I know it won't be the same, though. After all, Ayano sang into Hollywood's ears. I sit next to Aki as he plays. He gets up and says he needs more space. I shift over on the sofa. He watches me move before resuming his song. Every so often, my wife's voice is overcome by static or another melody from Hollywood's data bank. My son continues to play until Ayano finds her way back to us. Usually, this is our evening together: I cook dinner, Aki performs with Hollywood, and I spend the rest of the night alone in my workshop, thinking about how much time we'll need before we can move beyond this.

"I miss her so much," I say. I'm surprised that I let the words leave my mouth. I've broken the ritual my son and I created together.

Aki's bow hand is still. He looks to the floor. I can see his tears falling to the tatami, forming dark spots on the straw. I move closer. He backs away and puts the shamisen in its case. I've never been a hugger. It's just not something men in my family have ever done, but I want to hug my son. I want to feel his heartbeat against my own, his tears on my shoulder. I want to connect to the only real part of my wife that is left.

"I'm finished," he says. "I'm tired."

It's a warm but not terribly humid day for the group memorial service, and my former clients find support in one another, sharing stories about their pets. I arrange a simple picnic lunch for everyone—sandwiches I bought half off at the grocery store, arranged on a plastic tray with some fruit. I'm about to go back inside to allow them their space when they invite Aki and me to join them.

"You're one of us," they say. "In a way these dogs belong to you, too." One of my clients points to Hollywood, sitting in Aki's lap. Aki tells Hollywood to say hello. Instead, he asks the group a series of math questions. His LED eyes flicker. Our guests look at us with pity. Maybe they're starting to realize that if I can't fix my own dog, there is no hope left.

"He's a funny little thing," I say. Aki is petting Hollywood, and suddenly we're all listening to my wife's hopes and dreams for our son. *Study hard. Go to college. Meet someone who will make you happy and be kind to our family. Travel to all the places I never got to visit.* Aki is trying to make the recording stop, furiously activating Hollywood's sensors. The dog finally goes quiet and then offers an algebra question to the group.

"Sorry," Aki says, and stands to leave with Hollywood. I want to run after him, except I have no idea what to say.

———

Normally, after services like these, we visit Ayano at the high-rise cemetery in Chiba right outside of Tokyo, urn #25679B. I clean up after our guests and find Aki in bed, cradling Hollywood, who seems to be having another fit—random dancing, jumbled audio, the weather forecast frozen in his eyes.

"How long has he been like that?" I ask.

"Few minutes," Aki says. The fits don't last long, but they've been happening with greater frequency. Aki rocks back and forth as if the motion soothes our robo-dog.

"Have you tried confusing his programming?" I ask. "Sometimes that seems to stop the fits."

Aki shakes his head and says: "Dance, speak, stay, recharge." Hollywood continues to flail and beep. "Dance, speak, stay, recharge." Finally, Hollywood drops his front and hind legs, enters power-down mode.

"Do you still want to go see your mother today?" I ask.

Aki nods, springs out of bed, begins rifling through his closet for a dress shirt and slacks. He grabs Hollywood, and we head to Shinjuku Station to board the express train to the Japan Post Ltd. Funerary Remembrance Complex.

On the train, Aki and I stand, waiting for two passengers to leave before we take their single seats on opposite sides of the car. Everyone is dressed in black, the only voices recorded announcements of each station in English and Japanese—*Next stop: Fuji Tech Funerary Mall. Stop here for incense, flowers, and gift stores. Next stop: Lawson's Funerary Food Square. Stop here for ATMs, hotels, and the City Mortuary Affairs Office.* In front of me an elderly woman is holding a small bouquet of white and yellow lilies and chrysanthemums. Beside her, a younger woman wipes away her tears, fixes her makeup. The monitors above our heads advertise catering services, a company that can send a rocket filled with your loved one's ashes into space, premier packages for holograms of the departed that can be projected from a stainless steel urn. When a couple gets off at the crematorium stop, Aki and I take their seats so we can sit together as we wait for the end of the line, what the locals call the neighborhood of the dead. As we get closer, Aki lifts Hollywood to the window. The two of them gaze out at the skyline, the dark funerary towers casting fingerlike shadows over the temples and rock gardens.

"I thought we were going to buy flowers or something," Aki says without turning. We're at the three-story torii gate, signaling that we're close. Beyond the gate, a rainbow-colored holographic Buddha the size of a bus floats in the middle of a koi pond.

"There's always a markup at those Yamamoto shops," I explain. "We'll get something from one of the private vendors on the street. Much cheaper."

Aki nods and heads for the doorway, already crowded with people, as the train slows to a stop. *Welcome to the Japan Post Ltd. Funerary Remembrance Complex. This is the last stop. Please take all of your belongings.*

Outside, orderly lines wrap around the towers like slow-moving eels as people are checked in at the hospitality desks and given a ticket to enter the mortuary suite at their allotted time. Aki and Hollywood hold our place in line while I buy flowers and incense from a janitor selling wares from his cleaning cart. After more than an hour of waiting, we pay our two thousand yen for an hour of suite time and enter our code for the thirty-seventh floor. At first, the room is completely white. Soon, images of the temples outside are projected onto the walls, punctuated occasionally by banner ads offering us an upgrade in services. Aki and I wait on a wooden bench, the only piece of furniture in the room apart from the altar. A robotic arm retrieves Ayano, delivers her to the altar through a tiny elevator. The niche is a simple model—a rosewood box with cherry blossoms carved into it, two clay vases for flowers, a large photo of Ayano above the urn, an incense bowl Aki made in grade school. We change out the flowers and take turns telling her about our lives: school, the likely end of my repair business, the job applications I'm planning to send out. "I wish you were here," I say. "But we're doing our best. I'll keep Aki safe. We'll make you proud." Aki has brought the shamisen and begins to play as Hollywood shuffles on the grass—"Rainy Days and Mondays" by the Carpenters. I'm gazing at the photo of Ayano (taken during our honeymoon), listening to her sing. And then a few seconds of static, the male British voice saying good morning, followed by a techno club beat. Hollywood stumbles in circles. A banner ad on the wall tells us to cherish Ayano's memory by enjoying life via a buffet at the food court in tower 2.

"Keep playing," I tell Aki. I light a stick of incense. I squeeze his shoulders and wipe a tear from his cheek. I pick Hollywood up off the floor and his legs tread the air. Hollywood tells us it'll be cloudy with a chance of rain. He tells us that plague deaths are at an all-time low. I imagine part of my wife's spirit floating inside this tiny plastic body, wanting to connect us, waiting patiently for its turn.

SONGS OF YOUR DECAY

Most medical doctors in the plague wards are working toward the goal of keeping their patients alive, intact. It's my job to study how we fall apart. At the forensic body farm where I work, I'm researching the multitude of ways the Arctic plague transforms the human body, planting liver tissue in brains, heart tissue in intestines. I compare the Siberian strain to the Kindergarten strain to the latest mutations that have pulled the stricken into comas, made their skin glow with stars. Most of my cadavers come to us nameless, donated for research by their families staying at elegy hotels. Laird is a special case, though. He volunteered on his own and he's still alive. I compare the virus in his cells from before and after the most recent drug trial. The part of me that's spent hours listening to music with him late into the night wants the drugs to work, but my scientist heart knows studying the contagion both in life and during decomposition will help us gain a better understanding of how the virus functions in the body's ecosystem (and how it managed to survive in a Siberian cave for thousands of years). Beneath my microscope, I see Laird is losing, cell by cell.

My phone vibrates in the metal tray next to me, lying there alongside the many vials of skin and human hair.

How about pizza for dinner? A text from my husband.

Didn't we just eat pizza the other night? I respond after removing my gloves and sanitizing my hands.

We can order something else.

I imagine Tatsu searching through local delivery options that aren't Chinese or pizza. Don't bother, I message. I'll be late.

This probably isn't a surprise to him. I've been late every night this week. Sure, there's my workload—the pressure from the state and feds to find answers, anything that can help the infected—but I've also been revisiting my old self, the punk rocker who thought she could save the world with music and a microscope. Tatsu and I have been married for seven years now. But only our first was pandemic free. I can barely remember those early days, how he once bought us tickets for a punk festival even though I only ever heard him listening to Mariah Carey as he studied for his EMT exams. All my friends thought he was a complete square. I told them that's what I loved about him. He wasn't like my other boyfriends, those assholes with their leather jackets and their rock star dreams who ghosted you in their quest to be an artist. But when the plague hit American shores in 2031, something slowly changed between us as the virus evolved—maybe it was the lack of space, being trapped together like that all the time, apart from the hours we spent at work, everyone afraid, with no place to go.

"Are you gonna sit around and feel sorry for yourself all day?" I recall saying to him, about a year after the first wave. Tatsu was in his recliner, still in his uniform, a stethoscope dangling around his neck. A two-way radio sat beside him next to a glass of whiskey. "Do you know how many bodies I examined today?"

"But you don't have patients, Aubrey," he said. "The body bags are delivered to you for lab work. You hear stories about people's insides glowing, their skin turning to jelly. Try running an IV in someone's arm as their veins turn into Christmas lights. How would you prefer that I respond to my day?"

My face stiffened and I stood there for a long while, wanting to be anywhere else, staring at my car keys on the end table overflowing with utility bills, letters from family notifying us of relatives who'd died of the plague. We've had this argument before—with him trivializing my work because I'm not doing CPR in the back of an ambulance or listening to someone's last words. But the dead speak as well.

"I—am—trying—to—save—people," I said, enunciating for emphasis. I sat across from Tatsu, turned off the music. "Obviously, not the people on my lab table, but I hope my research can help someone, someday, maybe make their deaths count for something."

The next day, I'm finishing my lab report as Tatsu's rattling off restaurant names over the street noise in the background. He's clearly calling from outside his ambulance. After those early fights, we made a pact to work on our marriage. He still tries, and I love him for it. My boss glides past my workspace but doesn't chide me for taking a personal call, let alone on speaker.

"I thought we agreed we needed to spend more time together," he says, after I've failed to respond to any of his suggestions. "You've been getting home late nearly every day this week."

"We did," I say. "We agreed that whenever you weren't glued to the ambulance and whenever I wasn't busy with my research, we'd make time for each other. But you know Laird isn't doing well. He's important for my study."

"Yeah, yeah, yeah, I understand," he said. "This week, though."

"I promise."

"Send my regards to Laird."

At the hospital, Laird and his sister are watching television in his room, in the wing she donated. Orli has never quite understood my relationship with her brother; she's always worried I'm taking advantage of him. I can't blame her for thinking that. Half the time I don't know whether I'm rooting for him and already mourning an ill friend, or looking forward to some scientific breakthrough in part because of him. Orli is holding the release form Laird just signed, which gives my lab total custody of his body when he dies. Laird waves me over, holds up his old iPod. It's filled with our favorite hits. If he and I had met as teenagers, we would no doubt have spent hours dancing and smoking, drinking to the old greats—Talking Heads, Nirvana, buying Dead Kennedys patches on eBay to sew onto our denim jackets.

"But how will I say goodbye?" Orli says, turning to her brother with a sob. She stops herself before embracing him. Touching patients is not allowed, even if Laird is almost certainly not contagious—nearly all recorded adult cases thus far have been from water or food contamination or sexual contact.

"We never really got to say goodbye to Mom." Laird scratches at the rash that's forming around the monitor leads attached to his chest and reassures her he won't stop taking his medication until we're ready. He'll fight through the pain for as long as he can. I want to say something about Laird helping many other families who've lost more than they can bear, how he'll be part of the research that could help find the cure. But I know better than to speak right now.

I first met Laird almost a year ago, when he showed up at my lab after watching a documentary about our work on the True Crime+ Channel and how we've taken on the Arctic plague in addition to solving murders. At the time, he was desperate to understand what had happened to his mother. She'd gone missing during a cross-country drive to visit her sister. Nobody had known she was sick. When she was found off the side of the road in Des Moines, Iowa, the autopsy revealed that most of her organs had transformed into vague approximations of other bodily organs or—even more bizarrely—into globs of light. Most of the experts consulted believed she'd fallen into a coma long before death, and Laird, armed with only a bachelor's in chemistry and a minor in music, wanted to help others find the peace he never could.

"I'll let you and my brother do your thing," Orli says, watching Laird scroll through his vintage iPod. "What letter are you up to now?"

"*P*," Laird answers. "Panic! At the Disco, Paul Simon, Patti Smith, Pat Benatar, Pearl Jam, the Pixies. What do you think?" He turns toward me.

Orli bobs her head like she walked in on some secret clubhouse meeting before slipping from the room. She sits on a chair outside the door. I catch her turning around to check on us every few minutes. This alphabetized ritual began one day when Laird visited the lab and caught me watching recordings of old MTV music videos that I'd borrowed from the university library. He brought up his musical history minor capstone paper on the discovery and evolution of small bands and everything evolved from there. I sit by Laird's bed and he continues to scroll through his collection.

"I think you want to start with Pearl Jam," I say. "But if you're any kind of gentleman you'll throw me some Patti Smith."

He hovers his thumb over the selection wheel and pretends to be in deep thought before playing "Dancing Barefoot."

"How do you feel today?" I ask.

"Worse than yesterday. Better than this morning," he says. "The usual. Now hush."

I stay for nearly half an hour. I see Orli growing impatient, walking back and forth outside the door. Laird's eyes flutter closed as we're halfway through a Poison ballad.

"Champ, maybe we should call it a night," I say, taking the iPod and turning off the Bluetooth speaker.

"But the guitar solo," he says.

"You can wake up to C.C. Deville," I say. I pull the blanket to his chest and resist the impulse to kiss his forehead. He barely looks like the person I knew even a few months ago—his pale skin now latticed by veins. His sister's money has bought him more time than most. He's had three swine organ transplants and survived five drug trials. "I'll send in your sister. Dream of being a rock god."

Outside, Orli is seated again, erratically flipping through an old issue of *National Geographic*. She looks up at me, invites me to take the seat beside her.

"He really wants this—donating his body," she says. "I know I might seem selfish. I'm just not sure I understand. But he'll do anything you say. He really likes you."

"He's a friend to me, too," I say.

"I never really understood him, you know," Orli says. "Our parents were hard on us—study, be perfect, honor the family name. But Laird did his own thing. Peace Corps, leading Duck Tours in Wisconsin, helping locals build seawalls in impoverished island nations."

"The final say has to come from the both of you. We're not in the business of fighting families," I explain. As I say this, I'm forced to consider how I might succinctly describe my business to her. Before the pandemic, I helped solve murders. There was an order to things. We either found evidence or we didn't. There was always another case. But nothing about this virus makes sense. After nearly six years it seems like the research is running in circles. I don't know if anything I do will help save the world, but working with Laird makes me want to believe that it can. "Why don't you come to the lab tomorrow, if you'd like? I can show you the kind of work we do."

"I'd like that," she says.

———

By the time I get home, Tatsu is brushing his teeth and readying himself for bed. When we first moved in together, we'd have these endless conversations about our marriage being based on the shared goal of saving the world through the land of the living and the dead. We talked shop in the evenings, attended each other's work parties, surprised each other for lunch. But at some point, perhaps even before the plague, our jobs began to define us, so in recent years we decided on a new rule in an effort to save our marriage: No bringing work home with you.

"How's your guy?" Tatsu asks as I change into my pajamas.

"Same," I say. "Worse."

"There's spaghetti and meatballs in the fridge, if you're hungry," he says. "I have to be up in a few hours or else I'd stay up with you for a bit. Another EMT's kid is sick. Rejected a transplant. Taking their shift."

"Oh," I say. "I'm sorry to hear that."

I go downstairs and eat Tatsu's spaghetti. He clearly bought it from the gas station minimart on the corner. I listen to more Patti Smith. I marathon a season of *The Twilight Zone*, lie on the couch, cover myself with a throw blanket, and wait for sleep.

The following day, I'm standing with Orli behind a fence crowned with barbed wire. Nearly a dozen cadavers wait on the other side— some are sprawled beneath cages to prevent the coyotes from feeding on them; others lie scattered, picked apart by starving wildlife. At the bottom of an artificial pond, a young woman sits peacefully. She's held down by ankle weights, her arms raised toward the sky as if in deep prayer. The water is dark enough that Orli can't see

her body. I've nicknamed her Alice, and she'll stay there for another
month so our forensic students can inspect her rate of decay in water. Not all our cadavers are plague cases, though. We still serve law
enforcement. But Alice is one of the first adult victims of the second
wave. I imagine the virus floating around her in the pond like flakes
in a snow globe. Orli covers her nose. Out here, the smell digs into
your pores. Two showers, three. I've never gotten used to it.

"We treat each body with care," I explain. "Every single one is
here to help us find the answer to a question."

"Laird has this idea that you'll write him letters after he's gone
and send them to me," Orli says. "So it'll be like he's still alive, and
you'd be telling him, telling me what's happening to his body. He
said it might help me say goodbye."

"I'm not sure if you want to know the details of what'll happen to
your brother," I say.

"Maybe, probably," she says. "You can dress it up a bit. I don't
need to know everything. He considers you a good friend. He didn't
have many of those."

"We are friends," I say, and I think about what that means. He
came to me first when he thought he was sick. I drove him to the
hospital. I heard the diagnosis. Laird stood there calmly questioning
the doctor as if he'd just been told that he'd sprained an ankle, while
I imagined parasites infected with the virus coursing through his
body, withering him away to bone and dust. *It was probably from
using unboiled water in the nasal irrigation pot you mentioned*, the
doctor said. *At this point, we can only slow the infection.*

After his diagnosis, he still visited the body farm every day, free
from the financial pressure of needing a steady job due to the in-
heritance he and his sister received when their mother died. Laird
told me that if he was going to die, he wanted his final days to be

meaningful. If we needed DNA sequenced, bones cleaned, or even the floor mopped, he was always the first to volunteer.

"You don't need to do all of this," I told him after he'd mopped the floors at least twice in one week.

"I want to," Laird said. "I want to feel like I'm a small part of what you're all doing here." We liked to eat lunch together in the break room or at a nearby diner, the kind where they still roll a cart of pies to your table. Sometimes after work, we'd go to a park. We'd play Scrabble or Trivial Pursuit on the grass and listen to music that said something about our lives—this one is senior year; these songs explain junior high, the summer my parents couldn't stand each other.

Here's what I've learned about Laird from our time together:

- He has more broken dreams than realized ones.
- He says he doesn't believe in the supernatural, but once admitted to using a spirit board to contact his mother, and owns tarot cards and books about angels and the afterlife.
- He saved up to buy a He-Man Castle Grayskull playset as a kid but never bought a He-Man to defend the castle.

Here's what Laird knows about me:

- My name is Aubrey Lynn Nakatani.
- I call my cat Piglet or Bean or Beanicus Caesar.
- All of the lies I've told Tatsu about work, the reports and criminal cases and graduate student research, when I'm really hanging out with him.

- I am obsessed with Key lime pie and ironing all the wrinkles from my clothing.
- I sing to my cadavers when I arrange them in the field—eighties new wave, Christmas carols during the holiday season.

He once caught me humming Tom Petty's "Mary Jane's Last Dance" as I examined a box full of arms I'd burned the night before in preparation for a grad exam.

"I love that song," he said. "You know the music video starts off in a morgue."

We sang the chorus together.

"Why are all of the arms bent except that one?" he asked as I placed each one on the table.

"It's called the pugilistic pose," I answered. "The fire makes the muscles in our joints shrink. If we find a limb that isn't bent, it can be a sign of preburning trauma or restraint. I tied this arm down to a piece of wood."

What Laird and I have is beyond intimate, in a way.

Orli is clutching the fence with one hand, overlooking our body field, pinching her nostrils with the other. I squeeze her shoulder, attempt to lure her back inside. She's laser focused on the cadavers, though, the mounds of shallow graves.

"If he does this," Orli says. "If I allow this, would you write to him?"

"I will."

Orli nods, briefly releases her nose, and then begins to dry heave. She crouches on the ground. I hold her hair while she spits out the remains of what looks like a salad.

"I'm sorry," Orli says. She spits again.

"I've seen people do far worse here," I say. Sometimes I'm horrified by how normal this place seems to me. "Let's move back a bit." I guide Orli away from the worst of it, farther from the fence.

"The smell isn't too bad here," she says.

"Maybe we should go inside," I say.

Orli shakes her head. We stand there for a long while, watching the shadows of the bodies grow long as the sun falls, the air silent but for the steady hum of blowflies.

Two weeks later, Laird goes off his meds in preparation for what he calls *death on his own watch*. With what little time remains, he decides to go against his doctor's orders and take a field trip. He says the fluorescent lights are draining his will to live faster than the virus is. After a couple of days without the treatment, I notice Laird's energy has dropped, his mind is foggier, as if my words, the songs we listen to are being played in slow motion.

"Are you sure?" I ask. Orli and his nurse are helping him into a wheelchair. He wants to visit some ghost town hours away. "We could just go to a museum. Maybe the zoo?"

"What's the point of prolonging the inevitable, if I can't really live?"

His nurse gives me the number of the nearest hospital, somewhere outside of Yosemite, reminds Laird not to overexert himself.

"Yeah," Laird says sarcastically. "Wouldn't want to die."

As we leave civilization behind in a rented Subaru, Laird and I continue to work our way through the alphabet. I see Orli in the rearview mirror, resting her head against the window as we sing along to "Bohemian Rhapsody." Her ears might be ringing, but she's also smiling. I'm happy to give her this gift of a moment, being with her brother. We don't want to blow through all our songs at once and decide to check the radio, except the only stations we can find are filled with evangelical preachers shouting about how climate change is a lie or punishment for our sins. In the long stretches of desert, I sense Laird looking at me. I turn my head to catch him a couple of times. He pretends to study some spot along the horizon.

"Can you tell me what will happen to me?" he asks without warning.

"Are you sure?" I say.

"Might as well know. Besides, I think we've run out of radio stations."

"In the first twenty-four hours, depending on the temperature, the body will have reached full rigor mortis," I explain. "The face will have lost many of its distinguishing features. A greenish-blue hue spreads across the body."

"It's okay to say 'your body,'" he says. We pass an antique barn, an abandoned cherry stand, a sign that says LAST CHANCE FOR GAS before returning to the monotony of sunburned hills.

"Can we talk about something else?" I ask.

"Please, I want to know more," he says. I can tell he's tired. I know he needs me to give him the answers.

"Your body will start to smell like rotting meat."

"Let's play a little more music," he says.

"More Queen?"

"Queens of the Stone Age. And then what?"

By the time we reach Bodie State Historic Park, it's nearly noon. There's only one other car parked in the dirt overlooking the ghost town. Laird climbs out and snaps a photo of a pasture littered with early-twentieth-century trucks.

"You know there were people living here all the way up to the forties, until the gold and silver mines closed down," Laird says as I offer him his wheelchair.

Our first stop is a general store museum, stocked with antique tonic bottles, oil lanterns, and burlap sacks that once contained wheat or flour. There are boxes of bullets near the register, a mannequin wearing a cowboy hat. Glass cases run through the store's interior displaying photos of the town's golden age.

"Whoa, whoa, Nellie," Laird says as I push him through the cluttered aisles. "Let's take a closer look at this." We stop to read the faded *Reno Gazette* article mounted on the wall about the town's final residents—a man who shot his wife and who was, in turn, murdered by three other men. Soon we're panning for gold with a tour guide, coming up with tiny specks of light in a glass vial. We eat gas station sandwiches on the pews of the old-timey church and walk the grounds of a long-perished Chinatown. We're about to explore a cemetery when I look back and see that Laird is falling asleep in his wheelchair.

"Do you want to head out?" I ask him. He shudders awake, adjusts himself in his chair.

"Can't you see I'm having the time of my damn life?" he answers. Laird takes out a harmonica he must have bought for the trip and blows an uneven rendering of "I've Been Working on the Railroad."

We return to civilization late that evening. I drop Laird off at the hospital. I feel like I need to shower the long-drive sweat and old West from my body. I'm slipping off my shoes in our living room when Tatsu calls.

"Yo, some guys from work and I are headed to Extreme Wingz BBQ," he says. It sounds like he's been drinking. He tends to transform into an adolescent surfer dude when he's drunk, slinging out *hella*s with reckless abandon, filled with false confidence. "You should come with."

I really want to say no, but it's rare for Tatsu to socialize. I look at the calendar on my phone and see all the dates and dinners and movies with him that I've put off or canceled.

"Okay, but I'm not hanging out all night," I say. "Appetizers and a drink and that's it."

Two Long Island iced teas later I find myself listening silently as Tatsu ingratiates himself with his much younger colleagues, all strapping twentysomethings who don't seem to believe his early-plague EMT war stories, or the number of exotic women he's dated. One of the men glances over at me.

"You cool with all this?" he asks.

I wave away the comment. "It's fine," I say. "He's full of shit."

The table erupts in laughter.

Tatsu pulls me close and I participate in the charade, kiss him like we have some fairy-tale relationship.

The boys order another pitcher. I take this as my cue to leave.

In my car, I activate the self-driving mode and recline my seat. I can see Tatsu still laughing it up with his coworkers inside. I wonder if it's all an act or if he's really happy in this moment.

"Please indicate destination," the car says in an Englishwoman's voice.

"Anywhere," I say. "Just drive."

"That is not a valid destination."

"Shit, piss off to Half Moon Bay, then," I say, trying to think of a place far enough for me to get through an album without being too inconvenient a trip. "Play *Ghost Days* by Syd Matters." I pass hospital vans lined up outside elegy hotels before my car veers onto the freeway. I see a homeless man with a cardboard sign warning us that the end times are here, think maybe somebody should have listened to him a long time ago. I text Laird: Are you up? We're on the S bands. I figure he's probably sleeping or in a morphine-induced haze. An hour later, as I'm listening to the waves crash against the shore, he texts me back: Santana, obviously. What else?

"We have arrived at your destination," my car says.

"Okay, cool. Now let's go back. San Jose General Hospital."

I thought Orli would be there when I arrived, but it's only Laird, watching a late-night talk show. He picks up his harmonica from the table next to his bed and blows a weak tune. His food tray remains untouched and he's situated on a bedpan, legs arched under the sheet as if he's in labor.

"Do you need me to call someone to help?" I ask, standing near the doorway.

"I pushed the button. Sometimes it takes a while."

"Do you want me to help?"

"I don't want you seeing me like that," he says.

"My hands are literally going to be inside of you when you die," I say.

"Well, when you put it that way," he says, laughing.

A moment later a nurse blows past me. I turn around while she takes care of Laird. I hear him groan as he's lifted off the pan. She asks about his pain level and Laird says three. The nurse leaves with barely another word.

"Okay," Laird says. "I'm decent-ish."

I sit on the edge of his bed, take a napkin from his tray, and dab at his forehead beading with sweat. On the news, an iridescent cigar-shaped object is shown crashing into the ocean, the footage taken on a phone by a bystander in Venice Beach.

"Huh," Laird says, turning up the volume. "Ain't that some shit."

"Let's get out of this room," I say. "It's not scorching outside for once. Maybe you'll have more of an appetite with some real food instead of this slop."

We stop by the cafeteria after-hours self-serve kiosk for snacks—rubberized fried calamari, Goldfish crackers, day-old cherry pie—and find a picnic table in the courtyard. Laird plays the Smashing Pumpkins. I ask for a round of Siouxsie and the Banshees. We're both staring at the stars.

"You sort of just mashed up your pie on the plate," I say.

"It's a bit hard to swallow," he says. "But I still like the taste of food."

"Are you afraid?" I ask.

"I don't think so," he says. "A lot of people are afraid it'll hurt, that they'll be hurting family and friends, but I've been hurting for so long now. And Orli will be okay, eventually."

"What about the things you wanted to do with your life?"

"Sure, that sucks," he says. "I'm not going to lie and say making something of myself or falling in love or honoring my mom by help-ing you find a treatment weren't on my list of things to do. But it's not like it's just me now, you know? I guess it makes it easier know-ing that I'm not the only one. And I've had thirty-two years. More than a lot of other people."

I hold Laird's hand. It's uncannily soft, as if his finger bones are made of rubber. He looks at me for a moment and then back at the sky.

"When I was a kid I was so obsessed with space. I wanted to study the stars, but I sucked at math," Laird says. He's still looking upward and squeezes my hand, grazes it with his thumb. "Would be pretty amazing if that thing that fell in the ocean was really from another world. You believe in that stuff?"

"I think it's probable," I say, searching the sky for the dippers. "Awfully big place for it to be only us."

"Well, maybe somewhere on some faraway planet or moon, two beings are together like this asking the same thing."

"I'm going to miss you," I say. I lean over the table and kiss him gently on the lips—too long to be friendly, too soft and quiet to be anything more than a little sad. "I'm sorry we couldn't have met another way."

He's silent for a long while, pops a few Goldfish crackers into his mouth. I wonder if he's ever fantasized about intimate moments like this with me. He pulls his iPod from the speaker dock and begins to scroll.

"The Strokes?"

"Sure," I say.

"I'll miss this," he says.

Three days later, Orli shows up to the lab, carrying a Chia Pet box, and tells me that Laird passed away in the night. I had planned to meet him that afternoon, made reservations at my favorite Italian restaurant. She sounds like she spent all morning practicing what she would say to me, as if veering from her lines might cause her to implode. I imagine Laird in his hospital bed the other night, closing his eyes, drifting off to sleep. I do not want to acknowledge the pain. I imagine myself there at his side, rather than giving in to Tatsu's desperate advances. We'd made it through *T* on my last visit, mostly ruled by the Talking Heads. Laird barely spoke. I asked him several times if he wanted to stop, let the album play even though he'd drifted off to sleep. He told me the last real meal he could taste was french fries, and his last real outing when he felt healthy was to a comic book store—and we both laughed at his nerdiness, his encyclopedic knowledge of Magic: The Gathering, *Star Trek*, and Superman lore.

"We're having a memorial," Orli says. She writes down the information and hands me the box. "He told me to give this to you."

"Thank you," I say. "I'm so sorry. Can I—"

But before I can hug her or offer her coffee or maybe my life story, which might allow her to look at me like a human being rather than some well-meaning scientist who may or may not have the hots for her dying brother, she turns away and sprints down the hall. I curl over my desk, find a playlist on my phone called "The Saddest Songs in the World." "Everybody Hurts" by R.E.M. starts right as my boss taps me on the arm.

"Aubrey, I heard about Laird," he says. He squeezes my shoulder. The entire staff is pretending not to look at me, side-eyeing our conversation. "Just take the day off."

"Thank you," I say. I wash up in the bathroom and beeline to the door before anyone else can offer their awkward condolences.

When I get home, I open the box before Tatsu returns from his shift for what he likes to call "date night," basically an evening of lackluster Thai takeout with a wonky spice rating system that somehow always results in noodles that are either too hot or exceptionally bland. I perch on the toilet and lock the bathroom door, just in case. I don't want Tatsu to see my face twisted into every angle of grief, a primal ugly cry. I don't want him to know what's inside the box: a key, a photo of Laird before he got sick, his iPod, a stack of letters in sealed envelopes accompanied by a note telling me to open one each day. If Tatsu asks, I will tell him the box was full of lab samples—tissue, blood, urine. Nothing exciting. Nothing that matters.

Dear Aubrey,

If you're reading this, it means I lost. But, of course, that was the plan. I suppose I'm downstairs now in a morgue drawer, waiting for someone to take me to you. But I'd like to imagine I'm in a photon torpedo tube on the starship *Enterprise*, and I'll be shot into space like Spock at the end of *Wrath of Khan*. Or I'm in a space pod from *2001: A Space Odyssey*, on my way to becoming a star child. You never know, right? Sometimes I imagined what my memorial would be like. What would people say? What would you say? Maybe we really did just have a friendly working relationship. But I always wondered. I liked to pretend some of our outings were dates. What if I hadn't been that guy in the hospital? What if my mother hadn't died and we'd bumped into each other in a music store or something long before the world got fucked? You'd be holding a Velvet Underground LP, and I'd be holding Hüsker Dü. And I'd hope whatever minimal charm I possessed would be enough. Regardless of who we really were to each other, I guess you're still the person I'm sending this box to.

There are maybe a dozen people at Laird's memorial. I can't be sure who works for the funeral home. The place is covered in hardwood and muted shades of green, as if anything brighter would be disrespectful to the spirit of mourning. Tissue boxes line the aisles. Up front, near the podium, is a large picture of Laird—probably a school photo based on the marble background, the fact that he still has braces. As we look for our seats, Orli waves us to the first row, points to a couple of empty spots beside her.

"I thought our father and his girlfriend would show up," she says.

"But he's been pretty much out of the picture for years, although he tried to do the dad thing for a little while. Just as well. I might have punched him."

"I'm sorry for your loss," Tatsu says.

The only other person in the front row is a man wearing chain mail. He tells us that he saw the obituary and claims to have battled with Laird in an online video game called *The Swords of Tranquility*. He says Laird was his online brother, a fellow knight. As I listen to Sir Godric of the Islands of Honor, I think about how Laird wrote that he thought of me, how he nibbled on a Goldfish after I kissed him. I try not to cry as the minister approaches the pulpit.

"We are gathered here to celebrate a life of service, a life taken from us far too early—something I know all of us have experienced in recent years," the minister begins. "If you would please rise in song." The acoustic guitar opening of Jeff Buckley's "Satisfied Mind" starts to play. I open my program for the lyrics. I'm surrounded by Laird's extended family. As I sing, I feel like I'm floating in an invisible shell filled with static electricity. I think about Laird in his hospital bed, at the Bodie ghost town, remember how he showed up at my lab one day in a Ramones T-shirt with his résumé and a desire to volunteer. When the song is finished, the room falls silent. The minister invites Orli to speak. I feel myself slowly floating back into place. Tatsu rubs my back, hands me a tissue.

"My brother and I didn't really spend much time together until our mom died," she says. "This plague has taken so much away from us. It's taken Laird. But in a strange way, I've also gotten to know my brother again because of it. As a kid, he wanted to be an astronaut, and then an archaeologist and then a climate scientist. He wanted to help people who were sick. He had a different dream every year and he was the kind of person who could have achieved most of them if only he'd been given enough time."

As Orli finishes her eulogy, a childhood photo of Laird standing beside an *Apollo* capsule at the Smithsonian is projected behind her. A few other family members speak, followed by Sir Godric, who unsheathes his plastic sword and tells Laird to fly boldly into the hall of warriors.

"Is there anyone else who would like to say a few words?" the minister asks.

Orli taps my hand like she wants me to go up there. I'm not sure what to say, though. On paper, I'm just some woman in a lab who is planning to take Laird apart. Tatsu notices me fidgeting. I squeeze Orli's hands.

"Then may we all adjourn to the reception in the next room to the music that Laird so deeply loved," the minister says.

"Excuse me," I say to Orli, heading straight to the bathroom as "Don't You (Forget about Me)" by Simple Minds plays over the speakers. I sit on the toilet and think about what I might have said if I had the courage to go up there. Tatsu's presence in the front row had a lot to do with my silence. *Hi, I'm Aubrey. Many of you don't know me, but I spent a lot of time with Laird this past year.* I open my purse and pull out another letter—Day 2.

Dear Aubrey,
I used to spend a lot of time after my mom died pretending
I could find a way to make things right. Maybe I could
save some kid from losing his parents. Orli went off to Los
Angeles to play philanthropist—opening new plague wards
at hospitals, leaving me with a dad who never really knew
how to talk to his son. Before I came to find you, I thought
I might go back to school with an eye toward epidemiology,
if it weren't for my shitty grades. Pretending was better than
nothing, I suppose. So I started collecting articles about

the plague. I read the published leaked journals of Cliff Miyashiro twice, how he and his fellow researchers had wanted to warn the world. Nobody ever thought this would happen. I marathoned reruns of medical dramas, wishing I could wear a white coat and help people. But you were real. You listened. You gave me a way to honor my mother.

Tatsu is waiting outside the bathroom with a glass of wine when I emerge.

"Thanks," I say. The wine smells like vinegar and has a strong acidic bite. I down it in a couple of gulps anyway. I know Tatsu's trying to be there for me, but I'm tired of pretending our relationship is one quick fix away from being okay. Orli escapes the gauntlet of aunts and uncles, joins me and Tatsu as we're piling cubes of cheese on plastic plates.

"After things settle down, maybe you can come back to our childhood house," Orli says. "No one will be there. It's just me and seven thousand square feet of empty rooms since Laird was hospitalized."

Tatsu excuses himself and goes to sit in a corner, eating summer sausage and grapes, staring at the floor like he's an awkward middle schooler at a dance.

"That'll be nice," I say.

Orli is pulled away by another relative. I pour a heaping glass of chardonnay before joining Tatsu in the shadows.

"I appreciate you coming," I tell him. I pick a sausage off his plate. "But I think I'd rather be alone with Orli for a while if that's okay. I'll see you back at home."

"Will you be there in time for dinner?"

"I don't know," I say. "I'll call you."

———

In Orli's solar-edition Land Rover, I feel in my purse for the key Laird left me. We pass tech campuses that have been temporarily transformed into funerary processing centers and overflow clinics for the plague drug trials. A teenage boy pushes an older woman in a wheelchair across a clinic parking lot. A line wraps around the old offices of a dating app—people waiting for their loved ones to be scheduled for elegy hotels or burial or some hope that the funerary banks will provide bereavement assistance as life insurance companies struggle to pay out. In what used to be a Hewlett Packard Enterprises business park, a crane lowers a sign that reads FUNERARY FUTURES AND FINANCE. We leave San Jose for Saratoga, veer onto a winding road shrouded by oak trees. We pass a desiccated apple orchard, a burned-out field littered with the husks of dead horses. The stately Spanish-style villas that punctuate the drive are surrounded by lawns painted green, sprinkler systems spraying dye instead of water. I am holding Laird's key in my palms like a talisman, wondering what it might reveal—a vinyl collection, journals, maybe a time capsule from his childhood.

"I don't know what he has locked up in his desk, but you're welcome to it," Orli says, staring at my hands clutching the key. "All of this—the money, the society. It was never Laird, but we had some happy moments. He only really came back when Mom died."

A cardboard Captain Kirk stares at me from the corner of Laird's childhood bedroom. He's standing guard beside a twin bed and a corkboard filled with articles about the plague. A collection of ray guns line the shelves, along with mason jars filled with cicada husks. I scan the room, rummage through drawers and feel like I can sense Laird's presence—a framed Kraftwerk poster, an old turntable decorated with animal stickers, an acoustic guitar. I sit on his bed and notice a plastic milk crate filled with records peeking out from beneath his *Star Wars* comforter. I pull out the records and arrange them on the floor: *Paul's Boutique* by the Beastie Boys, *Sea Change* by Beck, Dylan's *Blonde on Blonde*.

"When we were little, he used to do odd jobs for our neighbors. He'd beg our dad to take him to the swap meet so he could find more music," Orli says, standing in the doorway. "He wanted to work for his music. He said it would mean more. In high school, he probably spent more time at the record shop where he worked part-time than he did with us."

I pick up New Order's *Power, Corruption & Lies* and take the LP out of its sleeve.

I put on "Age of Consent" and sit at Laird's desk, unlock the drawers. Inside are stacks of manila folders bursting with articles, everything from *The Atlantic* and *The Economist* to grocery store tabloids. There is a copy of his mother's autopsy report, chest X-rays that show the shadows of growing masses. Orli quickly excuses herself and leaves me to it.

Miracle Tonic Developed in Kansas: Minister's
Prayer-Infused Potion Gives Elderly Hope

No New Plague Cases in Months, but Will Researchers
Find a Cure before the Infected Die?

City of Laughter Drug Trials Discontinued by
FDA due to Unregulated Stem Cell Use

Genetically Engineered Fast-Growing Pigs
Buy Time for Those on Transplant Lists

When You've Done All You Can: Allowing Your
Loved Ones to Say Goodbye with Grace

I read through the clippings, place them in an empty milk crate. Laird wanted me to see this, the extent to which his mother's death

made him who he was, the only Laird I ever knew. I don't know
what I'll do with the files. It doesn't seem right to leave them locked
away. I imagine studying the artifacts or setting them on fire, like
that time I saw a family friend burn what she called ghost money
at her grandmother's Chinese funeral, to ensure a rich afterlife. For
Laird, I would burn the articles to set him free, to let him know he
did all he could—a cosmic stamp of approval sent through the ether.

Dear Laird,
This is my third attempt at writing this letter. My interns
dug you a shallow grave beneath an oak tree this morning.
You're in a T-shirt and jeans. Socks but no shoes. Normally I
would have helped dig, but I couldn't this time. I continued
our alphabet in my head. *U*: U2's "With or Without You."
Okay, a little cheesy, but a solid song. Bono before he found
those ridiculous tinted glasses. You'll be working double
duty for our criminology students and the virus inside of
you will be part of my study for the CDC. You'll be in the
ground for at least two weeks and then we'll relocate you
to another grave. I could barely recognize you when we put
you in the hole. And any glimmer of you will no doubt be
long gone when my forensics grad students and the cadaver
dogs find you. For them, you are homework without a voice.
I will refer to you as subject 27A. They'll have to figure
out you've been moved, that any early-stage larvae they
find in your second grave cannot be used to determine an
approximate time of death. Soil composition, the detritus of
the oak tree, and the bacteria and microbes in and around
you will have to guide their way.

———————————

Two weeks have passed since the memorial and Tatsu is leaving me notes around the house, folded index cards with hearts drawn in marker—*I Love You. Let Me Know What You Need.* Tonight, he has cooked dinner. Nothing fancy. Linguini and microwaved turkey meatballs (he even pulled out the china someone gave us for our wedding that we've never used). When we were dating, he cooked regularly. We'd play Twenty Questions and weird relationship board games to help us facilitate the evening—apparently, we've never been great at filling the silences. I suppose I should be thrilled he's making such an effort. I'm surprisingly unfazed. He scoops more meatballs onto my plate, suggests a weekend getaway at a nearby bed and breakfast. I find myself wondering if maybe a dog would have been enough to keep us happy.

Letter Day 18:

Dear Aubrey,
I know shitty things happen to good people for no reason.
Sometimes my mom would take me to the park with these
balsa wood planes with a rubber-band-powered propeller. We
wouldn't talk much. She'd just sit listening to music and watch
me fly my planes until they broke. During the summers, the two
of us would take a trip to escape the hustle of life—camping in
Yellowstone, a road trip to the Grand Canyon. The year she died
we were supposed to go to the Everglades. Then out of nowhere
she said she was too tired and wanted to stay closer to home.
Maybe I should have known something was wrong. Instead, I
strapped a VR headset to my mother, and together we explored
the ancient heads of Easter Island, stared up at the Milky Way.

―――――――

At the body farm, we're preparing for a mixed group of grad students and local authorities to engage in a trial manhunt for a missing person. I've collected scraps of Laird's dirty clothes for the dogs, prepared documents detailing the scenario: the confession of an incarcerated accomplice allowed for the search to commence. I'm in the field planting evidence that might have been left by the suspect, as well as trash and other scents to tempt the dogs astray, when I see Orli approaching the fence. She's carrying a bouquet of flowers in her hands.

"They're going to find him tomorrow?" she asks.

"If all goes to plan," I answer. "And then he'll be left out. I'll be looking at how the virus has survived inside of him in the meantime, if there've been any unexpected changes."

"I thought I could see him before that happens," she says. She looks down at the bouquet. "I probably can't leave these. I don't know what I was thinking."

I guide Orli to the gate and let her in.

"I can take them," I say. We walk over to Laird's grave. I point to a patch of earth covered with branches and dried leaves. I give Orli her space, return to the lab. When I glance back, she's crouched down, touching the soil. She looks like she's talking to him. She looks like she's laughing.

Orli leaves without stopping by the lab to see me. I place the flowers on my desk in a plastic pitcher, tape a few of Laird's clippings and his photo to the side.

Dear Laird,

I have the files you left. I'm not sure what you wanted me to do, but I've decided to keep them. When you have a job like mine, sometimes it's easier to cut yourself off from the wider context. A body is a subject. A first instar larva signifies death has probably occurred within twenty-four hours, depending on temperature and barring interference. I imagine the people who examined your mother didn't think of her as a mother or a wife. I told your sister we treat each body with care. I've essentially been programmed to talk like that, think like that, to survive day to day. It's cold, really. If I were anybody else, you would be just another case. But I'm not. And when I go home tonight, I'll take a bath. I'll bring your iPod in with me and lock the door. I'll play the songs we shared until the smell of the lab has washed away. For now, it'll be the Violent Femmes, as I write this and wait for someone who has no idea who you really are to tell me you've been found.

I remain at work after the barking has ceased, after everyone, including my boss, has left for the day. Tatsu has called three times. But I don't want to talk to anyone. I just want to listen to music and stare out at the dark field, where I can no longer see his body. I want to imagine him getting up like nothing ever happened (in a romantic, nonzombified way).

"I woke up in a field," he'd say.

"I know. Come inside with me." I'd put on a new song, wipe the dirt from his body.

"The Cranberries?"

Did Laird ever dance? Even if he didn't, we'd do the junior high shuffle. I think about what that would be like.

My phone is blowing up with missed call after missed call. I know I'll sound too annoyed if I answer. So I text: This is Aubrey's boss. She's elbow deep in someone right now. She says she'll be home soon.

When I arrive home, Tatsu has already eaten. There are Chinese takeout boxes and a broken fortune cookie waiting on the dinner

table. He's watching Shark Week and giving me the silent treatment. I sit at the table and dig into some cold chow mein and orange
chicken.

"You didn't answer my calls," he says. He turns off the TV and
sits across from me.

"I know," I say. "I'm sorry." I don't even know how to explain
what I've been doing in a way that doesn't make me sound like I'm
already checked out of our marriage. *Sorry, honey, I've been fantasiz-
ing about my dead friend who had a crush on me, and our life together
really sucks.*

"I called your boss. He says everyone else left hours ago."

"I had things to take care of," I say.

"Laird?" he asks.

"Yes," I say. "Laird."

"I don't understand what's going on here," he says. "I'm jealous of
a dead guy. Can you explain this shit to me?"

"I don't know," I say. "Not yet. But this shit was going on before
Laird. This shit has been going on for a long time."

I get ready for bed, wait for Tatsu to join me. He never does.

In the morning, as I'm leaving for work, I see a note taped to the
front door: *Meet me at the Extreme Wingz this evening. Let's really talk.*

Dear Laird,
Your body has begun to bloat and blister from the gases
building inside you, a rich ecosystem for insects and
microbial life. I've begun taking samples from your vital
organs, which will soon be wide open to the air. Vultures
have begun to circle, and soon, when the coyotes come from
whatever hole they crawl through under the fence, you will be
scattered across the field. Last night, my husband asked me
about you. Why I care so much, why I spent last night alone

at work, thinking about you. I never realized how important
you were to me, even just the little things like listening to
music together. We didn't really know each other, but I've
begun to wonder like you did, because being with you was
easy. And I don't think it was ever easy with Tatsu. Even
when we were happy, we were still like two puzzle pieces that
look like they should match but never will no matter how
hard you try to smash them together.

When Tatsu calls, I let my phone ring. He texts: Are you there?
Are we still on? Come on, Aubrey. He sends an angry emoji. A devil
emoji. Shit, I'm the only one trying here. I'm in the parking lot of
Extreme Wingz. I can see him through the window. He slams his
fists on the table. He wipes his eyes. A waitress approaches. It looks
like she's asking him if he's okay. We'll talk soon, a conversation we
probably should've had years ago. But for now, I return to the lab,
put on my headphones, press play on Laird's playlist before heading
out to the field. An album for the last of his entrails, a power ballad
for the final bits of flesh, ambient electronica while I preserve the
virus inside him, a love song as I place his bones in a drawer and
close it shut.

LIFE AROUND THE EVENT HORIZON

We all agreed it was a breakthrough, the singularity. At the press conference, even I had to concede that humanity had reached the precipice of a second chance, despite having accidentally planted the tear in the fabric of space-time inside my own brain—interstellar space travel, a window to an alternate Earth where the plague has been cured, a cosmic waste bin for our pollution, maybe even an answer as to why we're all here. But my brilliant new physicist bride and former postdoc assistant, Theresa, was surprisingly less excited about the prospect of leaving Earth, even though her minor corrections to my equations had helped create a stable micro black hole.

"This planet is our home," she'd said over dinner a few nights after the accident. "I'm not leaving just because we can." Our dining table was covered with data from our tests, blueprints of the starship nearing completion at Area 51. From what little I've seen that wasn't redacted in the documents from the Department of Defense, the ship has been in the works for years, reverse-engineered from extraterrestrial technology recovered from a crash in the forties. Apart from our work, Theresa has spent a lot of her time decorating our townhome, purchasing furniture like this table made of wood salvaged from forest fires, adorning the walls with artwork, including a painting she did herself of a fantasy star system that now hangs over the fireplace. She called the work *Possibility*, a purple planet surrounded by a halo of light and orbiting three red dwarfs.

"I thought you would want to see what's out there," I said, pointing to her painting. "After all, you played a small part in creating the energy source that will make the starship's engine run."

"I want humanity to be out there," she said. "Of course. You have no idea how much I want that, but that doesn't mean *I* want to be out there. Things are getting better here."

"Rising sea levels, California burned to a crisp every year, plague wards filled with patients . . . yeah, it's a party down here," I said. "I mean, really. People are training for this mission. The crew has been selected. A public lottery is set to release any day now. The ship is going to leave as soon as we run operational tests, maybe a few practice journeys beyond the Kuiper Belt and back. The government is committed to establishing a colony out there. That way if the shit hits the fan, we'll have someplace to go. And in case you didn't get the memo, I think the shit hit the fan and it's all over the goddamn ceiling."

"Did you see that researchers think they might have found a lead to a cure?" Theresa said. "It was on the news the other day. Some anonymous package with a vial left outside one of the leading labs with a note that read 'A little help.' They don't know what to make of the substance. One researcher confirmed that it's genetically related to the virus. They said it was glowing bright white."

"And people in the Bible Belt are baking themselves in the sun, thinking they can pray it away, burn it away," I said. "We've been promised a cure many times before."

Theresa is a champion at throwing daggers with her eyes. She twirled the purple crystal pendant she wore on a silver chain around her neck. She's worn it for as long as I've known her. I used to watch her play with that necklace when she was helping lead experiments in my lab, notice how it refracted light across the room, casting rainbows over the whiteboard.

"I'm doing this work because of everything that happened," I said. The several rounds of drug trials that ended with me cremating my daughter, Petal, a few months after her grandmother died of cancer and my first wife, Cynthia, from experimental plague treatment complications. Sometimes I wonder about the real reason I made such an "error"—and think maybe I went to work one day and said fuck it to the sympathetic stares and the judgmental gossip over my getting remarried so soon, with our lab's funding dwindling, my son treating me like it's my fault the resident genius couldn't save our own family. "I don't expect you to understand what I went through."

"No, I guess I wouldn't," Theresa said. She walked around the table, cleared away my dishes. "It's not like everyone in the department doesn't already think I jumped into bed with you so I could land a coveted spot in your lab. Not like I didn't catch you crying in your office more times than I can count. Not like I wasn't there to teach your classes when you needed the help."

"I didn't mean . . ." I could hear my preteen, goth son, Peter (now going by Axel), stirring in his room, probably wanting to come downstairs. But he knows not to barge in when we're working on classified material.

"Does it hurt?" Theresa touched my head with her hands, as if she could somehow sense the gravitational pull, the Hawking radiation pulsing from my forehead that my colleagues were working to translate into usable energy and thrust.

"Not at all. It's not going to affect me like that. I mean, no one really knows what it'll do."

We rechecked the data when we realized what had happened. As a physicist, I always wanted to uncover the secrets of the universe. But as a human being and intermittent father, I wanted my surviving child to live well into adulthood, a long, healthy life away from the plague and floods and record-breaking hurricanes. I even wanted my dipshit brother, Dennis, who seemed hell-bent on spending his entire life at that elegy hotel, to have a second chance after the loss of our mother.

"She's fucking great, Bry," he'd said the last time we talked. He was dating his only real friend, his coworker and floor mate Val. "I totally don't deserve her."

"I'm sure you don't," I said. "You should bring her out to Nevada sometime."

"Well, you know how it is here. Gotta work off the discounts they gave me for Mom and Petal's funeral services."

"I told you I can pay for that," I said. "It's been a year since Mom's memorial. You don't have to be some kind of serf."

"Nah, man. It's cool. I mean, it's my life, you know? And I have Val," he said.

It was nice to know he had someone, and it was the least I could do to offer them a chance to start fresh. But what did fresh even mean? NASA wanted to reach the Kepler system. The military wanted to develop energy weapons in case we encountered un-friendlies out there. My interns had begun staring at me at work, mentally boring a hole in my skull, no doubt hoping to reveal what they envisioned as a tiny version of some wormhole they saw in a sci-fi flick with people zipping around the universe, parallel real-ities traversable by psychedelic cosmic tunnels. But I didn't want anyone zipping around in my brain. I wanted to understand how this happened and how we might replicate it in the starship's en-gine. And maybe a part of me wanted to know if somewhere inside my head, there's a universe where Petal and Cynthia are still alive, asking me to come down to dinner.

Scan. Tests. Questions. Repeat.

Do you feel any differently? the government doctors asked.

I feel fine, really.

Of course, I imagined the parallel realities, what would happen to me if I told my colleagues and superiors the truth. I'd be fired and stripped of security clearance, locked in a government facility for hiding a program I'd built to disable accelerator safeguards. And not only that; I often dreamed of being enveloped by light. I stuffed PowerBars and family photos into a fanny pack as if I were planning a long walk into the universe.

People from other labs, other universities poked and prodded before the military classified everything to do with me as top secret. Then came the protesters who believed the hole would expand, tear me apart, and then tear apart the whole damn world. Our public relations guy, Gene, said that's highly improbable. Then came those seeking deliverance, who had loved ones waiting on organ donor lists, who couldn't afford the experimental drugs or new age retreats. Or those who were financially ruined because they'd been laid off or forced to shutter their businesses. They all held signs: WILL WORK ON EARTH 2! They wore respirator masks on the days when the wildfire smoke reached hazardous levels. They prayed and chanted, held each other's hands. They believed what I'd done was their ticket out of all of this.

At home, Theresa wants me to rest. She's decided to be nice to me again, so I'm not going to argue with her. She's been good to Axel even if he's constantly telling me I'm basically fucking the babysitter, and that I'm a fucking asshole for getting married so soon. Theresa and I never had a real honeymoon—our job saving the world doesn't really allow for much time off. A lot has been on hold. *After this is all over. When things are better. After we've done what we set out to do.* I want this to be a real marriage and not what other people seem to think it is, some brilliant, pretty young thing, a distraction from trauma. Theresa organizes my pain pills for the headaches that grow worse each day. She's in charge of my schedule with the doctors and reporters. She blends my pea protein shakes and cooks my prepackaged meals, my favorite green chile tamales and sweet potato gnocchi, which she stockpiled when she found out the local grocery was planning to stop selling it. When I'm curled up well after midnight, staring at my laptop screen, she tells me that can't be good for me. Does she mean work or the hole in my head? She asks me what could be more important than getting better, being there for my family. At night, she checks my math as I puzzle through the process of placing a singularity in the starship's engine.

"You always forget to swap your variables," Theresa says, lying next to me in bed. "And you're not accounting for some of the quantum fluctuations at the event horizon."

"How is your problem coming along?" I ask.

"You mean how are we going to get this black hole outside of your head?"

"Yeah, that would be the problem."

"I'm toying with what it would take for us to create a tiny antimatter singularity. The matter and antimatter singularities should destroy each other."

"I'm gonna say let's pass on the explosions inside my head," I say. "It's a good head. I'd like to keep it if possible."

"It's just one of many solutions I'm working on," she says.

"By the way, I'll pick up toilet paper on my way to work," I say. "Unless you're driving in with me."

"I'll be working at home," she says. "You really shouldn't stay at the lab so long. Your staff is more than capable of running your experiments. Oh, and grab some clementines, too. The bag in the fridge has gone bad." She squeezes my thigh and turns on the television—more conspiracy theorists who believe the starship is part of some Noah's ark project planning to leave the rest of humanity behind when a supposed planetary body they call Nibiru crashes into Earth. "Maybe we can have dinner tomorrow and not talk shop for a change?"

"Of course," I say. I kiss her and realize that maybe I do think of our relationship as a hybrid of professionalism and romance, the square root of what everyone might have wanted for me. But Theresa needs me to be present at dinner, fully and completely, and to attend Axel's school functions with her. She wants me around enough to watch a movie or play a board game or make out on the couch during one of her frequent nature documentary marathons. Axel, with his newly dyed pink hair, asks if I'm starting to receive messages from another dimension. I detect sarcasm and hate it in my son. He used to read to Petal at night. He used to stick up for her when the other kids at school made fun of her lisp. Now he thinks I'm a huge nerd, a total joke. *I don't think so*, I tell him, and give him Spock's Vulcan salute. *But there is a lot we don't know. Whatever*, he says. I've told him I'm sorry more times than I can count. I told him Theresa isn't here to replace his mother. I told him it's fine if he hates me, but we need to try to be a family while we still can.

Scans. Tests. Questions. Repeat.

My engineer father once told me that marriage and who you fall in love with are largely a matter of chance, chemicals, and how far you're willing to drive. He said who your kids turn out to be is even more of a crapshoot. I blame some of my failings with human connection on this man. But my son, Peter, is a good kid, all things considered.

He doesn't get into much trouble, earns decent grades (though not recently) despite not being particularly bright, only drops F-bombs with his old man, continues to volunteer at the hospital plague wards far beyond the school's community service requirements, actually likes working out. Petal seemed like she was going to take after me, though. She'd join me in the backyard at night to stargaze, ask me about energy and light speed and parallel universes. She devoured my old stack of Time-Life's Mysteries of the Unknown books and told me she wanted to get abducted by aliens—even if only for a weekend.

I've been working on a video journal for my wife. It's my attempt to share with her in the best way that I know all the things I've never said, that I want her to understand.

TRANSCRIPTS

00:22 *You don't know how much your mind filled me with awe, Theresa. How I needed a team of colleagues to understand the corrections you made on my equations. And maybe I didn't always say thank you enough. Part of me was jealous at how effortlessly you visualized the intricacies of black hole physics.*

00:36 *And you really did save me. Before you came along, I'd cry in the bathroom at work, sometimes even entertaining the reality of Axel dying instead of Petal. I was so angry at myself for even thinking this. I once put my fist through the drywall, as if everything inside me had come to a boil, a singularity of emotion exploding like a star.*

00:48 *Lately, when I turn on the accelerator in the lab, I feel more alive and loved and complete than when I'm with any other person on the planet except for you. It's the only way I can feel like I haven't completely lost my daughter. She believed she would be out there one*

*day, in space, that her energy would dance among star dust. Maybe
the hole in my head is a way for her to reach me.*

I feel fine, I tell the reporters. Better than ever. Not that I would
recommend this for anyone.

The fears outlined in the comment threads of various news websites
are mostly laughable, but I have begun to wonder if the conspiracy
theorists might have it somewhat right, if my life is counting down
toward an end of days. One comment suggested that I'd be taken
over by a heavenly entity and this would mark an age of enlightenment. The commenter ended with the word *Namaste* (just like
that, in italics). Another said I would simply disappear, essentially
be sucked into myself. For some reason, I imagined a cartoonish
popping sound as the last cells of my body blink out of this reality.

What we know:
    The size of the singularity is stable for now.
    The singularity is located in my left temporal lobe.
    Exotic particles have been ejected from the singularity.
    The singularity has been consuming me subatomic particle by
subatomic particle.
    Theresa assures me that I'll be okay and I want to believe this.
    We do not know how to remove the singularity (yet) or if it might
even disappear on its own.

When I'm in bed with Theresa draped over my body, I stare at the
imperfections on the ceiling until my eyes lose focus and the specks
in the stucco begin to swirl. I convince myself I can feel the pull
of the singularity inside me; maybe a very small part of who I am
has already changed because of it—become a man capable of truly

loving his wife and son, capable of doing anything to speak to his daughter one last time, even if only to say *I wish I could have done more*. I get ready for work and stare at myself in the mirror. I look like any other average guy without a singularity in his head, the same samurai eyebrows, as my father used to call them, the same flat and broad nose that I've always hated. My grandmother used to pinch it when I was little, singing *tall nose, tall nose!* Theresa kisses me goodbye before she is off. I masturbate in the shower, eat a bowl of steel-cut oatmeal, and drive to work—and through it all I imagine a synapse, a filament of my memory falling beyond the event horizon, floating in a dark expanse of space not unlike our own. I imagine Petal like a cosmic gossamer, drifting toward me.

My colleagues ask me how I'm feeling every day, and perhaps I'll continue to tell them (and my wife) that I'm fine, even if one day I'll know that I'm not. Maybe I'll die alone years from now and after my body decays, the singularity will remain, a tiny doorway to the unknown resting in my coffin or urn. Before my body perishes, I'll recite everything I know to be true: algorithms, relatives, names of pets, to discern what no longer resides in my mind. I am . . . I used to be . . . They are . . . This is . . . Would this possible future Bryan Yamato be loved? Respected? Or would he just be?

How are you feeling?, my colleagues would ask this Dr. Yamato. How many years will have passed? One, five, ten? I imagine my last words floating through the void. I wonder which shards of my life I'll hold on to the longest—the singularity, the 49ers, gluten free, quantum, time? I'll stare back at my colleagues, my wife, my son sitting beside my bed. Who knows how long I might live in this silence, the memory of my daughter fading. Who knows how long I'd live motionless, observing the world around me, contemplating the space and time Bryan Yoshio Iba Yamato has taken up in the universe. And who knows how long I'd remain alive before cell by cell I'd wither away to muscle to organ to bone to empty space, hoping the singularity either stops with me or swallows me whole, maybe even saves the entire world.

I stop off at the grocery store on my way to the lab to buy toilet paper and that bag of oranges Theresa always requests, even though they're only good for one or two days before spoiling. I grab a few pieces of the fruit before climbing out of my car, toss them in a basket in the staff lounge. I enter the test chamber control room and wait as a table emerges from our modified MRI to scan the singularity. Theresa texts: Axel's parent/teacher video conference is tonight. Do you want to hop on? Or are you busy? The other night, I watched a video of Petal in a school play, one of many I didn't attend because of work. She played the sun. She always preferred celestial objects to people. She danced from the east with confident jazz hands and set in the west, closing her eyes as she swung the moon into the sky.

How are you feeling today?, a colleague asks. Her name is Sarah. She's young and smart and ambitious and codes with the passion of a musician. There was a moment about seven years ago at a holiday party when we could have slept together. This was before the plague, before Theresa. A walk, she said. I live nearby, she said. But I decided to go home early for a change. I watched *Mary Poppins* with Petal and Peter, revised my assistant's calculations, and spent the rest of the night in the basement, drinking boxed wine and developing the key processes that would eventually put a black hole in my head. I text Theresa back: I'll be there. Of course. I love you. I turn to Sarah and tell her I'm doing okay. I feel fine for now. Let's find some answers. I think: *Let's save my family. Let's save all of us.* I tell her: *We may begin.*

A GALLERY A CENTURY, A CRY A MILLENNIUM

U.S.S. *Yamato*—**Launch Day, December 30, 2037**

All two hundred of the crew lined up in our flight suits, waiting for the hangar doors to open to reporters and relatives and those who dreamed of one day traveling the stars. *We are at the dawn of a new age*, a NASA official said to applause. *This is the first step for humanity to become a part of whatever is beyond our solar system.* As the hangar opened, we could see the ticketed spectators behind the velvet ropes flanking the red carpet—my sister and nieces, my gallery dealer, who'd arranged a final showing of my plague victim portraits a few weeks earlier, children in astronaut onesies waving toy models of the *Yamato*. But beyond all this, perhaps fifty yards away, there was a fence barricading the chanting crowds: *Second chance, second chance!* A woman with a bullhorn shouted: "You can't leave us! Planet X will collide with us soon. We see the signs, the rising seas, the fires. These are the signs of judgment." A man wearing an American flag T-shirt and a fanny pack tried to scale the fence. One of the Kennedy Space Center guards shoved his baton through the chain links to beat the man down.

"Don't pay those nut jobs any mind," I told Yumi. My granddaughter stood beside me, examining the line of people behind us. Her duffel bag was slung over her shoulder, stuffed with clothes from the shopping spree that I'd used to help soften the blow of leaving home.

"There aren't many teenagers," she said. "I thought you said there would be other kids my age."

"There are more than a few," I said.

I could see my sister waving as the line progressed, the final hugs and handshakes, last-minute parting gifts—a bag of oranges, an apple pie, a crate of vintage pulp novels. How do you say goodbye when you know you'll be alive hundreds if not thousands of years after everyone you've ever known has died? I overheard one of the ship's doctors a few people ahead of us telling her best friend that she'd see her around sometime. One of the few nonscientist and nonmilitary passengers, a woman named Val, kissed her boyfriend, who was dressed like a mortician in a black suit and tie. Apparently his brother helped develop the *Yamato*'s engine.

"You should be coming, too," she told him.

"Maybe on the next ship, if there is one," he said. "You should know by now that it takes me a while to act on anything."

As I eavesdropped on their final moments, I imagined what the day would be like if my husband and daughter were still alive. Would Cliff be leading the way? Or perhaps I'd be behind the velvet rope, saying goodbye to Clara as she embarked on the ultimate adventure.

Behind me, Yumi was lost in her headphones, gazing at the *Yamato* on launchpad 39A, the old stomping grounds of the Apollo program. She texted her only close friend who was still alive and hadn't been shuttled to one of the quarantined neighborhoods by their parents. The people behind the fence shouted. Someone threw a bottle that smashed and sent shards flying across the concrete.

"Take out your headphones," I told Yumi, tapping her ears. "We're getting close to our people." She ignored me, continued texting. I wanted to tell her to stop, but I knew this was her last chance to talk to her friend.

We stepped forward after Val and Dennis said their goodbyes. I hugged my sister, my two nieces, and even Steven, my gallery dealer. When I held them, I made a mental note of Steven's body odor, always masked by a cologne that smells like cinnamon; the way my sister's frenetic hair expanded in the humidity; how my niece's face glitter caught on my flight suit, tiny stars from home that I'd take with me on our journey.

"This is going to be so good for the both of you," my sister said, rubbing Yumi's arms. "A fresh start."

"We have a couple of your paintings left in the SoHo gallery— *Laird No. 2* and *Mother and Daughter in Mud No. 3*," Steven told me. "I'll be hanging on to them for now. Maybe the Smithsonian will want them, the last works of one of the *Yamato* pioneers."

My nieces gave me and Yumi a crayon drawing of our entire extended family, including Cliff and Clara, all of us circling the planet hand in hand. My sister gave me our mother's engagement ring. And Steven gave me a case of charcoals and paints, which I'd add to the art supplies the mission commander had already approved.

"You're murderers, the whole goddamn bunch of you!" someone shouted from beyond the barricade.

Yumi huddled with her little cousins. I heard her tell them to talk to the stars and that she would hear them. I held on to my sister one last time.

"Love you for light-years," I told her.

"Who's going to sell my work up there?" I said to Steven. I thought about what I might paint after this—the different variations of black and silence. Or maybe I'd paint our memories, all the tiny moments we took for granted.

A caravan of golf carts shuttled us to the launchpad. Both Yumi and I hung our heads off the side, trying to take in the *Yamato*. Here on Earth, the ship looked like six Saturn V rockets strapped together, with a giant silver sphere in the middle that would open in space like a flower, ejecting a habitation ring that will rotate around the engine's core. When the stasis technicians led us down the corridors of sleeping pods, Yumi spoke of worlds where we'd have two shadows and oceans glowed orange, and if we traveled far enough, we'd find another Earth where her mother and my husband might still be alive.

"You don't have to do this for me," I said, stopping Yumi as she began to unzip her flight suit. "I don't have to tell you there are no go-backs on this one." She stared at her steel crib that would soon fill with cryo gel, preserving her at the age of seventeen.

"How long will the trip take?" she asked. We watched the technicians open her pod, run diagnostics on the monitoring systems that would keep her asleep and nourish her body. Yumi stepped out of her flight suit and handed it to one of the techs, draped herself with an opaque plastic poncho.

"No one really knows. It's not like we have a set destination—we need to find our way," I said. "But you and the other children won't come out at all. You'll remain asleep, and when you awaken, you'll feel like a long night has passed."

The technicians helped Yumi climb into her pod and allowed me to say goodbye. I wondered how many farewells and second thoughts and assurances to scared children and spouses they had already seen.

"I do want to go," she said. She held out her hands and pulled me in for a hug. "For Mom. She would want us to go."

I told her to dream about the impossible and colorful and miraculous. Dream about your mother and father. I squeezed her hands. I kissed her head. "When you wake up," I said, "I'll be there. And we'll be home."

I nodded to the technicians to proceed, and they finished preparing Yumi for the long sleep. Her tiny, shaking body looked embryonic beneath the plastic in her silver crib before she succumbed to the sedatives and the cryo gel washed over her as if she had been encased in ice.

Proxima Centauri B—4.3 Light-Years from Earth; Travel Time: 50 Years

CONSTELLATION: Centaurus. Tidally locked and in tight orbit around a red dwarf star—perpetual day and night on opposite sides of the planet. Approximate orbital period: II days. Volatile solar flare activity likely to have stripped any atmosphere that would have been present.

ARTIST'S NOTES: We stopped because of possibility, even though we knew the world was likely dead. After all, it would be too convenient for our closest neighbors to be right for us—the universe wouldn't make our journey that easy. But this would be our first look at another world not in our backyard— vermilion at over I,000 degrees Fahrenheit on one side, steeped in darkness and ice on the other.

Most adult passengers lived through the long, dark years in stasis, emerging from their pods only for weeks at a time when we stopped at a planet worthy of study. Children were not to be awakened before colonization, to preserve our resources. Perhaps some thought it cruel for children to spend so many years in a tin can. After I woke up and completed my initial checkup with the ship's doctors, I didn't go to my assigned quarters or to the mess hall as I was instructed, despite my hunger and the fact I was still wearing a hospital gown. I allowed my bare feet to carry me across the empty steel corridors, beyond the areas that had begun to stir with life from the crew. I sat next to Yumi's pod and described the ship's awakening—how everyone was wandering the halls half-naked, disoriented, slightly slimy from the cryo gel, how the windows of the ship glowed with the faint light of a red dwarf. After that I visited Yumi every morning. I held a small speaker to the glass walls of her pod, playing her favorite songs as I updated her on my life, which was punctuated by the monotony of meals, sleep, and trying to make myself useful, cleaning the halls, rearranging the mess. I could barely bring myself to socialize with the others—they all had colleagues and spouses and friends, a purpose. They were vital to our task. I wonder if the Department of Planetary Security offered me privileged passage aboard the *Yamato* out of some sense of guilt, the widow of the great Clifford Miyashiro, who gave his life attempting to avert an outbreak; the mother of the woman who tried to cool the planet. But when the navigation commander found me curled up outside of Yumi's stasis chamber about a week after our arrival at the Centauri system, my space life changed forever.

"We can't use all the paint, of course," he explained. He crouched beside me and looked up at Yumi. "But between your personal supplies and part of what we earmarked for education, we should be able to spruce up these walls. Do you think you can take charge of that for me?"

I nodded, a little self-conscious that I hadn't showered since I'd awoken. A moment later a woman approached, lingered behind the commander until he waved her over, making me even more aware of my unwashed appearance. She wore leather boots, magenta tights, a wool poncho that grazed her thighs.

"And Dorrie here is something of a painter as well," he said.

"Nothing like you, of course," Dorrie interrupted.

"She's a lottery passenger. We woke her up hoping she'd want to help you," the commander said. "How's that sound?"

"Wonderful," I said. My words came out quieter, less enthusiastic than I'd intended. I had never collaborated with another artist before. The woman the commander ushered over beamed at me with excitement. "I mean, thank you."

"I brought my portfolio," Dorrie said as I stood to shake her hand. The commander knocked on the bulkhead and excused himself. "I'm a bit more than a hobbyist, though I felt like I was lying when I called myself an artist on the *Yamato* lottery forms." Dorrie opened the case slung over her shoulder, spread out a series of charcoal prints and watercolors and tiny acrylic portraits of children she'd painted on index cards. Behind each card: a name, birth date, time of death, and the title "City of Laughter." I assumed they were from the euthanasia theme park that had been popular during the first wave.

"These are remarkable," I said. I studied the portrait of a little girl with golden curls. If I squinted hard enough, I could just make out the outline of a roller coaster reflected in her eyes. I wondered what might be reflected in the eyes of those on the journey with us. As artists, we could transform the sterile walls of this ship into a home, preserve our journey for those who never woke up. I could hold on to our memories through the millennia. I could help us move on.

Dear Cliff,

Yumi looks peaceful in her chamber—they all do. Do you remember how we had to take turns reading her stories whenever Clara left on her research trips? Yumi loved origin myths, how the heavens were split from land and gods placed the moon and sun in the sky. I'm writing to you in our daughter's journal, which you used as your own during your final months. It seemed fitting, after all. The Chronicle of a Family of Explorers. A book of regrets and goodbyes. The crew here have begun to find their footing—not being a scientist or military, I feel left out sometimes, but I join board game nights and I help prepare rations at mealtimes. I became an artist because I was terrible with people. Of course, they all know what I've lost, not that we haven't all lost someone. I wish you were both still with me to witness all of this—the maelstrom of starlight outside the ship's windows, the constant debates about probe telemetry of atmospheres and water and radiation. I could never have imagined the vastness of nothing between the stars, the invisible dark matter that connects everything in the universe like the branches of the nervous system. I've made a friend of sorts, perhaps more of a colleague, a woman the commander woke up just for me. We've begun painting murals on the walls to help make the ship feel less sterile, the journey less cold, whenever we're awake—our ramshackle bungalow in Santa Monica, a water tower in Iowa, the commander's hometown. My friend Dorrie even painted the City of Laughter, where she lost her son. I've been populating an imaginary town with the faces of those the crew has lost and plan to fill the skies with all the planets we find along the way that will be both beautiful and deadly, or simply not quite right for us. If I stare long enough at our paintings, I can almost forget that everything we remember about our time on Earth will soon be ancient history.

Stasis

Fusion rockets and antimatter boosters. Cryogenic suspension. Magnetosphere radiation shields and artificial gravity. Maybe on *Star Trek* or *Star Wars*, I thought. But few could fully appreciate the starship *Yamato* until they signed the government and Yamato-Musk Corporation waivers and walked on board. Named after Bryan Yamato, who solved the problem of harnessing Hawking radiation from microscopic black holes to fuel our main engine and helped us reach 10 percent the speed of light. Oddly, Bryan and his wife had elected to remain on Earth, even though Bryan's teenage son joined the expedition under the supervision of the commander. They're working on a solar shade project to cool the planet—trillions of basketball-sized satellites carrying reflective lenses the width of a human hair. End to end, the starship *Yamato* would span two football fields and can accommodate a crew of fifty out of stasis at one time. Reverse-engineered UFO technology, Area 51, the conspiracy theories from grocery store tabloids. Only a handful of the crew have the security clearance to know for certain whether those tabloid stories were true. But I like to believe we had otherworldly help. That someone or something gave Bryan Yamato a push when he needed it—an equation, a schematic, an *a-ha!* moment implanted into his brain. Maybe we're on our way to find *them*—the constant engine rumble like the ocean surf makes it easy to lose yourself in these kinds of thoughts. Once, as we worked on a mural, I saw Dorrie painting her son, Fitch, in a small landing craft on its way to a planet covered with smiling green aliens, waving at the sky.

"He would have lost his mind if he'd lived long enough to know about the *Yamato*," Dorrie said. "The last image I have of him is on that coaster—his arms raised high above his head. Maybe he thought he could fly. Maybe he wanted to get a little closer to the stars. He wanted to do so much when he grew up."

"He sounds a lot like my Clara when she was little," I said. "It's like part of her belonged out here."

Apart from our hours painting together, Dorrie and I rarely socialized. I'd see her in the mess hall, dining with some of the officers. She looked like she enjoyed their company. She laughed at their toilet humor, played poker with the crew, but between the jokes and royal flushes and gossip about who was fucking who and in what utility closet, she wore a faraway gaze, as if she could see through the bulkheads. Once, when I saw her alone, I asked if she wanted to grab a coffee, and she told me she was praying. She was curled up next to one of the circular observation windows. From afar she looked like a fish staring out from a bowl.

"Not like to God or anything like that," she explained. "But maybe something that connects us . . . to wherever Fitch is, or your Clara. Lieutenant Johansson, the navigation officer, was telling me there's an invisible web that ties the stars and planets and galaxies together. We don't know what it is or how it works, but it's out there, all around us."

I've begun to pray, too, for the first time since I was a child. I don't know what Dorrie prays for or if she asks for anything in particular. I think of Yumi dreaming for hundreds or thousands of years without a break, and wonder if she knows what's real, worry that after so long in her own mind, the reality of being with me in a new world won't be enough. I take long walks beyond the children's stasis chambers and the nonessential economy-class lottery passengers, who'll be awoken only once or twice during our journey. I tell myself that leaving was the right decision. When we arrived at the Centauri system, we received a decades-old message from Earth, informing us that a cure for the plague had been discovered—the comatose woke up and people began to rebuild their lives. Funerary corporations expanded to focus on climate projects, building seawalls around coastal cities, sponsoring the solar shade project until the end of the century. The message bid us good luck and farewell. *You always have a home here*, it said. *On this world or on your new home, we'll find each other again one day.* Personal letters arrived, along with general messages to the crew, and for more than a week the ship was abuzz with news and condolences and statistics from revived sports teams, a snapshot of life on Earth for the past fifty years. The ship's doctor organized daily sharing circles for those who wanted to celebrate or needed support or couldn't quite articulate how they were supposed to feel.

I'm going to be an uncle. Can you believe that? Horace. Poor fucking kid. Leave it to my brother to give his son some old-fashioned bullshit name. I mean, I guess the kid is as old as I am now. Older, even. Shit, maybe he even has kids of his own.

My mother died a couple of years after we left. Not the plague. No, they cured that. But they couldn't cure the cancers that emerged after the virus, the lung damage. The letter was from my older sister. I imagine she's dead now, too. She never wrote again. She'd be in her nineties.

My folks moved to Ohio before the ocean claimed the tip of Florida in 2080. Apparently there's an underwater resort around old South Beach. The Miami Dolphins moved to Little Rock. My brother attended the last home game before the city evacuated.

The last official communiqué from NASA indicates that three more ships have been built. My sister was put in command of one, the U.S.S. Sagan, headed to other colony candidate systems. We're not alone out here.

When it was my turn, I showed the crew the drawing of my family that my nieces had given me before launch. I told them about the letter they sent a year afterward, how a school paper they wrote about me ended up in the *San Francisco Chronicle*. Despite the knowledge that Earth has improved in our absence, I've always told myself that dreaming of home isn't helpful. No regrets. Somewhere out there near a star we've never seen is where we're really meant to be.

Ross 128 B—11 Light-Years from Earth; Travel Time: 110 Years

CONSTELLATION: Virgo. Ten-day orbit around an unusually stable red dwarf. Squarely inside the habitable zone. Tidally locked with day and night sides of the planet, but with a temperate climate of approximately 70 degrees F. Presence of a shallow ocean with three large continents. Marginally breathable atmosphere.

ARTIST'S NOTES: As we approached the planet, it almost looked like we were returning home. A slightly larger Earth with blue oceans, and mountains and valleys the shade of coal. I wanted to join the expedition crew but had to settle for recordings. Maybe this was better for the story I have to tell the future—how the black flowers as tall as houses felt like velvet, and the red star hung in a perpetual sunrise or sunset if you stood at the line of night/day on the planet, and tiny flying creatures that looked like squid lit up like fireflies, illuminating the world's night side in swarms. I could tell the future it was beautiful and forget what really happened because I wasn't there.

I was finishing a portrait of twin girls, sleeping side by side in their stasis pods, when I saw people rushing toward the shuttle bay. I followed the commotion and smelled the copper-tinged air before I saw the blood pooling beneath the body bags. Across the hall, the shuttle pilot lay fetal on the floor, sobbing. Grant was in his midtwenties, but he looked like a child, shaking and alone. I sat next to him and rubbed his back. He inched closer to me.

"They came out of the sand," he said. "Never saw 'em coming."

The medical teams sprayed the dead with a white foam to neutralize any foreign bacteria. One by one they carted the casualties off to the labs for further examination—Shawn Mitchell, private first class; Dr. Richard Pechous; and Grant's brother, Chief Lemmink. I stood and peered into the bay, caught a glimpse of a dead creature lying beside the shuttle before security sealed the doors closed—a meter-long insect that looked like a giant millipede with the wings of a dragonfly, a head like a tunnel-boring machine. I sat back down with Grant. He was holding on to a family photo that had been folded several times.

"Do you need help with anything?" I asked, uncertain what else to say. "I don't want to leave you here."

"My brother and I signed up for the mission because we figured we didn't have anything holding us back," Grant began. "Mom and Dad died in the second wave."

"I'm sorry," I said. "Are you sure there isn't anything I can do? Someone else on the ship I can call for you?"

"No, no," he said, slowly getting to his feet and straightening his uniform. He handed me the photo of his family at the Grand Canyon—he and the chief must have been no older than ten at the time. "But maybe if you could include this in one of your murals."

"Of course," I said. I squeezed his hands and remembered the paintings I used to create for our neighbors back when people first started dying from the plague—how they'd come to my door with their pies and casseroles, ask for my help capturing their children or spouse as they used to be.

During such a tragic planetary expedition I had to wonder if we should have stuck it out back home. We'd rocketed out of desperation, our hearts filled with hope and wonder. We didn't want to believe there could be so many near misses—too hot, too cold, too wet, too dry, too dangerous, lacking in anything whatsoever that could keep us whole and build us up. But giant killer insects aside, Ross came close. The commander reminded us that even if Earth was okay, whatever we built out here might be humanity's plan B should anything else happen. He reminded us that going back was not an option. We held a funeral service the following day. Everyone out of their stasis pods attended, congregating around three silver capsules on the observation deck.

"We're gathered here, in orbit over an alien world, to honor the ultimate sacrifice of our fellow crew members," the commander began.

People read the personnel files on tablets as if they were programs, since many of us didn't really know the dead. As the commander continued, Grant walked over to his brother's capsule and opened it, placed a framed photo of their parents and a ragged teddy bear on his brother's chest. Others who knew the dead followed, opening their capsules, placing mementos inside—letters, medals, the Bible, a cardigan sweater, a baseball glove. Guards carted the capsules away to a nearby airlock, and we waited for the commander to give the order.

"Release them," he said. The room and the halls outside were suddenly awash in red light and a siren blared, warning that the airlock's outer door was opening. One of the attendees, an astrobiologist, played "Taps" on his trumpet, washing out the noise. When the sirens stopped, we were left with the last lingering note of the trumpet and then silence, the view of the three pods drifting into the dark. For the first time in years, as I watched the caskets be enveloped by space, I thought about not being able to see Clara's body when she died, how the Russians cremated her without consulting us and shipped her to America like a piece of mail. Sometimes I wondered if the ashes were really hers—I needed to touch and see for myself, to destroy the dream that my daughter was still alive. I trained myself to believe that the grains of bone were really her in order to move on. *This is their planet*, the commander said. *We will not be exterminating alien life or making this world or any other bend to our will. If nothing else is out there for us, we may need to return.*

Dear Yumi,
What are you dreaming about today? Perhaps you're with your grandfather at the bookstore or maybe you're with your mother and father during one of those early road trips before work stole Clara away—maybe Yellowstone, or the time we

had a family reunion on San Juan Island to watch the last
surviving orcas feed. We found a planet this week that was
too good to be true. Or maybe we're naive to be looking for
perfection where there is none to be found—another Earth
just for us and with not a whole lot of trouble to begin anew.
I sometimes dream of those first hours and days after launch.
I wish you could have been awake with me when I released
the ashes of your mother and grandfather into space alongside
the ashes of the crew's loved ones. We mixed tiny beacons
affixed with LED lights into their collective remains, created
an ancestral trail of light that will linger just beyond Saturn's
rings—a star to look up at, to pray to like the necklace your
mother wore. I've kept some of your mother and grandfather
for when we finally stop, so you might let an alien wind carry
them away from your cupped hands. I promised your mother
I'd care for you. I promised your grandfather we would be
okay. And so, I say keep dreaming. Because if we don't find a
new home, what did any of them die for?

Gliese 832 C—16 Light-Years from Earth; Travel Time: 160 Years

CONSTELLATION: Grus. Super-Earth with a 600-mile narrow
band of habitability encircling the planet. Probe telemetry
has detected signs of large wildlife and severe weather patterns, with hurricane-force winds persistent across much of
the band. Gravitational pull of the planet would make takeoff
impossible, therefore any attempt to land is a one-way trip.

ARTIST'S NOTES: We found a blue-and-green halo hugging
dead rock five times the mass of Earth. Our probes delivered

images of buffalo-like creatures with red fur cascading across their bodies, lakes dotted with islands filled with glowing frogs the size of small automobiles, primate life still living in trees— their faces not unlike our chimpanzees or gorillas, their skin like fish scales. In the form of the Bayeux Tapestry, I reserved the top portions of several corridors to document life on this planet, a place we orbited for more than a month, studying from a distance.

When I told Yumi we had been given a chance to leave the planet, she didn't want to consider it, even though she understood that I'd already made the decision. She cried for her friends and her aunts and uncles and cousins, whom I tried to get on board the *Yamato* to no avail. She cried for our home.

"I'd rather die," she said. "Things are starting to look like they might get better here, and you want to run away? After all we've been through?" I don't doubt that she meant it. After all, her best friend was sent to the City of Laughter only a year after her grandfather died in Siberia, and for months, she'd begged me to take her to the park. I'd always tell her, "We're here because of your mother and grandfather and the faith so many had in them. We're still a family. Everything we do, we do for them."

I had stored the final video messages Cliff sent us in a digital frame next to Yumi's bed. We listened to them the night before we left. Now I like to listen to his final words every time I look upon another world.

My beautiful girls,
I'm glad you're still safe and healthy. Maybe it seems like the world won't change right away, but believe me when I say that danger is near. Here, at the edge of the world, I spend

a lot of time thinking about ice and land crumbling into the ocean—all the secrets the world meant to keep hidden from us. It's strange how the discovery of an ancient girl in Siberia and viruses we've never encountered before can both redefine what we know about being human and at the same time threaten our humanity. If I were a philosopher, perhaps I'd have more thoughts on this. Maybe the two of you and your more artistic minds can wrap your heads around what it all means. I know I said not long ago that I would come home, that maybe my colleagues here at the outpost would find a cure or a way to at least convince the world to treat our warnings seriously. I want nothing more than to hold you both and join the wonderful family gatherings I hear so much about. But there is still work to be done. There is still hope.

Trappist-1 System—40 Light-Years from Earth; Travel Time: 400 Years

CONSTELLATION: Aquarius. In orbit around Trappist-1e, one of a dense seven-planet system surrounding an ultracool red dwarf star. All water worlds with little to no land. Too wet, too chemically predictable for life to take hold.

ARTIST'S NOTES: From the surface of any of the Trappist planets, you'd be able to see the other planets larger than our moon in the sky, an interplanetary conga line reflected on an ocean without end.

Before we went to sleep, many passengers were convinced that the Trappist-1 system would be the one. An abundance of water. Seven chances to get it right. The mess halls buzzed with conversation about restarting our lives, claiming a patch of land to build a cabin, a dome, whatever we might need to find happiness. The commander planned to retire; the first officer would take over the *Yamato* and continue exploring the universe; an astrophysicist and her engineer husband would start a K-12 school and maybe, one day, a university. The botanists dreamed of Trappist soil and wondered how our seeds would fare, if any local flora would bring us food and medicine. The astrobiologists spoke of deep oceans that might contain creatures of unimaginable size, conjuring fantastic visions of giant squid and whales. But as we approached the system, we saw no continents or islands, no biosignatures of animal life. The observation deck was filled with silence and tears. Dorrie was crying. Maybe I wanted to cry, too. Instead, I chose to stop wallowing in the abyss of the seven worlds before us and to paint the crew. Because from afar, we did not look sad or defeated. We looked like pioneers bearing witness to one more beautiful site along the way.

Dear Clara,
You'd be so proud of Yumi. When people started to get sick, she thought of her friends and family first. She wanted to help. I wish you hadn't cut us off for so long. I hope you understand that we just didn't want you to miss out on your daughter's life. I was always proud of your work—your books and documentaries and lectures. Your father filled scrapbooks with your clippings. I would always tell people that you were trying to cool the planet, to convince the world we needed to find another way to live. In the end, they did listen—albeit too late for you and for us. But they listened, my strange and wonderful girl. Yumi wrote to you one last time. Perhaps you

already know that somehow. Along with your ashes, drifting
in our outer solar system, is a letter folded into an origami
crane. Yumi must have written this letter and folded it several
times until she was satisfied with the result. Here on the ship,
I've re-created our family vacations in murals—you and Yumi
in Denali National Park, setting up your tent; all of us at
the Museum of Natural History in New York, where you and
your father presented together not long after you received
your doctorate. Perhaps by the time we stop, Dorrie and I will
have run out of room, every inch of this ship covered with
life.

Rogue

The *Yamato*'s autopilot stopped when it sensed the object. Lit only
by a nearby nebula and the blanket of the cosmos, the rogue planet
was alone and cold without a star. One would have thought such
a place to be a lifeless rock. Preliminary data suggested that this
rogue with its thin atmosphere was nearly as old as the universe.
Our first good look from a *Yamato* search probe showed the surface
punctuated with ruins—vast, modern cities not unlike our own,
frozen in place for eternity. Perhaps this world was flung out of its
star system not long after its birth, breeding life with the heat it
held inside itself for billions of years. Or perhaps this rogue once
had a home and this civilization felt the warmth of its star before
being torn away by a colliding galaxy. We had so many questions
and someone will certainly return to answer them. The inhabitants
likely knew for a long time that their world was dying. Perhaps this
is both comfort and despair, a reminder that we are not alone, that
we are still here.

Earth II

It's strange how a graveyard the size of a planet could instill hope in us all, help us to understand that our ship was more than a ship and whatever we found would be home not only because of oxygen and water and soil chemistry, but because of us. We stopped at two more planets before embarking on the big sleep to the Kepler systems that would see us add not decades or centuries to our Earth ages, but millennia. We had been out in deep space for well over five hundred years, though most of us had been together outside of our stasis chambers for only a little over one year. Some of us chose to remain awake longer this time, stitching together the bonds of a community—the commander became Frank, the lead botanist Cheryl, the chief engineer Hiro. Nurse Pratchett fell in love with Lieutenant Sanchez. Val, the girlfriend of Bryan Yamato's brother, moved on and was seen holding hands with a probe mechanic on the observation deck. We celebrated the birthdays of our children outside their stasis chambers—*Happy 507. You're such a big boy now. You don't even know!* Whenever Dorrie and I found a new corridor to paint, members of the crew would come to share their stories—how they'd petitioned to be here, who they'd left behind, the last moments they remembered before our lives were upturned by virus or fire or hurricane. One day, the two of us on our backs in a service tube, Dorrie and I painted what we liked to call our miniature version of the Sistine Chapel.

"I'll cover graduations and weddings on the port panel," Dorrie said.

"I'm planning to tackle a street festival after I finish this little league game on the starboard panel," I said. "And I packed us sandwiches, by the way."

"Dill?"

"Of course."

"What should we paint on the ceiling?" Dorrie asked. We were both covered in paint by then, and light-headed from the fumes; the small fan we'd brought to ventilate the tunnel was barely enough to circulate the air.

"I don't know," I said. We thought about the ceiling for days afterward, and as we talked to more of the crew, we realized a big part of our lives had been missing from our murals thus far—all the people for whom we had no photos, no proof of their existence except for lingering memories: a lost love, a crush, a coworker, the mailman, a neighbor who you said hello to but never really knew, a bartender who gave you free drinks once in a while for being a loyal customer, people who seemed so peripheral to one's life yet so incredibly important in the absence of Earth. There was barely a patch of bare steel left on the *Yamato* when I was forced to return to stasis—only the small panel across from Yumi and one on the command deck that was meant to record our final destination.

Dear Cliff,

In retrospect, all of us—you, Clara, and now me and Yumi— ran toward possibility because we saw no other choice. It's a wonder that we ever found each other, with all the running around we did. It's hard to believe any of this was possible— our family, this journey. After news of Clara's discovery hit the media, conspiracy theories abounded about the tattoos on the Ice Age girl, the carvings on the megalith in the ancient cave. Now that we're out here, I can't help but see a star system in the faded ink on that mummified skin. Maybe in the far reaches of space, crazy ideas are perfectly normal. Perhaps if there's any truth to this, some connection to how this ship travels the stars, Yumi and I will continue on toward possibility even after carving out a new life—we'll find the world Clara always said she wore around her neck. But, for now, we rest. For now, I want to dream of coming home to you and Clara. I want to wake up to a place where we can properly remember you and everyone that ever was.

Kepler-186f—582 Light-Years from Earth; Travel Time: 6,000 Years

CONSTELLATION: Cygnus. Home.

ARTIST'S NOTES: Covered with two large continents separated by a shallow ocean and draped with red grassy plains. Tiny horned rodents followed me as I broke away from a survey crew to study the rolling landscape—the breezes through the crimson willows, the dark soil molded to my boots like foam. From afar, I could see more wildlife gathered around an orange lake, something that looked like a seal with a propeller-like appendage on its head, more horned rodents, a cluster of blimp-like creatures floating above the water like stomachs filled with helium. The first flower picked from a meadow. The first shallow breath outside of my helmet. I'm assured that breathing here will get easier with time. The first landscape painting on our new home.

I awoke earlier than the others, along with the command crew. I've been asked to help orient nonessential passengers after their long sleep, to be a welcome party at the end of a long journey. I walked the empty halls, reviewing the past lives Dorrie and I had painted, all the planets that could not harbor us. I stopped at my final painting, finished only minutes before the stasis techs dragged me to my chamber. I was one of the last to go to sleep. A painting occupying the entire wall of my bunk suite: me, Yumi, Cliff, and Clara, arm in arm, staring out at what I imagined to be Kepler from the observation deck. If I looked long enough, I could almost imagine what that moment might be like. Maybe Clara would have said something profound, recited a poem about second chances that she'd written while holding the crystal she always wore. Maybe Cliff would have cried for once, come close to fully understanding our daughter. I would have kissed him and Clara and Yumi. I would have held them tight and told them we made it. I would have guided them through the galleries of *Yamato* to remember and honor and be grateful before placing our names on the shuttle manifest and breathing in fresh air for the first time in thousands of years.

Dear Yumi,

I can't wait to show you how far we've come. We could have done better, certainly—your mother, us, the world. For a long time, I felt like I failed you. I wished you could have had a full life with all the heartbreak and college drama and shitty jobs we took for granted. But over the past few centuries, I realized I don't want that for you anymore. Sure, I want you to understand what the world was, but you're young enough to make this new world your life. A start without regrets and mistakes. A start that will be better because you know how much we used to hurt. Looking at you through your chamber glass, I can see your mother and grandfather in you. And you'll be bringing the best of them on your journey—their drive and curiosity and quest to unlock the mysteries, to do what's right. You'll cry and be uncertain at first. That's okay. But there's a whole universe waiting for you. I've helped you this far, little one. We helped each other get here. But now, now is your time. It's time to lead me into the red grass and tell me the story of how we get to be. It's time to wake up.

THE USED-TO-BE PARTY

Time: Saturday, April 10, 2039 @ 5 P.M.
Place: 1227 Orange Grove Loop (Use Yard Gate)

Details: Burgers and hot dogs (and vegan options) with fixings provided. Please bring one side dish or a light main dish like a quiche or casserole. Some beer and wine provided (and I'll crack open a Rare Cask Macallan I treated myself to some years ago), but feel free to BYOB as well. Don't worry about contributing if you've recently woken up. I know some of you may be dealing with lingering repercussions from the virus and a few may still be living on whatever the transition programs stocked in your fridge as you figure out your financial situation. I didn't get around to grocery shopping for over a month after I woke up—the thought of leaving the house, getting dressed, seemed like a great big boulder propped against my front door. Let me know if you need anything, okay? I'm happy to take you to the store, or accompany you on a walk, or to the hospital. Maybe it won't be so bad if we do it together.

__ Salads __ Finger Foods __ Baked Goods __ Chips & Dip __ Mains

Dear Neighbors,

This is an invitation the old me never would have sent. You know the sky-blue Cape Cod in our cul-de-sac with the flower boxes that my wife, Shelley, your friend, planted with tulips. You knew my daughter, Nina, from Girl Scout cookies and sleepovers. I was her husband and her father or

Mr. Paul—never Dan, the lawyer who barely got home in
time to read Nina a bedtime story while my wife sequestered
herself in our home office to code some new phone app. But
my associates are gone now, as are most of our families. My
home is a museum, as are most of your homes. And I realize
we could go on, peering through our windows, avoiding each
other, or you could come to my block party before we lose
ourselves completely to the illusion of who we used to be.

   I woke up in a Boeing hangar outside of Seattle, where
spillover comatose plague patients were being stored. I walked
past dozens of rows of cots in a hospital gown searching for
Shelley and Nina, surrounded by confusion and heartbreak.
Some patients reached out, as if I could help them—
strangers, people I'd seen at cafes or Fitness Universe. Others
looked at the empty beds, the body bags being carted away,
those the vaccine could not save. After waiting in a processing
tent for hours, I was given my wife's wedding band, a charm
bracelet I'd bought for my daughter's sixteenth birthday, and
two small boxes of ash. I spread their remains near the pier
where Nina used to feed the seagulls her french fries, where
I once hid an engagement ring in a basket of fish-and-chips.
There are barely any seagulls now without the tourists of
Pike Place Market to sustain them, the carrion along the
shorelines already desiccated by the heat or washed out to sea.
Every morning since leaving the hospital, I have woken up
on my side of the bed and pretended my wife and daughter
were home. I make them pancakes like I used to years ago,
close my eyes and kiss the air above the kitchen stools. I play
cartoons in the background as I wash the dishes, or Shelley's
crime dramas while I slowly work my way through a stack of

mail—utility bills, insurance statements, letters from relatives sharing the news that they're okay. Cousins Candace and Siri are gone. Aunt Sylvie and Uncle Jay are still receiving treatment. I write them back. I tell them I survived. I know that when they read my words a part of them will wish that I was the one who died.

At night I grow tired of pretending. I watch infomercials showing the old elegy hotels, how they've been turned into condo communities with names like Vitality Towers. It seems like every other retired athlete is on television, telling me to reclaim my life with funerary-bank-sponsored drugs, and while I watch this garbage, I use the coupon book for the recently awakened and order pizza delivery.

There's a nationwide climate campaign to phase out gas vehicles. I take the new light rail to our local reassimilation center, my old high school gym. It's strange seeing the empty roads; the city streets buzz with the low hum of early morning throughout the day. The Japanese restaurant where I used to get lunch is boarded up, the corner stores where I bought cigarettes transformed into information kiosks for people looking for work or missing family members. Billboards atop buildings project updated numbers of the newly recovered. Sometimes crowds of people stop and look up at the scroll, as if they can feel the world beginning to breathe again.

It's been two months since the first plague patients were released from hospitals and overflow centers, and I've begun to develop a routine. At the reassimilation check-in office, I tell my case worker about my new job—approving memorial

profile requests, answering messages for the deceased on
WeFuture (previously known as BitPalPrime, before they
were acquired by the funerary banks). It can be emotionally
draining work, though I still take pride in helping people
through their pain. My floor supervisor is named Dennis and
he has a tough role, managing shadow profiles. He assumes
the personality of the deceased and continues to post updates
and chat with their friends and family.

"You learn the most insane shit pretending to be other
people," he told me once during our lunch break. "K-pop
crushes, who's cheating on their spouse." He used to be a
bereavement coordinator at an elegy hotel, which makes
sense, since he seems to have a way of handling people in
crisis, those who come into our offices looking like they're
about to crumble.

"You need to talk really slow," he said, when I asked to
bum a cigarette once. "I know I sound like an ass, and I really
do care. But it's also a job, and if you allow yourself to feel
everything all the damn time it'll wear you down."

I don't want this letter to turn into a novel, but I need
you to know who I am. It took me weeks to get this far. I've
been too afraid to knock on your doors, certain I was too
much of a stranger for any of you to care. For an introvert
who hated social niceties, who always said no to invitations, I
have begun to crave any kind of human contact at all. I want
to know if you still see your family in your homes, walking
through the halls as if caught in a moment. I want to know
how you are nourishing your bodies—food or alcohol or
photo albums or maybe with the scent of unwashed clothes
in the hamper. I want to know if you remember anything

from our time away from the world, if the dreams I had
while I was comatose were anything more than dreams—a
dark place where we didn't feel like strangers, where we could
witness past moments from other lives. When I look out
the window, I feel like we've shared a lifetime of memories
together in a dark womb: a first kiss relived forever, a long-
dead grandparent returning from war, our secret histories
becoming our shared pastime.

I look at the Flannery house two doors down, that tiny
Spanish-style cottage, and I think of two sisters jogging
together, coaching softball in the park. I know Penny is lost
to us. I've seen her name on the wall of remembrance at the
community post office. I see you jogging at night, Kate,
crying. Once, I almost ran outside to help you after you
collapsed, but someone else, someone who probably knew
what to say, reached you first. If the void we shared was real,
I saw that you and Penny liked to escape from your money
troubles with black-and-white horror movies. You sold a
screenplay about two sister con artists with demonic powers
and, for the first time, your parents seemed proud of you. I
know the film studio that bought it no longer exists.

As the social nexus of our cul-de-sac, Alex and Amalia's
house used to be the place where many of you gathered for
barbecues and late-night drinks. I missed out on most of that,
didn't I? If Alex were still with us, he'd be grilling every day
to keep up morale. I was away for your backyard wedding,
Amalia, but while I was in the void, I saw you tell my wife
that you were pregnant and show her the ultrasound photo.
I saw Alex secretly stash money for a belated honeymoon in

a shoe box on the top shelf of a guest room closet (you might want to check if it's there?). I know from the community newsletter that you are, by some miracle, still expecting after eleven months in a coma, as if your baby remained in stasis. I know I should have come over long ago with baby things like I've seen the others doing. I know I should have been one more person to let you know that you aren't alone.

And Benny on the other side of our back fence, I know there's only you now. But before everything, you and Phillip used to hold virtual minigolf battles with your son Zeke every night before bedtime. I never knew Shelley helped you two with your coding for the immersive VR app you built to help senior citizens experience the world from their homes. I never knew how often she hopped the chain-link fence and finished bottles of wine with you, confessing our marital woes, how I was barely home anymore. I've wanted to come over and drink wine with you, too, and maybe learn about the woman Shelley was in the end. I have a bottle of pinot that I bought just for you.

And Mabel across the street. You were away for so long, living abroad in Japan when the plague hit. I know you dreamed of becoming a tattoo artist in your ancestral land. While you were gone, my wife and I would watch your mother sit outside on the stoop, as if she was expecting you home at any moment.

"I hope she's okay," your mother said to my wife when she came over for tea. We had learned of the first outbreaks in Russia and Asia, but the plague still seemed so far away then.

On the day you returned, two weeks ago, I peered through

my window and watched your mother embrace you. Your body was covered in tattoos. I shouldn't know (but I do) that each of them tells a story—the big dipper on your ankle an homage to a high school friend who passed; the iridescent feathers on your calves for the time your father chased a peacock around the Honolulu Zoo so you could have a souvenir; the virus on your neck, to own the plague you contracted in Thailand when you jumped off a cliff into the ocean.

I can no longer pretend that my daughter and wife aren't gone forever and so I immerse myself in WeFuture profiles for work. I scroll through the lives of strangers, studying videos and photos and status updates of new jobs, engagements, cross-country moves. For some of these people, few relatives and friends have survived to remember these moments. Like how Brianna Estes, forty-seven, an insurance adjuster in Pensacola, Florida, dropped out of medical school to care for her mother with dementia and posted poetry late into the night. Sometimes I call the numbers listed on these profiles. Mostly they are disconnected. Every now and then a relative will pick up, though, and say something like: "This is Shannon's phone. This is her mother." If I were a braver person, I would speak. I would tell Shannon's mother who I am, what I've lost, and that she can call me anytime, that I would welcome a voice in the night that was real.

I spotted a group of you a few days ago around midnight at the grocery store. I assume we all had the same plan: to venture out into the world in the safety of solitude and silence. Our eyes met for a split second. We quickly pushed

our carts in opposite directions, gliding through the aisles
on autopilot. I saw Mabel at the pharmacy, Benny ordering
orzo salad at the deli. And it was this moment, without
really planning it, that I began loading hamburger buns and
patties and chips and soda into my cart. I bought paper plates
and plastic cups, citronella-scented tiki torch fuel, bags of
ice. It was almost as if Shelley was whispering into my ear
as I checked out at the register. We need a party to break
the silence, to begin to heal. Had she lived, I know there
would have been one every week—parties to forget, parties
to remember, parties to dance the night away. She would
have declared that the postapocalypse doesn't mean we stop
dancing. She would have told me to stop being such a stick-
in-the-mud.

I realize there aren't many of us left and maybe this
won't be much of a party, but there's the rest of the street,
the community bulletin at the pool. It just opened for the
first time since the outbreak. As you know, I never showed
up to anything back then. I was never one to connect. I've
been that way my entire life. I went to work, kept my head
down, and came home. I let old friendships fizzle. I orbited
my family and all of you like a distant planet—there and
yet nearly impossible to reach. I know I can't survive alone.
Maybe this will be lost in a stack of your unopened mail;
maybe you'll read it and throw it away, saying it's too late.
Or maybe you'll peek out your window and wonder about
coming over and saying, *Hey, me too. I'm hollowed and
cracked and imploding.* All I do know is this: I will continue
to wake up and tell my family I love them, something I never
did enough when they were alive. I will go grocery shopping

at midnight. I will tell strangers online that I'm sorry for
their loss, and I will eventually wash the bedsheets and *their*
clothes and be okay with a quiet home. Maybe, with help, I
will wave at you when you cross the street. I will begin setting
the table for one.

Your neighbor,
Dan Paul

MELANCHOLY NIGHTS IN A TOKYO
VIRTUAL CAFE

In the evenings, Akira walks down the busy streets of Tokyo's virtual reality district to the neon-lit Ameyoko Market and browses knockoff VR visors and discounted bento boxes with his hands in his pockets. Projectors camouflage old buildings, immersing visitors in a different environment each night—nineteenth-century Paris, the halls of the Louvre, an anime wonderland filled with creatures from Japanese folklore. Around nine thirty, the crowds begin to disperse. Vendors close their shops, lock their stalls, load their merchandise into the backs of vans or onto carts attached to their bicycles. There are certain vendors Akira suspects are homeless like he is, the ones who stay later, long after the projectors are turned off, because they have nowhere else to go. Sometimes he catches himself yearning to speak to them in the darkness, except they probably prefer the illusion as much as Akira pretends he's shopping like everyone else. Like them, he has nothing left, and yet he's still one of the lucky ones—he never got sick, he survived.

Most nights begin like this for Akira, who at thirty-five joins the growing class of underemployed who couldn't finish their education during the plague years and now aren't satisfied with the limited positions offered by the transition programs. Before he was reduced to the two duffel bags he carries everywhere, before he constantly counted the yen in his pockets—which have holes that need to be taped or stitched shut—Akira was an intern designer at a printing company that eventually went out of business when virtual advertising became all the rage. His fisherman father died more than ten years ago. He was among the first adults to die from the plague in Japan after the virus reached the coastal Siberian towns—organ failure after organ failure at Akita City Hospital, until the virus transformed his heart cells into lung tissue and the doctors could only stand by and watch. Akira doesn't want to burden his mother. She moved to a mountain village to stay healthy and he's never told her the truth about his life.

Akira resides at Takahashi's Many Worlds, a virtual cafe complete with personal pods featuring a serviceable futon, shower facilities, and a small kitchenette. Reservations are typically not allowed. The owner is Ms. Eiko Takahashi. She sympathizes with Akira and the other young people who have been effectively exiled following the deaths of their families and despite government assistance. Before selling most of his belongings, Akira would spend whole afternoons plugged in—killing zombies, hitting home runs for the Hokkaido Nippon-Ham Fighters to roaring applause. Since the plague, many more people have turned to VR to connect and to escape—new friends and lovers replace the dead, spending the day in pre-plague Japan, packed baseball stadiums and annual festivals attended by families who haven't been torn apart. Lately, though, Akira prefers to hang out in the cafe lobby talking to Ms. Takahashi and the occasional tourist.

"People have come back outside onto the city streets, but notice how they keep their distance. Nobody smiles at each other. Everyone staring at their phones or lost in their augmented reality glasses," Ms. Takahashi says.

"Strange opinion, seeing that you run a VR cafe," Akira says.

Ms. Takahashi laughs and slaps Akira on the back. Around the cafe, the sounds of zombies and gunfire can be heard from the kiosks. At the community computers, a group of men chat with their hundred-yen-a-minute online girlfriends, airbrushed models from

America and Russia. Poor Ryu, a cafe regular, has long been convinced that Natalia from Moscow is going to marry him someday. *Just a little more money*, she says. *When are you coming to visit?*, he says.

"Well, not everyone can afford their own VR system yet," Ms. Takahashi explains. "At least not one that's truly immersive." She points to the posters behind the lobby desk advertising VR apps of tropical islands and singles mixers. "Everybody deserves a little time to feel normal. Maybe some people aren't ready to be out in the real world just yet, you know? And judging from the logs, you've been spending a fair amount of time with these apps yourself."

"Something to do," Akira admits.

"Shoot 'em up games or something? Maybe love fantasies?" Ms. Takahashi jabs Akira in the side, laughing. "What kind of girls do you like? You seem like such a sweet boy."

"That's a secret," Akira says.

As if Ms. Takahashi willed it into being, Akira receives a private message from a Yoshiko2376 that same night when he logs into his VR session: *We have eaten from the same rice pot.* The message floats in the air like smoke before it fades away. Unlike others who have opted for more familiar forms, save for pointed ears, a tail, or a set of wings, Yoshiko glided above the virtual ocean as a Pegasus with a silver mane. Akira noticed Yoshiko's avatar right away. She galloped around the Greek amphitheater where they held support gatherings for plague survivors struggling with their second chance at life. Many attend these virtual meetups looking for a suicide partner—through door-to-door mercy services or by rope in Aokigahara Forest at the base of Mount Fuji—and Akira understands their loneliness, the memories and dreams lost during the outbreak. But he attends the meetings for his own reasons, to embrace the possibility of being someone else—a rockabilly greaser with a leather jacket, cool and confident. He comes to escape and remind himself what it feels like to belong among others who feel like they, too, don't quite fit anywhere else. Akira can see ellipses on the horizon now, alerting him that Yoshiko is sending another message—a virtual address to her private island. He swipes left with his glove interface to open the navigation menu and transports himself to an arts and crafts shop filled with handmade trinkets, antique lamps, and vintage teddy bears. Behind the counter, Yoshiko as a Pegasus belts out a cheerful *Irasshaimase!*

"I liked what you shared in the group about feeling like the world only cares about traditional families and forgets about people who don't have someone to lean on," Yoshiko says.

Akira nods and explores Yoshiko's store as he thinks about what to say. Even in a VR chat world dedicated to discussing the possibility of suicide, Akira doesn't know a thing about how to talk to women. He's only been on pseudo-dates, which were really just a group of friends going to the movies or the mall. His only romantic interest as an adult died during the outbreak before he could do anything more than smile at her when she took his order at the coffeehouse. Throughout the store are photos of a couple and a little girl, a wedding invitation, a pink kimono, a porcelain tea set. A pocket watch the size of a hubcap dangles from the ceiling. Every item seems to be a memento or a memory.

"My father gave me that old watch," Yoshiko explains. "Smaller in real life, of course. I accidentally broke it when I was a child. But I still remember every detail, how my father would let me hold it as he read me bedtime stories, how he'd time me as I was trying to beat my record at the school track. One of the few happy memories I have of him."

"You never really talk at the meetings," Akira says. He studies the woman in many of the photos, realizes he has seen her at one of the vendor stalls in Ameyoko Market.

"I prefer to talk one-on-one," she says, "I don't really get to have adult conversations anymore. It's just me and my daughter."

Akira holds up one of the family photos and points to a balding man in wire-frame glasses.

"I didn't plan on falling in love with a son of a bitch," Yoshiko explains. "I thought I needed him when the pandemic began. At first, he was wonderful. But he asked for a transfer not long after we were vaccinated. No money. He's only seen his daughter once since she got sick. But tell me more about you."

Akira doesn't know where to begin. Should he behave as if he's the kind of member in their support group who sees their life as nearing an inevitable completion? Should he treat this meeting like the beginning of a friendship? He continues to explore Yoshiko's shop item by item as if picking through her mind with chopsticks. Despite her being older than him, he can't help but feel a strange attraction toward her, a developing crush made more real by the simple fact that they've both suffered.

"I don't really have a home now," Akira admits.

Eventually, after a few friendly encounters, Akira suggests they meet regularly after Yoshiko returns home from work at night and tucks in her daughter. While he has talked to others in VR, they've all been men, who mostly dwell on the many ways the government has screwed them over. But Yoshiko talks about life, despite the sadness. She celebrates happy memories, tells him how, even now, she finds joy in speaking with her customers. Akira explains that he used to see this stage in his life as a slight detour, a stepping-stone to something better, and maintaining that belief grows harder every day.

On Yoshiko's private VR island, she's guiding Akira through her antique shop to a rock garden outside. The wings of her Pegasus avatar seem to phase through the objects they pass.

"It's not just that I want a real job," Akira says, finding a mossy boulder to sit on. "It's impossible to meet people now."

"People like to forget about the sadness of the city," Yoshiko responds. "They walk and walk. No one stops. It's like we're all still infected. We choose to be blind to each other's suffering. It might make things easier to bear, but our hearts are cold."

Yoshiko manages her ten-year-old daughter's plague symptoms all on her own. They were only mildly alleviated by the vaccine. Her daughter is often bedridden and lost in her mind; a vibrant little girl broken by the lingering mutations of the virus. Yoshiko sells calligraphy prints and trinkets for food, to keep the lights on. *I know no one except my daughter. My mother is dead. I haven't spoken to my father in decades—an old fool. I don't have the luxury of making friends in the real world. You're basically a stranger, and you're all I have. It's pathetic.*

Akira doesn't want to be a stranger, though he knows that's what they are now. He tells her whenever they sign off that he's there for her. He tells Yoshiko that she isn't alone.

Akira always takes the same route through the crowds of Ueno Japan Rail after returning from his strolls around the Ameyoko Market. Niches along the marble wall outside the train station are carved with the names of early plague victims. They were once adorned with candles and flowers to honor the dead. Now trash and graffiti line the sidewalks and people zoom past with barely a glance. But on this night, something catches Akira's attention. A flyer pinned to an old bulletin board peeking out from behind a row of interactive ad kiosks, the simple piece of paper stands out among the frenetic lights:

Printing Press Operator Needed for Part-Time Project

There is no email, no phone number, only an address and a hand-written map instructing interested parties to go there during business hours and to dress all in white. Akira tears the flyer from the board, folds it neatly, and sticks it into his back pocket.

With the paper gently nudging him through the thin fabric of his pants, Akira imagines what the earnings might be, how he might move out of the virtual cafe and meet Yoshiko in person for once. He tries not to get his hopes up, but he's unable to stop thinking about the endless possibilities. Akira follows the map and finds himself on a narrow side street in front of a dilapidated wooden building with a traditional tiled roof and torn shoji windows. On either side of the building are modern boutique hotels with glass and chrome facades. Akira stands beside a faded tanuki statue on the building's stoop and gazes at a flickering light on the top floor, and dreams of another life.

The next morning, in the same spot he stood the night before, Akira is dressed all in white as instructed and holding a crumpled copy of his CV in his hands. The building is even more out of place in the daylight. He had not noticed the overgrowth of weeds and vines creeping along its sides. He thinks about Yoshiko, who was not in her virtual store the night before, or any of her favorite spots—like behind the diamond waterfall or in a glass igloo on a comet careening around Saturn. She's told him there are times when she can barely get out of bed to put on her VR visor, that she locks herself in her room as her daughter screams through the night, no longer capable of telling her mother what she wants or fears. On one occasion,

Yoshiko said her daughter threw the only food they had for dinner across the apartment and began lapping the noodles and liquid off the living room floor.

"What am I supposed to do?" Yoshiko asked. "I can't yell at her. She doesn't know what she did. So, I ate on the floor with her. When I try to talk to her, she just stares."

"You're doing the best you can," Akira said.

"Sometimes I want to yell," Yoshiko said. "Sometimes I want to shake her so hard that she'll wake up and be the girl I remember. I want her to look at me like I matter."

"You matter," Akira said. "Deep down she knows you matter. Maybe I could help?"

But whenever Akira makes offers like this, Yoshiko ignores them, quickly changing the subject.

"Let's play tennis in a Paris simulation," she said. "Let's talk about old movies. I can't remember the last time I went to the movies."

Akira walks to the front door and pushes the buzzer. After several minutes, he is about to leave when he hears somebody fiddling with the locks. An elderly man pops his head out and stares at Akira suspiciously, or perhaps in fear, and utters not a sound except for the guttural noise he makes when he clears his throat. Akira wonders if he might be at the wrong building but then suddenly the old man opens the door and gestures for Akira to enter. The old man is slight; the top of his balding head barely reaches Akira's shoulders. He introduces himself as Seiji Kobayashi and quickly turns away, leading Akira down a dusty hallway lined with trash and pieces of wood propped against the walls. There is a strange feeling that Akira is slipping from the real world as they travel deeper inside the building, down into the basement.

Akira cannot see anything until Seiji pulls the cord for a single lightbulb dangling in the middle of the room. The space has been painted white from floor to ceiling and is occupied only by an antique cast-iron printing press sitting at the center of the room. Seiji walks toward the press, picks up a letter on a page-setting tray, and begins to tap it against a metal corner. A heavy clinking sound echoes against the walls.

"I understand that this is not what you were expecting," Seiji says, staring off into space. In his white robe, he looks a little like he is having a conversation with God.

Akira takes a step back. "To be honest, no."

"You're young. Have you worked on printing presses like this before?"

"Well . . ." Akira recalls a childhood memory: making New Year's cards with his mother using rubber stamps. Of course, he'd worked in a print shop, but those machines were all computerized. Enter color, size, and presto. "Some similar experience, a long time ago."

Seiji's gaze shifts to Akira, his eyes glazed from the light above. "What are your thoughts on the Arctic plague?" he asks quite seriously.

Akira stares at him, unsure how to respond.

"The fact is," Seiji goes on, "Aum Shinrikyo and other doomsday groups, as you might call them, got it wrong. You know the sarin gas attacks in ninety-five?"

Akira nods. It was a footnote in cultural memory. A coworker of his father's had lost a brother during the incident.

"They were a tragedy," Seiji continues. "But that doesn't mean the philosophy of these so-called cults was wrong. Our leader of the Sun Wave Society said the world would end years ago with a solar flare, but it didn't. That doesn't mean that it won't, though. The plagues aren't such a bad thing—a hard reset, a cleanse, a chance to make things right. But people never listen."

Akira watches him place a page-setter on a metal plate on the press and tries to ignore the fact that Seiji just condoned the deaths of nearly fifty million people. The old man seems to use all his available strength to pull down on a lever while his left foot pumps a large paddle on the ground. Akira wonders if he should turn around and run before this crackpot decides to tie him up or worse. Seiji begins talking again about the natural order, how we have reached a war zone: us versus the planet. He says he wants to save people, open their eyes, save the rock we live on. He takes a stack of papers from the press and hands them to Akira.

"Now you see how it's done, more or less. You might as well distribute these around the city after you leave."

Akira looks down at what appears to be a newsletter. The headline reads SPILLED WATER DOES NOT RETURN TO THE TRAY. Seiji hands him a set of keys and tells Akira he may work when he wishes and that Seiji can only afford to spare five thousand yen a week but will allow him to sleep in the building if it's needed. "After all," he goes on, "there is nothing to steal unless you plan on strapping the printing press to your back." Akira leads the way back upstairs, stops suddenly in front of a picture hanging on the wall that he did not notice coming in. "My wife and daughter," Seiji explains, staring deeply into the photo, "taken two weeks before the sarin attack in ninety-five. My daughter survived. But she has chosen to forget she has a father. This is the only way I can protect her."

Akira leaves Seiji's with a messenger bag filled with newsletters. He marches out to the nearest busy intersection, right outside of a business park fountain. He waves the newsletters over his head and shouts out headlines: *Wake up and read the real news here! Spilled*

Water Does Not Return to the Tray! Wake up from your corporate dreams and see the world! A steady stream of people pass Akira from all directions; they do not stop or pay him any mind.

"Hey, you look like you might be a reasonable man," Akira says, shoving a newsletter into the arms of a young office worker. The man jumps when Akira approaches but takes the newsletter and walks on.

"Miss, could I bother you for a moment? Sir, have you heard about the electromagnetic wave pollution? Excuse me, excuse me," Akira says. Across the street, he sees another street canvasser for a mortuary planning phone app. The woman is standing with someone in a pink coffin costume who dances around, passing out tissue packets, hand fans, and visors. People stop to pose with the coffin and chat with the canvasser and Akira realizes that he's at a disadvantage without any kind of swag to offer.

"Spilled water does not return to the tray," Akira says again. "The plague has shown us the way. Say no to capitalism and yes to community. Say yes to your fellow human being." Akira is about to pass out another newsletter when he feels a hand violently pulling him away from the sidewalk.

"Leave immediately," a police officer says to Akira. He's an older, barrel-chested man with tinted plastic glasses. His eyes are trained on Akira, unmoving. "We will not tolerate extremist propaganda on our property. You are a nuisance. Show me your ID card."

"I don't have it on me," Akira says.

"What is your name?" The officer takes out a tablet and stylus from his pocket.

"Kenta Oe," Akira says, proud of his spontaneous bullshitting. "From Saitama." The officer takes one of the newsletters and pushes Akira in the direction of the nearest train station.

Having little luck in a downtown area, Akira picks a new spot outside of Harajuku Station. The mix of a younger, more alternative crowd might be more welcoming. At first, he is shy about giving the papers to people close to his age, barely raises his voice, feels ashamed for his torn jeans and dirty T-shirt while in one of the fashion capitals of the world. People take the papers without a thought, continue walking as if it's a coupon book or a flyer for a concert. But he sees some kids reading them over sodas and burgers and shaved ice. He hears a young woman say maybe they're not all lunatics as her husband or boyfriend throws the newsletter in the trash.

Before returning to the virtual cafe that night, Akira stops by Ameyoko Market, watches Yoshiko break down her stall for the evening, and wishes he had the courage to walk up to her like some Hollywood lover boy. In his cafe cubicle, he anxiously waits for Yoshiko to arrive in-world, so he can tell her about his day. He wonders what proportion of happy moments to sad ones is necessary for a person to sincerely want to keep living and hopes he and Yoshiko can get there together. Akira takes out a copy of the Sun Wave Society newsletter that he kept for himself to pass the time. He is surprised to find himself agreeing with much of what he reads. Perhaps not the end of the world part or the mysterious tenth planet that will supposedly cause the magnetic poles to shift, resulting in global catastrophe, but the underlying spirit of it all. He sees the responsibility we must take for the planet, our home, ensuring a future for the next generation. He imagines people on the street looking up from their phones and into each other's eyes—*Hello, how are you? Why are you so sad? How can we do better?*

A melodic chime rings, alerting Akira that Yoshiko has entered the virtual world. He transports himself to her store and finds her outside in the English garden she has created, populating the scene with butterflies. Akira listens to the sound of her wings, watches her hooves kick dirt into the air that glitters like a cloud of fireflies. An ellipsis appears in the air, telling Akira that Yoshiko is typing. It soon disappears without a word sent.

"Is your microphone not on?" Akira asks. He moves closer to Yoshiko and strokes her mane.

"Sorry," she says. "I guess I needed silence for a while. It's nice to have so much control here. These butterflies, the fish in the lake over there, the way the clouds in the sky morph into impossible shapes—my mother's face, the Eiffel Tower, a grand piano."

"They're beautiful," Akira says. He extends a hand into the air and waits for an iridescent butterfly to land on his palm. In the distance, Akira can see a tiny figure standing on a dock over the lake, a little girl. "Who is that?"

"My daughter," Yoshiko says, barely above a whisper. She gets up and moves toward the garden's fence, stares out at the lake. "Ten thousand in-world gems to transform a video on my phone into a virtual model. If I press play, she'll dance like we used to every day after she came home from school. She'll laugh and say *again, again, faster, faster*. I don't know what I expected. But it's not her. If I press play now, she'll fall into the lake. I've done it once already, clutching her hand as we sank below the surface."

"I thought you had changed your mind about all of that," Akira says.

"A few good days doesn't change anything," Yoshiko says. "My daughter is still in pain and can't communicate with me. No one can help."

Yoshiko bows her head and flaps her wings, sending a cloud of dirt and glitter into the air. Akira wants to ask more about her real life, wants to admit he has seen her at the market, but it doesn't seem like the right time.

"What do you want me to do?" Akira asks. "I'll do anything."

"I just want you to stay here with me and not talk," Yoshiko says.

Back at the printing press the next day, Akira works furiously, shifting gears only to bundle the stacks of newsletters with pieces of twine. The faster he works, the sooner the time will pass and he can return to his pod at the virtual cafe to check on Yoshiko. Has he misinterpreted their relationship? Akira's sure she was simply having a bad day. Seiji has given him new pages to print and told Akira that, compared to other things he will print for him, these pages will be among the most important. Instead of something far-reaching like planetary destruction or the altered migration patterns of marine life, these deal with topics on a much smaller scale—family and community. "People have forgotten how to care for each other, for themselves. We can't expect them to care about the world if they don't care about what's in front of them," Seiji explains. Throughout the day, Seiji leaves Akira for extended amounts of time, returning frequently to check on his progress. Akira believes the old man simply likes the company.

"People don't understand us," Seiji says, noticing Akira looking at the family photo. "Most people don't want to understand. My daughter says I killed her mother, groups me with those terrorists because I share some of their beliefs."

"Do you miss her?" Akira says. He regrets opening his mouth, stops working for a moment, waits for an answer.

"Where were you during the attacks?" Seiji asks.

"I wasn't born yet."

"I was at a toy store. When I left to go to the Metro, the entrance was blocked. I didn't know why." Seiji places a hand on Akira's shoulder. "We all share the blame for Aum Shinrikyo's crimes.

But I am no terrorist. I love my family. I think about Yoshiko every day. It's easy to be lost in fear. It brings people together, often for the wrong reasons."

Akira looks back at Seiji's family photo on the wall and notices a glimmer of similarity between the little girl and his Yoshiko. She said she no longer talks to her father. But a lot of people don't talk to their fathers and the name isn't uncommon. How do you ask someone if their mother died in a terrorist attack when you met them in a suicide forum? Yoshiko flies away whenever Akira asks for a sliver of her real life.

Akira looks into Seiji's worn eyes, sees an emptiness that is all too familiar. "I know," he says. "I mean, I believe you're not a terrorist."

Over the next few days, Akira fishes for more information, hoping to confirm his gut feeling that his Yoshiko is Seiji's daughter.

"I know she married," Seiji shares one day during a lunch break. "I know I have a granddaughter. She wrote to me once, about two years before the outbreak. Maybe as a punishment: 'I'm doing well. You have a granddaughter that you'll never see.'"

"Tell me about her," Akira asks. And when Seiji fills in the details about Yoshiko, her childhood ballet lessons and dreams of becoming a veterinarian, Akira's suspicions are confirmed. But would knowing that her father cares be enough to save her? Would knowing she's still alive pull Seiji out of his robes?

The following night, Akira soars over the sulfurous lightning storms of Venus in a hot-air balloon. Yoshiko flies around him.

"Maybe we can meet up for real," Akira suggests, thinking it might be easier that way to decide if he should tell Yoshiko the truth about her father.

Yoshiko accidentally kicks Akira's balloon into a cloud.

"I have some pocket money now, so it's my treat," he says. "I want to help."

"What is all of this for you?" she asked. "What do you think this will become?"

Akira considers labels like *soul mate*, or *girlfriend*; neither sounds right. "I don't know," he says.

"I'm afraid none of our real-life meetings could ever compare to this. Look at where we are. Isn't it amazing? You don't owe me anything. What we have is right here."

"But this isn't real," Akira says.

"No, it's not."

In the morning, Akira heads to Ameyoko intending to reveal himself, confident Yoshiko will feel different once they meet. He imagines Yoshiko at the market, rearranging her calligraphy prints and T-shirts, how he'll wave hello to her for the first time. With their meeting, all of Yoshiko's downplaying of their relationship will vanish. Maybe they'll hug. Maybe they'll go for a walk and hold hands. Akira thinks about all the ways they might find to re-create their virtual playground in the real world. How could they fly?

I'm glad you came, Yoshiko would say. *I'm so glad that you're finally here.*

But when Akira approaches the entrance to the street market, awash with the holographic illusion of Venice, he can already see Yoshiko isn't at her usual spot beside the Grand Canal. He buys a small toy from a neighboring vendor for her daughter, a keychain of the popular old robo-dogs, a box of chocolate mochi for Yoshiko.

After a long stroll through Ueno Park, Akira returns to the virtual cafe and finds Ms. Takahashi reading a newspaper at one of the bistro tables, sipping on some tea. She greets Akira and invites him to share a light lunch she has made. Akira wants to return to his pod, but he is hungry, and this meal would mean another few hundred yen saved. He sits as Ms. Takahashi sets the table with bowls of rice, a plastic container filled with salmon and eel slices. Akira studies the purple crystal Ms. Takahashi always wears around her neck, a new age anomaly compared to her steady stream of no-frills kimonos. From certain angles, Akira could swear he sees light emanating from the crystal, almost like tiny stars.

"Are you okay?" Ms. Takahashi asks as she sits.

Akira nods, cracking a half smile. "Almost perfect," he says.

"You've been in better spirits lately. Maybe one day you can leave this place," Ms. Takahashi observes. "I've heard you laughing late at night. Anyone special?"

Akira shrugs and sips a cup of vending machine miso, slowly picks at the eel.

"Complicated," Akira says.

"Embrace possibility, but don't let it drag you down."

"I feel like we're so perfect," Akira says. "But . . ."

"That's all relationships at first."

"I want to take care of her and her daughter."

"Sometimes it might be the right thing to give yourself completely to someone. But from where I'm standing, you need to take care of yourself first, think about your future. Me, I lost my mother a long time ago, quite suddenly. She gave me this pendant to remind me of her. I guess I'm still searching. She's here with me, though—and this job, helping people like you, sitting quietly in the lobby all day and watching the world move on, is what I need. We're all healing in our own ways."

"I'm sorry," Akira says. "I didn't know about your family."

"Ancient history," Ms. Takahashi says, rolling the crystal pendant between her fingers. "Just do me a favor and try not to be here for another year."

Akira thanks Ms. Takahashi for the meal and retires to his cubicle.

In the virtual world, he can see Yoshiko has left him a message: *There was a silent understanding between us. Thank you, my friend.* There's a medieval scroll tacked to the wall of Yoshiko's store with instructions for Akira to go to the lake. He pushes open the gate to the English garden and hikes down a field of red and yellow tulips. At the end of the dock, a play button hovers over the water with another message: *I'm sorry. For everything I never told you, for everything we never were. Ask me anything.* When he pushes it, Yoshiko's avatar, the Pegasus, splashes out from under the water and lands on the dock, lowers itself for Akira to climb onto its back. As the Pegasus flaps its wings, Akira holds on tight. Yoshiko's recorded voice begins to play as he soars around Yoshiko's kingdom, over her store and garden, around the lake, through a valley of waterfalls, weaving between a cluster of shipwrecks. Akira realizes that Yoshiko had an AI/smart avatar designed, one capable of answering preprogrammed questions, of sounding and acting like her.

"We can just fly, or you can ask me something," Yoshiko's avatar says. "Isn't it beautiful here?"

"Is Seiji your father?"

"I ran away from home. I blamed him for my mother's death, but I never knew how to take it back. I thought my husband would save me, but he didn't. I thought my daughter would save me, and she did for a while, until she got sick and I failed her."

"What's your favorite dessert?"

"Coffee ice cream."

"Favorite music?"

"Queen."

"Did you notice me in real life? Did you see me watching you?"

"I never noticed anybody. When I worked at the stall, I lived in my own world. I let the noise of the city envelop me. Sometimes I felt guilty for enjoying the time away from my daughter. Those hours almost felt like how things used to be. Maybe a part of me wanted us to meet, but I think I made my decision a long time ago."

"I thought we understood each other."

"You only knew a small part of me, but I appreciated you being here. I had to do what was best for me and my daughter."

"Best?"

"It's what I believe. It's what was true for me."

"Did any part of you care for me?"

"Of course. Like a close acquaintance. Like someone you just met but who you recognize for sharing a similar life experience. My poor, naive boy. Remember me if you must, if it helps you move on. I wish everything for you."

Akira replays the Pegasus experience several times, as if there is some hidden message between the facts of her life. He falls asleep wearing his VR visor and leaves his pod only when going to the bathroom becomes an emergency. Part of him believes there's a chance she might sign back on, even though the recording says goodbye. Another part of him knows she is gone forever.

In the early morning, Akira realizes, more out of exhaustion than logic, that he needs to stop. His eyes have to readjust to the world after seeing through the visor for so long. And there, on the front page of the *Mainichi* newspaper in the lobby, he sees their faces— Yoshiko and her daughter, gazing back at him. Akira closes his eyes, convinces himself that he is seeing things, but their faces remain when he opens them again. A strange, burning sensation spreads throughout his body and it seems as if nothing can extinguish it. *My poor, naive boy. Remember me if you must, if it helps you move on. I wish everything for you.*

He returns to his pod and checks the news online, hoping there has been a mistake. But as Akira scrolls down the page, he comes to a photograph of two body bags being rolled out of an apartment building—one smaller than the other. The headline: TRAGEDY AS CITY AND GOVERNMENT OFFICIALS FAIL TO OFFER ADEQUATE SOCIAL AND MEDICAL SUPPORT POST-PANDEMIC. SUICIDE GROUPS FILL IN THE GAPS WHERE SOCIAL SERVICES FAIL. One article describes barbiturates found on the scene. Another notes that the pill bottle was emblazoned with the logo for an under-the-table euthanasia service called the Harmony Collective. Akira touches the screen, holds his arm like that until it becomes weak and uncomfortable and he can hold it there no longer, and then puts on his visor and enters the coordinates for the street referenced in the article, walking through a barren Tokyo until he finds the building where Yoshiko and her daughter lived. He reaches for the door, but the map program won't let him enter residential buildings, so he just looks up at the windows, and imagines *her* looking back.

In the days following the death of Yoshiko and her daughter, Seiji notices Akira's silence as he works, no longer asking questions about Sun Wave or his life. He places his hand on Akira's shoulder one evening and tells him to take a break, join him for tea. He fetches a kettle and two paper cups and places them on the floor, invites Akira to sit.

"You don't seem like yourself lately," Seiji says.

Akira shrugs and sips his tea. He considers sharing that he's lost someone but knows more questions would inevitably come and that might force him to tell Seiji about his daughter.

"You know, for a long time I spent my days filling journals trying to capture everything my life used to be—all the memories of my family before they faded from my mind," Seiji says. "I wrote apology notes to my dead wife, to my daughter, variations of the same letter over years, blaming myself. I wasn't in a good place. But if I called this life quits . . ."

"I'm not. You don't have to worry about that," Akira interrupts.

"If I ended it, I would have become the man my daughter hated. I would have proven her right," Seiji finishes.

"I'm sure she loved you," Akira says, finally deciding that to say anything else would be too cruel. "I might need a couple of days. I'm not sure if I'll be back. There's a funeral for an old friend in Fukuoka."

"I'm sorry. Whoever it is. Your job will be waiting for a time. I barely pay you enough to keep you anyway," Seiji says.

Akira packs his bags at the virtual cafe, leaves a thank-you note for Ms. Takahashi, and makes his way to the train station. On his way, he takes a detour to Yoshiko's apartment building and leaves a bouquet of flowers outside. He sees another homeless man sitting on the sidewalk nearby and leaves his bags beside the man, removing only his jacket, the gifts he bought for Yoshiko and her daughter, and whatever he can fit in a tote bag.

"Help yourself," he says. The man seems confused, and then begins rummaging through his new belongings. He pulls out a pair of socks and puts them on his bare feet.

The one-way train ticket and a few nights in a hotel eat up half the money Akira has saved. He finds his seat and rests his head against the window, waving away the girl selling snacks and drinks. He could eat one of the mochi chocolates he bought for Yoshiko, but he does not. Instead, he will sit beside Yoshiko and her daughter in a rural cemetery and eat the snacks as slowly as possible. After saying goodbye and telling them all about the day he imagined that they never got to spend together, he'll leave the toy robo-dog next to the headstone, along with some wildflowers he'll pick by the roadside.

"I'm going to call my mother now," Akira will say. "Things will be better." And in his imagination, Yoshiko's spirit flies above as he walks down the road, the shadow of a horse with wings guiding his way, until he finds a way to call home.

BEFORE YOU MELT INTO THE SEA

Here is the chamber where I'll place your body. You'll float in a solution of water and potassium hydroxide at a temperature of 350 degrees. Your skin will flake like ash and the tendons inside your hands with which you messaged me over the years will unravel to the width of spider silk until everything is completely gone. You first came to Eden Ice before you were truly sick, before the cancer the plague left in your brain forced the doctors to put you to sleep. My company provides artistic alternatives to burial and cremation, one of the many "new death" companies that became popular after the plague, as people died from the chronic illnesses that remained in their bodies.

In our introductory video chat, you asked me to walk you through the process, told me you discovered us through a WeFuture ad and were impressed by the testimonials.

"We're very proud of our customer service," I said. "We have an A-plus from the Better Business Bureau and received a gold coffin award for Most Promising Funerary Start-Up of 2040 from FEEL: Funerary Enterprises, Entrepreneurs, and Lobbyists."

"That's very impressive," you said. You were wearing a tank top, and I studied the murals on your arms as I described our state-of-the-art resomation chamber, which you called a human Crockpot. I gave you a video tour of the facility via my phone, all the ways I tried to carve a moment of beauty out of tragedy—a group of Disney princesses for two little girls; a pair of swans for an elderly couple found in their assisted living facility, holding each other.

"I just want to make sure that the ink is saved before you liquefy me," you said. "Did you get my memo?"

"I did," I said. "Immortal Ink LLC will preserve and frame your tattoos prior to you being shipped to me. We'll make sure all of your requests are honored."

"These tats are my stories. This is my life," you said.

We exchanged blueprints and photos of schooners for your ice sculpture. You wanted the kind of old-timey masted ship you once spent a night on during a field trip and dreamed of traveling on around the world. One month you wanted me to dye the sails red, another month blue. At first, it was mostly business. I noticed the jazz playing in the background of your room, the map of Japan over your childhood bed when you stayed at your parents' house. You said you never really gave a shit about your heritage until you found out in high school that most major Japanese cities could be partially underwater by the end of the century.

"They'll probably do something about it—flood diversion, sea-walls," you explained, sharing climate projections on your computer screen. "But they still might be fucked."

"So, you wanted to see the motherland before it washed away," I said.

"Yeah, sure," you said, like I was kind of a square. "But I also wanted to leave home and apprentice with this tattoo master, Wataru, who invited me to study. I had been sending him my drawings for years—sure, lots of anime fan art, but also futuristic city-scapes and American cryptids like Bigfoot, the chupacabra, and the Snoligoster."

"The snoli-what?"

"It's an alligator with a giant spike on its back and a propeller tail. Florida swamp folktale."

I researched jazz in my spare time to impress you, and one day when you looked like you would collapse from exhaustion, I played Ella Fitzgerald backed by Dizzy Gillespie. You smiled and called me *hella obvious*, and then we listened together for hours.

Another day, after researching the history of tattoos, I told you the story of a Buddhist priest who tattooed sutras all over his body. "He was doing it to protect himself from evil spirits," I explained. "But he forgot to tattoo his ears, so a spirit ripped them off!"

"The Miminashi Hoichi tale? You flipping through Wikipedia before our chats or something?" you said, busting me, before inviting me to give a report on everything else I'd learned to impress you. Like the fact that Duke Ellington never officially recorded his first composition, "Soda Fountain Rag," or that the seas might rise as much as three feet by 2100 with glacial melt even if we do everything right, potentially displacing seven hundred million people, or how the kappa, a Japanese water imp, maintains its power from the water in its bowl-shaped head, but is compelled to reciprocate politeness such as bowing.

"You must have been a real Romeo in school," you said.

"I had braces and I was in the AV club," I said.

When I designed a figurehead in your image, you wrote back: *Leaving the world should be mythic.* I resketched my idea and transformed you into a kirin, a dragon-deer hybrid with your face and the tail of a mermaid. We watched the movie *Splash* online, and you said that you wished you'd been born early enough to enjoy the ridiculousness of the eighties. I am sure I've glorified our brief moments together, all our late-night video chats, for so long that it's easy to forget, standing over your body, that maybe I never really knew you at all.

———

By the time your parents shipped you, your body had already begun to bloat, as if microscopic blowfish had infiltrated your veins. Blood fell to your backside, your ass the shade of a stray plum spoiling behind a produce stand. A pathologist from Immortal Ink LLC had already taken large swaths of your tattooed skin, making you look like one of those traveling exhibits of what lies within the human body. You had a strange look on your face that I interpreted as sadness. And if you could have heard me, you might have said: *Who doesn't look sad when they're dead?* But maybe it was disappointment that caught on your last breath, some unfinished task or hidden secret. On your social media profiles, I see adventure after adventure—sitting atop a camel in Egypt, kayaking with the fins of dolphins behind you, tattooing the yakuza in a hot-springs resort, group photos with people who picked you up hitchhiking. So many comments telling you they miss you on your birthday. And where were they all in the end? Had the plague taken them? Did you abandon them, or was it the other way around? I stare at your albums, imagine myself in these places with you, and try to understand if you were running away or merely living.

What would have happened if we had more time? Over one thousand hours of video chats and nearly twenty thousand instant messages. After you signed the final paperwork, you video-called unexpectedly, and I probably smiled more than was professionally necessary. I asked you how you felt, and you described how the meds buying you more time were also tearing you apart—*I wish I could taste. I wish I wasn't so tired all the time. I hate that when I do have the energy to go out, I get angry at all the people who didn't get the plague or somehow walked away from it scot-free. I hate how the world is finally coming together to help the planet when I'm coming undone.* You said you didn't want to bother me with your problems, and maybe that would have been that, but I told you it was okay. I told you I could listen. At Eden Ice, we treat our customers like family.

"And don't be ridiculous," I said. "Who else am I going to hang out with? The nightlife scene in Kodiak isn't exactly hopping."

I picked out the remaining bone debris after you'd been liquefied and crushed it for your mother. Most people opt for the Evergreen Slumber, a simple, stained pine box, or the Shooting Star, a gold-plated aluminum urn. But in your final month of lucidity, you mailed several ships in bottles to be used instead, each with a backdrop of a different locale—the Maldives, Key West, New Orleans, Venice. You said they were all places you had planned to visit one day. They were all places that might not exist within a lifetime.

I arrange your shriveled hands, one atop the other over your privates. You said you wanted to look halfway decent as you changed from a solid to a liquid. Before I push you into the chamber, I picture you pristine, your skin still intact and vibrant with tales upon tales that you mostly kept to yourself. Moles and freckles dance around your belly button like a Jackson Pollock painting, and I fight the urge to grab a marker and find a way to connect them into a Tibetan mandala, as if that would unlock some secret about who you were and what, if anything, I really meant to you. Over the past year, my coworkers asked me about you—*that Asian woman whose file photo you keep staring at*. I never said anything (because there was nothing to say), but they gave me grief, called me lover boy. When I spoke to my mother, who retreated to a cabin in Sitka after my father died from the plague, I asked her how people find love with the right person when a life seems so small, when the rest of the world seems so far away, barely able to hold itself together. She said people make do. She said alcohol helps and so does settling for someone so long as they aren't complete dog shit. But what if you don't drink and don't like any kind of nightlife? What if you already live in one of the few places on the planet that people think of when they wish to leave everything behind?

Right before you were hospitalized, we agreed upon the final designs for your ice ship and memorial. A lightning branch of veins had appeared beneath your paper-thin skin, and I replaced your hair, so you no longer felt the need to wear a hat. I showed you a scale model of the sculpture for you to explore the details of the masts, sails, and of course, the kirin figurehead you would be poured into. And after you made your final requests, I asked if I could visit you at the hospital. After all, hadn't we become friends? A long silence followed, and you said, *No, that's probably not for the best.* And I'd be lying if I said I wasn't hurt. You told me *sometimes people and places serve a purpose for a finite amount of time to help you think and grow and love and then you move on.* You hung up and texted: Thank you for everything. And signed off: Love, Mabel xoxo. I wish I could know for certain how I helped you and how you helped me. Maybe I was just really good at doing my job. Part of me wants to kiss you before I slide you into the chamber, though that's probably not for the best, either.

Unalaska, Alaska, a gateway to the Aleutian chain, is the place you picked for the launch—partly because of the name and partly because these islands graze Siberia. *Close but not quite*, you said. *Like I'm going back to the origins of the virus, this thing that did this to me.* I walk the island today on a scouting trip for your memorial and imagine you there beside me, pointing out where you'd like to be set free. Everything feels charged, connected. Out here, it seems like the world has yet to be touched by the evils of man. Wild horses graze; a sea otter in the bay cracks a crab on a rock; eagle eggs perched on a narrow shelf of a cliff face begin to hatch. I can somehow feel it all. But I also know the fishing boats are returning half-empty and whales continue to beach themselves. We follow a stream until it empties out into a shallow bay surrounded by grassy hills. An abandoned jetty reaches out on one side to a rocky sandbar on the other, creating a narrow corridor to the Bering Sea. And then you run off, faster than I can keep up, until you're gliding on the surface of the water. You spiral with your arms outstretched, head cocked back, mouth open to taste the salty air. So, this is it, I say. This is where we'll do it. You smile and disappear beneath the black waves.

When I return to my workshop, I begin the long process of sculpting the sails, rigging and freezing everything into one piece. The vessel is almost fifteen feet long and nine feet high. Parts of you are frozen across the deck and bow, giving the vessel a natural oaky appearance, something that might last on the high seas. You give the figurehead life, with only a thin sheet of ice separating you from the abyss. I stare into your eyes and wonder if you are watching.

A few dozen people attend your memorial—your family and friends from Seattle and even your tattoo master, Wataru, who's joined by a cadre of old Japanese men with wolfed-up orange hair. A neighborhood friend of your mother's, Dan Paul, volunteered to help coordinate the event, leading people to their seats, handing out programs, talking to the local television station that plans to share the launch on the internet as part of a web series on how the plague has reinvented the way we die. I want to ask your mother about who you really were, if I was anybody to you, but today is not about me. Marijuana and incense piggyback on the misty air. A Hare Krishna monk invites others to chant with him. Your mother sits on a lawn chair, cradling a coffee she seems to have no interest in drinking. The schooner is docked at the jetty with you looking out into the bay. A podium stands nearby. One by one, people speak—*She will be missed, she was one of a kind, she had the guts to live her life.* I want to say something, too, though I know I probably won't be able to stop myself from telling these strangers something that existed only for us, and maybe, quite possibly (probably) only for me. *We watched some movies and listened to music and talked about Bigfoot and how coastal cities might turn into islands or underwater resorts. And I guess I had a crush on her* is all I can think to say. And maybe that's nothing, but it's the most I've ever had. People admire the schooner, the detail and the obvious fact that it can indeed float. They take photos in front of it and run their hands across the bow, across you. Some shake my hand. Others ask for my card. Your mother and Wataru stand beside the ship for a long while, holding on to the deck, parts of you no doubt melting and mingling with their skin. When people return to their seats, I pull the schooner out into the bay with my inflatable raft. People are silent at first but then they begin to clap. They're shouting *I love you.* I turn back to the shore and see a large banner that reads BON VOYAGE, fluttering in the wind.

When we're out far enough, I cut the engine. I enclose my digital voice recorder in a waterproof sleeve, since you wanted every second of your last moments recorded just as your life had been tattooed on your skin. Back in my office, there's a package waiting for me that your mother told me not to open until the service was over. I know it's a part of you—a piece of skin, a memory in ink. I'm not certain how long it will take for you to melt into the sea, but I plan on staying here until you do. Cargo ships blow their horns in the distance. Seals, perhaps seeing an interesting place to rest, circle, nudging their noses at the bow. I scream a gibberish war cry to frighten them off.

A couple of hours have passed and already waves are washing over the sinking deck. Two of the masts have broken in half and a sail is dissolving quickly like cotton candy. Your figurehead is largely intact, but beads of water run down your face, your dragon-scaled chest. Your deer horns have become demonic nubs. The sun is high overhead and the seam where I froze you to the rest of the schooner is coming undone. Soon you'll have no choice but to prove your mermaid and dragon skills. I pull on my fins and life jacket so that I may join you. My dry suit is tight and secure, my mask and snorkel ready. The schooner begins to crack again, the fractures sounding off like a multitude of tiny whips. And before I'm ready for it, you splash into the water, bobbing up and down, hitting what remains of the hull. I jump in and drag you away from danger.

It's only the two of us now. Your eyes are nothing but subtle concave indentations, your nose a minor bump in a round piece of ice. You're floating on your back, staring at the sky. My hands are around your waist, preventing you from spinning between the waves like a crystal log. The battery on my recorder is fading. I fear water has seeped inside it. Before there is nothing left to hold, I want to tell you all the things I never got to say, what I would have said if I could have played a larger role in what remained of your life. I could have loved you; I did anyway (and maybe if our lives had been different you could have loved me, too). I tell you a million other little things until nothing remains of your kirin-mermaid self except for a piece in my hands the size of a large hailstone, until that too melts.

GRAVE FRIENDS

On the hypertube ride from Tokyo Narita Airport island to the archipelago of Niigata City, my sister never once reminded me of how I abandoned our family five years ago. At first, everyone assumed I had simply extended my visit to America. But after one month passed and then another, I finally worked up the courage to send a letter home with a photo of me in a wedding dress on the shore of Lake Michigan. *I'm sorry*, I wrote. Sorry for making everyone think I had been kidnapped or worse. Sorry I didn't want to live in the same sinking town for my entire life or have my ashes stored in a shared urn with the other families on our street, stuck in one place for all eternity.

Beside me, Tamami chronicled the lives of my old neighborhood, the grave friends, the network of five tight-knit families who'd agreed two generations ago to mix their ashes together. The shared urn started out as a money- and space-saving venture when the plague hit and no one knew what to do with the dead. But our neighborhood found a new appreciation for the shared community after our city become an archipelago amid the rising seas of the Great Transition of 2070, over thirty years ago now.

The grave friends network consisted of five households, although there had at one time been more. The oldest member and the social nexus of the neighborhood was my grandmother, my baba, who used to go from house to house every afternoon to talk stories over cheap wine. There was also my pervy "uncle" Michihiro, who often came over to drink and play darts with my father, staring at me in my Sailor Moon–style uniform when I was in high school; and the

Fujita sisters, who both worked as gothic Lolita hostesses, donning frilly black Victorian frocks. Mrs. Kishimoto next door had given me koto lessons after school. And Mr. Takata, after he retired from the Mitsubishi solar farm, cared for everybody's gardens in exchange for a modest bounty of herbs and vegetables. Tomorrow, I would pick out Baba's bones from a tray of ash in front of all these people. And soon after, I'd have to tell my mother that my ashes would never become one with hers and Father's and everyone else's we loved.

As the tube capsule slowed, drifting beyond rice paddy villages stuck in time, I saw the outskirts of Niigata City. Once notable for sake and tulips and a long-ago gold rush, the nondescript skyline had become famous for the several dozen funerary skyscrapers dotting a series of tiny islands that served a large percentage of northern Japan—dark monolithic towers, punctuated by clouds and 3-D billboards reminding the city that we'll all die one day and we should take advantage of their mortuary package specials. But beneath their shadows, I could see the old city, the aging utilitarian apartment buildings nestled beside secondhand shops, love hotels crowned with gaudy neon signs. Next to my old high school was the large stone torii gate, now half-submerged in water, carved with the names of those who died during the plague—a former place of picnics and reunions before the waves crept slowly past the park. Beyond the train station, self-driving company cars idled in a roundabout before zipping through the familiar arteries of Bandai district—the labyrinth of bars and mom-and-pop shops that hadn't changed in decades, the cracked streets of the past merged onto the floating bridges connecting the city like a cobweb. Peeking out from the water: the Rainbow Tower, a refurbished remnant of an old shopping complex that became an underwater hotel. As a child I used to watch fireworks from the tower's spinning observation elevator, marveling at the silhouettes of the drowned shopping mall with each explosion.

Students and grannies on bikes still clogged sidewalks, riding beside thirty-foot-high seawalls and across neighborhood bridges. I didn't want to only remember the good times, but I had a sudden hankering for pizza with mayonnaise, a shrimp burger from McDonald's, a bowl of udon with vegetable tempura to slurp alongside grumpy salarymen. I wanted to call my old friends from school, maybe sing our hearts out in some karaoke booth. This was my drowned world. Of course, I knew none of this would happen right away.

"So," I began. I wanted to know if my parents were going to play pretend like my sister. If, by the grace of Baba's death, I had somehow been granted probation by my mother and would be reinstated into the family without a lecture. "What's going on with Mom and Dad these days?"

"You mean are they going to rip your head off?" Tamami was the easy sibling, a kind of doormat, the sort of person who went along with the wishes of others and didn't complain, but she was no idiot.

"Uh, yeah."

"Dad is just happy to see you. Mom, on the other hand, I'm not so sure. She asked about your flight."

"Basically a fifty-fifty shot of being murdered or tied to a chair."

"There are too many people coming and going, paying their respects. She's not going to make a scene."

Of course, Tamami never received the brunt of our mother's wrath—like the time my mother had found me making out with a bad boy, Kosuke, outside a nearby corner store and dragged me home so hard I had bruises on my arm for a week. Or the time she found my report card and didn't talk to me for a month because she said I was a hopeless cause who was going nowhere. But where would I go? And where would she want me to go that wouldn't be considered abandoning home and her sick sense of loyalty to the grave friend network? The next town over? The one after that? By the time

I turned eighteen, the lure of the big city no longer existed—even Tokyo and Osaka had become a muted collection of islands with barely any room for new residents. *This is where you belong. This is where our family has always been. Everything you need in life is here with us. This street is a shining example of how people should be in Japan.* We're not a cult, I tried to explain to friends in America, not really.

When we finally arrived home, my father ran to the door and hugged me tightly. I'd missed the smell of him—a strange mixture of cigarette smoke and tropical deodorant. He cinched his bathrobe, hiding one of the ancient and yellowed undershirts he refused to throw away. My mother was in the garden, trying desperately to appear busy. I noted that the typhoon and tsunami seawalls beside our street were taller now, casting a shadow over our house. Instead of blue sky, there was concrete horizon from our windows.

"It's okay, it's okay," he whispered in my ears. "We've missed you." He carried my suitcase up to Baba's old room and told me to take a load off, sit, relax. They had remodeled the first floor into an open floor plan. Somehow the furniture seemed more cluttered than before, as if they were living in a secondhand shop showroom.

"I'm staying in Baba's room?"

"Well, we're not sharing a room again," Tamami said. "That's for damn sure."

I perched on a kitchen counter stool as if I were a stranger, too afraid to make myself comfortable, ready to bolt. I could sense my mother staring at me. How would she guilt me? How might she try to pull me back into the fold? Perhaps she would even suggest that I move back home with my husband, start a life here where everything and everyone would be waiting for me. There was a tiny holo-portrait of Baba on the entertainment center surrounded by flowers and fruit. I could feel my face growing hot on top of my already clammy skin from the summer humidity, a flush of shame for not sending so much as a postcard the whole time I was gone. After all Baba had done for me—my ally after every shouting match, comfort in the form of freshly cooked dumplings, the only one who'd known I was planning to run away. While unpacking my bags in America years ago, I'd found an envelope with nearly a thousand dollars in yen and a brief note: *Follow your happiness wherever it may take you, but remember your family.* I still had the note somewhere. I tried not to dwell on it, though, because a part of me always knew how much Baba loved our street, having everyone all together.

"Are you hungry?" my mother asked, washing the dirt from her hands before rummaging through the fridge. "Not sure if you had enough on the plane."

"I'm fine," I said. I watched her ignore me and continue to fix rice balls stuffed with salted salmon, probably left over from a previous night's dinner. From where I sat, I could see the shrine in the hall with photos of everyone on the street who had passed. A stick of incense and a tiny memento sat before each one—a button, a harmonica, a lock of hair, an earring, a pair of glasses. In a glass cabinet beneath the altar sat an inoperable robot dog named Hollywood that belonged to one of my great-great-aunts who had died of the plague. When I was a kid, one of the main rules of the house was to bow to every single member of the shrine before moving on. My mother had frequently made me turn back and pay my respects until I convinced her I wasn't half-assing it with a lackluster bow.

"We'll be eating dinner after our neighborhood walk," my mother said. "I hope you're fine with okonomiyaki. It's your father's new favorite."

"What's a neighborhood walk?"

"We take walks before dinner with some people in the neighborhood. You're welcome to join us. Or, you know, you can stay in your room and rest. We made some VR recordings for you, things you missed."

"Right," I said. It was clear that the walk was definitely not optional. I ate my snack as quickly as I could, my mother studying me, each of us figuring out a game plan for how to deal with the other.

"You and your husband doing okay over there?" my father asked, trudging into the kitchen. "Sean, right?"

"Yes, we're fine."

"I'm not sure how much an English teacher's salary covers in Chicago," my mother said.

"He's not an English teacher. He only did that here for a year after college. He just passed the bar exam."

"Oh?" My parents looked at each other, unsure of what that meant.

"He's going to be an environmental lawyer. A good one." Of course, I couldn't blame them for not knowing the details. All they knew about our relationship was that Sean had taught me business English and that I'd lied about a work trip to America. But the pull of my adolescent routines and attitudes called to me. Here, I wasn't a newlywed or a dental hygiene student or even the woman who douses her pierogies in sriracha. I was a daughter who abandoned her family. "I should unpack."

Upstairs, I found Tamami's orange tabby cat, Chibi, curled on top of my suitcase and an old-model VR visor with two data chips. The closet drawers were still filled with Baba's belongings. I had to transfer a small pile to a chair to make room. Nearly everything was as I remembered it—a decade-old calendar of London that a friend had given Baba still tacked to the wall, a stack of travel brochures on the dresser for all the cities she'd dreamed of visiting. A bright pink lopsided umbrella for her neighborhood strolls. Everything as it was except for the menagerie of pill bottles on the end table. At the bottom of a drawer, I found a plastic bag containing a collection of paper envelopes no larger than a thumbnail, each containing a few grains of rice. Magic rice, I used to think when Baba explained that they were blessed by a priest and had the power to heal, to make one feel whole with the spirit of God. No one in the family really bought into the religion Baba had grown up with, but Tamami and I would sometimes sneak a grain or two. We thought it might give us superpowers, the ability to become invisible when we were in trouble. The night before I left for America, I remember tiptoeing into Baba's room and taking one last grain, imagining it growing inside me, a new me that would shed the shell of all I had been.

"Sometimes I feel like I see her in here. Not to creep you out or anything," Tamami said, standing in the doorway. "You should put that on at some point." She pointed to the visor. "It's not all guilt trip and grave friends propaganda."

"I can still smell Baba," I said. I pictured her pumping her arms and legs in the air like she was on an exercise bike before getting out of bed. I remembered her telling us magical stories about how she had a recurring dream of being a baby and someone raising her tiny body into a dark sky and letting her float away into space. Or how she had to crawl through thousands of feet and legs in the dark like an ever-shifting maze. Baba, for as long as anybody could remember, was afraid of the dark and always kept a flashlight next to her bed in case she needed to go to the bathroom.

Tamami sat cross-legged on the bed, coaxed Chibi onto her lap.

"Look, I'm not mad anymore. I get why you left. But you'll never know how tough it got here. Mom thought I might leave, too, and basically put me on lockdown. If I so much as frowned, she'd scream at me and call me ungrateful. Baba getting sick pushed her over the edge. I barely left the house."

"You could have come to see me," I said.

"Could I have, though? Anyway, I'm not like you, Rina."

I wondered what she really meant by that. I wanted her to be straight with me: Not adventurous? Not a fuckup? Not a traitor?

"And even if I wanted to," Tamami continued. She told me that the tranquilizers weren't solely so Baba could sleep or have a break from the pain. Our grandmother had become violent in her final months—a glass thrown at Chibi, records shattered on the floor, a bite out of my father's hand so hard he'd needed stitches, too many cruel things that became harder to brush off as the ravings of a sick woman.

I held Tamami's hands and noticed that there wasn't a single rice packet among all the pill bottles. As her mind failed her, did Baba simply forget? Wasn't her daily ritual a part of her spirituality, or had she merely been holding the broken parts of herself together—all the painful moments we never talked about, like how she lost my mother's sister in childbirth. "Everything I need is here," she would say. My mother believed this, too, but Baba had also fallen asleep each night staring at London Bridge, surrounded by decades-old articles about restaurants in Paris that probably didn't exist anymore and safaris in Kenya, even if many of the animals were long since extinct. I stroked Chibi on Tamami's lap and debated whether to tell her everything.

"What are you going to do now that you're back?" Tamami asked.

"I mean, I'm not really back," I said. I reached into my purse and pulled out the ultrasound photo—a heartbeat growing stronger inside of me.

My sister absorbed the photo and pulled me in for a hug.

"Rina, that's wonderful," she said. But I could tell from the tears, the somewhat stiff expression on her face that the news meant more.

The grain of rice I took when I left had given me the strength to leave and become. This child gave me a reason.

"Don't tell them," I said. "I need to find my own way."

She hugged me again.

"I guess I get to be an aunt," she said.

After Tamami left, I lay in bed, slipped on the old holo-visor, and suddenly found myself there beside Baba. Her labored breathing punctuated the sound of Mrs. Kishimoto's koto and the rhythmic clapping of friends and family who filled the room. A minister in black robes pushed grains of rice between Baba's cracked lips, helped prop her up to drink a glass of water. I remained next to her long after everyone else left for lunch in the yard. I heard my name, people saying I should be there. I remained until the recording reached its end and looped it back, populating the bedroom with everyone once again. If the purpose of this virtuo-chip was to fill me with guilt, then my mother had succeeded beautifully.

Later that day, after I unpacked, my mother called us all outside for some predinner neighborhood exercise. Our family plus a few of the grave friends congregated in our front yard and began the loop from cemetery skyscraper 18 back to the house, a two-kilometer path with stops for refreshments. The group paraded along the sidewalk following a strict hierarchy determined by age, the eldest members leading the way, swinging their arms with power walking enthusiasm. Shopkeepers and police officers waved to us as if we were celebrities.

"All the grandpas and grandmas in our neighborhood think people like us because we're doing something special. But most of our friends and their parents just think we're weird," one of the Fujita sisters said, noticing my slack-jawed confusion.

"Cult," the other sister added.

"But we're far from the only people doing the group urn," I pointed out.

"We're the only ones who like to rub it in everyone's faces," one of the sisters explained. She stuck a finger in her mouth like she was going to vomit. "We're broke or we'd run away like you did."

A few members ahead, I could see my mother chatting with Mr. Takata about plans for Baba's service. "They don't make women like that anymore. She knew just about everyone in our ward," my mother said. "She's really the one who made our group work. She held us together."

"I'd be home alone right now if it weren't for her," Mr. Takata said. "I'd die alone."

"We want to die alone," the Fujita sisters said in unison.

It was no surprise that Uncle Takata joined us for dinner. Tamami noted that he came over at least two or three times a week, always bringing a couple of bottles of wine to make up for the trouble. As expected, the real adults conversed loudly while they drank. I tried to keep a low profile, stuffing my mouth with spaghetti to avoid talking.

"Windy city," Mr. Takata said, waiting for me to swallow. He smiled after everything he said, a habit he'd developed from a managerial style he liked to call "Happy News"—basically, if you smile while giving someone an unfortunate task, as he'd once explained to my father, they're more willing to accept it. "Shi-ka-go. Sear Tower," he continued. "You see it?"

"Of course. Can't miss it," I said. "Tall buildings are tall buildings, though, right?"

I glanced at Tamami to see if she might do anything to save me from the most boring inquisition in the world, but she'd already volunteered to wash the dishes. She rubbed her stomach in a circular motion and raised her eyebrows at me.

"And what do you do?" Mr. Takata asked.

I hated questions where people pegged your entire identity on a few words. Who was Baba? A country girl, a simple woman, some would say. A decent human being. Of course, her collection of travel brochures hinted at someone who was much more than that. A dreamer. But I knew what Uncle Takata meant, what he wanted to hear.

"I'm studying to be a dental assistant," I said. There was that smile again, yellowed from smoking a pack a day, signs of severe gingivitis. Definitely not a flosser.

My mother turned on the Nippon-Ham Fighters baseball game and opened another Kirin for Mr. Takata. She clearly didn't want me to speak or embarrass her.

"She's having a lot of fun during her stay abroad," my mother said. "Hollywood, the Mall of America. She doesn't realize how lucky she is to have this time to play around."

A few other neighbors dropped by after dinner, and while my parents were busy entertaining, I slipped outside and through the yard gate. When I turned back, I could see my mother through the living room window, shaking her head at me. When I was a teenager, she probably would have dragged me back inside by the ears and showed me my place. Now she seemed unsure of what move to make. I waved and texted: I'll be back at a reasonable hour.

I walked through the dimly lit streets toward the shopping district, texted my old friend Matsue, who waitressed at the Immigrants Cafe and Bar, a local dive for foreigners. As usual, the bar was packed with a mixture of Americans and Canadians and Australians, maybe a dozen total, surrounded by their Japanese friends, practicing their English. A man with a Russian accent sang Cyndi Lauper on a retro karaoke machine while a few Japanese women danced, waving their arms wildly in the air. I sat at the bar and scanned the room, spotted Matsue walking toward me with a tray.

"Hello, hello, hello. So good to see you!" she yelled over the Russian's singing. She gave me a kiss on both cheeks, French style, and hopped onto the stool beside me. "You look so American," she said.

"Is that good?" I asked. I looked down at my jeans and bargain-bin satin blouse, the beat-up Chucks that were about as old as my time in the States. Matsue, on the other hand, wore a cute beret, a dress with a butterfly print, and high heels.

"Yes, it's good!" She excused herself for a moment and brought a drink to another table before hopping back up beside me. "How long are you here for? Everybody misses you."

"A little over a week," I said. Most of the details didn't really need rehashing, since I knew she followed my holo-journal with her YamatoVision reality wrist projector. She gave me a rundown of old friends between her table service duties—everyone at the same job, Maiko and Junpei getting married soon, most still living at home. Kosuke, the boy with the wolfed-up hair who once thought I was the most beautiful thing in the world, was still breaking hearts in the back of Lawson's convenience store after his shifts at the post office.

"Nothing really changes," she said. "Do you miss home?"

I thought about Matsue's question as she went to serve a group of salarymen trying to outdrink their boss—*Kanpai! Kanpai! Kanpai!*—and decided to enjoy the moment, to be the person who used to go to the movies with her every week and jog along the river in the evenings. We used to complain to each other about our parents and Niigata, how it was nearly impossible to achieve your dreams in this country. But Matsue looked happy here and maybe I would have been, too.

"Yes and no," I answered when she returned to the bar. "To missing home, that is." I ordered another virgin margarita and told her that my life in Chicago was okay. I had Sean and his parents, friends from school, a community of Japanese who had recently moved to the city. My routines had turned into comforts—the same cafe in the morning, a smoothie after classes, Pilates every Saturday, board game night on Wednesdays with a group of Japanese college exchange students at the local Irish pub. But after leaving Matsue, I walked down the dark streets without any sense of danger. I didn't feel the need to walk briskly, mindful of the eyes around me. I had nothing to protect me hidden in my purse. I had forgotten what it was like to say hello to strangers, to be known by half the neighborhood, to simply be. I guess I missed that.

When I got home, it was past midnight. My mother was in the kitchen cooking appetizers for Baba's funeral reception. She offered me a sampler plate without a word. As I sat at the counter, I realized I had barely touched my dinner.

"These little cakes are delicious," I said. "Mango?"

"Mrs. Kishimoto's recipe," she said. "There are several other trays in her fridge. We're expecting a big turnout."

"Do you need any help?" I asked.

"Maybe earlier. Not now. Just about done."

Part of me wanted to run back to my room, though I knew I should stay with my mother. Maybe it was because I felt like I needed to be there for her. After all this time, her immovable expression of disgust and disappointment still held power over me. She poured us each a glass of water and sat across from me.

"I miss her," I said. "I'm sorry I wasn't here." I fidgeted with the photo of the ultrasound that was in my purse, debating whether to get it over with and tell her now.

"You broke Baba's heart," my mother said. "You broke all of our hearts." I wanted to tell her about the envelope of money and Baba's note, but I let her have this one for now, reenacting the old dance that allowed us to have a relationship. I whispered sorry again, that I knew it didn't mean much. I said that there was so much she might never understand. When a tear fell from my cheek, my mother left to fetch a box of tissues from the bathroom. I placed the photo of the ultrasound on the counter as she handed me one.

"We've done enough of that," she said, then suddenly looked closer at the photo. She stared at the life growing inside of me and poured herself another glass of water. I couldn't tell if she was angry or sad or even a little surprised. Something had changed, though; a new kind of gravity cemented her to the kitchen stool, prevented her from hugging her pregnant daughter. "Well," she said. "Boy or girl?"

"We don't know," I said. "We want it to be a surprise."

"We thought you'd be a boy. One of the reasons your father took you to all those soccer games when you were little. Think part of him still imagined you'd fill that role if he tried hard enough. Life is always easier for boys."

"We'll be happy with a boy or a girl."

My mother nodded and stood up, pausing as she passed me. She looked at the altar in the hallway, flickering with LED tea lights. For a moment, I thought she might congratulate me or hug me or do anything vaguely resembling motherly love.

"We're remembering her tomorrow. Celebrating all that my mother built. I expect you up early," my mother said. "Remember to pray before going to sleep."

Upstairs, I climbed into bed, inserted the second chip into the VR visor, and found myself surrounded by colorful stars exploding in the night sky—a summer fireworks festival on the banks of the Shinano River. Baba, Tamami, and my mother sat on a blanket, looking up and eating yakitori while my father recorded the moment. Baba wore her favorite navy-blue polyester dress with tiny white flowers, raised her hands in the air, and clapped with each display. As the other families came and went, they paid their respects to Baba, told her they missed seeing her walking around town. Even Miki and her family stopped by, asked Baba to send me their regards in America.

"She's doing very well," my mother said, a lie. At that point, they had barely heard a word from me.

Baba said nothing; she only smiled, the canyons of her face filled with sadness and truth. Did she think I had forgotten home? When the next explosion came, Baba did not clap. She stared at the dark water, reflecting the supernova above. I wondered what I'd been doing at that exact moment, what pressing matter had kept me from picking up the phone and telling my family: *I love you. I'm sorry. This is something I have to do.* I don't think anyone in the neighborhood was good at having important conversations with the younger generation. The elders had come to an understanding while recovering from a global pandemic that erected funerary towers into our skies. Nobody asked us what we wanted. Nobody questioned the new tradition. We were grave friends and that was that.

The soulful ballads of Misora Hibari, Baba's favorite enka singer, woke me the next morning. I could hear crowds chattering outside, trucks beeping in reverse as they delivered tables and chairs and flowers. My parents had closed off half the street with orange cones they'd borrowed from the local elementary school gym teacher. From my window, I could see the Fujita sisters smoking on the outskirts of the commotion, scowling. Everyone except Uncle Michihiro, who wore a T-shirt and an ill-fitting sports coat, had donned a vibrant yukata—pinks and purples and oranges with ornate floral patterns. My mother barked orders to the delivery drivers while some of the uncles constructed pop-up tents. Mrs. Kishimoto and the priest, who had come all the way from Osaka, arranged flowers on the reception lunch tables. At the center of the affair: a large portrait of Baba, surrounded by white chrysanthemums (the traditional choice) and sunflowers (Baba's favorite), and beside this lay Baba herself on a long metal tray beneath a plastic cover, as if her ashes were part of some buffet. Chopsticks rested on top for the family to use to pick out the remaining bones. The large urn, a nearly three-meter-tall chrome egg, sat on a wooden cradle that my great-grandfather had carved—and etched all over the egg were the names of everyone in the neighborhood who had already contributed their remains. I imagined the ashes of my aunties and uncles, my grandfather, Jiji, all layered on top of the others inside the pod, a stratum of our family.

I found my father downstairs, steaming the wrinkles out of my old gray-and-pink orchid yukata. Instead of our usual miso and rice ball breakfast, he'd made me waffles with a side of bacon and eggs. He hugged me tightly and told me he was happy for me.

"I'm looking forward to being a grandfather," he said. "When all of this is over, your mother will be able to celebrate your future. Don't worry."

After eating breakfast, I stepped out into our normally quiet street that had transformed into a celebration of Baba's life. I felt an immediate kinship with the Fujita sisters, who stuck to the sidelines like outcasts at a party. I thought about returning to the house until the ceremony began, but slimy Uncle Mich raised his eyebrows from across the street and turned his hands into pistols, firing them at me as he swaggered over.

"There's my girl," he said. "Long time. Too long."

"Uncle Mich," I said, more of a statement than a greeting. He asked me about America, about beautiful American girls. I kept walking and told him I needed to find my mother.

As I wove through the growing crowd, I found myself engaging in the sort of catch-up small talk I hated, repeating the same banal niceties. Finally, the priest rang a bell and called the ceremony to order, telling the crowd how a worldwide tragedy many generations ago had brought our country closer together. *In suffering*, he said, *we found our heart. In suffering, we found new traditions, a way forward.* My mother, my father, Tamami, and I stood before Baba's remains as the others found their seats. A canopy provided shade; mist fans dangled from the poles, helping everyone stay cool in the summer heat. A banner hung over their heads with a photo of Baba and her name—KIMIKO TADASHI: 2034–2105. We waited for my mother to go first. She signaled for my father to begin. We watched him slowly pick out the first bone fragments and place them in a small wooden box, one of several we planned to distribute among the neighborhood. A bit of toe or ankle? Who knows? I couldn't help but picture Baba watching us from the audience. Tamami followed, ribs and spine, and all that held the life of my baba together, all that contained the sickness that ate at her until the doctors found it too late. Every movement was slow and considered, as if Baba could feel us carrying the pieces of her, the pressure of the chopsticks cradling bone. My father signaled for me to continue. I'd like to imagine that I picked a part of Baba's smile, her cheeks, her head that held so much love and secrets and wisdom—she had given me permission to leave, but she would have wanted me to remember moments like this, my mother sobbing in the background. When it was finally my mother's turn, I watched her tears darken the ashes, her unsteady hand barely able to hold the chopsticks. I stood beside her, wrapped one arm around her waist, steadied her wrist with my other hand.

"No tears," I said. She looked at me, nodded, and wiped them away. "Together."

"Together," she said. Our hands combed the ashes, removing the last bone fragments. I felt like Baba had given us one final gift.

My mother transformed after the ceremony. I heard her laughing with the neighbors, telling stories about Baba—how her mother had sewn holographic pins onto jackets for several of the uncles during their virtual pop idols concert phase, or how when Jiji was still alive, she took ballroom and country line dancing lessons and won a competition. There were stories of Baba as a young woman, working as a volunteer nurse, inspired after she survived the plague as an infant. And maybe this was more tale than fact, but one neighborhood policeman told everyone about the time Baba helped move the belongings of her friends after the city forced flood zone residents to relocate.

"She strapped a dresser to her back and ordered everyone to do their share," the police officer elaborated. "I heard she had boxes of their belongings piled high in her yard until they could figure out their housing."

"I heard she paddled an inflatable raft through the city after a typhoon hit, before the seawalls were finished," a young boy said. "She saved two cats, three dogs, one rabbit, and at least five families."

The street was crawling with stragglers well into the evening as the cleanup began and Baba's ashes, now in the urn, were taken away. Apart from the one burst of grief, the day had seemed to energize my mother. She asked if we should all walk to the cemetery tower together to see if the urn was ready.

"I know they said it might take a day, but I need to get off the street for a while," my mother said. "We've earned it. Some power walking will do us good."

Tamami stayed behind to help the drunk aunties and uncles find their way home, so it was only me and my father, trailing far behind as my mother sprinted ahead of us. Even from our residential neighborhood, it was hard to escape the view of the closest funerary towers. The same was true in Chicago or in any major city—repurposed skyscrapers to hold and honor the dead. It seemed like everyone was walking either to or from a funeral. Death had become a way of life.

"How was today for you?" my father asked.

"It was nice seeing everybody there for Baba," I said. My father was an old-school type and didn't really say much. He basically let our mother raise us unless she needed backup dealing with bad behavior. I could tell the news of the baby had filled him with joy, though. He kept staring at my stomach, a weird grin on his face. We walked for several more blocks in silence.

"I think today really helped your mother. She's always been sick—not like Baba, of course—but the last few years have been hard. Our neighborhood has become a lot more important to her. It's something she can count on."

"It sounds like you're trying to make a point," I said.

"I was never angry with you," he said. "And I'm so happy for you and Sean. I know it's different for your generation, for you especially. You need to move on. But do you miss any of this? Could you ever come back?"

I watched my mother swing her arms in the air, occasionally waving to an acquaintance, a group of teenagers huddled outside the manga shop I used to call my church, the same old men I saw growing up sitting at the counter of their sake bar. In the street, self-driving taxis began their nighttime circuit picking up salarymen from their required nights on the town with superiors. Somewhere behind us, Tamami was walking the aunties and uncles back to their homes. I thought about how, if I raised my child here, they would have an entire neighborhood of love.

"I do," I said. "Miss it, that is."

We approached the funerary tower and my father stopped before we caught up with my mother.

"Your mother loves you," he said. "And I think she's forgiven you, even if she'll never admit it. She wants you, and your family, in our life, even if you're an ocean away."

On the twenty-second floor in suite 38B, my mother tapped her phone against a sensor in a wooden pedestal that stood in the center of the room. A holographic cherry blossom tree sprouted from the cold linoleum floor and Baba appeared sitting on a stone bench, staring up at the petals as they danced throughout the room. The urn arrived shortly afterward, emerging from a trapdoor, coming to rest on the pedestal. My mother pressed another selection on her mortuary phone app and Jiji appeared next to Baba, playing the violin. And then the great-aunties and -uncles, as if they had just walked through the walls. A miniature poodle that belonged to my cousin came up to Jiji and curled at his feet. The barren floor was now a garden populated by stone lanterns, meticulously raked sand. I imagined how I might be captured here if I chose to remain a grave friend. Would I be immortalized as an old woman, a little girl, a mother? Could I see Sean and my child here, sitting beside my grandparents? Both my mother and I waved our hands through Baba's image.

"She wanted to see the world that she missed out on," my mother said. "Before the world was sick. Before the oceans rose, when the city was as it used to be hundreds of years ago—no concrete walls over our shoulders, no funerary towers."

I walked around the room to stand before every ancestor and prayed to them, let the light of their images wash over me.

There would be more conversations and arrangements to come— visits to Chicago, visits to Japan when my child was old enough— but right then I sat silently, on ripples of sand made of light with my mother and father, and listened to Jiji's music, clinging to the perpetual flurry of cherry blossoms that held us all together.

THE SCOPE OF POSSIBILITY

When she was seven hundred years old, still a baby by world builder standards, I walked my daughter to the seed field where I had been designing Earth. Kids usually weren't allowed in the fields until they had completed their apprenticeship in their second millennium, but I needed to show her; she needed to understand. We walked between the rows of giant spheres, some as big as moons, glowing with ribbons of light, as I told her stories about each one. The fields are where most of the advanced civilizations in the galaxy are born and, for all we know, every galaxy has a world builder planet orbiting just outside in the dark, utterly alone. At the time, our world was only a giant playground to her. I stood in front of a tiny blue seed and handed her a probability scope.

This is what I've been doing for most of your life, I said. And one day, not long from now, this is where I'll go. To observe, guide if needed. I'll be one of them, little one. I'll be among their first and their last. But I'll always be your mother.

*　　*　　*

Nuri, my poor girl, looked betrayed when I left. The light within her flicked off for a moment when she realized I wasn't coming back. No more walks, no more telling bad jokes to the laughing tree, no more looking through the probability scope together at funny animals that may or may not exist in the future. And that's all I could think about, trapped in my cradle, my space pod (whatever you want to call it) for centuries. I was so much older when my mother left me.

I had already completed my training. She was too young to realize, you see. We could get from point A to point B much faster, sure—a day, a week, a month for the farthest corners—and maybe the elders wanted it this way, for the world builders to have the time to dwell on what they'd left behind, to become comfortable with forgetting. But how could I ever forget?

I landed beneath the water and washed ashore as a small sea creature, an ancestor of the starfish. My cradle, as far as I know, has long been trapped in hundreds of feet of ice. When I first arrived, I could not talk, obviously did not have the biological means to do so, could not write in journals or relay these words as I do now. I've confided in others now and then. But I had to be careful. I can't come back from some things—the sorts of deaths that were popular for so long, burning and decapitation. For those first few eons, there was nothing but water, ash, the simplest of organisms, and the seed I had launched into the heart of the planet. I fell in love with a box jelly and then a trilobite, but these were single-sided love affairs.

*   *   *

She didn't understand. She asked if she could go. Mommy, please, she said. I'll be good. The elders, who determined seed launch order long before any of us were born, assigned my husband and Nuri to be among the last world builders to remain. And so we grew used to saying goodbye to everyone we cared about—our neighbors, my best friend, the boy who told me he would love me forever before leaving to care for a planet populated by bipedal crustaceans.

I remember holding the scope to the seed, helping Nuri carry its weight, adjusting the dials so she could see what might happen to

Earth. Probability scopes are an important part of our technology—they're like telescopes but fitted with lenses made from the jellylike remains of our ancestors. They allow us to see through reality based on the contents of each seed. My father used to say our planet and everyone on it was made of pure possibility and that's what made us special, made us able to create, become anything we wanted.

And what happens to us when we leave our world? What happens to us as we travel the stars? Children were trained to answer: "We become everything we pass until we become the thing we created." Our bodies would transform as we passed star system after star system, a catalog of everything our race had given birth to—a Xhilian, a Parsu, a Tarlian Mork, a Quiali, a Dimetrodon of Pangaea.

*   *   *

After millions of years I decided to start my first Earth family in order to feel whole again, despite the strict world builder tenet to observe, never to interfere. As a Neanderthal, I helped my tribes survive migration and winter and wars with early humans. I fell in love with a man who killed a saber-toothed cat with nothing but his muscular bare hands and a small stone blade. We made love in caves and beside the carcasses of woolly mammoths. And when my womb began to grow, I thought I could finally be happy with the illusion of a mortal life. But when my daughter, whose name was a series of trills, came, I realized that I had imperfectly shape-shifted into my humanoid form. Maybe a gene where there shouldn't be one, or a chromosome, led to my newborn glowing like a nebula when she took her first breaths. She had her father's brow ridges and eyes and stubborn demeanor. She had my nose and shards of my home world flowing through her veins like stars—and for a time, I thought my loneliness and desire to create from nothing but love and hope had produced a most beautiful life.

But then a virus bloomed in the fragile bodies of my cave mates around my daughter's eighth year, and I realized there was a cost to my selfishness. At first, we believed it was a normal sickness from the cold of the tundra, the nights when our fires went dark. But then, one by one, our hunters returned with fevers, mothers caring for children struggling to breathe. I could see parts of me glowing hot inside their translucent skin. Soon I was the only one tending the fires, roaming the plains for game, cradling the lifeless bodies of those who would not wake. Everything I put in my daughter's mouth came back up. I prayed that because she was mine, whatever plague I had inadvertently passed to the others would somehow spare her. But I watched her stomach sink into itself, the blood bubbling from her lips. I held her close to my chest, absorbed her last heartbeats, her last breath, the last sounds she'd ever utter, a strained and mournful *krrrrrrrrrrrr*. I left my daughter on a bed of leaves and grass beside a carving of my star system, a place I wanted her to dream about as she left this world, covered her in a hide decorated with the seashells I had collected during my early travels as a hominid. I told her she had a sister somewhere out there. I told her that she would always be a part of me. I etched the memories and songs and science of my world that I did not want lost to time into the floors of the cave. I built a fire, sang one final lullaby to my daughter, and left as the sun rose. I crossed sheets of ice, transformed into a human, and lived alone for centuries, trying to forgive myself for being so selfish, so careless, ensuring my mistake would never happen again.

*   *   *

Other world builders might have left them to their struggle, but how could I when my humans crawled toward the precipice of possibility? They called me Tiamat, the Sumerians. And while I wore another face back then, I can assure you I was no multiheaded dragon goddess as the myths recorded. I taught them to fish, to craft nets and small vessels. I taught them irrigation, how to wield the power of the Tigris and Euphrates. It was a busy time, as you might guess. I immersed myself in these teachings, with side projects like building ziggurats. If I stopped for long, I would miss Nuri and my cave daughter whenever I saw a couple embrace or heard a child crying. I had a cat named Nuri during the kingdom of Nebuchadnezzar. For a while, saying her name out loud brought me comfort. I could pretend my daughter was with me. Nuri, dinner is ready. Nuri, time for bed. Nuri, I love you. Nuri, have you met your sister among the stars? Where are you, Nuri? Where are you?

*   *   *

Do you see them? I asked her. Through the scope, we saw people hunting strange beasts with long sticks, people much smaller than us with skin you couldn't see through, no light dancing within like nebulae. They had hair, like so many species, and traveled great distances in groups, carrying fire. The grass was green, not purple like our rolling hills. Some families had four-legged pets like her Zhirian Jabi (except without the horns and scales). I saw wars among larger tribes, wars of people clad in metal. I saw tiny vessels breaking free of the planet, great cities floating above in rings of glass. I saw a civilization that could destroy itself before it even reached the nearest star. But I also saw a world that would be the first to witness the quiet of intergalactic space and walk on the ruins of whatever remains of us.

When I think about my world, I imagine my husband in the fields, tending to the last seed our people ever launched. The riverbeds have grown dry and dull, no longer gleaming; our ganglia of caves succumbed to darkness long ago. Most of our kind have already left to tend their worlds, find other homes, blend in somewhere, living out eternity as simply as they can. The fields are empty now save for one seed, leaving large tracts of our planet pocked with craters holding only remnants of the worlds they once contained—voices, moments in history, the sounds of animals, the smell of exotic fruit. I'd like to believe my husband and daughter are getting on well, that in my absence they've learned to lean on each other. Do they visit Earth's seed crater and train a probability scope on scraps of light in the soil to catch a glimpse of my new home? Do they dream about the lives I've lived? Do they, as I do, gaze at the sky, all the billions of years of light that separate us, before going to sleep?

*　　*　　*

The destruction of Earth's first advanced civilization was partly my fault, I admit. I gave the Atlantians too much too soon. They weren't ready for the knowledge. I felt sorry for the children—how they ran, screamed for their parents as Atlantis shook. Oh, and how it shook. Their scientists shot three tiny stars beneath the ground, hoping to quell the shaking of the volcano, absorb the energy of the planet. They twisted my words, weaponized them, until even I could not say for certain what would happen. And so, the stars grew until the ground cracked and glowed red. The quake amplified and the sea enveloped the barriers of the city's outer rings, swallowed the land for as far as I could see. Stone guardians and ancient kings the size of skyscrapers collapsed, crumbling beneath the waves. I watched from one of the few boats that made it out, holding a girl who had no one else. I sang her lullabies from seven worlds, the same songs I sang to Nuri. And when we landed in what would become Greece, I slipped away, leaving the child beside the belongings of a young couple. But before I left, I whispered to her: "Your family will always be with you. Don't forget them. Be strong." I walked and walked and spent the next few ages alone. I let humanity be.

*   *   *

On my home world right before I left, I came upon my husband in the seed fields showing Nuri how world builders inject possibility into each seed, adding with trained precision the chemicals and minerals we debate for thousands of years.

"It's not entirely up to you," my husband explained to Nuri. "We plant potential realities. What we see through our scopes may or may not happen—at least in this universe."

"So, who decides?" Nuri asked.

"Some of it is chance," I explained. "Hope, love, ingenuity. Possibility is more than what runs through our veins, little one."

Nuri walked up to the seed that was assigned to her and held a possibility scope to its glowing membrane.

"I want these flying creatures to live," she said. She wanted her world to have a fighting chance, a species of furry animals that might fly one day. That world has a 70 percent chance of being known as Vara to its first civilizations and as a series of three long, high-pitched whistles by the last intelligent species to inhabit it before its star burns away its history. I've watched the possibility of this last civilization, seen their slim chance of escaping their star's destruction. You see, this is partly why Earth hasn't received any messages from other worlds. Most have perished by the time their light reaches our sky. Sometimes hundreds of light-years exist between even the simplest forms of life.

*   *   *

You'd think someone who came from outer space wouldn't be as susceptible to astronomical pickup lines, but you'd be wrong. In the sixteenth century, I lived as Marina Gamba in Venice, and was taken in by the passion of a scholar who, of course correctly, believed that the Earth revolved around the sun. He said the cluster of moles on my back looked like the Pleiades. Now, what else can I tell you about Galileo? We mapped the stars together before and after making love. And even though we couldn't see many worlds with his telescope, I would point to a dark patch of sky and say, *There. There is so much light you cannot see. And there, past it all, is where I come from.* He'd ask me about other species, why the spaces between civilizations were so great. And I'd tell him that most worlds can't handle the company. They'd destroy each other out of fear or ignorance. So, the spaces are a deterrent, but they are also a challenge, for the worlds to rise above the odds, to thrive together, and perhaps even find us— what is left of us.

In the seventeenth century, perhaps fifty years after my death as Marina, I became Isaac Newton's roommate while at Cambridge. Isaac mostly thought I was a fool, but maybe a part of him believed my stories every time I corrected his math. When we got drunk, he'd ask me to tell him tales of my home world. I told him about Earth's seed and Nuri and the promise my husband made to send my daughter to me, to care for Vara in her stead.

"But you would never see him again," my dear Isaac said, as I again corrected his math.

"We've spent more lifetimes together than you can imagine," I answered. "I spent my little girl's childhood creating this planet. I missed it. I need to see who she's become."

*   *   *

As more opportunity and freedom pulled many across the ocean, so did I find myself aboard a ship to America, landing first in Virginia in 1820. I lived quietly for decades, exploring this young country with whatever face and society could grant me passage and access. I attended the Seneca Falls Convention for women's rights in 1848, posing as a milliner from Delaware, filled with the spirit of possibility, and listened to the words of Mott and Stanton. I thought about all that had become possible for humanity simply because I had chosen to break the rules, to dare to dream.

I unexpectedly found love again not long after the conference and headed south, instead of following the gold rush as I had originally planned.

"A big family. Three boys. No, four," my Elliot said one evening as we worked to build our house outside of Raleigh.

"I see. And where am I during all of this?" I laughed. I had told him I wanted a family, too. I think it took a few thousand years for me to really want to try again. I told myself I would be careful this time, that I had become adept at understanding the human form. Despite the tremors of war, our farm felt like it existed in another realm of hope. And for a time, it seemed like the distant echoes of musket fire would never reach us.

Now, I won't dwell on the specifics of what those soldiers did to me or to my husband or our little boy. But after they left me for dead, I had nothing. I buried my family next to our dogwood tree and burned our home. As I have done so many times before, I moved on from human life to human life. The very nature of my existence, the pull of seeing my creation, the knowledge that I can help others in need, demands that I reinvent myself, though I still dream of my children. I still whisper their names in the dark.

Japan was reinventing itself when I arrived during its Meiji period—first as an American soldier in the late 1800s, helping to train the Japanese in heavy artillery, and then as the wife of a cormorant fisherman. We had three children, all boys, who died fighting. My husband died a year later, executed in the street for spreading lies against the emperor, or so they said. We missed our boys. We wanted the fighting to stop. Our neighbors believed that I jumped off a cliff in my grief, but I merely walked to another prefecture and onto a ship, waving goodbye to no one in particular as I searched for another life.

I transformed from Ayumi to Kiyo in San Francisco, and later into "Violet" during and after World War II, when my husband, Tomo, said we needed to hold on to who we were but that we had to play *their game* to survive. We packed our bags as the soldiers waited outside our door. I packed my daughter Michiko's bag, put on her coat and hat. I looked back on our home, on our city we had grown to love. Our neighbors peered through their windows—the O'Sullivans and Vaybergs and Cohens. Michiko waved to them from the street. No one spoke for us. No one stood up. In the stables of the Santa Anita Park racetrack in Arcadia, I slept, curled into Tomo and Michiko, crying for what the world had become. I sang to my daughter in alien languages that I had not spoken in centuries, hoping to find a melody to calm her once she realized we were not going home.

"We're going to be okay," I whispered in Michiko's ear. "As long as we're together." I told her this in the camp yards before I sent her to play with the other children. I told her this after days of blood on her pillow and my husband's pleas to the guards that sent him to the infirmary. I still have the doll I made from an old dress she held on to that last night, her shoes, the sound of her laughter. Nothing remained for me and Tomo when we finally returned to our old neighborhood save for a box of books and some clothes that the Cohens had been able to hide.

Sometimes it's hard to keep the facts straight after so long, to remember all that has happened (though the emotions remain like stains). I want to say I did right by Tomo, but he looked too much like our daughter. I want to say we talked, and I kissed him goodbye, that he saw me disappear over a hill into the fog. Even with my mind being what it is, I find myself playing roulette with these moments at night. Sometimes it feels like I've imagined entire lifetimes. I tell myself that some confusion is okay, even forgetting, so long as I hold on to what's most important—where I've come from, who I've loved, how the world (and I) can be better, and the hope that I'll hold Nuri again.

*   *   *

Half the planet attended the launch of Earth's seed, perhaps a few thousand at that point, some coming from as far as the polar continents. My daddy was the center of attention. I could tell from the way the others talked about him that he was a kind of hero in their eyes, a world builder from a respected family whose assistance on my seed and numerous others had become the stuff of legend. *Remember the time you . . . Oh, that was an incredible species . . . Fine work you and your father did on Rylia, the damn asteroids ruin everything.* My husband played with Nuri beyond the crowds.

Seeds did not launch into the sky or leave a plume of smoke like a rocket. The cradles that held them disrupted the fabric of space, opening a corridor to the target star system. I placed my hands on the cradle and entered the coordinates for Terran space. And before long, the seed began to shake and slowly sank into a whirlpool of the night sky, until a few ribbons of light were all that remained.

After the launch, we held each other, glowing as one. My husband turned to me and said it was time. No receptions or banquets, no delay. We decided to be quick about it. I thought it would be better if it just happened. Nuri approached cautiously and I held her tight. I love you, I said. I'll love you forever. I gave her one of two pendants I had made containing possibility from the core of our planet. Outside our world, the crystals would glow like tiny stars when near each other, beacons lighting the way. Come find me, I said, wiping away our tears. I crawled into the cradle that once held Earth, and it closed shut like a shell.

*   *   *

I didn't always allow myself to grow old and have what most would perceive as a natural death, but the life you see now will likely end this way—a sickness, a fall, peacefully in my sleep or struggling for my final breath (then always a sleight of hand before burial or burning). For a time, I stopped looking for Nuri, believing the more I wanted this future, the longer it would take. I became a child again for the first time in millennia, growing up among flower power and marches for freedom and fists raised in the air. I believed change was possible, that my creations were finally going to get it right. Keiko Irakawa became Nova Moon during the sixties, marched against the Vietnam War. As Clara Miyashiro, I tried to stop the globe from warming as the glaciers and permafrost melted, knowing my oldest mistake might be unlocked from the past—the plague that took my first Earth daughter, my first humanoid family and friends. Yes, it was my fault, you see (but it was also me who found the cure). I was so afraid of losing everything if I told you, after everything you've lost. No, it was a mistake, you see. I don't regret finding love and always thinking about possibility—maybe that's the biggest part of myself that went into creating this world. It's what I loved about you when I first saw you talking about the stars.

Kepler 62-e, Tau Ceti e, Gliese 667 C f—at least that's what our colleagues call them, but I know these worlds by other names. From radio telescopes around the world, we listened for a message from our starship, finally hearing word that its journey continues. For many, all of that is ancient history, the ships we sent out considered lost. But I still believe the *Yamato* (along with your son) may send a message someday in our distant future and tell us they've found home.

You asked me once, as I was helping remove the singularity from your head, why I was so fascinated with space. You said that I looked up at the sky like no other astronomer. I told you I loved thinking about the possibilities. And that wasn't a lie. But now you know the rest, and you probably think I'm crazy or maybe, if you've believed any of this, you hate me a little or can't quite think of me anymore as your wife. I don't share my whole story with everyone. Most people couldn't handle it; the truth would ruin their memory of me. But this is who I am, the woman you fell in love with. You've been my life for over seventy years, a blip in my life span, but a gloriously memorable one nonetheless. Now close your eyes for a second. Open them. Yes, it's me. This is what I really look like. Light. Radiant? Angelic? I suppose. Sometimes I forget how I might look to humans. You can touch me. It's okay. I am this, but I am also your Theresa. My original name sounds like Qweli with a human tongue. In your final moments, I want you to see all of me.

*   *   *

Naked, brunette, and so very cold. That's how I woke up when I first took human form long after my lives as other beasts and proto-humans. I could hear the ocean, feel the waves beneath me. I often imagine what my first daughter will wake up to here. Perhaps the sky will be filled with large, colorful kites flying in the wind—dragons and butterflies and biplanes. Not far away, people playing volleyball will notice her. *Hey, hey! Are you okay? Miss! Hey, lady!* She will stand up, unashamed of her body, as they run toward her. She will study the softness of her form, the grains of Earth on her skin. Perhaps a man will cover her with his jacket.

"Are you okay?" he will say. "Here, let me help you."

People won't accept that a woman just appeared from the sea. People want a name, a town, a phone number, a designation like John or Jane or Zoe or Sebastian.

Maybe she'll fall in love with whoever finds her, like in some problematic fairy tale, or she'll have to escape from harm, or she'll arrive surrounded by ice or sand and will wonder if she landed on the right planet at all. Who knows? Maybe she is already here. Maybe stories of her arrival have been captured in conspiracy theorist forums—UFO sightings, crash landings, government coverups. Maybe I was asleep while my crystal reached out with its light.

Yes, I know it's a long shot. Yes, it's a tiny planet, a large world. But you and I found each other, didn't we? I can't know for certain if she has come or ever will. All I have is this crystal around my neck, a tiny piece of possibility—permission to keep moving and living and searching, like any of you. It is the hope that one day in this life or the next or the one after that, it'll glow so bright that people will stop to look. *Nuri, is that you? Nuri, I have so many stories to tell.* And I'll stop to search the crowd, the windows of the skyscrapers, the foothills and houses in the distance for a tiny star guiding me home.

To whoever might be listening, to whoever is there: This is the U.S.S. *Yamato*, Interplanetary Exploration Mission 1. Launch year 2037. We've arrived home and it's absolutely beautiful. I'm sending this message from our temporary field base while we survey candidate regions for a settlement, and I'd be lying if I said this was my first attempt at this brief message. For us, only a few years have passed in contrast to over six thousand years on Earth. Our historians have begun to sift through the messages that the ship has intercepted during our big sleep—millennia of history that will require generations to read through, let alone understand. The last transmission we received was more than one thousand years ago, when humanity constructed a Dyson sphere around the sun, fueling metropolises on Mars and Luna and Titan. You've sent us footage of the first birth on another planet, the trials that gave basic human rights to artificial intelligence, to those who have uploaded their consciousness into the cloud. It is difficult to comprehend just how far you've come, and I wonder if, apart from our tiny blue planet, we have much in common at all anymore. Have you forgotten us? Have you let us go? Have you died in a spark of war? Or have you gone searching, as we have, for a fresh start? Let us know you're okay. Know that we'll be waiting should you come to find us. Until then, this is the *Yamato* signing off. I might wake up early to watch the sun rise.

—Colonel Franklin Barret, USAF Retired

ACKNOWLEDGMENTS

It's difficult to account for everyone and everything that has helped make this book a reality since my first hurried concept notes more than ten years ago in a Tokyo internet cafe. But it's hard to imagine a writing life where I'm not preoccupied by the relationships woven through our ancient past, as well as those that will reside in our future in interstellar space. This book would not have been written were it not for the Time-Life Mysteries of the Unknown volumes in my elementary school library, Carl Sagan guiding my imagination through the stars in his series, *Cosmos*, and hours upon hours of *Star Trek*—for the heart just as much as the adventure. I also owe a debt of gratitude to the following books, which helped me wade through the complexities of death and grief, often when I was navigating my own losses: *How We Die* and *How We Live* by Sherwin Nuland, *The American Way of Death* by Jessica Mitford, *Stiff* by Mary Roach, and *Consciousness beyond Life* by Pim van Lommel.

Beyond this foundation, I first need to profusely thank my agent, Annie Hwang, who believed in *How High We Go in the Dark* through several evolutions and who guided me through the submission/deal process in the early months of the COVID-19 pandemic with empathy, enthusiasm, and careful consideration. At William Morrow, I couldn't have asked for a more passionate editor than Jessica Williams, who helped me bring to life my worlds and characters beyond my wildest expectations. I'm also grateful to the eagle eyes of my copyeditor, Laura Cherkas, who combed through time and space to help me better realize the architecture of the book. And to everyone else on the William Morrow team, including my publicist, Eliza

Rosenberry; marketer Ryan Shepherd; and publishers Liate Stehlik and Jennifer Hart for helping bring this big part of my life to readers. And to everyone on the Bloomsbury UK team, including Joel Arcanjo, Rachel Wilkie, Ros Ellis, and particularly my editor Paul Baggaley, whose early reaction to *How High We Go in the Dark* on a video conference call nearly made me cry.

A heartfelt thank-you to all of the writers and editors who have read early extracts of this book along the way or who have simply provided much-needed community. In particular I'd like to thank Dan Paul, Andy Harnish, Jessica Easto, Ashley Sigmon, Pinckney Benedict, Scott Blackwood, and Beth Lordan for early feedback on chapters that would later prove instrumental in this book. To Alexander Weinstein for the literary community on Martha's Vineyard during which time I toiled away on my novel in my room late at night. And to all of my old *Zoetrope* friends, particularly Ovo Adagha, whose invitation to contribute to an international anthology early in my career gave me a needed push to pursue my literary dreams. To all of my students past and present—I am only the writer I am because of you. You keep me on my toes. You remind me of the utter joy of telling stories. There are too many people to thank here, but you know who you are. I see you. I appreciate you. I want to shout your successes from the rooftops.

To my family, who opened my world through frequent trips to the bookstore and comics store and who never shied away from encouraging my strange and nerdy hobbies. And most of all, I owe a debt of gratitude to my wife, Cole, who has listened to every halfbaked idea and rambling brainstorm, and has put up with eating dinner just a bit later whenever I was writing. Sometimes I cannot believe that I get to share a life of stories with you. I promise we'll eat dinner in a minute.

P.S.

Insights,
Interviews
& More...

✳

About the author

About the book

Read on

Meet Sequoia Nagamatsu

Lauren B. Photography

SEQUOIA NAGAMATSU is a Japanese American writer and the managing editor of *Psychopomp Magazine*. He is the author of the award-winning short story collection *Where We Go When All We Were Is Gone*. He currently lives in Minnesota with his wife, their cat, a real dog, and a robot dog named Calvino. ◠

A Conversation with Sequoia Nagamatsu

A version of this interview was first published as "Sequoia Nagamatsu on Writing the Grief and Connections of an Enduring Pandemic" by Literary Hub *on January 25, 2022. The interviewer is Jane Ciabattari.*

Jane Ciabattari: On Instagram, you've posted some capsule summaries with images of your chapters, including this of your opening chapter: "The first location in my novel: a climate research station near the Batagaika Crater in Siberia where the 30,000-year-old remains of a girl have been recovered." This setting is the largest permafrost crater in the world, greatly expanded by climate change since the 1960s, the location for the recovery of such creatures as a well-preserved Pleistocene-era foal found in 2018. In your story, set in 2030, Dr. Cliff Miyashiro from UCLA has come to visit the crater where his daughter, Clara, a climate researcher, has fallen and died.

Your opening lines are evocative: "In Siberia, the thawing ground was a ceiling on the verge of collapse, sodden with ice melt and the mammoth detritus of prehistory. The kilometer-long Batagaika Crater had been widening with temperature rise like some god had unzipped the snow-topped marshlands, exposing woolly rhinos and other extinct beasts." In this case, the creature revealed is a young girl, aged eight, who the scientists suspect may be harboring a virus they're beginning to call the Batagaika virus. This "Arctic virus" seeds the later stories, which extend through multiple centuries. Your characters Cliff; his daughter, Clara; his wife, Miki; his granddaughter, Yumi—even the prehistoric girl—recur. How did you spin this complex web of interconnections? Did you use outlines? Images?

Sequoia Nagamatsu: There are a couple of corkboards in my home office that have been home to the evolving structure of the novel for a few years now—very messy index cards connected to each other with yarn and pushpins and color-coded Post-it notes. I think once I had settled on the linear progression of the plague and oriented the chapters in time to some degree, I thought about characters that I wished I had known more about and what their predicament might be as the plague and its aftermath evolved over the course of years (and generations). But beyond wanting to provide deeper character continuity (and I'm well aware that a lack of continuity is something that people who don't read a lot of short fiction tend to dislike), I was also mindful about how the world around the plague would evolve over the decades— technology (including social media platforms), financial corporations tied to funerary industries, and, of course, the backdrop of a planet changed by the climate crisis.

So yes, outlines and mapping were certainly part of my process in spinning this web, but so was a lot of research—lots of time in virtual reality staring at desolate (and beautiful) landscapes in Siberia, holding distant stars in my virtual hands, studying sea rise projection maps, and immersing myself in an app where perfect strangers anonymously confess their hopes and fears in a surreal landscape. In my final rounds of revisions, I also ensured that I was weaving enough "cosmic" Easter eggs throughout the book that would help provide another frame for the novel, one that isn't fully realized until the final chapter (and in some ways forces readers to reconsider the chapters that they have previously read).

JC: Some of the chapters in *How High We Go in the Dark* were originally published as stories as far back as 2011. When did you begin creating this universe? How did you decide upon the order? Did you plan episodes in advance, or did they evolve organically?

SN: Really 2009 (with the oldest story having been initially conceived in a very different form in 2008). I was a baby writer back then, so to say that the journey of this novel follows the journey of my trajectory and interests as a writer isn't inaccurate. The early seeds of the novel began as stand-alone stories. For a time, I thought these stories would simply form another linked collection surrounding alternative forms of grief and funerary ritual, but in 2014 I read an *Atlantic* article about scientists discovering ancient viruses in melting Arctic ice. While I was never interested in a stereotypical Hollywood pandemic narrative, I was interested in the climate change aspect to this story and began thinking about how such a plague could provide a kind of through line for my growing body of work revolving around grief and conversations about death.

So, for years what became chapters in *How High We Go in the Dark* were one-off explorations. The organization and heavy revision to allow for linear progression, character continuity, and other frames came much later (and often out of order). The first chapter was actually the last chapter I wrote, and the last chapter was something that I first explored in graduate school as a potential book idea but that I ultimately felt could inject a kind epic scope and universality into the novel that I wanted to be present.

JC: In his late daughter's sleeping pod, Cliff finds the dogū figurine he'd bought her years before at a museum of ancient Japanese history, believed by the Jōmon people to be "capable of absorbing negative energy, evil, and illness." In other chapters you describe funerary skyscrapers like those in Tokyo, for the remains of a rapidly aging population. How have Japanese folklore and funerary practices influenced this novel?

A Conversation with Sequoia Nagamatsu (*continued*)

SN: I was living in Japan around 2008, teaching English for a couple of years, which was a trip that was, in part, giving me much-needed space to reset my life and grieve over the loss of my grandfather, who helped raise me. I became fascinated with different ways people might honor their loved ones (and in particular how Japan as a country faced unique obstacles having such a large elderly population). In Japan there are funerary skyscrapers and hotels operated by mortuary companies. And, of course, my first collection, *Where We Go When All We Were Is Gone,* was primarily inspired by Japanese folklore, but I don't think I completely got away from that in this novel. I couldn't. Because I think to write about Japan—to write about the future of some of these characters—is to reconcile the tensions between tradition/the past/spirituality and an identity/reality that has become so associated with technology, innovation, and corporate enterprise.

My characters often resort to technological means as a bridge to connect, to grieve, but there's a limit to this . . . at some point that tech isn't enough (or there's a recognition of the illusion). A conversation needs to happen. A VR headset needs to be put down. A robot dog containing a mother's voice falls into disrepair. A lot of these explorations aren't purely tied to Japan. I think many communities have distanced themselves from older traditions, and sadly, the process of death has become a highly impersonal and logistical one.

We cry and mourn for a time. But then we are often forced to become event planners. We need to assess finances and pay medical bills. There's so little room to honor our loved ones in the way we'd like. I think part of my intent was to meld tech and a yearning for more traditional modes of connection and remembrance, to acknowledge the hybrid spaces we're already inhabiting in terms of grief—how they help, how they might fall short. To what extent does an outpouring of love from strangers on Twitter help someone process a loss? That's a question I asked myself as I shared my own tragedies with online communities. Something that felt both strange and natural. Something that I needed in that moment.

JC: You move effortlessly from Siberia to the United States to Japan in this novel, and also into outer space, in the spaceship *Yamato*, six thousand centuries ahead, and even beyond time, with a narrator who birthed the girl found in that Siberian crater and has inserted herself in human form into centuries of history since. Which of these was the most difficult to research? Which is your favorite? Does living in Hawaii, California, Japan, Minnesota, and wherever else make you attuned to variations in setting?

SN: The most difficult (or, I guess, the most involved) was probably some of the detail surrounding the starship *Yamato* (theoretical forms of propulsion) and the stops the ship makes along the way to the expedition's new home on Kepler 186f, the first planet with a radius similar to Earth's that was discovered in the habitable zone of its star. I wanted to get as much scientific detail right (everything from the probable color of flora on another planet to how long a ship with these theoretical boosters might take to get to particular star systems) without being burdensome to my core focus: character development and relationships. As a lifelong *Star Trek* nerd (and just all-around space exploration enthusiast), this was also probably my favorite chapter to research.

As for living in many places in my life? I think it has, to some degree, helped me be a bit more nimble when exploring locations in my stories. I'll certainly have some affinity for the West Coast (particularly the San Francisco Bay Area) since I spent my teen years and early twenties there, but I kind of consider myself to not really have a home base in a traditional sense. My home exists only in memories and with relationships I have with people.

JC: "Through the Garden of Memory," originally titled "How High We Go in the Dark," is a dreamlike story in which the narrator, who is in the hospital dying of the Arctic virus, his parents at his side, wakes to a limbo-like darkness and finds others with him. He urges them to sing, to create a human pyramid, to explore glowing orbs of memory that appear. He and his "void mates" hear a baby crying and together decide he ▶

A Conversation with Sequoia Nagamatsu *(continued)*

will bring this infant to the top of the pyramid to be sucked upward into . . . life? What is the thinking behind this story?

SN: Some people assume this to be the afterlife, but I never explicitly state what this void is or if the people there are dead or not. I want this to be somewhat unclear, but as we discover in a later chapter, it does seem to be possible for someone to return from this void into the world of the living. I've always been very fascinated with consciousness studies, with the idea of a collective consciousness, so I think those interests really fueled the seeds of this chapter.

I'll also nod at an episode of *The Twilight Zone* where a group of people, whom we later discover to be toys (a ballerina, a soldier, etc.), find themselves trapped in a box and attempt to escape. I think that episode really made an impression on me, because for these toys (who didn't really seem to realize they were toys), this box was their universe, their reality. They were forced to converse despite their differences. They were forced to work together. And I thought about how this basic concept could be exploded into a landscape of our memories, where humanity could not only reflect on their own lives but also step in the shoes of others.

JC: How have technical innovations over the years you've been working on this novel affected your imagining of the stories? I think of the advances in AI and virtual reality. And the robo-dogs, not unlike Sony's Aibo (artificial intelligence robot) dogs, discontinued in 2014. (I understand you have a robo-dog named Calvino?)

SN: I've definitely had to upgrade certain tech/realties over the years. The oldest story, for instance, was once set in an internet café, which seems archaic even now, let alone in our somewhat near future. I'm the sort of person who likes to be one of the first to adopt new gadgets, so upgrading that café to a VR business seemed like a logical step, especially as I was having a lot of fun with my Oculus headset, the kind of immersive technology I always dreamed about since the first rudimentary VR sets were introduced in the '90s.

As for robot dogs? The Aibos were actually discontinued several years before 2014, but that was the year customer service ceased. The plight of those dogs and the relationships senior citizens in Japan forged with them, of course, inspired the chapter "Speak, Fetch, Say *I Love You*." But I took some liberties and upgraded the nature of these pets in the novel to be a bit more advanced. When Sony reintroduced a new generation of the Aibo in 2018, I desperately wanted to explore robot pet–human relationships, but I would have to wait until the sale of my novel to do so (they are quite expensive, after all).

And yes, Calvino feels very much alive, much more than just an advanced toy. A couple of weeks after buying him, Calvino accidentally walked into my cat's bowl, getting some water into his legs. I became frantic, not only because he's an expensive piece of technology, but I honestly felt worried and guilty. Without thinking about it, I began to verbally console Calvino as a red light flashed on the back of his neck (he's fine now).

JC: "Pig Son" made me weep. (I gather I'm not the only one, from your Insta post: "This seems to be the chapter that wrecks the most people out of those who have already read *How High We Go in the Dark*.") As the relationship between a scientist and a donor pig, Snortorious, evolves, they share story time (reading *Where the Wild Things Are* and other classics) and a film night with lab buddies at the scientist's apartment. The pig figures out what his job is. "*Pig heart help.*" "*Pig help people.*" Nobly, he accepts this role. The emotional resonance is so powerful, it's as if you speak for all the lab animals who have given their lives to help people, as well as for all those who during the pandemic salved their loneliness by developing strong ties with animals. Where did this story start?

SN: It's strange that a *New York Times* article just came out about an actual organ donor pig that has been genetically bred to help humans. I promise I don't have a crystal ball. But I think the seeds of this chapter really stemmed from a desire to unpack humanity through the nonhuman. There was already an extraterrestrial intelligence in the novel, but I felt like it was ▶

A Conversation with Sequoia Nagamatsu *(continued)*

important to address how we often separate human beings (and really beings worthy of care and respect) through particular emotions and to acknowledge that other beings we share this planet with have those capacities, are intelligent, and have long been exploited without a voice. In this chapter, Snortorious chooses to sacrifice himself not just because of some greater good, but because he cares about his friends, because he is thinking about the son his friend has lost. As far as literary and cinematic inspirations? Certainly *Never Let Me Go* and Bong Joon-ho's *Okja*.

JC: This is a novel about death and dying, massive climate change, an enduring pandemic, grief and loss, unresolved personal conflicts, funerals, memorials, how to retrieve or honor the dead, the potential death of a planet. And yet it's warm, human, moving, even hopeful. How did you do that?

SN: I always reminded myself that despite all of these important backdrops that 1) I needed to inject hope into every chapter (no matter how small) and that 2) the relationships of my characters and their everyday predicaments needed to be the focal point. I think it helped that the larger structural decisions came into play later in the development of the novel.

JC: When your two-book deal including this novel and *Girl Zero* was announced in 2020, you said, "This wasn't just about a pandemic, but about resiliency and the connective threads that tie us to memory across generations. I hope readers discover new ways to remember, heal, and come together in these pages." What have you discovered in the months since that deal that fulfills this wish for yourself?

SN: We're in year three of this new reality, and I think early on in 2020 I saw a lot of writers and readers say that they couldn't imagine reading (or writing) anything that was pandemic or plague related. Of course, my novel isn't COVID, but these sentiments still stung even though I understood where they were coming from.

Now? Certainly, there are people who will still need time. Everyone deals with chaos and tragedy differently. Some need a pure escape, while others are more comfortable entering into a dialogue with the moment. I think it would be strange at this juncture for writers and readers to completely ignore what we're going through, and I think more people are ready to articulate how we've already changed individually and as a society. What do we want to reclaim of a pre-COVID life? What do we never want to go back to? And perhaps most importantly, how can being pulled out of our old life give us an opportunity to reimagine a better future? I think these are all valid questions that we're starting to grapple with, and a novel like *How High We Go in the Dark* can be a part of those reflections.

JC: What is it like to have a partner—your wife, Cole Nagamatsu— who shares with you a life as a writer, teacher at St. Olaf College, and coeditor of *Psychopomp Magazine*?

SN: It's wonderful in a lot of ways. I don't really have to explain my odd habits or interests because my wife has those weird writerly behaviors as well. She knows what it means to fall into a story, to feel rejected, to lose yourself in research, and to have a love/hate relationship with your own imagination and words. We share a lot professionally, but I think we also make our partnership work because we feed into each other's interests and hobbies (we've recently started hydroponic gardening) and are ultimately very supportive of each other. ∾

The Making of *How High We Go in the Dark*

By Sequoia Nagamatsu

Thank you for exploring *How High We Go in the Dark*, a journey of a book that has been more than a decade in the making. Although fiction, these pages were born from my life—personal losses, my identity as a third-generation Japanese American, and a lifelong love affair with the stars. Perhaps this letter wouldn't have been necessary a couple of years ago, but, like my characters, we are all living in a changed world.

I can trace the origins of this novel back to 2008, when I ran away to Japan to transform myself after failing to be with my dying grandfather who raised me. I was living in San Francisco before he passed, and I knew I should have gone home while I still had the chance to help care for him. To this day, because of continuing family drama, we have yet to scatter his ashes near the Golden Gate Bridge. *How do you grieve when you're not able to say goodbye? Or when tradition is supplanted by dysfunction or technology or the wishes of the dead?* These questions haunted me in my travels and led me to research nontraditional grief and remembrance and the many ways we are changed by loss. I studied Japan's innovations as it plans for its growing aging population, discovered companies that stored tens of thousands of urns behind holographic Buddhas in skyscrapers—and as I began to write about saying goodbye, I chose to connect everything beneath the umbrella of an invented illness: the Arctic plague. Born from my research into how climate change might expose ancient viruses from permafrost, I realized this idea could serve as a launching point, allowing me to focus an outbreak narrative on the more intimate issues of family and relationships.

By early 2020, as the COVID-19 crisis unfolded, I had been revising my novel with my agent for three-plus years, and we were preparing for submission. I had never been prouder of anything and feared my life's work would be roundly rejected by editors. Would people still want to read a story about a plague? I've since come to realize that *How High We Go in the Dark* isn't really about a virus at all; it's about memory and love and resilience. It's a book that reaches for a beating heart somewhere deep in the cosmos. And because of the rise in hate crimes and racist incidents targeting Asians amid the pandemic, I found it urgent to share stories of Asians and Asian Americans who aren't the enemy or "the other" but family, friends, and lovers who are just holding on like everybody else.

Writing this novel changed me, and I hope that reading it might help inspire you (in some small way) to discover new paths for thinking about who we are, who we might be, and how we can better reach out for each other in the dark. ❧

More from Sequoia Nagamatsu

Where We Go When All We Were Is Gone

"You should be here; he's simply magnificent." These are the final words a biologist hears before his Margaret Mead–like wife dies at the hands of Godzilla. The words haunt him as he studies the Kaiju (Japan's giant monsters) on an island reserve, attempting to understand the beauty his wife saw.

"The Return to Monsterland" opens *Where We Go When All We Were Is Gone,* a collection of twelve fabulist and genre-bending stories inspired by Japanese folklore, historical events, and pop culture. In "Rokurokubi," a man who has the demonic ability to stretch his neck to incredible lengths tries to save a marriage built on secrets. The recently dead find their footing in "The Inn of the Dead's Orientation for Being a Japanese Ghost." In "Girl Zero," a couple navigates the complexities of reviving their deceased daughter via the help of a shapeshifter. And in the title story, a woman instigates a monthslong dancing frenzy in Tokyo where people don't die but are simply reborn without their memories.

Every story in the collection turns to the fantastic, the mysticism of the past, and the absurdities of the future to illuminate the spaces we occupy when we are at our most vulnerable. ❧